DEAL IN DIVINITY

CHELY PENN

RIPTIDE
PUBLISHING

Riptide Publishing
PO Box 1537
Burnsville, NC 28714
www.riptidepublishing.com

Deal in Divinity

Cover art: Simone
Editor: Carole-ann Galloway
Layout: L.C. Chase, lcchase.com

ISBN: 978-1-62649-990-4

First edition
December, 2023

Also available in ebook:
ISBN: 978-1-62649-989-8

DEAL IN DIVINITY

CHELY PENN

RIPTIDE
PUBLISHING

A thank-you to my mother for being supportive of me writing this kind of stuff even when she shouldn't have. Another thanks to Michelle for dealing with me, and a third to Nevada for bullying me.

TABLE OF CONTENTS

CHAPTER ONE

A nder had made a horrible decision. Perhaps it would kill him.

Taking a deep breath, he stared at the towering wall that encircled the remnants of his hometown. The barrier was a ramshackle thing, strung together with anything sturdy enough to be nailed or welded down, by people desperate for shelter.

Over the past three years, the wall seemed to have gotten closer and closer to Ander, choking him every time he saw it. Like a collar on his neck—but a collar worth wearing. The soft chime in the air reminded him of that. The sound drifted down from the angels perched on the edges of the wall. They were the guardians that protected everyone from the monsters outside.

Ander was leaving that security. He hefted his bag on his back, eyebrows pinched together. The hot pavement under his tennis shoes led to the highway out of town, out into the changed world. The mere thought made his knees shake, and every cell in his body told him to turn around, go into his room, and sleep this stupid idea away. Told him it was fine to live his mundane, repetitive, and *solitary* life, because it kept him safe. It took a lot of effort to walk toward the gates.

A life safe doesn't mean a life worth living.

Ander scratched his neck in a nervous tic, fingers running across the feathers that stuck out from his skin like onyx shards. There were only a handful of them, and he was always tempted to yank them off. He resisted the urge—he didn't want to seem like a completely crazy person when he was talking to the Couriers.

Up ahead of him, a group of blends were putting packages and letters into soft tan bags that matched the dry Texas dirt. They stood in front of the silver gated arch that formed the entrance to the town. A bit of blood stained its edges, and Ander had to look away. Had to focus. His target was a younger Courier named Michael, who seemed like the friendliest from what Ander had been able to gather. He was a lean man with cropped white hair and the only one to carry a smile.

Ander headed his way. As he grew closer, Michael turned toward him slightly.

"Hello. What can I help you with?" He held out his hand.

Ander hesitated; he didn't often converse with purer blends.

Michael's eyes were a solid sapphire that glowed against his skin, which was a touch darker than Ander's own. He was beautiful, like all strong blends, and his allure made Ander's head spin. Somewhat hypnotized, he took Michael's hand, gripping it briefly with his own sweaty one, before letting go.

Michael smirked, eyes sparkling like waves crashing on the shore. "My name is Michael. Do you have a letter for me to deliver?"

"Uh. Uh, no, I don't. Thank you. No, I . . ." *Shit.* Ander had planned this speech for a week. Damn pretty blends and their dazzling faces. "I want to go with you." He blushed, heat lighting up his face.

"Go with me?" Michael repeated. "Haven't heard someone say that in a while. It's dangerous, especially for those whose blood runs on the more human side." He stared Ander down, studying the scruff on his neck. "Where is it you want to go?"

Ander couldn't tell if Michael was humoring him or genuinely interested. Either way, he hadn't been rejected. Yet.

"Atlasville."

Michael bit his lip. "The town deep down south?"

"Yes."

"That's slightly out of our jurisdiction. Like I said, *deep* down south."

"I know. I'd only travel with you as far as you go. Then I'd make my own way." Ander kept his voice firm. He had to. He barely stood five feet five inches, which combined with his black, curly hair, made him mimic a battered mop. The least he could do was sound confident.

"Atlasville is uncharted territory. We still don't know what went down there after the Gate broke. Demons could completely have it by now."

"I know," Ander said again. "And I know the dangers of demons. I wasn't in Gardners when this started—I was out there." His body stiffened at the memory.

"How'd you make it in here?"

"I heal crazy fast. It kept me alive in the beginning, so I know I can handle a bit." He stared hard at Michael.

Michael narrowed his eyes and scrunched his mouth. "I might remember you being brought through the gates. I thought you were dead."

Ander's stomach twisted in cold knots. "But I wasn't."

"You *barely* made it."

A pit grew in Ander's chest. If he had been luckier, if he had a little more angel blood in him, then Michael probably wouldn't hesitate, wouldn't recall him as a bloody mess being dragged into the safety of Gardners. He *had* barely made it. *If my rescue had been only minutes later . . .* Ander swallowed.

"Going back out there again after what the demons did to you the first time? Doesn't seem wise," Michael said after a moment. "People leave it up to us to do the running back and forth because it's dangerous."

"I know that. We've all seen people leave and not come back. But that's a risk I've come to terms with." Ander gritted his teeth. "You have to take me," he said louder.

"I do?" Michael had the slightest smirk on his face.

"Yes. There's no reason not to." Ander put his hand to his chest. "Like I said, I heal, so if things get bad, I'll probably survive it."

"Then what do you need us for?"

"You know where to go and how things have changed out there after all this time."

Michael was frowning now, and anxiety zipped through Ander's gut.

"Look, if I die, it's not on you," he blurted. "So take me, okay?"

All the Couriers were looking at him now. His feathers pricked up in embarrassment. So much for appearing brave.

"Are you going to be this annoying if we take you?" a Courier asked, crossing his arms.

"I'll be extra annoying if you don't." To his amazement, Ander managed not to stutter. "Please, take me."

There was a strange silence before the Courier rolled his eyes and motioned to Michael.

"Let the guy come. If he dies, he dies. We have a schedule to keep for the sane people of Gardners." The Courier turned around, walking through the arch. He glanced back for a moment. "But there's a reason not many people head out, besides us."

Up on the edges of the wall, seven angels turned their heads, apparently sensing the Couriers near the entrance. A shiver slunk down Ander's spine. He rarely looked at them, all massive bundles of white feathers and limbs, with dozens of eyes peering from each form. It was too much to focus on, even after all these years. But now, they were gazing at the group, and Ander had to stare solely at Michael in order to ease his nerves.

"Well," Michael said, as his party started to leave, a few of them giving Ander unreadable expressions. "I guess, yeah, you can come. It is dangerous, you being, well . . ."

"A weak blend?" Ander finished.

"Yeah. We don't get attacked by demons often anymore; we've held our own for a while, so they usually stay clear. But if they see you, if they see that maybe you're a weak link—" Michael started digging into one of the many pockets on his jacket. He pulled out a red bandanna and wrapped it around Ander's neck.

Ander froze as the fabric tightened. "What are you doing?"

"If they can't see the feathers, maybe they'll think you're a normal human. That'd be safer."

"That only means I'm weaker in their eyes, doesn't it? That's why all the normal humans are dead. Well, most of them."

Michael nodded but then leaned in close again, whispering into Ander's ear, his voice too soft and delicate for such a topic.

"Yes, but they won't be tempted by your blood."

Ander stiffened, his throat dry. "But I'm barely a blend. I thought they only liked, um, stronger blood."

"If you're coming with us, you need to know that it doesn't matter to them how much of you is angel—as long as they can taste it, they want it. A lot of them are addicts, and all blend blood is the same to them. Do you have everything you need?"

"You think I'd come unprepared?"

"I don't know what I think." Michael gave a forced chuckle. "I don't know what your plan is. But it looks like it's happening, so, I hope you're ready."

Ander's heart jumped. Holy shit. He was doing it. He was leaving Gardners and safety, all on a gamble. After years of stagnation, he was finally breaking free from the solitude that had encased him. But the price was monsters at his throat.

He took a deep breath. "I'm ready."

"All right." Michael motioned to the silver arch. "What's your name?"

"Ander Castillo."

"Well, Ander Castillo, come on; let's head out."

Ander glanced at the angels and saw they were still staring as the Couriers left, Michael and Ander at the end of the line. *Weird.* Ander turned his attention on the sky past the arches, the wide, creamy blue. It almost looked inviting.

Ander hadn't seen the world since the first days when the demons had broken out of Hell and he had crashed his way into Gardners. It was one of the few refuges, guarded by angels who'd appeared just as mysteriously and quickly as the demons. Anything out of their reach, past the barriers, was in danger.

At the entrance, a thick shadow fell from the arch, cast by the sun overhead. Once he crossed that darkness, that was it: he would be out *there.* He took a step, and his faded shoes hit the concrete on the other side.

The angels howled.

Ice sliced Ander to the bone as he and the Couriers froze. The angels had never made a noise like that. A scream, like a knife on rock.

Ander stared up, straight at one that was mostly a hoard of feathers with a strange skeletal-thin body barely visible underneath, then to the rest. They were all arched, as if prepared to jump. Adding to the strangeness, there was a chirring in the air. The angels were speaking, and Ander had never been able to grasp it. Their language was the whisper of a thousand leaves, the thrum of thunder, and the snap of lightning. *Otherworldly.*

"What was that about?" Ander muttered.

"I . . . I don't know," Michael said. "I don't understand angelic at all." His wings were partially unfurled now as if ready to fly.

Testing the waters, Ander took another step. The angels didn't do anything else, but they continued to watch, their bodies half-raised. They had never stopped anyone from leaving before. At least not since leaving had been approved.

One more step. The angels shifted, turning to each other. Ander ignored them; if he was doing something wrong, surely they would tell him in a way he could understand?

A few of the angels cooed amongst themselves, as if some agreement had been made. *Does that mean it's all right?* Ander looked back at them one more time. They only watched. But a strange feeling was in the air, a foreboding that elicited a shiver from him.

"That's weird," Michael said, grabbing Ander's shoulder. "But I guess it's okay. Let's go."

This was it.

He continued to walk forward, the Couriers and the world ahead of him, the angels behind. The highway stretched out up the overpasses, and thin roads spread like tendrils to long-abandoned houses. The scene was so desolate, so old, so hurt.

"Who are you looking for, anyway, if you don't mind me asking? Who's worth going out into demon territory?" Michael said, while peering over his shoulder at the angels.

Ander's breath hitched as he thought of comforting hands and sea-blue eyes. A memory from long ago but still ingrained in him. His heart ached. "Family," he said.

CHAPTER TWO

There was an unending heat that came with the journey. Ander had expected it, though walking in it was something else. It was always hot in the Texas sun, but in Gardners he'd at least had shade from buildings and trees. They'd trekked for seven hours so far and there had only been an endless emptiness in the landscape to match the blank sky. Nothing but dryness. Ander wiped sweat from his brow. Michael wasn't sweating at all, even though he was trudging the same burning path as Ander.

"Those things over there are demon carcasses. We'd move them, but the stench . . . it's too much." Michael motioned off into the distance, where vomit-colored lumps of flesh sat, rotting in the sun. Ander was too far away to smell them, but he could *feel* them. "And nothing but bugs will eat demon corpses, so they'll be there for some time."

"Did you guys kill them?"

"Not me, but the other Couriers. I wasn't one back then. I only started doing this a few months ago. Never been that good at flying, so I wanted to get better at it. These damn things make me feel clumsy compared to the others, though they are lovely." He flapped his wings for emphasis.

Ander twisted his mouth. They sure were. He'd been grateful for his ability when the gates had first broken, healing him from whatever pain the world threw at him. But when he'd entered the city, he had witnessed *true* power from those with real angel blood. Some had been blessed with gifts beyond understanding, strength immeasurable, hands that could weave fire or air. And he had waited, praying the same would be given to him.

Months and months in, he had been given a graze of feathers on his neck. And that had been that.

"How much angel blood do you think I have?" he asked.

"I don't know. Like one-tenth. Less? I'm not good at math or genetics. Which is unfortunate: I was going to be a teacher. Can you believe that?"

"At least you knew you'd probably get a job. I went for photography." He didn't mention the part where he'd dropped out.

"That sounds fun. I had to go work with teenagers all the time to get my degree. And then I realized I didn't really like kids." Michael laughed. "That's terrible right? An angel who doesn't like kids?"

"I mean, you didn't know you were part angel."

"True, but the blood was always there, right? You would think . . . it would have made us better people. Aren't angels supposed to be perfection or something?"

"You don't know what angels are supposed to be?" Ander tilted his head. Michael's face was stern around his eyes. "But you're one of the closest to them."

"I don't feel close at all to be honest. They seem so far away."

Ander swallowed dryly. Michael's face remained the same.

The air was sweltering, and in the middle of the sky, the sun was a burning eye, watching them. The heat blurred the top of the roads into a sizzling mess. Ander's arms and nose got a nice cherry red. He hadn't thought about sunscreen, though presumably he shouldn't need it. He hadn't burned so far in Gardners.

The outside was strange. He'd done a fair bit of traveling before the chaos, but this was different. Everything was a wounded clone of what he'd known before, a skeleton. Buildings were damaged, roads and cars empty; every so often they would pass by a human corpse, stripped of all flesh and blood. It was unnerving.

"Do you like doing this?" Ander asked, in an effort to distract himself. "Maybe-dying to make sure that someone a couple of miles away gets a letter from someone else?"

"Yeah, I do," Michael said without hesitation. "It provides some normality, you know? Writing to a friend or a loved one, knowing what's happening in other sanctuaries, it gives a sense of security. We used to do a lot of scavenging for supplies too. Have to travel farther and farther for that though now, when the time calls. Thankfully, the city gardens and farms have made it less needed."

"I've tried to help with those. But I seemed to mostly get in the way." Ander laughed dryly. "I was on weed-picking duty. Or washing dishes for the school."

"Hey, they're still jobs. Not everyone is suited for the harder things. Especially being a Courier."

Ander nodded, a tight knot in his throat. It wasn't the first time he'd been told he wasn't *fit* for something. Even when Gardners was forming and every able-bodied person had been needed, Ander had been put on the bench by blends far stronger than him.

He grimaced. "How far is the next town?"

"We're about three miles away now. This looks like a fairly safe trip; good for you." Michael nudged Ander's shoulder and chuckled. "I'm glad. I was worried."

"I told you, if something happened, you didn't have to worry about me," Ander said, staring at the ground.

"Yeah, but I wasn't going to just leave you for dead."

Ander bit his lip, still unable to look back at Michael. The guy was nicer than he had expected. Instead of being pissed that Ander had thrown himself in the middle of his trip, he seemed eager to chat, to explain things. Ander hadn't had this much conversation in months.

". . . Thank you for that." His face must've been so red. He hoped that Michael understood how much he meant his words. In the distance, the slight bumps of architecture that made the next town became visible.

"That's Afriel right?"

"Yeah."

"What was its name before?"

"Trenton. I think."

"That's a dramatic name change."

"Well, you know, they're very . . . angelic over there. They thought it would please their angels more. I don't think the angels care a bit, but as I said, I don't know what they are about."

"Do you think a Half does?"

"Maybe? Don't have one in our town anymore. Never got a chance to ask." Michael's voice had gone faint, his face gentle. Had he and the Half been close? Perhaps not a topic to press.

"How many angels does Afriel have? Three?" Ander asked, hoping his subject change wasn't too obvious.

"Yeah, not as many as us, though their town is about the same size. But they have a lot of strong blends, so they stay pretty safe."

"But don't they fight demons a lot?"

"They do. Causes them trouble, if you ask me. Go around fighting demons on purpose, they're going to start fighting you back unprovoked. Afriel seems to think it's their duty or something. They think demons all have to be wiped off the planet."

"Don't they? They're bad." Ander felt like an idiot for asking such a question, but Michael's evident disapproval made him curious.

"I mean, theoretically, yes. But I'm not so sure about all of them, all the time."

"Michael, are you talking shit again?" A Courier barked, whipping their head around.

"You saw how well Millstone was doing!" A blush crept up Michael's face as he glared at the Courier who'd called him out. Ander chuckled; he hadn't seen anything close to embarrassment cross Michael until now.

"Millstone was skeezy as shit. We ain't ever going back there. I don't care what anyone says."

"What is Millstone?" Ander asked slowly.

"It was . . . It's a town a bit further south. Not Atlasville-south, but you know, on the way." Michael waved his hands. "It happened to be near a different town we were delivering to, so we stopped by and were *vexed* by what we saw. And Louis in particular, well they didn't like it."

"The blends and demons there fuck," a red-haired woman in the group called out. Several of the others groaned in unison.

Ander stared. "Wait, what? What do you mean they . . . What?" He had seen demons, and nothing about them was appealing. They were masses of limbs and teeth and eyes. They were the size of cars and made sounds like broken glass skidding across rocks. There were a few that had human qualities, but they were still like animals, ripping out throats and spilling blood.

"It's obviously an anomaly, one that we would prefer to keep from the people of Gardners," Michael continued. "It was only that one town, that one incident. But . . . but demons are different than they used to be. Some of them, anyway. They talk like us, and they . . . I don't know, it was bizarre. They were easier to understand than any angel I've ever spoken to. It was strange, very strange. They were people, basically."

"But they're not," Louis said, turning around, their brown hair plastered to their ivory skin with sweat. "They're not people. They're demons. And you're a blend, and they would kill to get a hold of your blood so they could get high; don't forget that."

"You could talk to them? They talked to you? You had a conversation with a demon?" Ander paused, words getting stuck in his throat. "And didn't die? Why haven't you told anyone in Gardners?" He faced Michael, who appeared to be thinking.

"It's better not to know," Michael said after a moment. "It's too confusing, too stressful. The people of Gardners are safe and secure; we don't want to scare them for no reason and build up distrust. They wouldn't understand. If we said demons not only look like people but talk like one too, are more like us than we thought, they would probably start accusing each other of being demons in disguise. It'd be a witch hunt."

"Why are you telling me, then?"

"Like I said, now you're out here, you have to know," Michael took a deep breath. "And if you do . . . if you do get to Atlasville and back, I would appreciate it if you don't go around telling everyone. We will tell them, you know, eventually, on our own time."

Ander bit his lip. It didn't make sense to him. The world was changing again, and people were being left in the dark because . . . because it would stress them out too much? *Demons* taking over the planet was stressful. Lying wouldn't make anything easier; it would only worsen the few ties people had managed to keep with one another.

"I can tell you don't really agree with us," Michael said after a pause. "But we know what's best okay? We've been out here where others haven't. So, as I said"—his voice went dark—"it would be appreciated, and wise of you, to not say anything."

A chill crawled up Ander's spine, and he shifted in the sun. Had that been a threat or a simple warning? Was Michael holding more information Ander would need to survive?

"I don't think anyone would listen to me if I tried to tell them otherwise anyway." Ander shrugged. "I don't have any family or friends there. And people aren't keen on making new friends at the moment." He tried not to sound bitter. It wasn't like he was the only person who'd been knocked to the side after everything, but he wasn't a misery-loves-company fellow.

"People aren't as trusting anymore. They're rougher around the edges," Michael said solemnly. "More of a reason not to tell them."

"But you've been nice." Ander glanced at Michael. "And, well, I'm hoping I'll find others like you once we separate." He laughed nervously. "It would be comforting to have a friend along for the walk."

Michael hesitated for a moment. "I hope you find that friend."

"Hey, we're practically there," the redhead shouted, pointing at Afriel. It was odd to see another refuge in the world. Ander had known they existed, but it had seemed impossible, back in Gardners. The idea that more people lived and breathed just beyond the walls that encircled Afriel was enticing. A new town meant new people, perhaps kinder than the ones he'd been with. Shaped differently by the events than Gardners had been.

Ander picked up his pace. Before, traveling ten miles wouldn't have been a big deal, not with an air-conditioned car and a nice playlist. But now it meant hours walking under a sweltering sun.

Ander gritted his teeth; there was so much left to this venture, and he had to keep going. Just another mile or two left.

"Where are all the angels?" a silver-winged Courier asked.

The question hit Ander like a bucket of ice. Everyone stopped. He went cold down to the soles of his feet. A silence rippled among them all, a unified wave of fear.

Michael grabbed Ander's shoulder and gripped him tightly. "Don't let them see your feathers," he whispered.

That was all Michael got to say before something in the distance screeched. It was a sound Ander *wished* he could forget, an awful cry like metal against concrete. He took a step backward as he tried to pinpoint the source of the noise, but it was impossible to tell.

The ambush would have to be from ahead. To their sides were just empty streets and abandoned cars that were rusted and crushed almost to pancakes. The sidewalks were cracked and broken upward into the sky like stalagmites. Past them were ditches carved in the ground, overflowing with years of debris carried by the wind, then lodged in gravel and drainpipes.

Metal grinding to his right had him twisting to those trash-filled trenches. Like a blot of ink growing rapidly in water, a black mass of arms and legs pooled out from a drain. Ander froze. He was thrown back in time, to the very first day, the first night in a world where demons had cried in the darkness, yanked people out of cars, and tossed them in the air like toys.

Ander grabbed his own arm, his teeth clenched. Phantom pain pricked his skin.

The demon pulled itself out of the ditch, resembling a blob of tar. It was huge, slimy, the size of a bus, and glistening profusely in the high noon sun. There were hundreds of skinny black arms dripping off its body, dragging across the ground with wet *paps*. It screamed again, and this time Ander saw them: all over its gelatinous form, hundreds of mouths gaped, every single one full of sharp white teeth.

Then the demon threw itself at them.

Dozens of wings unfurled as one, in a sweeping gust of wind that kicked up dirt and debris. Ander was almost knocked backward as the Couriers leaped at the threat. They flew overhead, jerking the demon by its arms and ripping them off, flinging it back and forth to each other with their stunning strength, dodging its desperate flails as it shrieked.

Ander stood there, staring. He felt a pit in his stomach. Why couldn't he do that? Why couldn't he fly or . . . or something? There were thousands of these creatures out there, and he had no self-defense against them. He took a step backward. The cries from the fight faded in and out like a siren as the ground began to spin under his feet. *If the Couriers weren't here, I'd be dead.*

They needed to get out of there, take shelter. Ander looked back at Afriel, sweat dripping from his palms. It had probably been ravaged by this creature too—

Wait. It was supposed to be a town with three angels. Actual angels. And this demon couldn't even stop the Couriers tearing it apart. There was no way it could have taken down the angels that protected Afriel. So what had?

Static cracked through the sky. A Courier yelled in pain, white feathers spraying in the air as they tumbled to the pavement, landing with a sickening thud. Ander recoiled and scanned for the source of the attack in a panic, only for more shots to ring out in rapid fire, too many to count. The Couriers dropped like flies, thrashing, their wings flapping desperately.

Then Ander was hit. Electricity snapped up his spine, his body jerking as breath was ripped from his lungs. He staggered backward and pawed wildly at his side, finding the center of the pain: left, near his rib cage. Warm red blood soaked his hand.

Did I get shot?

Fire cracked across his knee, and he collapsed to the ground. From Afriel, a dozen creatures headed toward them. Ander groaned, tried to push himself up, but only managed to twitch a shoulder, his body was so racked with pain. But so were the others—to his left a Courier managed to get to their knees before crumbling forward.

And then the enemy was upon them.

"Look at this, boys," a voice hummed.

A woman had stepped to the front of the monsters. No, not a woman. She had a long snake-like tail that curled from her back, twisted into coils on the ground. And as she strutted closer, she gave a hyena-like cackle, showing off a row of shark teeth.

The other demon, the black blob, whimpered and clambered over to her. She pet its slimy sides, cooing at it like one would a child. "Shh, shh, Nevuro. You did good." She kissed it and it . . . purred? Then she plunged a foot down on a Courier, her heel digging into his skin, making him cry out in pain.

"Michael!" Ander yelled as the man writhed in agony. It was a mistake. The demon's head whipped over to him, and a smile crossed her face. It stretched too far, from sharp cheekbone to cheekbone.

"Oh, almost forgot about you over there. You didn't run over all heroically like the rest of your friends, did you? Don't blame you, Nevuro is a spooky fellow. Especially to a poor little human like yourself." She pointed a rifle at him and snickered before swinging it over her back. Had the electricity come from her as well? The bullet certainly had. "Tie up the blends, boys. We're going to have a party tonight."

Roughly, the other demons wrapped chains around the Couriers, hefting them up on their shoulders like bags of meat. Seven blends, snatched away almost effortlessly. *How is this happening?* Michael had said that nothing went wrong on deliveries anymore. And now in one fell swoop, everyone had been crushed. Had this group also taken down the angels? Was that possible?

Ander's stomach rolled. *Will Gardners be safe?*

"Not likely," the demon said, leaning down. "They're next."

Ander's eyes went wide. He could . . . he could feel her. She was in his head. A pressure in his skull, a heaviness he couldn't push away, like cold glass sliding against his brain. What was she?

"I'm a legit demon darling, and angels don't mean shit to me." She scratched a nail down the side of Ander's face, drawing blood. "Human blood, what a waste. Barely even tastes good."

Ander grunted. She propped a hand on her hip, eyes half-lidded as she brought her fingertip to her mouth, licking the red liquid.

Suddenly her pupils dilated.

"Oh, *holy shit*." She stood up, a grin splitting her face, every razor-sharp tooth revealed. A laugh crackled out. "Look what we've found here. Fuck *yeah*."

Ander furrowed his eyebrows. The hole in his chest deepened, a pit swallowing him. What the hell was going on? His eyes darted back to the Couriers, some of whom were trying to fight the demons, but the assault had clearly been brutal to all of them. Ander couldn't even move with the static from the bullet that had coursed through him, though his body was quick to heal.

One Courier tried to stand up and was greeted with a stab in the back. She sobbed, her voice echoing in the emptiness.

Ander grimaced. Why didn't his ability involve healing other people? Because if he could just get to them—

"Slow down, there." The demon shoved her boot into his back, and the sharp heel pinned him to the hard dirt. "You're not going anywhere." She licked her lips. "I've got big plans for you, Halfie."

Ander blinked. *Wait. What?*

CHAPTER THREE

Ander stumbled forward as he was yanked by the female demon in charge—Mayrez, they had called her. She had him tied up by leather ropes and was dragging him alongside her like a disobedient dog. He had felt like one when the demons had gone to bind him and he'd fought back to no avail.

He clenched his jaw so hard it felt like it would snap.

But this treatment was preferable compared to what the Couriers were dealing with. Their aggressive efforts had led to the demons knocking them out, piling them in the back of a cart like stacks of hay. If Ander had been able to fight like that, would he have been given the same fate? Or was Mayrez also giving him "special treatment" because of the insane ideas she had in her head?

What had she meant when she called him a "Halfie"? Halves were powerful, ethereal, and they flew. He was a fledgling bird at best.

He tried not to think about it too much, or of anything, since Mayrez could pry into his mind if she felt like it. Ander couldn't feel her now, but that didn't mean she wasn't there. He glanced nervously at her as she whistled, then back at the three other demons pulling the cart that carried the semiconscious Couriers.

What was going to happen to them? Would the demons kill them? Snap their necks like a can of cola and drink? Ander shuddered. *Is that what's going to happen to me?*

Okay, so the plan of getting to Atlasville without too many hiccups had been derailed. *But there has to be a way out of this.* The thought of leaving the Couriers behind made him nauseous, but he couldn't imagine saving them, not with his powers of shit-all. He had to focus on keeping himself alive. He straightened his shoulders, but they still shook.

This was his nightmare.

The gates to Afriel opened, and Ander's train of thought crashed to a halt. Demons. There were demons everywhere. Huge skeletal beings with skin so thin it hung off their bodies like wet tissue paper, clinging to bone—the ones Ander remembered so vividly on the day of the gates, the ones that made him want to die. Teeth and tendons snapped and clacked as other creatures moved on multiple limbs, no limbs, and throaty grunts and whispers filled the street. They clambered about the ruined and broken town like maggots squirming in a wound. The hair and feathers on his neck stood up.

As the group headed through the now-overrun city, the demons turned to them; one with the face of a decaying deer but about twice the size sniffed at them, then snorted, his breath a thick black smog. The eyes in its head wouldn't stop rotating wildly. It brought its mouth closer to Ander, opening it slightly, revealing rows of shark teeth. Further back, eyes plastered the lining of its cheek, staring. It smelled like sulfur, like Hell, like fear itself. Ander couldn't stop trembling. His own breath was lodged in his throat, and he couldn't look away from the demon as it got closer and closer, inches from his face.

"Back off," Mayrez said, smacking it on the nose. "This isn't for you, you fucking sack of shit." She smacked it again, and it cried out like a scratchy record, retreating on a lower body that appeared to be multiple human torsos fused together, walking on their arms like a centipede. Ander looked away; it was too much. He'd told himself back in Gardners that he could handle being face-to-face with these monsters again. But now it was taking everything he had not to curl up and cry.

People had been snatched from each other's arms by these creatures. Their families callously ripped apart and their guts strewn across streets. Ander had been there. How could he ever forget something like that? One day normal, next he'd been cowering in an alley as half a human corpse was tossed over him, sliding down the brick wall like a splattered tomato.

Suddenly, a demon skittered by while chewing a gnawed-on arm, and Ander dry-heaved. Fuck. He was a fucking idiot. Leaving Gardners had been a stupid, horrible, fucking terrible decision. He should have stayed there until he was a hundred and died of natural causes instead of heading off to get killed by one of *these*. These disgusting creatures that devastated everything around them.

Whatever remained of the original Afriel was hard to distinguish from the wreckage that now covered it. According to the Couriers, it had once been a beautiful refuge, but all Ander saw was a graveyard. Marks of death were everywhere: body parts scattered like littered cans, blood staining the dented carcasses. Fresh blood. This attack had been recent, Ander realized as his eyes darted around from building to building.

How had it happened? Why had no one been able to escape and warn any other city, especially Gardners, which was so close and so safe?

Ander was getting dizzy, and every step sent him swinging to the left or the right. Demons and bodies surrounded him, along with the smell of blood and rot. He closed his eyes, tried to breathe.

Then, there was a tap on his face and he blinked. Mayrez was smirking at him. She patted him again.

"Don't panic there, Halfie, you're going to be fine. I'm sure whoever pays for you will keep you in good condition." She gave him a peace sign and kept walking, yanking the rope hard enough to make him stumble.

"Wh-what?" *This can't be happening.* He frantically scanned his desolate surroundings for anyone else—an angel or blend, hell even a human. Anything besides a *demon*.

But there was no one. The Couriers were still out. It was only him, uselessly alone, surrounded by monsters that wanted to eat him in a town that reeked of decaying flesh.

"This is the joint," Mayrez said, coming to a stop outside a dingy bar with a falling sign. She pushed Ander forward, and he fell through the swinging door.

He stumbled to his feet and looked up, his hair flopping, sweat dripping down his forehead. At least thirty demons stared back at him from where they sat clustered around scattered tables and squashed up in damaged booths. There were strange ones, and the humanoid ones like Mayrez. Some of the latter resembled normal humans, but they carried an aura that left Ander feeling hot and trapped, like a rabbit with its leg caught, waiting for the hunter. Like the rabbit, he wanted to thump his feet onto the ground and dash.

Mayrez kicked him, forcing him down an empty path between the bar and the mess of a seating area. He chewed his lip and scanned for another exit, but it was hard to get a clear view of the place through all the demons. The building was definitely a bar, or at least it had been. The current guests probably weren't tossing vodka shots and leaving tabs open in here.

Frazzled anxiety scratched at his chest—fight or flight mode, and he would settle for whichever one was easiest. He walked faster, still searching for an escape, and Mayrez laughed. She yanked him up a set of stairs with the rope around his neck.

"What the hell is this, Mayrez?" a demon called out. "You said you were going to get us some nice blends. All I see is some human garbage."

"Calm down, boys, don't let your eyes betray you. We got a diamond in the rough here." Mayrez draped her arm around Ander and pinched his cheek, forcing him to gaze out at the crowd who were a blur of eyes and teeth. *Oh god, fuck.* He started hyperventilating, each pull of air hitting the back of his throat and making him swallow hard.

"Smile, boy, you want them to like you," Mayrez whispered between thin lips. She pulled him across to an empty stage. Where was everyone else? No one else was being forced through the swinging doors. Where were they taking the Couriers?

Why was he alone?

Again.

"I think you've gone crazy, May. Maybe you're hitting the stuff too hard, losing your brain. Now you'll only be a pretty face." The demon snorted, chuckling. He took a swig from a mug. Red dripped from it. Ander swung his head from mug to mug in every demon's hand. They were all drinking blood. Oh god.

"Fuck off," Mayrez said. "Now you don't get to bid, Laz."

"Oh, how unfortunate, I won't get to waste my salts on a fucking beanpole."

A few other demons laughed and Mayrez hissed. With her attention diverted, Ander tried to figure a way out. Obvious exit: where he came in. There were a sea of demons between him and it. Sharks in the water. *Elsewhere?* Windows to the left and right had bars on them.

Breathing was getting difficult. His jaw clenched. *Fuck.* He was freaking out. He was freaking the fuck out.

In the midst of his very reasonable panic attack, Mayrez slashed the side of his face. His blood splattered onto the stage as he doubled over, pain flaring across his cheek. What the *hell?*

"Taste it, you fucks," Mayrez snapped raising her free hand. Ander blinked furiously; she had gotten near his eye, and the world was faded, messy.

A demon close to the stage—dressed in an all-white suit— scoffed before swiping a smooth pale finger through the blood. He brought it to his lips, licked it softly with a sharp pink tongue. Immediately he lurched to his feet, his chair clattering behind him. "He's a Half."

"Are you kidding me!" a voice cried out. "There's no way that fucker's a Half!"

The whole bar echoed with voices, shouts. Demons started yelling things that Ander couldn't understand.

Mayrez cackled and smacked Ander's back. "I knew they'd love you."

"I'm not—I'm not a Half," Ander stammered, unsure how he managed to get the words out. "I don't . . . I mean look at me."

The crowd in front of him seemed to think otherwise, especially the man who had tasted his blood, the one now staring at him, hard. Ander took another step backward, thrashed his arms, rubbed against the leather that bound his wrists. He had to get out. He had to get out.

Nearby demons reached out their clawed hands, scraped Ander's blood to their mouths. As soon as they got a taste, they became ecstatic, murmuring to themselves, eyes fixated on Ander; wolves licking their chops for a bite of sheep. Every time he made eye contact with one of them, the cold panic in his chest built further, consuming him.

"What will the bets start at, friends? I'm not selling him for less than three hundred pounds of salt, unless one of you fuckers has a soul instead."

Ander bit harshly into his lip.

"Three hundred? You're crazy!"

"That's high even for an angel!"

"You're trying to pull a fast one!"

"I bet five hundred."

The room went quiet, which was somehow worse than the noise. The bet had come from the demon in the front, the demon in complete white. His eyes were a pale blue, like a dry day—empty.

Mayrez whistled. "Really liked that taste, huh, Micah?"

"Five hundred," Micah repeated. His hair was snow-white, and a ring of small and translucent horns made their way around the top, with two bigger ones in front. This demon appeared oddly angelic amongst the rest of the crowd. He fixed his jacket, and Ander could see specks of his own blood splattered on it. As if it was a canvas for his wound.

"Five-fifty," someone else shouted—Ander didn't see who. Micah's stare had captured him. He was lost in that stillness, trapped in the ice.

"Six-fifty!" Micah gritted his teeth. There was a frigid cold that came off him. Like the darkness of a winter blizzard. Like starvation, isolation, hopelessness. It made Ander want to hide, get away. He was not safe if this demon could see him, that much he was sure of. All of them were monsters, yet this one was something *worse*.

"Has he healed already?" a demon asked, just loud enough to prompt a few others to eye Ander more intently. He paled. Fuck. Well, there went any chance of him escaping unnoticed.

The murmur of the crowd turned to an eager buzz, and Ander's knees started to shake. Mayrez grabbed him by the chin, turned him toward her, and ran a thumb down his face where the slice had been.

"Shit." She wrapped her arm around Ander again and pulled him in close. "That starting price has doubled folks. We've got a healing angel here; you know what that means." She stuck out her tongue. "He's got a longer expiration date."

"A thousand!"

"Two thousand!"

"Fuck you!"

"Two thousand and five hundred!"

"You don't have that!"

"Let me see him!"

Demons started to claw over each other to get closer, a mass of teeth and claws. Mayrez snarled. "Hey, everyone, cool it!"

A demon began to yank himself onto the stage, only for Mayrez to drop Ander's ropes, dart forward, and shove him full force. He went tumbling into the crowd, but two more were already taking his place. They clambered onto the platform, and Mayrez huffed like a bull as she started to punt and toss the assailants before they made it halfway across the stage. She grabbed one by the skull and *crushed* it. "I said fuck off!"

For a second, the energy of the crowd wavered.

Ander inched backward.

He had to run. He didn't know how, or where the fuck he would go, but he had to go, and he had to go *now*.

He cautiously took another step back as Mayrez swiped at a nearby demon with a hiss, electricity flashing in the air, and the swarm reared back with wide eyes. *Where to go, where to go? Fuck, where— There.* Through a gap in the curtains, a dusty emergency exit sign gleamed above a doorway. He darted.

The chaos went from a storm to a hurricane. Suddenly every demon was full-out screeching in frenzied rage. He ignored them and flung himself through the exit doors. What a fucking stupid plan, maybe even more so than his original of leaving Gardners.

The fire escape was not an immediate out. Ander found himself running through a small hallway, which was stuffed to the brim with gadgets, chains, whips, collars—things that made his skin crawl. Far ahead of him was another door. That one *had* to go outside.

But what then? Just because I'm outside doesn't mean I'm free.

He ignored that thought and every other doubt and ran.

He had just managed to put a good distance between him and the first door, when the ground beneath him opened up.

Before he could hit whatever lay below, a figure slammed him into a stone wall, pinning him there. His head rang from the impact. Clawed fingers gripped his mouth, and the person whispered hotly into his ear, rough and low.

"Don't make a sound, fuzzball."

Ander's wide stare met bright aqua-green eyes that seemed to glow in the darkness. Overhead, there was clamoring, shouting, hisses, and cries. Mayrez was screaming at the top of her lungs. "Find that fucking Halfie right now or I'm killing all of you!"

The demon in front of him chuckled a bit, holding a finger to his lips. He had knife-like ears, and they twitched to the side, like a rabbit . . . or a puppy. The comparison confused Ander as soon as he thought it.

There was so much noise above him, all the demons yelling incomprehensibly. The ravenous screeches sent Ander's heart beating a thousand times a second, his breath slipping in panicked huffs between the demon's hand.

The demon, keeping his finger on his lips, slowly removed his other hand from Ander's mouth. He slid his claws to the binding around Ander's wrists, then paused. With a flick of his hand, the demon split the fabric open, freeing him. *What the hell?* Ander curled his sore hands to his chest with shaking breaths. The thrumming in his ears was making him dizzy, and his whole body was hot with adrenaline. He stared into the dark, body tense and mouth a firm line, waiting for the demon to bite him or do something, anything.

After a minute, the demon tugged one of his hands softly, urging him further into the strange and secret bottom floor.

Ander resisted for the shortest second. This was still a demon. The path was pitch-black and eerie, and he had no clue what was ten feet in front of him. However, he did know that above him monsters were ripping a building apart to find him so they could drink his blood. There was Micah. There was Mayrez.

So, unfortunately, following a mysterious demon into a tunnel seemed like the best option. He let the demon pull him into the darkness, taking his dwindling hope along.

CHAPTER FOUR

I t smelled musty and strange wherever they were. Every so often they would pass a light bulb strung up on the wall that let him glimpse a little of his surroundings. All he could tell was that the wiring was terrible and they appeared to be in cement tunnels. That wasn't exactly comforting.

In front of him, something swished back and forth; it had brushed his nose a few times. Ander guessed that the demon had a tail, but he couldn't make it out properly, even during the few times they dashed in front of a light source. It felt feathery.

The yelling and shouting overhead had slowly faded away, but they kept moving. Ander's shaking hadn't stopped; where was he being taken? Had he escaped just so this guy could devour him all by himself? Getting away from one demon seemed easier than getting away from twenty. But he still had no idea how.

Suddenly, they halted.

"Stay there," the demon said, letting go of Ander's hand, which Ander yanked back immediately. The casual contact with a *monster* had been unnerving. He stared uneasily in the darkness, as around him sounded the *thumps* of footsteps. *What on earth is he doing?* Something screeched, something broke, and then in a blinding flash, there was light. Ander jumped, squinting until the white faded away.

He was in a small room with brick walls and broken furniture scattered about—and a bar? As out of place as it seemed, there it was, a stained counter with dozens of dusty glass bottles behind it. Thin wooden chairs circled tables with moth-bitten checkerboard tablecloths. Above hung a chandelier coated with filth that clouded the crystal lights. Everything seemed old: the appearance, the smell, and the air itself. A tangible heaviness caked the place, made from dirt and grit.

Even with all of that, nothing was as surprising as the demon that stood a couple of feet from Ander. He wore no shirt, and his skin was a sun-earned sandy color with black patches on the shoulders like massive ink stains. The guy was muscled, probably from running around murdering people.

He also appeared younger than expected given how gravelly his voice was. He looked only a couple of years older than Ander. Ander didn't take that at face value though; the guy could be a thousand years old. Ander's understanding of demons was limited after all. What he did know was that they couldn't be trusted. He narrowed his eyes.

"Welcome to my secret little hovel, dust ball," the demon said, sliding over the top of the counter before coming to a stop. He crossed his legs and placed a hand on his stubbled chin, charcoal-gray hair flipping to the side. A sharp smile cut across his face that exuded an almost cheeky confidence. It was strange on a demon.

"Why did you bring me here?" Ander stepped backward, his hands skimming across an old turntable. He scanned for an obvious exit but found only the one they had come from. Was this room a dead end?

"Straight to the point, huh?" The demon chuckled, showing two rows of pointed teeth, one of the canines chipped. They all matched the two white horns on his head. "That's fair, that's fair. I mean, I didn't save you out of the goodness of my own heart, I'll tell you that much." He licked his lips, and Ander shivered.

"Are you going to kill me?" Oh god—he needed a weapon. He glanced down at the table with the record player; it had a drawer that was slightly open. Maybe something useful was stuffed inside. "Is that what this is about?"

"Pfft, what? No, dude." The demon waved his hand nonchalantly, as if they weren't talking about Ander's life. *Did he say dude?* "That would be completely . . . irresponsible of me. It would be pointless. A waste of your blood. No, no, I brought you here to one, save you, and two, offer you a proposition." He wiggled two fingers.

"A proposition?"

"Well, yeah. Duh." He swung his legs around and jumped off the counter. A long and gray tail swished behind him with a feathery mass of white and pale silver at the end, fanning out like a quill. "You're a Halfie, you little puffball. Do you know how long it's been since anyone has seen one? A bunch of them got murdered right in the beginning." He slid a sharp black claw across his throat. "Because some assholes couldn't control themselves when we got here. Then the remainder either joined up with the angels or . . . made deals."

"What does that mean?"

The demon had taken one step and then stopped. "What?"

"What do you mean they made deals?" Ander repeated. "What does that mean?"

"You know, a deal?" The demon waved his hands between the two of them. "A deal with a demon. An agreement, a pact?"

Ander simply stared. He had heard, of course, about deals with the devil and shit like that back before anyone thought demons were real. But that had only been through strange folklore talk, catchy country songs. However, as he looked into this demon's bright sea-foam eyes, he could tell there was more going on.

"Where have you been this whole time, buddy? Under a rock?" The demon raised an eyebrow.

Ander thought of the Couriers, to Michael, to all the things they had been hiding from the city. "Kind of? So I'm going to need you to elaborate."

"Okay, okay, then." The demon tilted his head, mouth scrunching for a moment. "A deal is what I said, an agreement. You ask something of me, I ask something in return, and then I am bound by that agreement, but so are you."

He took a step forward. Ander tried to retreat, but he'd already backed up as far as he could. He glanced over at the drawer; an object glistened inside it. Metal? "Bound how?"

"Bound by magic, or power, or whatever." The demon threw his hands up in the air. "I don't exactly know how it works either, but it *does*; that's the point. And you know what I want from you." He clicked his tongue. "So, I need to know what you want from me, and we can get this show on the road."

Ander chewed his lip. Was this a real thing? It didn't make sense. "Why not kill and eat me?"

"I already said, that's a waste. You're packed full of Halfie blood. Killing one of the few of you left, that diminishes the supply. Bad for everyone, but especially me." He placed his hands on his chest and took another step; he was only a foot away from Ander now. The height difference made Ander's heart race. "I want you all to myself, my own personal stock of blood, and that's what the deal will ensure. If you bind yourself to me, your blood becomes *only* for me. Another demon couldn't have you; your blood would be a poison to them." His eyes lit up. "It would kill them."

Ander's body fuzzed with what felt like static as his eyes grew wide. Fuck. This guy wanted to cart him around like a juice bottle. "What happens if I say no?"

The demon scowled. "Well. Then I wouldn't need you. And I'd toss you back up there. That would be unfortunate, I'd imagine. Mayrez is probably really pissed off."

Whelp. Ander's pickings were looking slim.

"But that won't happen, because of course you'll choose the option I'm giving you. After all, it's a win-win. There's got to be something you want, and I'm a demon—a fucking demon, kid. Power, riches, a couple of dead bodies? I'm your guy." He winked. "There's a reason people make deals with us, buddy; we are beneficial entrepreneurs. Wonderful trading partners. All you have to do is tell me what we're trading."

That was the problem. Ander didn't want anything; he simply wanted to make it to—

Wait.

"Anything?" he asked.

"Yeah, kid. Anything."

"I need to get somewhere." Ander fidgeted, glancing at the ground. How could he guarantee this wouldn't go south? If he worded it wrong, would it get twisted around like in some sick fairy tale?

"Bro, I can get you *anywhere*."

"But what happens when we get there?" Ander stared at the demon harshly. "What happens to the deal then? You keep taking my blood after that? For the rest of my life?"

"Ideally, yes. I'd take from you when I need it. Whenever I want."

Nausea hit Ander, bile at the back of his throat. He couldn't believe he was contemplating this. Letting a demon invade his body whenever it felt so inclined; a lifetime of someone pulling blood from his veins like oil from the cracked ground. But what choice did he have? He'd been torn away from the Couriers. Mayrez was after him. He was alone, he was lost, and he had nothing. This demon could get him out of that.

"I need to get to Atlasville."

"Oh, that's a bit far. You're on an adventure, huh?"

Ander glared. "I have someone I need to get to. And I need you to get me there, alive, safe, and unharmed. You have to do whatever it takes to protect me." He hesitated. "And promise—*swear*—to bring me to who I'm looking for."

"Who are we looking for?"

"His name is Ronan. He's important to me. He's my foster brother." Ander's face was hot. "I don't know if he's alive or not, but I have to find out. He's all I have left. He's all I've ever had—" His voice broke, catching him off guard. This was the first time he'd said so much about Ronan to anyone.

"I see," the demon mused. "Okay. All you need from me is a bodyguard of sorts. I can do that. We travel, I get you to Atlasville, we find this Ronan guy, and you become my meal ticket. It's a great plan. I am one hundred percent on board." He clapped his hands. "Let's make it official!"

"How—how do we do that?" Ander asked, shoulders tensing. All he could picture was a sick sacrifice involving slitting the throat of a bird or small mammal. Maybe dipping a paintbrush in the blood and drawing a pentagram on the floor. He didn't know a lot about the world of the occult.

The demon smirked. And kissed him.

Fire went through his body, from his face to his toes, ravaging him in a flash. The demon's claws grabbed Ander's upper thighs and *burned* him. The air was ripped from his lungs and replaced with flame. He couldn't think, he couldn't breathe. There was only the raging blaze, stripping everything in its path.

Then the demon pulled away, taking most of the inferno with him. Ander gasped. What the fuck had happened? His knees wouldn't quit shaking. And . . . there was a tendril of *fire* flickering in his chest. He pressed his fingers against the strange heat.

"You feel that, huh? Now it's official. I'm Sytri, your one and only beloved demon." Sytri took a bow, looking up with a smirk. "And you are?"

"A-Ander."

Ander's face grew hotter, his hands trembling. What specifically had happened inside of him to make *this* official? *Oh my god. I think I've made a horrible mistake.*

"Ander? That's pretty cute. I'm probably going to stick to calling you fuzzball, though. Or maybe dust bunny. Freckles? Maybe Halfie. It's nice and sweet. We'll figure it out." Sytri flicked his nose. Ander stayed plastered to the wall, trying to regain his breath.

What have I done?

CHAPTER FIVE

"Come on, fuzzball. You know what—that is my favorite. Fuzzball. That's good for you. Anyway, come on, fuzzball. This way out if we want to avoid Mayrez. And I promise you that we want to avoid Mayrez. Obviously." Sytri turned and pushed a shelf full of liquor bottles across the floor with one hand. It moved easily, and a darker path was on the other side. Great. The secret tunnel had more secret tunnels.

"What is this place?" Ander asked, eyeing the path. Even as he tried to distract himself, his hand kept going to his chest, feeling the erratic beat of his heart. He took a deep breath, slowly let it out. "You seem to know it well."

"It was, um, what do you call it? A place where your people went when the guys in charge made alcohol illegal. You know, the real-bar-under-the-fake-bar kind of thing? I found it a couple of days ago when I was snooping around. Lucky for you, huh? But that's beside the point. We have to leave now. Mayrez is like a blood hound. Ha! Pun. I made a pun. Get it? 'Cause she sells blood? Do you— You know what, never mind. You're slow. You going to be like this the whole trip?"

Before Ander could react, Sytri was behind him, shoving him into the tunnel. *He doesn't slow down.* The new path smelled sour and was a thousand times colder than the one they'd come from. Sytri's hands felt extra warm in comparison.

"We have like a mile to walk, so you can't be stopping and asking stuff every minute, okay? I super don't want to try and fight Mayrez. She's crazy, if you haven't noticed, and has a posse." Sytri flicked a switch on the wall, and dusty bulbs strung on the side lit up with a crackle. Everything took on an orange hue, and the passage before them seemed endless.

Ander swallowed. "Aren't all demons crazy?"

"Wow. Okay. Kinda rude but whatever. No, no, we're not all crazy. Look at me. I'm a well-adjusted individual."

"I, uh, I don't know about that honestly." Ander raised an eyebrow. *I think you only stop talking to breathe.*

"I saved your life! They would have torn you to shreds up there. Be nibbling on your thin-ass bones." Sytri smacked Ander's back. "Be grateful, dude."

"I'm sorry. But excuse me for not being excited that to stay alive I had to make a deal with a demon. I don't even fully understand the consequences besides the fact now there's some weird fire in my chest. Also, you used the deal to molest me, so . . . you know. Yeah." Ander scowled at Sytri the best he could. Unfortunately, he'd never been good at appearing pissed, even when he truly was.

"Molest? That kiss? It was absolutely necessary. There must be a physical connection to make the deal. And it has to be intimate. What? You wanted me to jerk you off instead?"

"No!" Ander took a quick step away from Sytri, his feathers fluffing up. He brought his hands to his face, trying to cover the blush on his cheeks.

"Well, then don't complain. Most demons want the whole shebang. That ain't my deal, though. And, anyway, you're cute and all, but not my type."

"I don't want to be your type! And you're not mine either!" His blush grew worse.

"See? So why are you upset about a kiss? Was it your first one?"

"It doesn't matter if it was or wasn't," Ander muttered, cheeks on fire. "People don't like being kissed out of nowhere!"

"Oh yeah. Humans take that kind of stuff more seriously. My bad." Sytri clicked his tongue. "But it was your first one, wasn't it?"

Ander scrunched his mouth shut and glared at the floor. There was silence from Sytri, and then he broke out into a cackle.

"Ha, I knew it!" The demon waved his hand. "So, you're like a *virgin*-virgin. Woof. You should be real glad you ran into a demon like me instead of an incubus."

An incubus? Ander's ears were burning. Could something truly be worse than Sytri? Ander had obviously made a deal with the most annoying being on the planet.

Sytri nudged Ander's shoulder. "Sorry to have stained your modesty. It sucks that you're miserable when I'm having a great time. This has been the most exciting thing to happen here in . . . months. And I'm super pumped to get me some of that Halfie blood."

"Please don't talk about my modesty or how you want to drink my blood."

"But I do."

"That's gross. That's real gross." Ander cringed. "How can it possibly taste good? And what does angel blood even taste like that makes it so much different than a human's?"

"Well, first off, pure angel blood is very off-limits. That shit will kill us. It's like concentrated innocence and it does not mix well with a demon. However, a Halfie, such as yourself, is the perfect blend of angel and human. A nice, nontoxic concoction of the best of both worlds. Enough kick for us to really feel it, without the dying part."

"Okay, so what, it gets you all high and that's worth risking your life over?"

"What? Dude. What? You think it's only about the high? Oh fuck, you guys don't know anything." Sytri laughed. "No wonder so many of you made deals right away. You don't know what the deal with angel blood is, do you?"

"No, of course not! How could I?"

"I mean, you have your cool angel powers now, right? So that tells you something about it."

"Actually, I don't—"

"Your blood gives you those abilities; angel blood is full of energy and life and purity and an essence out of this world. If we demons can get a hold of that, in a way that doesn't kill us, we get some of that too. We can *absorb* that. It's like salt for blends;

salt increases the angel in you, gives you a nice high. Blend blood increases our natural gifts, our strength, and gives us a nice high."

"What?"

"Yeah, dude. We get stronger off your blood. And I want me some of that." Sytri's tail swished back and forth like a dog's. The noir-themed feathers swayed ever so slightly with the movement. "And I was beginning to think every Halfie on the planet was either dead or had made a deal and I was shit out of luck and would have to settle for a blend that was . . . I don't know, only a quarter or something. But then Mayrez strolled in with you." Sytri wrapped an arm around Ander. "And my day got a whole lot brighter. Getting a deal with you is like winning the lottery. So yeah, I'm excited. And you should be too. I'm not a bad demon to make a deal with. Imagine if Mayrez had forced you to make one with her. Or Micah."

Ander recalled the all-white demon, the way his eyes had stared so deeply into him. It was enough to make Ander's skin crawl. Those eyes had a starving, savage hunger behind them. "How could they force me to make a deal?"

"All they need to do is get you to say yes and then make the connection." Sytri's tone went low for the briefest second. "They can force a blend to say yes. It's not that hard, if you think about it."

"Oh." Ander grimaced. What would Micah have done to him to make him say yes? Heavy fear spread throughout his chest, and he had to will it away. "Now that we've made a deal though, another demon can't force me into one, right?"

"Not until I'm dead they can't. And I promise you, I'd have to be for them to take you away from me."

The words sounded sweet, and for a moment Ander almost mistook them for kindness. However, Sytri's need to protect was based purely on his own personal gain. There was nothing caring about his declaration. Ander was his sheep, not to be feasted on by other wolves.

"You super don't seem to understand how this whole demon thing works; where have you been this whole time?" Sytri asked, raising an eyebrow.

"In my city. Gardners. I just kind of stayed there . . . It was safe."

"All right, yeah, I heard about that place. Full of angels and shit. A big no-demons-allowed zone. I guess it makes sense then that you wouldn't know a lot about us. So how long did you stay there?"

"Once I got in there? Until today."

"Oh. Buddy. You were not off to a great start, beginning your journey on the same day Mayrez decided to jump the Couriers. That is unfortunate."

"So she'd been planning it?"

"Yeah. She'd been keeping tabs on them for weeks. I told you, blend blood is running low and she wants more. The more she can get, the more she can sell, and the stronger she can get. She always sneaks a sip or two before she sells the blend off." Sytri nudged him. "I'm telling you, I got you out of there in the nick of time. Mayrez would have been lapping at your blood like a kitten with a saucer of milk."

"That's disgusting."

"I'll be nicer about it, I promise," Sytri said with a laugh. His pale gray hair skimmed across Ander's forehead as he leaned in close. "But, spoiler alert, I'm going to lap you up too."

"Don't say it like that!" Ander said, voice hitting an octave he hadn't known he could reach. He shoved Sytri away. "That's super creepy!" He wrapped his arms around his stomach, holding down the urge to vomit.

"It's the facts," Sytri said with a snort. "You made a deal and you're going to have to pay up, Halfie."

"Well, you have to stick to your part of the deal," Ander said defiantly.

"I can hold up my end of the bargain, no problem," Sytri said, putting a hand on his hip. "I'm aware you don't quite believe me, because you apparently know nothing about demons, but I'm a pretty tough dude."

"Did you just say, 'tough dude'?"

"Yeah. It's the truth."

Ander's mouth twisted as he studied Sytri. He wasn't acting violent like Mayrez nor disturbingly cold like Micah. He had the same aura all demons had, the wild electric air of a strange animal. But his lacked menace. In fact, being around him was like being in the presence of a very energetic housecat after escaping the maws of lions.

Ander watched him as they kept on walking, really observing the demon. His legs and body were lean and taut, like he worked out. He didn't have human ears, instead they were long and rabbit-like, covered in gray fur—the same color as his tail. This fur meshed into the stubble along the cut of his jaw.

Sytri tilted his head, his neck cracking. Ander winced.

The demon was so close to being a person. Just a little off. If there were more demons like him at Millstone, no wonder it threw the Couriers for a loop. It was easy to fear a creature that mimicked a human so well, that could talk to you sweetly before it killed. At least the huge monstrous ones couldn't mask their intentions behind a human facade.

"Dude, why are you looking at me so hardcore? You're freaking me out." Sytri's face was suddenly close, the glow of his seafoam eyes like a strange otherworldly fire. Ander couldn't stutter anything before Sytri started talking again, turning back toward their path. "You were vacant. Like a mannequin. What is that? Your thinking face?"

"No, I'm—"

"It's pretty dumb looking. But kind of cute, I guess. Not a good thinking face, though."

"Why are you constantly rude to me?"

"What? I said you were cute. How is that rude?" Sytri's ears folded downward a bit.

"Never mind. Ignore what I said. Are we almost out of this place?"

"Yeah. Yeah, we are."

Ander waited for Sytri to say something else but nothing came. Oh no. He had to go and hurt the demon's feelings of all things. And he shouldn't care, honestly. It was a *demon*.

But that demon was all that he had.

An uncomfortable silence crept in, the only sound coming from their footsteps hitting the cold, damp ground. The quiet wedged itself between Ander's heart and bones, pressed against him, icy and sharp. Thoughts spun in his head. Sytri hated him. He would abandon Ander here in this tunnel.

If he didn't just kill him outright.

Change the subject, keep a conversation going. "So, um, why do they trade us for salt? What does Mayrez need salt for? Like you said, it's an angel-and-blend drug," Ander asked, his voice a little raspy.

Sytri didn't answer immediately, and Ander chewed into a fingernail.

"She makes trades with angels sometimes." Sytri's voice almost made Ander jump. "A lot of angels are willing to barter for a good chunk of salt."

"Angels actually trade with her?" Ander scowled, though his stomach was in more knots than it had been seconds prior. "But angels—"

"What? Are the good guys?" Sytri scoffed. "Maybe. But they also want salt. And the bigger angels already laid claim to the mines and depositories. So, the smaller, way weaker ones, they have to bend their morals a bit to scratch their itch."

That was a truth Ander couldn't seem to swallow. But why else would Mayrez have been willing to trade for it? "The angels that protected my town wouldn't do that. Anything with high amounts of salt was banned. I think that's part of the reason they didn't let us out for so long, so we couldn't get our hands on it. Though people used to smuggle out soy sauce bottles from the stashes the angels hid away."

"What?" Sytri snorted, clearly failing to hold back a laugh. "Contraband soy sauce?"

"Our angels went through the town and plucked it out of houses and hands. The higher blends said it'd make us lose our humanity." Ander paused. "And they were right. Eventually, some people stole it, ate it, and changed—in a bad way. I didn't want any part of that."

"Even if it could have made you stronger?"

"Yes." Ander looked away, licking his lips. It had been tempting. "I want to be stronger. But I don't want to lose *me*." He shivered. "The people who ate it changed in a way that was more than physical. Something about *who they were* got warped. They got all weird and silent like angels are. And when they did talk, their voices were . . . hollow, empty. Eventually they got kicked out. The whole ordeal was pretty serious, and blends were more restricted than ever after that." He put his arms around himself.

"But weren't they wanting to become more like angels? Shouldn't that have been okay?" Sytri murmured.

"The angels don't think humans, even blends, should change in such a messed-up way."

"Bet it's because they don't want competition."

"Angels wouldn't make rules based on something like that. They're not demons."

"Fuck me, then."

"I didn't— I don't know. But angels only seem focused on protecting us. And demons seem to want to do the opposite; I mean, demons just tried to auction me off," Ander said, waving his hands. "Angels have never done that. And they never talk about people like we're property."

"Well, you said angels barely talk right? You don't know what they could be thinking. Maybe they do consider you all property. Maybe that's why they kept you locked up in a city."

"That's not why they did it!"

"Whatever helps you sleep at night. Anyway at least demons are honest—we say everything right there out in the open. That's not a bad thing in my opinion."

"I guess it isn't when you *aren't* saying weird things and you politely answer my questions. Even if I could understand the angels, I bet they wouldn't tell me anything useful." Ander paused. "So, what was Hell like?"

"Whoa, okay just shooting that question out, huh?"

"I've always wanted to know."

"You and every other human."

"How could we not?" Ander grinned.

"Seems like a waste to worry about." Sytri shrugged. "I guess it's a lot like Earth."

"But with fire?"

"What? No. No, why does everyone think it's full of fire?"

"I don't know, a lot of religions have it hot."

"It's not. It's a lot like Earth, really, but darker. And I mean darker literally—we don't have a sky. Only this blackness that goes on to who knows where. Asked Kyle once where it went, and he said it ended in a black hole. Don't know if he was messing with me."

"Kyle?"

"The boss of Hell."

"So, the Devil? The Devil's name is Kyle?"

"No. He's not . . . not the Devil you're thinking about. We have like a royalty system down there; the position of ruler is passed down through generations. Kyle is our current ruler. He's called the Darkest Soul. Real edgy title. He doesn't like it, though. He prefers to just be called Kyle. He's a very sweet kid."

"So, Hell is like Earth and it's ruled by a guy named Kyle?"

"Yes."

"That is not how I pictured Hell."

"Yeah. A lot of people don't. People are super shocked when they end up there. I mean, it's not like it *isn't* an absolute shithole. It's full of the really sadistic demons, like the ones that were crawling all over Earth and eating people. And some demons like me, the humanoid ones, still like torturing and shit cause they're old-timers."

Ander's stomach turned. "You tortured people?"

There was a pause and Sytri took a deep breath.

"I was different in Hell." A coldness permeated his voice. "Different than who I am now. Worse, for sure. But I wouldn't say I *tortured* people. Whatever. That's not the point. There were other things there besides demons." He shivered. "Things that wormed out from the sulfur sometimes and sent us hiding. And you're trapped with them. It's Hell and you're trapped."

Ander was still fixated on the first part. What did a demon consider *worse*? The thought traced its fingers down his spine, goosebumps blossoming in their wake. "What do you mean you were different?"

"Drop it okay?" Sytri growled.

Ander flinched. *Okay. Dropped.* "You said 'trapped'; you mean by the Gates? Like the actual Gates?"

"Yeah. They're huge. I mean fucking huge. Think of the tallest thing you've ever seen and fucking erase that from your mind because the gates of Hell tower over that shit. No one has ever seen the top of them. They just keep going, and they're the only constant source of light, always shining gold. Always in your peripheral. I was there once when every demon in Hell tried to break them. We couldn't. Couldn't even put a dent in them."

"So, who could?"

"I don't know."

"Oh."

"Yeah. *Oh.* Everyone wants to know who did it and how. I just woke up one day to everyone shouting, and saw that the gates were busted. There was a clear gap like someone had pushed them apart. I didn't think twice about running through it." Sytri turned toward Ander. "Why're you so curious?"

"Why wouldn't I be?" Ander twisted his mouth. "My whole life was destroyed because the gates broke."

"That makes sense. Sorry about that. Unfortunate that the best day of my life was probably your worst."

"*Probably?*"

"Definitely. My bad. If it means anything, I didn't go around eating anybody. I'm a new-age demon, and that's not my style."

Ander stared at Sytri, whose expression was impassive for once.

"Then what did you do?"

"When I got out?" Sytri stopped. In front of them was a thick wooden door, heavy and old. Sytri grabbed the handle and pulled. With a groan, it opened and soft sunlight poured through, bringing with it the smell of grass and hot air. Even the heat was refreshing; it was the sensation of freedom.

Sytri grinned wildly before stepping through, pulling Ander with him by the hand. They went through a small shed with broken windows that let the rays of light cut in, highlighting spiderwebs and dust. This place had clearly long been abandoned. Sytri closed the door behind them, opened another one in front, and a gust of warm wind hit them.

"I enjoyed this," Sytri finished.

They were in a cornfield that was barely holding on to life. The sun was thinking of setting, pink beginning to form around the horizon. It gave the whole world a warm tint, a glow that made Ander think of lemonade and strawberries. He turned to see that they had walked out from: a shack that was pressed up against a small hill, which was more of a mound of dirt than anything.

Sytri kept his hand intertwined with Ander's, gesturing at the sky with the other. "That shit right there," he said. "Is the best thing I've ever fucking seen. It was so dark in Hell. It was like living in those fucking tunnels. Everything was dark and dim, and I was so fucking angry all the time. Where I lived . . . made me furious. Desperate." Sytri gritted his teeth. "And everyone was always fighting, screaming, bleeding."

Ander stared at their fingers; Sytri was gripping him a little tighter. *He was different in Hell.* "What do you want to do now that you're not there?"

Sytri paused. "I don't know that part yet." He faced Ander, the sun glistening through his gray hair, his horns almost blindingly white. His body was outlined by the light, giving his tan skin a golden glow.

An odd pressure bubbled up in Ander's throat. It was a sensation so close to fear.

But he had no fear right now—though there were a million reasons why he should. Instead, the uncomfortable weight was an unknown. He furrowed his eyebrows and slipped his hand out of Sytri's.

What he did understand was that he had to be careful.

CHAPTER SIX

Sytri stretched out his arms and groaned as they trudged on through the cornfield, mostly barren orange ground with a bundle of stalks here and there. Ander stayed as close behind him as he could. Even though everything seemed all right for the moment, it could change.

After at least two solid hours of walking, the sun setting and the moon rising, he remained on guard. Every noise in the night was a threat unseen. Mayrez could still be searching for him for all he knew. When he blinked, in that brief darkness he could see her—vicious grin, claws like knives. Panic thrummed in his chest and he had to will it down. He had nothing out here in the open to protect him. Just Sytri.

A demon. Everything that Ander had been holding in his heart, his hatred, his fear, had been because of demons. They had desolated humanity and *reveled* in it. Cackled just like Sytri.

"Fuck man, we've been walking forever. Can't you get on my back and I can like super-speed us out of here?"

Annoyance cleared the anxiety in Ander's lungs. "I don't want you to super-speed me anywhere," he said, rolling his eyes. The idea of going piggyback across the state on a demon wasn't appealing. It would leave him more dependent on Sytri than he already was. "Do you . . . do you really call it super-speed?"

"What else am I supposed to call it?"

"I don't know."

"What about sonic speed? Ultra-fast."

"These all sound like video games moves," Ander said. "Do you say those in your head before you run?"

"No."

Ander held back a chuckle as Sytri's ears went down. The demon was clearly trying to not show his emotions, his face impassive; however, his body always gave him away. Or perhaps it was an act. But if it was, it was a good one. *Almost makes it hard to be afraid of him. Almost.*

"How far away do you think we are from Afriel?" Ander asked, not letting Sytri's bruised ego distract him. He looked up at the sky, where specks of stars had appeared; a bird flew overhead.

"Not far enough, because you refuse to let me carry you!"

"I'm already putting my life in your hands. I'd rather keep my body out of them."

"That's stupid. At some point you have to give me your blood. Where do you think my hands will be then?"

Ander clutched at his chest as if gripping pearls, and scowled. Sytri worded things so terribly. "We'll cross that bridge when we come to it."

"We're going to cross no bridges because you walk so damn slow! Can't you speed it up? Most blends aren't this slow."

"Well, I'm not like most blends."

"Yeah, you're a Halfie, so you should be faster."

Ander scrunched his mouth and stared at the darkening ground at his feet. Halfie. According to tales, Halves were beautiful, angels in human skin. Blends with eyes of light and wings of gold. Nothing about him seemed like a Half: his appearance, his abilities, *nothing.*

He touched his neck, scratched at his feathers. The demons had sure acted like Mayrez's claim was legitimate. They'd frenzied over his blood, become wild animals for it. *But then why am I so weak?*

"Are we positive I am a Half?" Ander asked.

Sytri's ears twitched. "What . . . what do you mean?"

"I just— I never thought I was."

"Of course you are. Mayrez knows her shit." Sytri turned, facing Ander but continuing to walk, backward. "What do you mean you didn't think you were?"

"Halves usually look more like . . . well, like they're a Half. I don't."

"Yeah, but that's fine. Sometimes that happens right?"

"Have you ever heard of a Half with such a mundane appearance?"

"Not personally, no, but I'm sure there are others." Sytri's tail pushed a stalk of corn out of his way. His bright eyes still stared at Ander. "What kind of angelic abilities do you have? Don't they make up for your lack of heavenly appearance?"

"I heal myself."

"And?"

"That's it."

"What the fuck." Sytri skidded to a stop. "You just heal yourself?"

"I mean, I don't even really heal myself. It sort of happens naturally."

"Are you kidding me?"

"No." Ander chewed his lip. "That's how it's always been. It's why I didn't think I was a Half." His face felt hot. "I didn't tell you that I was. Mayrez did." Halves were everything Ander admired. Everything he was not.

"Mayrez wouldn't lie about that. She wouldn't . . . she wouldn't have anything to gain from it." Sytri tapped his foot harshly onto the ground. "Would she? No. It would only piss off whoever she sold you to. They'd fucking kill her. And why would Micah lie?" He paced in a circle, his tail smacking everything out of his way with heavy thuds. "Nothing, though? Nothing? You're a Halfie with, like, fucking nothing? You might *not* actually be one?" He threw his arms out. "Are you fucking kidding me?"

"It's not like I wanted this! I wish I could do something, okay? Anything!" Ander snapped. "Do you know what it's like? Not being able to help anyone in this terrible world? I'm a nuisance to everyone. I might as well be a normal human. The Couriers got attacked, and all I could do was watch." He clenched his jaw. Even worse than that, now he'd abandoned them. A pit grew inside of his chest. *Michael wouldn't have left.*

He wanted to go back. But what could he possibly do?

"Let me taste your blood, then I'll know for sure," Sytri said, reaching out a clawed hand.

Ander smacked it away. "No."

"You've got to keep your part of the deal same as I do. That was the point of the fucking deal. And then I'll know for certain that Mayrez didn't somehow trick all of us."

Ander's heart raced as Sytri took a step closer. "I don't want to do that yet—" What if he really wasn't? What use would Sytri have for him then?

None. He'd kill me.

Sytri snatched his wrist, and Ander yelped, kicking him. The demon stumbled over broken corn and into the field, where he snapped a pile of stalks with a grunt.

Ander panted, his heartbeat pounding in his chest, body shaking. Sytri glanced upward, his pale green eyes glowing like an animal's in the darkness and moonlight.

They sent a shiver down Ander's spine. Sytri was a demon, plain and simple. His cheerful demeanor was a front to keep Ander by his side, nothing more. He was the same sort of creature that had snatched him and the other Couriers. One of the monsters who had almost ripped him apart for his blood.

Ander swallowed hard and forced back tears. He'd been an idiot to think for even a moment that he was safe with this monster.

"Halfie. I don't want to get forceful with you." Sytri pushed himself up off the ground. "We're supposed to be two buds on an adventure. Don't fuck it up by making me hate you."

"Don't you mess it up by making me hate *you*," Ander snapped back, taking a step away. "I'll give you my blood when I'm ready."

"It's just blood, dude. Mayrez drank some. Is this because you're a virgin?" Sytri raised an eyebrow. "Like, is giving blood similar to giving your body or—"

"They're not the same! It has nothing to do with that!" *I'm going to kill him.*

"Well then, what is it? We already made the deal. You can't break it. If you keep on resisting, you'll feel the backlash."

"Backlash?"

"It's the thing that makes sure we both stick to our part of the deal." Sytri tapped his chest. "If you start fighting it, the deal starts hurting. A lot." He huffed. "You don't want to feel it, fuzzball. I guarantee you that. And *I* need to make sure this deal wasn't a fucking waste for me. You're a so-called Halfie with no powers? Maybe Mayrez did trick everybody, and I ended up with some blend with only a smidge of angel blood."

Ander flinched. Now even a demon was telling him he was useless. Fuck, tears started breaking free, and painful cuts stung inside his chest.

It was hard to breathe.

"So get over here and let me find out if you're a Half or not, or I swear to god, I'll—"

Ander screamed as he was whipped into the air.

"Oh shit. Halfie!" Sytri yelled.

Streaks of fire ripped through his sides, and his legs flailed as the land swung beneath him. Rows of claws dug into his flesh. Above him was another demon. One of the physically *monstrous* ones.

Its face was shaped as if it had a beak, but where normal bone should be, it continued into pink and rotting flesh, swooping to a point. The mouth was full of gnarled teeth. As Ander stared in horror, a fat black tongue slid out and hit him in the face like a rubbery wet snake. He screeched, trying to keep it away from him, as saliva came off it in dense swathes. Fuck. He needed to force the demon to drop him.

He tried to tear the claws out of his body, but the demon's grip didn't budge. Ander scanned the monster up and down, desperate to find a weak point. Something fleshy and soft, like eyes. *Damn it*. Its head was attached to a disturbingly long and bony neck, keeping it out of Ander's reach.

The tongue smacked him in the face again, coating him in more saliva. Ander blanched. But then . . . *Soft? Check. Fleshy? Check.*

He grabbed it as hard as he could and yanked down, piercing it with his nails, drawing blood in spurts that oozed out of the slices. The demon gargled, his body tilting and jerking, and Ander yanked harder.

"Let go of me, you asshole!" he shouted. Even if the demon hadn't heard him, its pained scream showed that Ander's message had come across. It flitted closer to the ground and its claws loosened.

"Yeah, you asshole! Let go of him!"

A weight on Ander's leg brought him and the creature farther down. Sytri was hanging on his thigh and being slammed into cornstalk after cornstalk, his tail flapping wildly in the wind. If Ander wasn't afraid of death arriving at any moment, he would have laughed.

Sytri climbed up Ander's side, digging extra claws into him.

"That hurts!" Ander yelped.

"Sorry that me saving you is a little fucking painful, Halfie. Or would you rather I let the big fleshy bird demon eat you?" Sytri snapped. He hefted himself up and dug into the demon's bat-like wing before tearing it off. The demon's scream was like glass scraping on metal inside Ander's ears. His vision blurred as the demon shuddered with jerky, violent movements that sent the three of them toppling toward the earth.

Suddenly, Sytri was under Ander. He wrapped his arms around him, claws digging in. The sky was spinning, heaving.

Then they slammed into the solid ground.

The world cracked in Ander's skull like glass.

Seconds stretched out like years as Ander gripped Sytri's shoulders, burying his face in his chest. His lungs hurt and he gasped. Every bone ached. But Sytri had taken the brunt of the blow.

"Y-you okay?"

"Fuck, let's say I am," Sytri muttered. "What about you? Still in one piece?"

"Yeah I'm . . . Yeah." Ander waited a minute before the slight zip of electricity through his chest let him know that his body was already beginning to repair itself. The process would take a while, and he would feel it the whole time. It made his skin buzz like static on sheets. He cautiously lifted himself up and gazed down at Sytri. He was bleeding too, and it was strange. His blood was a soft green-blue, like his eyes, and had the same glow, like something toxic.

"Thank you."

"What else am I supposed to do? Let you get eaten?" Sytri scoffed. "We made a deal; even if you turn out to not be a Half, you're still my problem." He laughed, then took a long raspy breath. "And it looks like you love being a damsel in distress."

"I do not. I hate it."

"I've literally rescued you twice in less than twelve hours."

"It's not my fault," Ander grumbled, and then narrowed his eyes. "Seriously though, are you okay?" Sytri's breathing was thin, labored. He wasn't like Ander. He wouldn't heal as easily from his wounds. "You didn't have to take the fall. You know I can heal."

"Would you have been fine from that height?"

Ander glanced away. "I don't know." *Probably not.* The back of his head was still throbbing, and every other second the small *crick* of something moving back into place reverberated in his skull. He winced, hoping Sytri wouldn't see it.

"That's what I thought. You can't be risking things like that because you *might* be okay. Damn, dude. Anyway, as I said, I'm fine. I'm not a wimp." Sytri pushed himself up, as if to prove it. But he cringed, biting down on his bottom lip with sharp teeth. "I'm used to this kind of bullshit."

"You don't have to be a tough guy, you know?" Ander grumbled. Clearly Sytri didn't respect him, so why put on a cool guy routine?

Suddenly, Sytri tried to move again and Ander wobbled.

"Hey, man, you mind getting off of me?" Sytri nodded down.

Ander's ears grew hot. He was sitting on Sytri's lap. He flung himself to the ground. That was the most awkwardly intimate he'd been with anyone his entire life.

Sytri raised an eyebrow.

"So, uh, do you need a moment to rest?" Ander asked slowly, willing his blush to fade.

Sytri said nothing for a few seconds. Then, "Maybe a bit of one, yeah."

He'd been hurt. Bad. For Ander's sake.

"I'm . . . sorry that I threw a fit earlier."

"Whatever." Sytri rolled his eyes. "I don't get—"

"Guys! Maurice fell! I think someone got him!" a voice yelled out.

Sytri and Ander froze, then grimaced at each other.

Maurice? Sytri mouthed. The demon across from them groaned. "His name is Maurice?" Sytri hissed, frantically pointing at it.

"I don't know," Ander whispered back. "How would I know? You said the Devil's name was Kyle."

"First off, once again, not the Devil; secondly, that's different, his mother named— You know what, never mind. Not important right now."

"Maurice!" a different voice yelled. "Maurice, are you all right?"

The slightly-less-winged demon groaned again and quivered an arm into the air before it flopped back down.

"What kind of demon is named Maurice?" Sytri hissed. "That's so stupid. Aside from the royalty, we name ourselves. That's a stupid name, you asshole." He picked up a rock and tossed it at the demon. It whimpered.

"Sytri, stop it; he's hurt, you prick," Ander said, batting his hand.

"He just tried to kill you," Sytri snapped back in a low whisper.

"That's no reason to be a bully!"

"Are you kidding me? I thought we were bonding and you freaking—"

"Maurice!" a different voice chimed in. This one female. The big wounded demon cried back louder. "I think he's over here, you guys!"

"There's at least three of these assholes." Sytri grabbed Ander by the waist and stood up before crumpling over. "Shit. Shit."

"You're too hurt!"

"It's fine, I got this." Sytri shuffled his hands awkwardly. "Just stay close and I'll . . . I'll figure something out, okay? I'm not a fucking run-of-the-mill-demon." He spat on the ground.

Ander scowled. "You're too dramatic, you jerk. Not a second ago you said you needed a rest." The voices grew closer, louder; it sounded like there was a fourth one now too. They were surrounded in a cornfield by demons like some stupid B-flick horror movie. He shifted in place. Maurice continued to flop around, garbling in pain.

"You shut up!" Sytri hissed at Maurice, pointing at him. "This is your fucking fault, you idiot."

Maurice whined loudly and painfully into the night air.

"Maurice!" the woman yelled. There was running, feet on hard dirt.

Sytri was outnumbered and wounded. If Ander had only been willing earlier with his blood, perhaps this whole situation could have been avoided. They could have—

Wait. "My blood."

"What?" Sytri asked as he tried to stand up again and managed to hold a rather slumped stance.

"That's what you wanted right? That was the point of this? Well, take it! If my blood really is Half, it gives you a boost or something? Like steroids? I don't know—just do it!"

"What happened to Maurice?" a voice cried out.

Ander whipped his head around to see a man on the other side of their crash site, his eyes wide. His body was lean and appeared stretched, like elongated bones shoved in skin far too small. A body a skeleton had stolen. Each limb was about three times the length it should have been, his arms dragging on the ground.

For a second, Ander was paralyzed, overwhelmed by the demon's size, the rage that oozed off it as it searched for them. Then, pain hit him.

Sytri's teeth had snapped down on his arm, splitting flesh and hitting bone. Fire raced through Ander's body, traveling through his veins in bursts. Every movement he made fueled the flames.

He groaned, pulling away.

Then Ander was dropped, his body slumping to the ground, his face hitting cold dirt that was almost a reprieve from the inferno.

After a minute, he looked up with weary eyes, trying to force himself to stay awake. But everything hurt, and his bones were the kindling to the forest fire inside.

Sytri was a barely visible spot of gray in the moonlight. But a darkness stretched out from his silhouette, writhing and striking. Something screamed out so loudly, so painfully, that even in his half-dead state Ander's hair stood on end. Liquid sprayed into the air, followed by terrified sobbing.

His vision started to flicker, the edges going dark.

Sytri better be okay.

Then he blacked out.

CHAPTER SEVEN

A nder heard the soft hush of wind first, followed by the trill of birds. His eyes blinked open to sunlight slipping through blinds, forming bars of pale gold across his face and over a wall. *Way too much light this early in the morning.* Even worse, the air was sticky with heat. He took a deep breath and then rolled over, an ache stretching across his shoulders, his face pressing against a warm body. Wait. When had that got there?

Ander shoved himself from it, his hands pressing into the scarred tan skin, causing the figure to grumble and snarl. The mattress beneath them creaked, metal springs bending more than they were meant to, probably far past their prime. It was a futon. And the figure was Sytri.

The night before came back to him, and he shivered.

Somehow, they had lived.

But where were they now? Ander surveyed the area. It was obviously a living room—it had all the fixings, for the most part. There was a dusty TV, an upside-down table with a filthy rug underneath. He stopped on a pile of paper towels, stained with blood, both his and Sytri's from the mixed colors. All the red on the towels suggested his wound had been *deep*, but as he grazed his hand over where it had been, there was only a tender spot.

Would he have healed as smoothly without Sytri's medical care? Ander grimaced.

Sytri snored loudly. One of his arms was folded above his head, and his legs were splayed out. The other arm was curled over Ander's waist, and claws softly clung to his hips. It was strange to see him resting. *Not running around or running his mouth.*

Upon closer inspection, the first thing that stood out was how fit Sytri appeared, his skin showing the sharp ridge of muscles on his arms and stomach. Ander blushed; he usually never paid attention to someone's physique like this, but it was hard not to, sitting next to a shirtless Sytri. What weird fuckboy decision was it to just always be shirtless? Thin scars were etched across his skin; he didn't heal the way Ander did, it seemed. His wounds left reminders. What had attacked Sytri and left him with scars? Other demons, most likely.

He focused elsewhere, on the ink-like spots on Sytri's shoulders, then his gaze wandered up to Sytri's lean neck and angled jaw. His hair was translucent in some places, the charcoal gray faded to a jewellike opacity. The tail feathers were the same. The gold piercings that hung from his soft animal ears matched a slim bracelet on his arm. Had that been a fashion choice on Sytri's part? He didn't seem like the type to think about fashion, but Ander highly doubted it was a coincidence. The style was charming and dorky at the same time.

Sytri was . . . different. That was for sure. He seemed far from the type of demons that had traumatized Ander. Even further from Mayrez.

Mayrez. Ander shuddered again. What was she doing to the Couriers? What would she have done to him?

He tentatively touched his wrist, tracing phantom lines. With closed eyes, he took a deep breath. Mayrez's claws weren't ensnaring him, and he wasn't trapped on a stage. He was here, in this house. With Sytri.

Another demon.

He seemed kinder compared to the other horrors, but he had demanded Ander's blood to strengthen his own.

Ander placed his hand on Sytri's, the one that hung around his waist. A pulse beat calmly underneath his palms. Was a part of Ander in there still, the part that had somehow kept them alive? *Was it enough for him to want to keep me safe, to bring me here?*

And where exactly had Sytri brought him? This place was a disaster; abandoned when the demons arrived, presumably. There were clothes strewn about, suitcases half-packed. Whoever had lived here had left as quickly as they could. To go where? Where did one go when the world was ending? Were they alive right now, holed up away in some safe city? Or had they been dragged from their homes into the jaws of a monster? That's what had happened to most.

Cautiously, Ander slipped away from Sytri, trying to ignore the infinitesimal way their skin touched. Sytri grunted like a restless dog. Ander slunk to the floor; it gave in to his weight, creaking underneath him, and he winced, looking back at Sytri, who was evidently still sleeping. His mouth was open, showing his sharp teeth. Ander thought for a moment about the previous day, about the pain and fire those fangs had brought him, and shuddered.

Thankfully their temporary home provided a distraction. He drew his gaze from Sytri and slipped out the room. After all those years trapped in Gardners, the chance to explore someplace new was enticing, even if it was only a random house.

He stopped to stare at picture frames on walls, at drawings stuck to the fridge with magnets in the shape of fruit. People had lived here in a tranquility they no longer could.

There were buildings in Gardners, yes, but they were rough refuges more than anything else. There were no TVs plugged into sockets or study rooms lined with books and glass vases. The buildings were crammed with canned goods, blankets, clothes, and medical supplies. Some items of sentimental value remained of course, what survivors had managed to cling to like pieces of wood out at sea. But it wasn't the same. There was always a sense of practicality in their homes, that they'd been made to provide shelter and nothing more. This home was a reminder of the untroubled life he had lived in the past. It was packed with video games and figurines, piles of cookbooks and a collection of fancy shoes. Photos on shelves showed a family of three had lived here. A wife and husband, and a daughter going off to college soon. Or maybe she had already left? There was a story. Everything had a story.

Ander found himself in the daughter's room and felt like an intruder instantly. It was the most personal of them all. Pictures were stuck to the walls and pinned to cork boards. She had an assortment of clay succulents lined up on the windowsill and a whole row of books on how to learn Italian on a shelf. There was no unifying theme to the room, just passion. Just a place filled with things she loved.

On her bedside table was a camera. Ander stared at it for a moment. It was one of those instant Fujifilms that had come back during the era of retro and early nineties nostalgia. He had a similar build; well, he had before. His chest went hollow. That gift was long gone.

This camera was bright blue, with a thick white strap hanging off it. Ander reached out.

"What are you doing?"

"Fuck!" Ander jumped. He whipped his head around to see Sytri standing in the doorway, leaning against the frame.

Sytri yawned, his tail flipping softly behind him.

"You gave me a heart attack."

"You going to take that?" Sytri asked, motioning to the camera, completely ignoring Ander's comment.

"What? I— No. I shouldn't."

"Why?"

"It's not mine."

"So? Are you telling me since this all started you've never taken anything from someone's house?" Sytri raised an eyebrow.

"No. But it's— That's not something I *need*. It's something I want. And what if she comes back? What if she's alive and one day she comes back home with her family and they're ready to start their life again and then she finds out someone stole her camera?"

"Dude, in that very specific and unlikely scenario, I think she'd just be fucking glad to be home."

"But what if it was important?"

"More important than being alive?"

"You know what I mean."

"Not really." Sytri shrugged. "Why do you want it anyway?"

"I—I did photography in college. I like taking photos. Haven't had the opportunity to do that in a while." Ander shrugged. "It seemed like it would be nice. To do it again. That would be dumb though, wouldn't it? To take photos when we're all just trying to stay alive. I mean, it was a pretty pointless thing to do even before the world got overrun with monsters." He laughed. He'd always found his choice of degree to be ridiculous. So had most people. A passion degree, not practical. "Ronan said I should have picked out a better one, you know, to get a real job. But he still supported my choice in the end."

"Ronan?"

"My foster brother."

"Well, what did he know? Your whole world ended. What good would being a lawyer have done you?" Sytri walked forward, wrapped his tail around the camera and pressed it into Ander's hand. Ander gripped the thick plastic, clutching it to his chest. Sytri shrugged dramatically. "Were you fucking going to debate your way out of getting eaten alive?"

"I mean, I don't think you should plan your life around the world ending."

"You should," Sytri said, pointing at Ander. "To an extent, anyway, because how much would it have sucked for you to spend your whole life doing something you hate only for you to die the next day and you never did a damn thing you liked? Take some pictures, you nerd." He held up his hands. "Who the fuck you going to do anything for at this point if not yourself?"

Ander looked down at the camera and back at Sytri, who was glaring at him now. He couldn't stop himself from laughing.

"What? What is it?" Sytri said with a scowl.

"Nothing. You're just the world's worst life coach." Ander held the camera a little tighter. It felt nice to hold one again, to own anything again. Pretty much all of his possessions had been in the bag that Mayrez had taken from him. He held down Power and was pleasantly surprised when the camera *ding*ed to life.

"It work?" Sytri asked.

"Yeah, strong batteries, huh?" Ander replied softly. "Smile." He swung the camera upward, and Sytri gave a huge and tacky grin. With a flash, the scene was captured. After a delicate clicking, a small photo rolled out from the bottom of the camera. Ander tugged it free and held it up.

Sytri stepped behind him. "I look good."

"Pfft, I guess so." Ander chuckled. It was a nice picture, he would admit. He had always been a fan of spur-of-the moment photography, to capture candid emotions. No fancy poses or set-up scenery. He brought the photo closer. "Back before everything happened. Ronan bought me this *really* nice camera for class. Like two thousand dollars, which I thought was absurd. Considering he was one of the most adamant that I pick a more practical career."

His heart twisted and his throat went dry. It was one of his most vivid memories: Ronan, smug grin on his face as he watched Ander unwrap the gift. As soon as Ander had realized what his present was, he'd gasped and Ronan had broken into laughter, as fresh and clear as a stream rippling by. Ander had that sound on repeat in his head.

"Even if he didn't like what I did sometimes, he always made sure that if I was going to do it, I'd succeed." Ander glanced over at Sytri. "But I think I kept letting him down."

"How?"

"For one, I quit college."

"Well, that's not that big of a deal."

"Is it not?" Ander replied with the smallest smile.

"Not anymore."

"Good point. Though, if he was mad, he didn't show it. He helped me get a job afterward, organize paying off those pointless loans. I still took photos too. I had that nice camera after all." He admired the thin paper in his hands. "In the beginning, when the worst of it happened, I lost it. Never bothered even thinking about it again, really. This is the first picture I've taken in more than three years."

"That's a long time for someone who wanted a photography degree, isn't it?"

"I'd say it's been a bit of wait." His chest was tight as he stared at the picture of Sytri. The demon wore a genuinely happy smile, full of shark teeth and bright eyes. There was silence as Ander tried to place the emotion he was feeling. His first picture in a long time was of a demon. He couldn't have predicted that at all. Even more so, that the demon had *saved* him.

"Thanks . . . for rescuing me," Ander murmured, his face warm. "Are you okay? How did you get us out of there? There were so many demons after us."

"I told you, I'm strong. I can handle myself." Sytri gave a cocky grin. "I was more worried about you, bleeding all over the place. You feeling all right now? You were out for hours."

"I'm good," Ander said quickly. Neck still hurt, body was still buzzed—maybe something inside him was still being fixed. But nothing to worry Sytri about.

"I'm glad. Had me fretting. Anyway, some more good news: you're definitely a half, Halfie."

Ander had to process that for a minute. "What?"

"Mayrez was right: you got halfie blood. I might have had a little trouble getting us out of that pinch if you had been anything else. But nope, you got Grade-A perfect blood."

"But . . . but how? Look at me!" Ander waved at himself, the strap of the camera swinging wildly. "I can't do anything!"

"I don't know, dude, but I promise you, she's right. Your blood is like . . . I don't know . . . It's fucking addicting." Sytri seemed dazed for a moment, a heavy hunger in his voice. Ander's whole body grew hot. Then Sytri chuckled. "Oh, sorry, that's kind of weird for you, right?"

"A-absolutely weird," Ander stuttered, looking anywhere besides Sytri. His hands settled on the camera. "I still don't understand it. Halves are supposed to be all-powerful, and I'm all not." He brushed a hand against his neck, ruffling his feathers.

"You're more than you think. And I'm—I'm sorry that I blew up when I thought you weren't. I tend to do that." Sytri's eyes darkened for a second. "I'm working on it."

"I didn't like it." Ander hesitated. "You felt like Mayrez."

"Don't want that," Sytri said through gritted teeth.

"Me neither. I like you much better like this, not yelling." Ander gave a strained grin. "How about you work on the anger part and I'll work on not being so reluctant to give you my blood. I mean, especially now that I know it works." He flushed. "Which, why . . . why did it feel like that? Why was it so . . . hot?" Fuck, why couldn't his brain process his thoughts a bit better before letting them jump out of his mouth?

"You sealed a deal with a demon. What did you think it would feel like? By protecting you, I had already initiated my part. By finally letting me have a taste, you were doing your part. You completed the agreement. It's like . . . official-official now. What you *felt*, was *me*."

What did that mean? "Then . . . then did you feel me?"

"Yeah."

"What did I feel like?"

Turned out Sytri could blush. His face was suddenly overcome by an electric blue hue. Ander stared at him wide-eyed and thought of bioluminescent waves in a dark ocean. The strange cyan glow was undeniably attractive. Shit. He leaned back on his heels, his feathers fuzzing up.

"Soft. Cold. Like liquid silk." Sytri bit his lip and laughed nervously. "I've never felt something like that." Like a goddamn model, he flipped his hair back.

Ander turned away, chewing on a fingernail. His whole body was too hot. He was suffocating in it. "I don't know what that means," he said. "I don't understand why . . . I don't know. We should go, shouldn't we? While it's daylight?" He put the camera strap over his neck, fumbled with the device.

"Sure, I guess," Sytri muttered after a moment.

Ander closed his eyes and took a deep breath. He had to stay on track. Losing focus could mean losing any chance he had of finding Ronan.

They went to the living room, Ander giving one last look to the house, the photos, the memories of what had once been. Perhaps one day the world could be like that again, with him and Ronan together. His heart twisted with an unreachable longing.

Then he opened the front door and faced the bright and burning sun.

CHAPTER EIGHT

"This rain is fucking awful!" Sytri yelled. Thunder roared overhead, nearly drowning out his words even though Ander was sitting on his back. Ander shivered violently, gritting his teeth. The wind was howling and rain was coming down in icy sheets, freezing him to the bone, drenching his small frame.

The hot Texas sun had cursed them for over a week after they'd left the house, making Ander sick from heat exhaustion. He'd thought there couldn't be anything worse than the horrible burning. Then an ocean had fallen on them. It had been without warning—in an instant the summer sky had been blanketed by black clouds.

It had been almost half an hour now and the storm was relentless.

Ander had shoved his camera into a new backpack he'd lifted from a convenience store a day or two ago. He patted it, scared that even in the thick cloth and leather the camera would end up soaked in the torrent they were facing. He didn't want to lose it so soon.

"We have to find somewhere to stop!" Ander shouted as loudly as he could.

"I'm looking!" Sytri yelled back.

Ander clung tighter to Sytri—it was hard to hang on when he was shivering so severely. He glanced to the side of the overpass and only saw darkness below and above them; the road resembled an inky river, overflowing. He hadn't known it could rain so quickly without warning.

"There's a gas station up ahead," Sytri said after a moment. The demon's speed picked up, his desperate footsteps splashing through the water. He wrapped his tail around Ander's wrist, holding him. There was a comfort in it.

Up ahead, the gas station sat near the edge of the road, Its windows black, its lot vacant. Vines had crawled up the sides, like thick cracks. In the storm, it looked haunted, empty and dark, with only a periodic flash of lightening illuminating it. A sign with plastic lettering caught Ander's eye during one of those moments. Where a gas station would usually have the prices or deals listed, there was a jumble of words.

"Welcome to the Cast. May your . . ." Ander read. The rest had tilted and fallen askew, some gone altogether. He tried to piece together the sentence from the few letters that remained but couldn't.

"Out of the rain, out of the rain," Sytri muttered as they got closer to the shelter. He darted between the useless pumps and burst through the glass doors, making a tiny bell ring. Ander slid off Sytri's back, and they both shook themselves like dogs.

"It's so terrible out there," Ander muttered. Even with the door closed behind them, the rain hammering on the roof echoed throughout the empty building. He pressed his hands against the glass and gazed outside. It was all dark, then white lightning streaked through the sky, making the rivers of water glisten like oil. "When do you think it'll stop?"

"Feels like never." Sytri stuck out his tongue. "I hate this kind of weather. Reminds me of Hell."

"It rained in Hell?"

"Yeah. Just like this. If it rained, it was always a storm." Sytri's long ears tilted to the side, flicked. He raised his head and glanced around. "Give me a second."

Sytri scavenged about the small gas station, his tail whipping back and forth, nose sniffing the air. It was almost entirely black inside the store, but Sytri's lean form was visible as a silhouette at times. Lightning sporadically brightened everything, cast their shadows across the room, along with the shadow of the huge sign outside.

"What is it?" Ander asked, his fingertips still pressed against the cold glass door. His breath fogged it up. It was freezing.

"Smells like angels in here."

"Angels?" Ander perked up. Angels meant safety. He listened for bells, anything, but if there was any noise, the rain and storm drowned it out.

Sytri was seriously absorbed with whatever scent was in the air. His ears kept on flicking at the ends. He tiptoed around the edges of the room.

"I'm not sure. Everything smells like water and mold." Sytri sniffed again. "It's hard to tell. And the storm is so loud I can't focus."

"Well, even if it's an angel, they're all right, right?"

"Depends on who you're asking. I'm a demon, fuzzball. They don't really like us." Sytri's eyes darted around the room, emitting a soft green glow; an animal searching for prey or predators. "Also, angels are very classy folks. They don't usually make their nests in gas stations." He opened a back door and peered inside before closing it. "They like churches, schools, mansions; they like regal things."

"By 'nest' do you mean like an actual nest or like . . ."

"Sort of. Demons, we make like hovels. We like to be away, ya know? It's nature, I think, or whatever. We may hate Hell, but we are bonded to it. We like to be close to the ground, underneath it if possible. It's comforting for us. But angels, they like to be up and out in the open. High. Literally touching the heavens if they can."

"Guess that's why the angels in Gardners always rested atop the gate."

"Yeah, they're big ol' birds basically. So, like I said, abandoned gas station? Not an angel's home. No reason for it to smell like one."

"Maybe the angel just stopped by?"

"No. Rain would've washed out the scent if it was just a one-time-visit thing. This angel has been staying here." Sytri walked behind the counter and searched around, before lifting a huge advertisement poster on the wall. There was a hole on the other side—a large, car-sized hole. "Well, would ya look at that." Sytri grinned triumphantly and pointed at it. "Knew something was fishy."

"Secret holes carved into a wall don't seem like the sort of oddity we should investigate, if I can voice my opinion," Ander said, peering over the counter's edge. There was a soft light coming from it, illuminating Sytri and the dust in the air.

"Don't you think it's weird that an angel would make a secret hole in a wall in the first place? Like I said, that's not their MO. It's very suspicious."

How was something being suspicious more of a reason to investigate? Life wasn't a video game; one didn't walk into every room they found in the hopes of cool treasure.

Sytri waltzed behind the poster, which flitted closed again.

"Damn it, Sytri!" Ander swore, starting to follow him. Lightning flashed, and for a second, Ander saw something in his peripheral vision. Out on the sign—a shadow, a figure. He whipped his head around as lightning flashed again. Nothing.

The hair on his arms stood up. His stomach churned. *Please let that be a trick of the light.*

"Sytri!" Ander whispered, hurrying to the poster. As he pushed it back, he was startled to see that past the wall was a staircase, going deep into the earth. And no sight of the demon. "Sytri," Ander squeaked again. He took a tentative step down, calling out to Sytri a third time to no answer. "Damn it, damn it." Ander hurried forward, a mixture of fear for himself and for Sytri driving him. What if Sytri had fallen into a trap? He seemed like the sort of guy who would fall into a trap.

"We have a situation outside," Ander said lowly. The staircase was tight, close, and he was alone. For a split second the narrow space was overlaid with the horrible hallway he had fled from Mayrez through. His breath halted in his chest, and he closed his eyes, waiting for the memory to stop. Stupid, stupid to think of that now. He shivered and kept to the sides of the stairs, finally reaching the bottom floor. "Sytri, where did you go—"

He saw only white. He took a step back, bumping into the wall behind him, and stared at the vast and unending stretch of white. It took him a moment to adjust to the color, to the sight, but then he realized what it was. Bags. Piles and piles of bags. They were stacked on top of each other, to the ceiling. Hundreds of them, each one about the size of Ander's torso.

"What is all this?" Ander muttered.

"Salt."

"What?" Ander looked to the side where a huge board covered the wall, pins and tacks stuck in it haphazardly. It resembled a conspiracy board. Beside it was a desk where an old radio crackled faintly with static. Sytri was standing in front of the board, staring at it with cold eyes. Ander walked over to him, the static buzzing in his ears. "Did you say salt?"

"Yeah."

"So, the angel has a drug problem."

"Maybe." Sytri glanced at the salt and then focused back on the board. "Maybe not. There's too much here for one angel."

"What do you mean?"

Sytri faced Ander, his expression unpleasantly serious. "They're a trader."

"Like Mayrez?" Ander grimaced.

"Working with Mayrez. I told you, she has a good deal with a group of angels down here. I think we're wandering into their territory."

"So, she comes here, then?" Ander whispered. Suddenly, he felt watched. As if she were hiding somewhere in the room. He swallowed hard and stepped closer to Sytri.

"I'm sure of it. I smell her," Sytri said with disgust. Before Ander could talk, he spoke again. "Don't worry, she's not here. Scent's faint." He looked back at the board. "The rain is probably from the angel. Declaring their nest or presence. So traders or enemies know that they're close. But only an angel of rank would claim their nest so boldly."

"What do you mean, 'rank'?"

"Angels have ranks. Just like demons." Sytri waved his hand as if it were common knowledge. "I'm a demon, higher-up from me would be an Archdemon. Then a Carnivale. A higher ranked angel would be like an Archangel, Throne, or Seraph. You know."

"I do not."

"What the fuck, man?"

Ander fumed. "Once again, I've been living in Gardners and the angels told me zilch."

"Oh yeah. Shit. Weird, what's the benefit of not explaining anything?"

"I tried asking that too." Ander paused. "Anyway, what about the ranks? What about Mayrez?"

"It's harder for the higher ranks of angels and demons to get here. Earth wasn't made for them. They have too much of an essence, for lack of a better word. Especially those coming from Heaven. Their Gate isn't open, so they need permission to get through. If they force themselves, they can get hurt. Isn't quite as difficult for demons since our Gate was broken. Even demons like Mayrez who are about to hit that Archdemon status can make it through pretty easily."

Ander's shoulders tensed, and he could feel himself scowling. He didn't like that, not one bit.

Sytri smiled gently, grazed his hand against Ander's. "Don't worry; like I said, I'm strong too. And with your blood, I'm only going to get stronger."

Ander nodded, but the tension simply moved down his chest, hurting his lungs. "But whatever lives here is stronger than the angels I've seen? Stronger than Mayrez? Working with her?"

"I think. I don't know. I haven't seen anything higher than your basic entry-level angel either. I didn't think they were allowed to pass through." Sytri tapped the board in front of him. "Much less that they'd be making deals with Mayrez."

"What would she have that they would want?"

"The blends. She only deals in salt and blends, and these guys already have the salt." He gestured at the pile of it.

"Opposite question, then: What do *they* have that *she* wants? She wouldn't want the salt right?" Ander asked.

"No. And I've never actually seen what she gets from angels in return. So, what would it be?" Sytri paused. "Maybe this angel is strong enough to pull out souls."

"What?"

"You know everybody has a soul or is made of one—like angels are. Stronger angels or demons can pull one out and eat it. They'd have to be way stronger than Mayrez, though."

Ander was having a hell of a moment. What the absolute fuck did it mean to *eat* a *soul*? That would put an *end* to a person, wouldn't it?

Sytri wasn't even facing him as he continued, this idea apparently nothing at all. "But it can't be *that* strong if it lives in a place like this. A higher rank wouldn't let itself live in the actual ground. Though, then I don't know what they could give her."

"Are you positive it couldn't rip out my soul?"

"Nothing like that could be on Earth. At least, not in this room. It'd be huge, as big as the building." Sytri turned from the board and jolted as he saw Ander's expression. "Hey, it's okay, all right? I promise. No soul-stealing angels in here. I wouldn't let them get you anyway." He smiled awkwardly, placing a hand on Ander's shoulder. "Got it?"

Ideally that sort of being wouldn't exist in the first place, but Ander nodded and tried to focus on something else. No time to dwell on the soul-stealing monsters that apparently lurked in other planes of existence. There were beasts on Earth he had to worry about.

"If Mayrez could get her hands on a— a soul, what would she gain from it?"

"Power." Sytri lingered on the word. "Besides a shit ton of Halfie blood, souls are the only real way to move up in rank." He tilted his head in Ander's direction. "Your soul, I'm sure, would be enough for me to become an Archdemon. You know, if I could pull it out. But it's a horrible thing to do to someone; it ends them, pure and simple. A soul is all anyone truly is. It's your life and afterlife." Sytri snapped his fingers. "But like I said, no angel could be strong enough here. Even if there were, I can't imagine one that would willingly give a soul to a demon." For a moment, his voice wavered.

Ander didn't like it; Sytri had confirmed his thoughts. He stared back at the map, with all the thumbtacks. Someone had furiously scribbled on it with a marker. Most of it seemed meaningless or was unreadable altogether. However, two words stuck out to him, scrawled over and over. The Cast. What did that mean? A shiver ran through him. He fumbled with his backpack and took out his camera.

"What are you doing?"

"This is . . . important," Ander said slowly. He snapped a photo. Took a step to the side, snapped another. Repeat. Then another. The map, the salt, all of it screamed bad news. If what Sytri said was true, about this place being an angel's nest, about them working with Mayrez, then it had to be a detestable partnership. "Maybe the angels in Gardners will know what to do about this when we get back. These photos might help if they can decipher the map."

Ander stepped away, splaying the photos out, making sure they matched up the way they should. A perfect copy of the map in front of him, made of twenty different photographs. Carefully, he gathered them up and put them deep in his bag.

Sytri was flipping through a notebook on the desk, making a disgruntled huff every so often. "Definitely selling blends," he murmured.

Ander looked back at the salt piled up by the walls; every satchel was sealed tight, wrapped with thick, heavy twine. Even with that, some loose salt was scattered around the edges, like gold coins encircling treasure. Ander stepped toward it. He couldn't remember the last time he'd eaten pure salt. Long ago. He'd seen the blends in Gardners who consumed too much. The price was steep for someone who valued themselves more than strength. Now, staring at a plethora of salt, with Sytri's words in his head, he was curious. What would happen if he dipped his hand into a bag and consumed? As a Half, what could salt do for him?

Would he be strong enough to defend himself from Mayrez?

If he was stronger, she'd never snatch him again.

"Fuzzball, what are you doing?" Sytri asked, breaking Ander's thoughts.

His hand was hovering near the salt. When had that happened? A shiver crawled up his spine as he tried to find words that wouldn't alarm Sytri. "I . . . It's a currency right? Maybe we can use it." Ander curled his fingers. He grabbed one of the smaller bags, which was cinched tightly, still heavy, and tossed it into his backpack. Cold settled in his stomach.

"Okay . . . just be careful all right? That stuff can be dangerous if you—"

There was a crash above them, followed by the sound of shattering glass. Instantly, Ander was assaulted by the clamor of bells: piercing and sharp, an orchestra so powerful it blindsided him. He collapsed on the ground, head spinning, the sound vibrating his body.

"Fuzzball, are you okay?" Sytri asked, grabbing Ander by the shoulders and pulling him close.

The ringing wouldn't stop. A grinding crunch came from the direction of the stairs, the clang of the bells growing louder with it. There was almost a tune to them, a cruel and mocking rhythm of pain.

Then a black hand curled around the edges of the doorframe, before a long and slender black figure heaved themselves out. They were taller than the room, unravelling their body and limbs to fit properly inside. A solid void of a beast. They tilted their head, white eyes shining down on Ander and Sytri, blindingly so. The static of a lost radio came from their body in waves. On the sides of their head two horns connected at the top, making a perfectly thin circle. Like a halo. Ander blinked.

What have I found hiding away?

The voice made Ander flinch. It came from everywhere and nowhere all at once. It was gravelly, haunting, a whisper between ancient and cankered earth. Older than a beginning. Sytri growled, snapping his teeth, shoving Ander behind him.

The being's eyes focused on Ander. Directly at Ander.

Small brethren, why are you here? Did my storm scare you? Its waters ushered you into my humble shelter. I'm sorry it's not quite fitting of our kind. I had to put this all somewhere. Somewhere our kind would not look.

They waved their hand at the huge collection of salt. Each finger was as long as one of Ander's arms, but thinner. Branches burnt in a fire.

"Nice stash you got there," Sytri retorted. "Now if you excuse me, we'll be making our way out of here."

But we've only just met. It would be rude of you, wouldn't it? To enter someone's home when they're gone and leave when they arrive.

They didn't so much as glance at Sytri. They kept staring down Ander, who thought back to what Sytri had said. That the angel must have been trading its salt for blends—or worse, tearing out souls.

And while the thought of an angel doing such an act seemed impossible, now as this creature stood before him, Ander could believe them capable. Yes, there were the bells, the flowing and calming sensation, the purity angels emitted that cooed one to sleep. However, at the same time, a rotten filth spilled from their words, seeped along the floor and wrapped around Ander's heart, letting fear pour out through its grasp. The angel was a mixture of two extremes that made Ander retch.

He swallowed his nausea, body shaking, and stared at the angel. "It would be very rude. I guess we can stay for a second."

"Halfie, what the fuck?"

What a pleasant idea. We can chat. Angel to angel. About all the wonders. All the emptiness. All the light.

Their eyes burned brighter, and Ander couldn't see anything else. He yelped as the angel's hands ran across his chest. Sytri snarled again, but Ander pushed him backward, putting himself between Sytri and the angel.

"Sytri, give me a moment," Ander muttered. If Sytri just started attacking, it would spell disaster for them both. More importantly, Sytri would definitely get himself killed. It was clear from the way the angel looked at them that Ander might be allowed to live, but Sytri meant nothing. Sytri was a demon, and the angel obviously did not care for his presence.

What is your name little blend?

"Ander Castillo. And you?"

I always tell company to call me Tephera before they leave. So I at least hear my name from them once.

"Once?"

I usually never hear from company a second time.

Ander gulped. "Sounds lonely."

Oh, it is. It is. It is.

They sounded truly upset. Despite the situation, for an instant Ander felt sorry for them. Maybe the creepiness coming off Tephera was just how they were, not what they were. But his heart told him that was not the case, that his gut instinct was not wrong. Tephera the angel was broken and something nightmarish oozed through their cracks.

It was easier in Heaven. I had a position, a place to where I would always see Souls, constantly surrounded by them, so many Souls, beautiful and damaged. Here on Earth I must barter for company from disgusting and vile demons. I must do as my Creator wishes. And she wishes strange things.

Fire ripped across Ander's sides, and he cried out in pain. Tephera's claws had wrapped around him like barbed wire, lifting him into the air.

"Halfie!"

"Sytri, stop," Ander snapped. He could feel Tephera's strength. He could feel everything about the angel. It was a massive weight on his mind, dark water that poured down his veins. The strange stream connected the two of them and slipped him feelings and memories that weren't his own. The angel was old beyond measure, like cold and cracked stone deep in the earth, rough to the touch. They were untouchable.

Sytri could not kill this creature.

Yet, with all Tephera's strength, Ander could feel blistering wounds deep inside them. Living in a realm like this was agonizing to Tephera, poisoning them. They needed the infinity of the heavens. What would bring them to the cramped basement of a gas station?

"Why are you here?" Ander asked. "This isn't where you live. It's something else."

It is something else.

"What is it?"

It is where I see if they can be pure of Blood.

"What does that mean?"

The angel squeezed, crushing the air out of Ander's lungs. He wheezed, and his insides suddenly felt full of needles.

Purity for the Cast.

Fingers pried at Ander's mouth, forcing it open with a painful *crack*. Ander gurgled a yell as Tephera slipped salt from their hands and down his throat. It was like an unending stream of liquid fire was being poured into him, lighting him aflame from the inside out.

"That's it, let go of him, you bastard!" Sytri yelled. "Halfie, I don't know what fucking shit you tried to pull, but it's over! My way now."

Ander heaved. Black liquid spilled from his mouth. "What the fuck," he rasped through the ooze.

Good. Pour it out. Be ripe for us. Be pure.

What was happening? *I've never seen other blends throw up fucking black. Oh god, am I going to die?* His organs were melting and twisting. They had turned into molten metal that churned violently at every sound and touch. He heaved again, the thick, inky ooze falling from his mouth, choking him, killing him. His body arched and jerked against his will at every torturous spill.

Tephera lifted him closer to their face. Ander was a few inches away now, staring into their bright eyes, which were unblinking, ever-seeing. The opposite of his own, which were out of focus.

Black ink kept falling out of Ander's mouth. How was he breathing?

So much in you. Ready to get out. What sins have you been hiding little blend? What festers in that heart of yours?

Tephera's fingers pressed against Ander's chest, and he saw white as pain flooded him. He threw up again, harder than before; it felt like it was taking his esophagus with it, like he had nothing left to throw up, insides included.

Suddenly, there was only the smell of Ronan, the ghost touch of his hand on Ander's.

Your sins are piling. Ah, they're so unexpected.

Ronan. Ronan. Ronan. Every feeling about him that Ander had ever buried was now exposed, raw and pulsing. The crackling desire that had come every time their skin had grazed. The overflowing adoration and devotion. All of it burned across him.

More salt was shoved down his throat. *If you survive the Culling, you will be such a fine addition. There is a strong angel underneath the filth.*

"You asshole!"

Tephera screeched, and Ander was thrown to the ground. He looked up, dazed, to see Sytri clinging to Tephera's face, with his whole fucking arm shoved into one of Tephera's eyes before he ripped it out, claw covered in white blood.

Tephera's screeching was a radio turned to every wrong station. The sound raced from one decibel to next, each more high-pitched than the last.

My fucking ears are going to bleed.

Sytri threw himself off the angel and turned to Ander, eyes wild. He snatched Ander, flung him onto his back, and bolted up the stairs as Tephera continued to screech. Ander tried not to heave again but failed, black splattering the ground as he did his best not to hit Sytri.

"Sorry. Sorry," Ander muttered. "I thought . . . I thought maybe I could talk to them or catch them off guard. I don't know. They're strong, Sytri, really strong. Don't let them get you." Thoughts of Ronan rose unbidden in his mind again, and he had to shove them away. What had Tephera done to him? What had they tugged on?

"Shut up. Let's just get out of here, okay, Halfie?" Sytri grunted as they burst from the front door and into the rain. In an instant they were under a river of water again, and Ander could already barely see a damn thing in the dark.

The storm was stronger now and seemed to cover every inch of air and earth. Lightning flashed around Ander and Sytri, followed by thunder so loud it shook the ground.

Ander looked behind to see Tephera breaking the door to the gas station, sending it flying. Their bright, lighthouse eyes tore into the pitch-black rain and gazed down upon them. From one eye spilled a waterfall of florescent white.

They were pissed.

"Sytri, going the fastest you can would be really good right now," Ander yelled as Tephera charged at them. A skeleton running like a dog, savage and bloodthirsty.

"Oh, thanks for telling me, fuzzball, I was thinking about taking a fucking leisurely stroll!" Sytri screamed.

"My blood!" Ander shoved his hand near Sytri's mouth. "It's a boost, right? Take it."

Tephera was getting closer.

"What? No! You're already dying from it fucking stuffing you with salt. If I take more of your blood it will fuck you up. I can't risk you—"

"We'll both die out here if you don't!" Ander yelled, his voice desperate. He pushed his wrist against Sytri's mouth as hard as he could. "So do it and get us out of here."

Tephera's breath was on his neck, the angel towering over him, their ancient static screech in his ears. They would snatch him, they would take him like Mayrez had, but unlike then, this would be the end. Tephera would be inescapable.

Large fingers slid down his spine, and Ander's breath hitched, his body paralyzed. *This is it.*

Then, Sytri tore into Ander's wrist, snapping it like a glow stick. Ander cried out, before biting on his lip to stifle the sob and acid that rose in the back of his throat.

Not a millisecond later, Sytri tossed Ander with huge black and liquid-like arms that tore from his shoulders.

Ander blinked, mind blank as he went flying, then he crashed into the side of a tree, his lower back taking the brunt of the blow. He gasped and fell over with a yelp. *Fuck, fuck, that hurt.* As he struggled to pull in air, he glanced upward. Through the dense rain, he could make out Sytri, his strange, ever-growing shadow arms fighting back against Tephera's own. They wouldn't be enough. When Tephera had held him, Ander had *seen* what they were—an unimaginable force.

But there Sytri was, trying his goddamn hardest. And if Ander were a smart guy, he would take this as a chance to run ahead.

Ander was a fucking stupid guy.

He leaned against the tree, racking his brain on what to do. How could he take on an angel of this magnitude?

At that moment, Tephera swung Sytri to the ground like an axe, ripping off one of his shadow arms. They clambered on top of his fallen form like a spider. Ander's eyes went wide, and he stumbled forward. *No, no, fucking no.* He wasn't going to let Sytri die for him, he *wasn't.*

"Tephera!" Ander yelled, his voice breaking, barely audible through the storm. He ran as much as he could, his body straining against the pain, but he slipped on the slick concrete and fell to his knees, blood spilling out and mixing with the rain.

He grimaced and stood up again, wiping away the grime on his face. His chest burned; a fire lit inside his lungs. "Tephera, you son of a bitch! Leave Sytri alone!"

Tephera froze, their head turning a complete one-eighty to face Ander. All lights on him.

"Halfie, what are you doing?" Sytri screamed. "You were supposed to make a break for it."

Tephera took one giant step forward, their whole body slinking closer like a marionette doll. Ander gulped.

My brethren, you're something new. Tephera jolted closer. *You understand the need for your Purity.*

Ander reached into his backpack. Tephera seemed unaware and didn't attempt to stop him. They just leaned down, their eyes illuminating Ander and only Ander in the dark rain as Sytri staggered behind the angel, mouth in a snarl. Glowing eyes stared right into Ander's core. The bleeding one cascaded white into the earth.

The Cast needs you.

Tephera's hands curled around the side of Ander's body. Sytri was almost to them. Ander could see the soft green of his eyes shining in the light.

Come with me.

"Fuck off," Ander growled. He flung the bag of salt straight into Tephera's wounded eye; the tie came undone, letting salt fall freely and everywhere inside the pulsing wound. Instantly Tephera screeched, digging their fingers into the socket desperately, sending their white blood flying.

Sytri snatched Ander and ran. He didn't look back, bolting away from the scene as fast as he could. But Ander could only stare at the sight behind them, unblinking. Watching the angel screech static, scraping at their eye, tearing themselves apart.

He watched until Tephera was out of sight, until their cries were drowned out by the rain. For a second, right at the end, when Tephera resembled a stick figure, Ander thought a mouth split across that solid black face. But it could have been a trick of the light or the dark.

Ander clung to Sytri's shoulders and kept staring, just in case Tephera sprung from the darkness. In case those long spindly arms grabbed at him again.

Ander stared until his eyes burned.

CHAPTER NINE

Sytri kept running as they left the storm and rain, as the heavy clouds faded away to a clear night sky flecked with stars and the smear of the Milky Way. It wasn't until Ander saw blue-blood-smeared footsteps behind them that he broke from his daze and called out to Sytri. It took more than one desperate broken cry to get his attention.

But Sytri finally halted. With shaking legs, he looked around for a minute. Then, in silence, he trekked slowly farther down the road, to a cluster of crashed cars. Sniffing around, he grunted, lifted Ander up with his shadow arms, and placed him inside the back of a van that had fallen halfway into a ditch.

Ander landed on an old mattress, kicking up dust. He sat there, his heart racing, his body still tense. How could an *angel* invoke such terror in him? They were clearly one, so ethereal and far away like space. *Or far away like the depths of the ocean, crushing and dark.*

Sytri prowled outside for a bit, sniffing the air, before he crawled into the van, closing the door behind him. The windows let a fair amount of the stars and moonlight in, so they weren't in complete darkness. They sat there, staring at each other, unblinking.

Sytri spoke first. "I'm sorry."

Ander jerked his head. "Wh-what? Why?"

"I wasn't— I didn't protect you the way I should have. Even with your blood, that angel, they were so strong, and I couldn't—" One of Sytri's legs was shaking restlessly, the slight squeak it made in the mattress was the only background noise.

"We got out alive, Sytri, that's all I care about. We made it out, okay? And you did so much. You did everything you could."

"It wasn't enough." Sytri's voice cracked. "And I'm not . . . I'm not used to it not being enough. I thought that I could make sure nothing would happen to you. I was positive that I would always be able to do something, but you were the one who managed to give us an advantage, a way to get out, and that's the only reason we're alive. Because you were smart and because I ran away." He stared at the floor of the van.

Ander paused. Was this fear or pride talking? It might have been both. He reached forward, put his hand on Sytri's knee. Sytri gazed up at him. There was so much in his eyes that Ander couldn't understand.

"I wasn't smart, I was guessing. We were lucky it happened to work. And you did save me; you threw me ahead, so I could run away. But how could I have done that? How could I have left you behind?"

"It's not part of the deal for you to worry about me."

"So?"

Sytri stared harder, making Ander's face grow hot. Finally, Sytri spoke again. "So why would you?"

"Be-because it's the right thing to do," Ander stammered. "Because you're risking your life for me; why wouldn't I do the same? We're in this together, right? We're a team." Ander's chest was heavy. *Or do I simply not want to be alone?*

"That doesn't make sense," Sytri muttered. "You're not required to help me. It's not— Fuck, fuzzball." He leaned back on the palms of his hands. His sharp claws pricked into the grungy blanket underneath them.

"Do you not think we're a team?" Ander asked weakly. Maybe he had overestimated Sytri's affection. Maybe he was only a demon after all. Maybe this whole front was just that. It wouldn't be the first time in his life that Ander had seen more than he should have in the kindness of a stranger.

He retracted his hand from Sytri, clenching his fists. Way to be an idiot. He barely knew Sytri. And the demon hadn't thrown him out of harm's way because he cared about him. It was because the deal gave him no other choice.

"I think we're friends."

Ander's heart thumped. He swung his head up, his eyes wide, face flushed. Sytri was scowling, his eyebrows pressed together. He was blushing for the second time. Sweeter this time.

"Yeah?" Ander said, unable to stop himself from laughing. It was akin to a giggle, and it made him hyperaware of himself. There was a lightness in his chest, a fluffy, dumb, and messy feeling. It had his head spinning. It softly blew away the tension.

"Yeah."

"That's fine, right?" Ander asked. "We can be friends."

"I don't think I have a choice." Sytri still looked displeased about this new-found information. He pointed at Ander suddenly. "Don't make me regret it."

"I won't," Ander promised. "I would never. I'll have your back too. The best I can, for the world's most useless blend." He chuckled.

"You weren't useless today, were you? You're the reason we're alive, the reason that Tephera fucker is half-blind now." Sytri snorted.

"Hey! You were the one that gouged out their eye, that wasn't me."

"But Tephera is an angel. I'm sure they would've healed from that eventually. You though, shoving salt in its eye? Super not going to heal right. You literally poured salt in their wound. That shit will mess you up." He paused. "Which, by the way, how are *you* feeling after all that garbage he shoved down your throat?" He glanced at Ander, one eyebrow raised.

"I, uh, I'm okay. I actually feel calm. Well, compared to how I usually am." Ander pulled at his shirt; it was stained with that black vomit. He wanted to take it off and never look at it again. "What was that?"

"I don't know for certain. I've seen blends throw up the black before; never that much though. Mayrez said it was human sin. But she could've been fucking with me." Sytri shrugged.

"Sin? As a physical thing?" Was *that* what all the ink-like liquid he'd vomited up had been? And when Tephera had probed his mind . . . had they been searching for more sin to tease out? Ander's pulse raced as the images Tephera had tugged on flickered through his head again. Instinctively he pushed them away. "I've seen blends change when they take salt. Maybe losing their sin causes that? Whatever that means. I feel the same though." *Physically at least.*

"That's good. But what was all that garbage Tephera was saying? Purifying you? Weird shit. What would they be purifying you into?" Sytri gritted his teeth. "Don't like it. Tell me if you start feeling strange, weak, or anything. Maybe they laced the salt— Can you do that? I'm not a scientist."

"If they can, I don't have a clue what they would lace it with." Ander studied Sytri's shoulders. "Speaking of, I didn't know you could do that arm thing. Is it my blood that lets you?"

"Oh, no— I mean, yes? I've always been able to do it somewhat. They were never especially durable or strong though. Couldn't do it for long either. But your blood is like an energy shot, makes it a lot easier." Sytri tilted his head, and from his shoulder one of the inky black arms stretched out. Its claws touched the edge of Ander's face. It was an odd sensation, like being brushed by cold clay. Ander carefully put his hand around it: a weight moved under the layer of ice, similar to running water in a hose. Such a strange thing. Though it wasn't stranger than anything else that he'd seen so far.

"What does it feel like to you?" Ander asked. "Like a normal arm?"

"Not quite. It's more like my tail. There's a fluidity to it that my arms don't have. It's flexible." Sytri twisted it to the side, letting it curve at an angle that no human arm could. Ander let go, and Sytri retracted the shadow. The arm disappeared back into the black ink patch on his shoulder like it had never existed at all. "The more of your blood I drink over time, the more I think I'll be able to use it, let it grow. And who knows, maybe I'll get some other cool stuff. I've seen it happen to other demons. They get enough blend blood and eventually they have so much shit going on." He smirked. "And then I can protect you better. I'll be a total badass."

"I wish it worked the same way for me," Ander said. "I wish I had something I could do to be stronger." *If I took salt, could I be amazing?* But what had been the black gunk—his humanity? What had Tephera meant when they uttered those sinister words? It all seemed too dark.

"Don't worry about it." Sytri smiled. "I've got this."

He kept saying that. He'd said that since the beginning, and Ander had hated it then, but he hated it even more now. If he and Sytri were going to be actual friends, then Ander wanted them to be equals.

But he *couldn't* be on par with Sytri. He wasn't capable. Discomfort nestled in his chest even as he stifled back a yawn.

"You should get some sleep," Sytri said. "I'll keep watch for the night. I think we're safe, though. I didn't smell anything. This tract of land seems pretty void of life. And no people means no angels and no demons.

"All right," Ander said weakly. "Wake me up when it's bright out or I'll have a heatstroke in my sleep." It wasn't hot yet, but as soon as the sun hit the sky that would change rapidly.

"You got it, boss." Sytri propped himself up by the van window and looked out into the night, his tail flicking back and forth in the darkness.

Ander slid under the dirty and dusty blanket. Far too self-consciously, he took off his sticky and stained shirt under the cover. He felt a billion times better, even if now his skin was touching a gritty blanket. He wrapped it around himself tightly, making sure every square inch of his body was draped in it.

"What kind of angel was Tephera?" he asked softly. "If they weren't a normal one?"

"I think they were an Archangel."

"Is that real high up?"

"Eh. No. There's still quite a bit above them." Sytri laughed. "But nothing else past an Archangel could get through. No way."

Sytri didn't sound completely convinced, though. Ander chewed on that. Tephera seemed like one of the most powerful things walking on Earth; how could something be beyond them.

Ander couldn't ponder long. He would get nightmares, if he wasn't going to already.

"I better find Ronan after all of this," he whispered.

"He worth it so far?" Sytri asked.

"He's worth anything." It was quiet for a moment. Only crickets. "You know, when a foster family wanted to get rid of me, there were signs. They'd slowly stop talking to me and try to distance themselves. Maybe they think it'll hurt you less when they let you go. But Ronan wouldn't let his family." Ander sighed, his throat tight. "For the first time, I had someone who wanted me around. Someone who had my back."

"How'd he stop them from sending you back?"

"They loved him. Everyone loved Ronan. Our parents adopted him after only having him for a year. All he had to do was make it clear he would never forgive them if they sent me back. So, I had a *home* because he put his foot down." Ander paused. "We were always together after that. While we were in college, we shared an apartment. He stayed with me. Through everything."

"Then why were you guys separated? When this all happened?"

"He went back home to visit his mom and dad. Mine too, I suppose. But I didn't visit them often, and never without him. I got too nervous being in their house."

"Seems like a lot of things make you nervous," Sytri replied quietly. "And you still risked this trip? For someone who could be dead?"

"Didn't look like I had anything left to lose." Ander bit his lip. There was too much weight in those words. Too much backing. He rolled over, feeling cold all over again. "I had no one in Gardners, this whole time."

"No friends?"

"No."

"I feel that." Sytri's voice was low.

"In Gardners, I was safe, but that wasn't enough. All I could think about, every minute, every day, was Ronan. I kept on thinking that maybe he was still alive, that I didn't have to be by myself, that I could have him back. Eventually, it got to me. I either had to go find out or—" Ander stopped himself. "I had to go find out."

"Even with nothing to indicate he could be alive?"

"Yes."

"That's some real dangerous thinking." Sytri tsked. "But I get it. You loved him, right?"

Ander closed his eyes. "Yeah. I—I love him."

His body was tense and his hands were sweating. He knew that Sytri wasn't prying, but it felt like it. Ronan was private information, buried deep inside, never to be mentioned. That's how it had to be. Anything else was . . . dangerous.

"Like good brothers would. So that's why you want to find him. I'm kind of jealous. I never had any siblings."

"I had lots," Ander said weakly. "But Ronan is the only one who liked me."

"Well, the rest didn't know what they were missing."

"Yeah, they did. That's why they didn't bother, but Ronan is strong enough to put up with me. He's great. Great enough that I made this trip, fueled by idiotic optimism. I do feel a bit bad dragging you into it though."

Silence again.

But only for a moment. "You didn't drag me into this. I'm the one who proposed the deal, and I agreed to the terms of it. And I don't regret it so far, Ander." Heat was behind Sytri's speech.

"Sounding real fancy over there, Sytri." Ander smirked, warm from embarrassment. He pressed his face into the mattress. He couldn't look at Sytri. It was as though there were a tight line in the air between them and turning around could snap it. His stomach stirred. "But . . . but thank you." He wanted to say more, much more than that, yet the fear that had plagued him his whole life was cutting his sentences short.

After a moment, the tension grew slack enough that he risked a glance at Sytri, who thankfully wasn't watching him. That would have been too awkward. His glance turned to a gaze as he studied Sytri's form at the window. The way his horns seemed to glow in the moonlight as he kept watch with neon and piercing eyes. The otherworldliness about him was mesmerizing. It made Ander's throat dry.

If I had to make a deal with a demon, I'm glad it was with Sytri.

CHAPTER TEN

"How do you read a map?" Sytri asked, holding the thin piece of paper out in front of him. He turned it to the side, flipped it over, and back again.

Ander sighed and took it from his claws. "The fact that's not a question I need to ask is a very good reason why *I* should keep the map." He looked at the paper and then around them; they were making their way through a small and abandoned town. Legitimately abandoned this time, Ander prayed. Over the past month while checking out similar towns, they had run into a few feral demons whose only goal had been to eat and murder—sometimes in that order. There didn't seem to be any decent folk this side of Texas.

"We'll stay on this road," Ander said after a moment. "And in a mile or so we can take some side roads to avoid bigger towns that are probably crawling with angels or demons." After Tephera, Ander wasn't keen on running into angels either. "And then we'll be about two days away from Atlasville." *From Ronan.*

"Hell yeah, almost there."

"Almost there." Ander scratched at the feathers on his neck, one of them ripping out. He flinched, and his eyes drew to the signs around him before grimacing. "There's another one of those billboards." He nodded to the left. A billboard of a regular woman talking about her bank had been vandalized, her eyes painted a solid white and a halo circled above her head. The thick paint had spilled down her face like a sad rain. An advertisement for the Cast, whatever that was.

The Cast Welcomes All Who Are Pure.

"What do you think it means?" Ander asked.

"Something stupid. Whatever Tephera was talking about. Something only an angel would think of. No offense."

"None taken." Ander sighed, adding another checkmark to the map. He had started keeping tabs whenever they ran into an advertisement for the Cast, and the dots were steadily increasing. Not a great sign. He reached into his backpack and pulled out his makeshift map, made of the photos he'd taken at Tephera's lair. He'd carefully attached them together with thick, clear tape. "The Cast has some paths they take up ahead; we should avoid those completely. I don't want to risk running into these guys." He frowned. "Or Mayrez."

There were a lot of symbols on Tephera's map that Ander still didn't understand. Which was a pain because he wanted to make sure they avoided the Cast completely. Steering clear of anyone associated with Mayrez and Tephera seemed wise. His sleep had been plagued by nightmares of her auction and the angel's grip.

"All right. Avoid, avoid, avoid; stay out of everyone's fucking way. I can go with that," Sytri said after a moment, clapping his hands. "Though how am I supposed to show off that I've gotten a lot tougher if you don't let me fight anyone?"

Ander rolled his eyes. Every day since their run in with Tephera, he'd given Sytri a bit of his blood. According to Sytri, taking a small dose over time was making him stronger without getting him high as hell.

"If we run into a fight, we run into a fight. We're not going to go around trying to start them," Ander huffed. One would have thought, after Tephera, Sytri would have been scared into place. "You're getting too full of yourself based on nothing."

"I'm just saying, I'm pretty sure I could take on some tough fuckers this time around. Maybe get a second round with Tephera."

"Sytri, I like you, but you're an idiot."

"I don't think friends call friends idiots." Sytri laughed. He wrapped his tail around Ander's elbow, and the gray feathers grazed his skin. "Fuzzball, you should be nicer to me."

"I'm always nice to you," Ander retorted, shoving Sytri to the side.

"I'd beg to disagree. Just the other day you tried to make me wear a shirt."

"It's weird that you don't, and it's distracting."

"*Distracting*? Halfie, what are you implying?"

"It was a joke! A joke!" Ander groaned, face hot. Though he claimed it had been in jest, the words had escaped without a filter. That had been a recurring annoyance as of late. The more he talked to Sytri, the more words spilled out of him. Ander had never been the type to keep talking. Now here he was, saying so many things they were drowning him.

"All right, sure, whatever you say, but don't blame me if—" Sytri's tail went stiff, his ears high and alert.

Ander instinctively stepped closer to him and gripped one of Sytri's arms. He'd been snatched more often than he would have liked on this journey. "What is it?" he whispered.

"Shh." Sytri put a finger to his lips. "I think I found something you'll like."

"What?" Ander twisted his mouth.

Sytri slunk across the street, stepping over bits of rubble and tall weeds that curled out of cracked pavement, Ander trailing behind. Their shadows spread over the roads and sidewalks like paint drips.

Sytri sniffed the air again, head swiveling like a cat.

Ander scowled. "Hey, clarify, please? What do you mean something I'll 'like'?"

"What it sounds like." Sytri shrugged. He turned down a barren alley and kept smelling, his tail twitching. Then he crossed over into dark grass, and Ander stopped at the edge. Like many things in the world, the park in front of him had been overtaken by the foliage within it. Grass stood waist-high, its thick weedy stalks reaching for sunlight and the hiss and buzz of insects coming from it in heavy waves. Ander itched just looking at it.

In the distance, there was a small pond that had seen better days. Garbage and debris had lodged along its sides. A slide had been turned over and was rusted and covered with graffiti. Trees overhead made the park one of the darker spots they had crossed. It was feral, lost to time. What about this would he possibly like?

"Sytri . . . Sytri where are you going?" The jerk had crept his way into the middle of the park while Ander still stood at the rim.

"Shh!" Sytri reiterated, bringing a finger to his mouth once again.

Ander glanced around nervously. He didn't like having space between him and Sytri. It made him feel vulnerable, like there were unseen creatures watching him. But the streets seemed empty save for litter and long-abandoned cars. Silence everywhere. It was reminiscent of the moment right before Mayrez's attack. A chill washed over him, and he wrapped his arms around himself before looking back at Sytri.

He was gone.

"Sytri?"

Nothing. Ander furrowed his eyebrows; his chest dropped. His eyes darted from one spot to the next. Then, a shift in the grass as something stirred. The feathers of Sytri's tail peeked over the edge of the plants. The grass rustled furiously as Sytri sprinted; a few birds flew off with panicked, loud chirps.

Ander chewed on his lip. "Sytri, what are you—"

Sytri jerked upward from the grass. A rabbit between his teeth.

"Oh my god."

The bundle of meat and fluff fell from Sytri's mouth and into his hand. Grinning victoriously, Sytri held his prize into the air. "Got it!"

"Sytri, what the fuck!"

"What?" Sytri tilted his head and strolled out of the grass, brushing his pants, then wiped the rabbit blood off his mouth. "A bit of salt and pepper and this will be a good meal. Not too much salt though, I guess." He smiled sheepishly. The rabbit was a plump mound of fur in his hand, its body made of rolls. "You were complaining you were hungry earlier." His voice was earnest, bright.

Ander paused. Sytri had caught it for him? That was unexpectedly thoughtful. Though his gratitude turned to a shiver as the rabbit's eyes stared blankly back at him. "Did you have to catch it with your mouth?"

"Is there another way?"

"Your hands?"

"Pft. What kind of predator catches their prey with their hands?" Sytri rolled his eyes. "You're ridiculous." He hesitated. "Do you not like rabbit?" There was a slight dip in the corner of his mouth; his ears went a little flat.

"I've . . . I've never had it. Guess we'll find out. Don't know how to cook it though." Ander scrunched his mouth. "Or skin it."

"I got that; I'm a decent cook, I think. Don't tell me if I'm not. Come on." Sytri motioned Ander to follow, the rabbit still in his hands. Ander had to ignore the lifeless animal. Sytri had meant well, even if Ander wasn't quite capable of handling it. But dead things weren't pleasant. Even when they were being presented as a gift—perhaps less so that way.

Sytri gestured ahead of them. "That house we scrounged through earlier had a fireplace remember? I can cook it up in there."

Ander smiled softly to himself. So far, he'd been eating whatever remained in gas stations and convenience stores. The meals were quick and made the most sense, even if Ander was sick of snacking on expired crackers. And Sytri, well Sytri never ate much at all. He had said demons worked like crocodiles in that regard.

They backtracked to the old brick building a few blocks down. It was strange; they usually didn't reenter a house once they'd searched it for supplies. Ander crouched next to the fireplace, dry wood still inside. He grabbed a book off the ground and tore out a few pages. Then he pulled a lighter from his bag and let the small flame eat at the paper.

Once he tossed the paper onto the wood, it clung there and a blaze began spreading. Ander stared at the fire, entranced as it crackled and curls of smoke snaked up. Then he turned to the room. Pictures on every wall showed it had been lived in by an elderly couple, which made Ander uneasy. He was not only a trespasser in their home once now, but twice.

*Clink*ing came from the kitchen. Ander glanced at the fire one more time, but it seemed safe enough behind a metal gate. He went to find Sytri and immediately regretted it.

"Oh no," he said, holding up his hands, squinting his eyes shut.

"I have to skin it, Ander. What, you want to eat fur?" Sytri mocked.

"Why are you using your claws?"

"It's easier. I have control over my claws. Does everything I do disgust you?"

"No! I just— I don't know. It's normal to not want to see a dead animal being dissected in front of you."

"Skinned. Not dissected." Sytri slid the claw on his thumb under the fur of the rabbit, then sliced upward to the neck. Ander clenched his jaw as Sytri pushed the skin upward with a slight ripping sound.

"How do you know how to do that?"

"Been doing it a lot since I came to Earth."

"Really?"

"Yeah. I don't have to eat as often as you, but when I do, I like meat, ya know?" He laughed drily. "I used to not even cook it; that had to grow on me. Aren't you lucky?" Sytri grabbed a knife on the table and quickly chopped off the feet. Ander gasped and turned around again.

Sytri coughed. "Sorry, should have warned you. Definitely don't look for the next part."

Ander crossed his arms and stared into the living room, back at the fire, focusing on the flames. There was another loud chop, then the *squelch* of meat sliding. He winced at a thud.

"You ate them raw?"

"I ate things raw in Hell."

Things. Meat unspecified. Ander didn't like that. Sytri didn't seem to either, so Ander didn't press the subject.

"Can I turn around now?"

"Not unless you want to see some organs."

"I prefer to see organs as rarely as possible."

"Wimp." Sytri snickered and Ander rolled his eyes. The fire had grown. A little warm blaze in one room, a home-cooked meal being made in the next. *Normalcy.* Despite his lingering nausea, everything seemed so quaint in that moment. Something twinged in his chest.

"Thanks, Sytri."

"Huh?"

"For doing this for me. It seems like a lot of work." Ander flinched at another thud. "Or at least it sounds like it. I never cooked back in Gardners. Food was rationed tight, so only the stronger blends got to prepare and distribute it on regulated days. To make sure there was no theft going on. But it never seemed like a fun task."

"Eh. I like cooking, actually. I started teaching myself when I got to Earth and being meticulous about something turned out to be good for me. There's a soothing quality to it, and I never really am otherwise."

Ander didn't know what to make of that. Sytri often said things he didn't understand. He *wanted* to know what Sytri meant this time though, what brought him to this point, made him the way he was. "How were you before?"

"A lot cruder." Sytri's voice was sharp. "Can you hand me a water bottle? I need to rinse it."

"Yeah, give me a second." Ander took one of the last bottles out of his backpack. "We better find more soon. I can't go without water." He held his arm backward, waving the bottle until Sytri grabbed it.

"I know, I know. We will. At the very least we can boil some from a stream. There was one nearby on the map. Or I can get into one of the water towers. Don't worry. We'll find you water." More chopping, the slap of meat, dripping water, a splat. "Couldn't find any salt. Who would've thought?" Sytri laughed. "But I found other things. You know, non-drug things."

Ander tentatively turned his head. The skinned rabbit was now slices of fat meat; Sytri was dusting pepper on them. The sight caught Ander off guard. One moment the rabbit had been a bloody carcass, the next it was a meal in the making. This whole cooking thing was . . . charming?

It was like being in an actual home: Sytri cooking, expression serious as he watched pinches of seasoning fall on the meat.

Emotion swelled painfully in Ander's chest.

"All right, now we got something," Sytri said triumphantly. He tossed the sections of meat onto a cast-iron skillet. "Let's get cooking." He grinned, and Ander couldn't help but grin back.

They headed into the living room. Sytri sat by the fire, sliding the skillet over the flames. It hissed for a moment before dying down. Ander sat next to him, watching the fire curl around the metal like dying leaves.

"You're always surprising me," he said, with a laugh. "Cooking?"

"Hey. No one else was doing it. And unlike you, my appetite isn't satiated by expired pasta boxes and suspiciously long-lasting cans of fake meat."

"I wasn't happy eating that food. It's just what we found along the way." Ander stuck out his tongue. The smell of the meat was slowly getting to him. He tried to remember the last properly cooked meal he'd had; it must have been before the gates opened. "This feels special."

"If I knew you were going to get so emotional, I'd have been cooking more often."

"I'm not getting emotional!"

"Yes, you are, over there fluffed up like an excited chicken." Sytri snorted. "I'll cook for you every day if you're going to be cute about it."

"Sytri!" Ander finally turned to him, and froze.

Sytri was already staring at him, eyes serious but bright. The flame of the fire painted him with orange light and deep shadows. It showed the strength of his jaw, the furrow of his brow. His tail was curled behind him, feathers moving slightly. Worst of all, the glow *really* highlighted his fucking bare chest, the bane of Ander's existence.

Sytri smirked and Ander's heart fluttered. Sytri was going to be the death of him. *Too attractive.*

"Here, be careful, don't burn your tongue." Sytri held up a piece of the meat.

Ander blinked, reached, and yanked his hands back with a yelp. "Sytri, it's hot."

"Well, yeah. I just took it off the skillet."

"Too hot for me to hold."

"You and your weak skin." Sytri brought it to his mouth and blew on it. He'd never done something that softly before. The gesture was hypnotizing.

Ander gulped. "Sorry I'm not a demon used to the fires of Hell."

"I told you there's not actually fire there. At least, not a lot?"

"Oh, so there are *some*? You liar!"

"It's not like what you were thinking." Sytri grinned, teeth showing. "You jerk. We don't have lakes of lava or anything." He brought the piece of meat toward Ander's face. "Come on, I want you to taste it. I cooked it for you, dude."

Ander shifted. There was an earnest plea in Sytri's eyes. It was strange though, leaning forward to take a bite from his hand.

It was tough meat, charred a bit. But . . . "It's fucking delicious," Ander said. "Oh my god."

Sytri's face was bright blue. "I didn't think you were going to eat it from my hand."

A moment of silence. Ander wanted to scream. His face was hotter than the fire beside them now. He managed to transfer the urge to hide into a squeaky laugh instead.

It was mirrored by a sharp cry from outside.

Sytri immediately bolted to the door, swinging it open with a snarl on his face. Ander snatched his bag up, heart racing. Why couldn't there be one town that was void of danger?

Cautiously, Sytri stepped outside and, for a moment, there was silence again. Ander wondered if he'd imagined the dreadful screeching, but there was no way they both had. "What was that?"

"Don't know for sure, but we should leave. It sounded like an angel." Sytri grabbed Ander's hand and dragged him down the sidewalk, fast. "Don't want to deal with one of those assholes again."

As they ran, there was only the patter of their own feet hitting the concrete. The screech had stopped.

Maybe it had died? That worried Ander more. What could kill an angel in one blow?

They reached a crossway, and Sytri stopped, surveying streets. Ander followed his line of sight. Empty. Everything seemed as empty as it had been before. Then, the terrible cry again, but a thousand times louder.

Overhead, out of nowhere, a woman appeared in the sky with a bang, a flash of light, and a burst of smoke . Huge white wings spread out from her back, sparkling like gems in the sun. Her scarred, tanned hands clutched the throat of an angel. It was a mass of wings and eyes that screeched like the striking of bells.

They crashed into the building next to Sytri and Ander. Wood, brick, and glass shot into the air like shrapnel, and Sytri shoved Ander behind his back as debris rained down on them. Ander gripped Sytri's wrist and scowled.

"Stop covering for me! We've been over this—I'll heal!"

"How well will you heal from fucking glass in your brain?" Sytri said, wincing as he brushed off splinters of wood. Ander bristled but glanced at the ground as Sytri continued, "Anyway, this doesn't seem like our fight. We could just get the fuck out of here."

"We can do that." Ander cringed as the woman punched the angel further into the dirt. Blood went flying. But as Sytri said, it wasn't their battle. The best decision was to leave immediately.

Sytri and Ander turned, only for a demon to stumble onto the pavement right in front of them.

"Delilah!" the demon shouted. Then he reeled back and glared at Ander and Sytri. He was taller than Sytri, and his eyes were pitch-black against his snow-white skin.

Ander instinctively reached for Sytri's hand.

"Who the fuck are you?" the demon snapped.

"Whoa, buddy, calm the fuck down. We have nothing to do with this," Sytri snapped back. "You're the one who burst in and ruined our dinner."

"Ruined your— Delilah!" He ran past them, shoving Sytri on the way.

Sytri scoffed, glaring at the demon momentarily. "What an asshole. Okay, whatever, let's go—"

Two figures smashed into Ander and Sytri, and they all collided into the building next-door in a rush of air, pain, and debris. Ander swallowed a yell. It *hurt*.

"Ah, what the fuck," Sytri groaned. He wrapped his tail around Ander and pulled him close. "Fuzzball, you okay?"

"Yeah, I'm okay. I told you that I would be." Ander coughed, staring at his arm, which was decorated with shards of glass. "I've healed from way worse than this."

"It still hurts you. Don't be an idiot." Sytri shook himself, bits of concrete falling off.

Ander scowled before taking a deep breath. Then he grabbed one of the glass shards, shut his eyes, and wrenched it out. His jaw clenched at the sting.

Movement to the right drew his attention—the woman and her demon, who had been tossed with them, were picking themselves off the ground, groaning.

Across the street stood the large angel, tattered and torn, but all its eyes focused on the quartet. It cried out into the air, its wings shaking. All its feathers unfurled, and underneath was a skeletal white body littered with eyes. Childlike screams echoed from its body, and it grew louder and louder, shriller and shriller.

"Sytri," Ander said, eyes locked straight ahead. His heart pounded in his chest. *Looks like the fight is our problem now.* He pulled the largest shard out of his skin with a wince before lifting the wound to Sytri's mouth.

Sytri didn't need any instructions. He lapped at the gash, blood painting his tongue. In a second, the huge black arms from his shoulders shot out, gripping the edges of the window frame.

"I got this," Sytri snarled. With that, he turned and darted out the window. Ander breathed heavily, a tight knot in his throat. He crawled closer to the window and watched as Sytri fought against the creature, which was so large next to him. Ander's stomach rolled; Sytri seemed to be holding his own but the tides could always turn. And Ander had already given him all that he had.

"Oh shit, he's kicking that bastard's ass."

Ander jumped and his feathers twitched. He'd forgotten about the others. The woman was standing beside him, along with the demon, who was brushing the dirt and dust off himself. "Y-yeah?" Ander stuttered.

"Ya going to go out there and help?" the woman asked, motioning to Sytri. She squinted for a moment, and her dark-brown eyes stopped on Ander's neck, on his little patch of fluff. "Eh. I guess you don't have a lot of angel blood, do you?"

Ander's face burned. *I have more than you think.*

"Whatever, don't worry, we'll go finish this. Come on, Cerberus." She patted the demon's back, and the two of them hopped out of the building.

Ander was left alone. He rubbed his hand against his feathers. They were so soft, so fragile and thin as his fingers grazed past. *A sign of my weakness.* His chest tightened, and he leaned over the bare window frame, watching the fight again. Sytri tore at the angel with his hands before tossing it into the air, then the woman darted upward only to knock it back down into the reach of the two demons. Cerberus had three tails, each one ending in a metallic spike that stabbed into the angel wildly. It was being ripped apart.

Ander should have been glad—someone was out there to help Sytri not get hurt—but he wanted to be the one to help.

The fight ended within minutes, the angel slumping to the ground as Cerberus managed to pierce straight through its chest multiple times. With a grunt, he wiped the blood off on his jeans, and the woman wrapped her arm around him, pulling him in close for a hug.

Ander stepped out from the store but found himself frozen. The three of them stood there catching their breaths, the perfect embodiment of strength and survival. He craved that kind of tenacity. A pang twisted his chest. There seemed an impassable circle around them, one someone like him hadn't a chance of crossing.

Sytri met his eyes and grinned brightly before running over to him. "Check it out, the quickest fight ever, huh? I'd like to think it was all me, but I'll admit, that guy's got a cool appendage. I wish my tail was half as useful. And that woman? Damn, she's the fastest person I've ever met."

Ander nodded and glanced over at the two newcomers. The woman's wings fluttered in the air, huge and magnificent, blinding. They'd be perfect on an angel. But no bells rang from her—she was only a blend. So much strength radiated from her, though. Her stance showed off her fine muscles.

She talked to her demon for a moment before they both looked back over at Ander and Sytri. Ander stiffened, awkwardly putting an arm around Sytri's waist.

"So, what are you guys doing, traveling out here? Just the two of you?" The woman asked, walking over to them. "Not that I mind at all since you really helped us out right then. That angel was bad news. Jumped us out of nowhere."

"Uh, I'm searching for someone. In a nearby town." Ander checked Sytri and then looked back at the two strangers. They didn't seem like enemies, but it felt best to not give away too much information. "Why would the angel attack you unprovoked?"

"That's what they do around here to Partners."

"Partners. Oh." Ander studied Sytri. *Partner.* His feathers fuzzed up.

"You said you're searching for someone? Friend, family? How far away?"

"What's with all the questions?" Sytri asked roughly.

The woman laughed. "Sorry, I get it, I get it—have to be on your toes. I'm only asking because you two seem nice enough, and we've got a town not far from here. You know, if you needed to take a break." She paused. "Or needed a place to stay in general."

"What?" Sytri and Ander asked together.

"We'd appreciate a good demon and blend pair like y'all." Her gaze was solely focused on Sytri, though. "We're always searching for more. Especially ones that get along. Ain't enough of us out there. Not with the fucking Cast crawling about." Clear distaste rolled off her tongue.

Ander tilted his head. That name again. "The Cast?"

"The fucking folks ruining everything. The angel that just attacked us was with them. We usually don't collide like that, but when we do, it's messy. I'm sure you must've bumped into them by now if you're this far into their territory."

"We ran into an angel named Tephera along the way. They clearly were a part of The Cast," Ander said.

"Holy shit, you ran into Tephera and lived? Your demon must be fucking tough. We lost way too many when that asshole moved nearby." The woman whistled.

"Actually, Ander did a really cool—" Sytri started.

"Like I said, we need that kind of energy. I'm not saying you have to help us out, but you can stop by and relax with us. We're Partner-friendly; in fact, we're Partner-positive, and you're not going to find another place like that for a while. You can consider us a nice rest stop along your journey." The woman walked forward and held out her hand to Sytri. It was covered in callouses, her arms shining with sweat. "I'm Delilah." She brushed back her dark black hair with her other hand.

"Sytri," Sytri said, shaking her hand eagerly. He clapped a hand on Ander's back. "And this is Ander. My blend." He grinned a hugely stupid grin, pushed Ander forward like a trophy.

Instinctively, Ander wanted to hide.

"Pretty tiny blend, huh?" Delilah laughed. She held out the same hand to Ander, and he grabbed it as strongly as he could. Her grip fucking murdered him. He kept a blank face, though. Delilah snorted before waving. "Come on, follow us, get a night's sleep in a place where you don't have to keep peering over your shoulder."

"What do you think, Ander?" Sytri asked, gazing down at him. Ander wanted to say a number of things; he couldn't think of a reason not to at least give it a shot, though. At the very least, they seemed to dislike the Cast. And friends, in this time, could be a huge blessing.

"I guess we can rest there," Ander said after a moment.

"Sweet, come on then, we'll show you the way." She started walking forward with long strides, and Cerberus followed her, his three tails swishing back and forth softly. "You're going to love it, I promise."

"What's it called?" Sytri asked. "I haven't heard of a deal, uh, Partner-friendly town."

"Millstone."

Ander stumbled. Oh. The town the Couriers had warned him about. The town of debauchery and filth. *Oh fuck.*

CHAPTER ELEVEN

I t was hard to not be on edge as they walked. Even though Delilah and Cerberus seemed kind enough, Ander wasn't able to label them *friendlies* yet. He stayed close to Sytri and focused on the path ahead. Delilah led them off the main road, further and further down gravel lines and into the depths of trees and foothills. Eventually, they headed into dense forest where the sunlight only managed to sprinkle its way through the leaves.

"We're in Big Bend now, aren't we?" Ander said as he surveyed the area briefly.

"Yeah, you know your stuff, huh?" Delilah said. "Been here before then, I take it?"

"I used to visit it as a kid, with my . . . family." Ander gazed vacantly at the ground, at the uneven and rocky tract of land. Trips to the national park had been tolerable at best. He had always been slow, and everyone had seemed impatient with him no matter how hard he'd tried to keep up. Except for Ronan, who had stuck by his side, seemingly unbothered by Ander's small strides.

If Ander closed his eyes, he would be back there for just a moment. Ronan keeping pace with him, orange and brown leaves scattered at their feet, sunlight shimmering off his blond hair like a halo. The cold chill that came with the fall meant every time they'd spoken, there had been puffs of steam. Before demons and angels, before the end of the world. A trip where when Ander had stumbled, Ronan had reached out a hand, guided him until he was steady once more.

Ander breathed out; eyes open. He was close to home—close to Ronan. "It's easy to get lost here."

"That's sort of the point. It's good to be hard to find." Delilah laughed, then rubbed one of her shoulders and groaned. "We don't want to be getting into fights all the time. You lose lives that way. We thought if we stayed away from everyone, they would leave us alone. For a while, that very simple plan worked. Until the Cast."

Ander stared straight ahead at the shadows hanging from the trees and spreading across the ground. They grew as the sun started to set.

"What did they do?" he asked softly.

"Ruined everything," Cerberus muttered. Ander jumped a little at the sound of his voice. It was gravelly, deep, and he hadn't said a word to them since they'd started walking.

"The Cast is our number one priority right now. We need them out of our land, but those bastards won't budge," Delilah said.

Sytri raised an eyebrow. "Thought you said you don't pick fights."

"We don't," Delilah retorted. "They pick fights with every fucking thing. The Cast isn't a joke. They're a fucking cult. A bunch of blends led by angels who're obsessed with the idea of purity or whatever—"

Ander had gone cold. He could feel Tephera's grip around his torso. *"Purity for the Cast."*

"—and they kill anything that's not an angel or blend. Not just demons, but humans too if they find them."

"What?" Thoughts of Tephera had dragged Ander from the conversation. "The angels tell them to do that? Aren't they supposed to protect mankind? *Tephera would have killed Sytri for sure, but a human?* Ander's skin crawled—maybe Tephera *would.* What did Ander even know anymore?

"Mankind isn't *pure* enough for them. These angels and blends in the Cast believe that this whole apocalypse was planned by their God. So that angels could finally claim the Earth and turn it into a perfect world. It's a bunch of bullshit." Delilah turned and glared. "Don't listen to them."

"Wh— I won't. I . . . I have Sytri, why would I think that all demons need to be killed? Sytri's my . . . he's my Partner." He glanced at Sytri.

"Yeah, you say that now, but once those cultist crazies start whispering to you, it's like a Siren's song, digs into your insecurities, pries at all those places in your mind you thought you hid so well." Delilah's eyes snapped back to the road. "What I'm saying is, I'm trusting you and Sytri right now; don't make me regret it. Don't prove yourself weak."

Tension built inside of Ander. His neck became stiff. Where did Delilah even get off, acting like she distrusted them? She was leading them into deep, dark woods. Not the other way around.

"Ander's not weak." Sytri placed an arm on Ander's shoulders, glaring at Delilah. "He's not going to be fucking seduced by some asshole with wings, all right? Give him credit."

"I'm just saying, I need you to be—"

"You don't need to say anything. Ander wouldn't abandon me to join a damn cult."

"I wouldn't," Ander said loudly, though it strained him. But he had to prove himself to Delilah, to make Sytri's words hold more ground. He grinned at his demon, who was smirking right back, shadows curled around his form. His bright seafoam-green eyes contrasted against their dark rim like diamonds, matching the leaves of the huge trees behind him. His grin was too perfect, his face too proud to be staring at Ander. Why was he so beautiful, and how could someone so gorgeous gaze at Ander like that?

"All right, all right, didn't mean to step on anybody's toes there." Delilah scoffed "It's just I can see the fluff on your neck there, buddy. Weaker angels and blends are easily manipulated by the higher-ups. Even I can fall victim to them." There was an edge to her voice.

"Well, that sounds like a *you* problem," Sytri said, rolling his eyes. "Ander's not a wimp." He snapped his teeth, and tension threaded through the whole group.

Okay, everyone needs to settle down.

"Anyway, what's Millstone like?" Ander interjected.

There was a heavy pause before Delilah said a little curtly, "We're actually almost there; see all that woodwork up there?" She pointed ahead of them, and Ander could vaguely make out the shape she was talking about. It seemed like a mass of branches and trees. "We're not in the middle of nowhere for no reason."

As they neared the mass, it became clear it was far more complex than a pile of sticks.

"Shit," Sytri muttered.

The wall towered with the trees, some sixty feet into the sky and stretched out for maybe a solid mile altogether. Larger than Ander had expected, especially for something he'd thought to be jammed in the woods. But *jammed* was the entirely wrong word. Trees had somehow been woven together to form a structure that swayed with the natural wave of the forest.

"How long did it take to make this? How did you have the time with all the chaos?" Ander muttered, placing a hand on the wood. Even though the wall had been formed by people, it blended in so well with the world around it.

"We didn't make Millstone when all the shit was going down; it took a few months for us to find each other. But as soon as we did, we kind of got to work and kept at it. Until we made what we wanted." Delilah laughed. She knocked on one of the large trunks that composed the barrier, hard and quick.

"Delilah?" a voice called out. "You're back? Oh. You found newbies!"

Suddenly, in front of them, a gate started lowering. It had been so uniform with the structure that Ander hadn't noticed it. They moved to the side to let it fall.

As they walked through the entrance, there were deep-red bricks; the barricade was reinforced. Past the barrier was the town of Millstone, and it took Ander's breath away. Instead of the borderline dismal conditions of the other towns he and Sytri had passed, it was gorgeous and filled with a luscious green. Small houses had been built, evenly spaced apart, with tiny gardens in front of them, and cobblestone paths led from one to another. Millstone hadn't been patched together from the remains of a forgotten society. This was a town that had been fully formed from the ground up; it had been taken care of, nurtured, and it was glowing from it.

Blends and demons walked around, apparently undisturbed by their entrance. On one side of the gate a demon sat in a chair, flipping through a magazine. Across from him a blend was furiously scribbling in a notebook. Ander couldn't remember the last time he'd seen someone look so casual. His body grew warm at the sight of it; the tension fell from his shoulders.

Ahead of him, a group of younger men and women were chatting on a wooden bench and taking bites out of sandwiches. Just eating leisurely, instead of scurrying back to their houses with their divvied-out rations. To his right, a woman left her house with a basket of laundry and began to hang it out to dry as she hummed. No dark lines under her eyes. Instead of clinging to the arms of their parents, children were running past, chasing each other. Some had small wings.

The whole thing was too serene. Ander felt like he was dreaming, that he'd stepped into a utopia that couldn't possibly exist. His eyes darted back and forth from one group of people to the next, unable to stop admiring. Everything was so perfect.

"It's almost like how it used to be."

"Yeah," Delilah said.

Ander faced her glowing grin. "How did you do all of it?"

"I told you, once you quit trying to pick fights with everyone, you have a lot of time to work on where you live. We don't see demons as inherently bad, or angels as inherently good, because that's not true. Or if it was, it sure isn't anymore." Delilah smacked Cerberus's back.

"People like the Cast, on the other hand, don't agree with us," Cerberus added. "And then there are demons who are traitors to their own kind and sell blends to those angels. There's been one by the name of Mayrez who's become a fucking handful."

Ander and Sytri looked at each other, Sytri's mouth already in a snarl.

"Are you fucking kidding me? She has her grimy little claws deep in shit even down here?" he growled. "I knew the girl liked to travel, but I didn't think it would be this far south."

"You said she had customers in the south," Ander said, jaw clenched. "We saw Tephera. It would make sense that whatever this Cast cult is, that's who she's been selling to. We had guessed it and seems we were right." *Unfortunately.* Ander stared around him at the contented people living in peace and serenity. Mayrez would snap them all in chains in an instant. Just like that, the smallest sign of society would be crushed again. Ice filled Ander's veins.

"You know her too, huh? Figures. We assumed she'd been grabbing people from pretty far off. She attacked us before, to kidnap blends. It didn't go well for either of us, but she keeps a distance from us now when she makes her way through."

"She hasn't tried again since the first time? Why?"

"From what we can tell, she likes the element of surprise. If she doesn't have it, then she decides her targets aren't worth the risk."

"But she still comes down here?" Ander asked.

"Yeah, every few months to drop off a dozen or so blends wherever the Cast are." Delilah narrowed her eyes. "The Cast wants recruits, in any way possible. You either join them willingly or they force you. And if somehow you can't be forced, they kill you. Simple as that."

Is that the Couriers' fate? Michael's? Ander bit his lip. He had abandoned them, and now it seemed they would either be sold off to a demon or some crazed cult. It would have been his end as well, had it not been for Sytri. What if he'd been caught back when they were in Tephera's nest?

"Wait." Ander flung his bag to the ground and tossed clothes and cans to the cobblestone path before taking out his taped-together map. "I took these pictures when we stumbled into Tephera's lair." He unfolded the photos, held it out in front of him. "Mayrez's name is on it. It's like a guide, a schedule of some sort."

Delilah stared for a second before snatching the pictures. Her wide eyes scanned across the them, working out the interconnecting lines, the circles and stars. Then she looked up at Ander, and there was a suspicious twist in her upper lip.

"You walked into Tephera's *nest*? And you got out? I thought you just stumbled into them, but you found their Nest?" She eyed the photos. "Do they know you took these pictures?"

"N-no, I had put them back in my bag before they found us."

"Holy shit. This will definitely change the game. Someone here will be able to figure out what the markings mean." She held the map out to Cerberus. "Give this to Vega, ASAP."

Cerberus glanced at it and then back to Ander before nodding and running off.

Delilah put her hands on her hips, leaned on one leg. "Well, I'm pleasantly surprised. I didn't expect such substantial events today. Finding new Partners, who have an actual map of Mayrez's trading routes."

Ander couldn't stop the small grin that formed at the corners of his mouth as Delilah beamed at him. He'd done something to help souls other than himself.

"If we can use that map to figure out the next time she crawls through our territory on the way to the Cast, if we have the element of surprise, maybe we can finally stop that cretin and save some fellow blends. It'd really weaken the Cast, cutting off their main source of new recruits. If we can, you might become my new favorite around here, An . . ."

"Ander," he stuttered, not even mad that Delilah had already forgotten his name. "It's Ander. And I hope you can. Let me know if you need help with it. I can't forgive Mayrez for what she put me through." He grimaced. She'd done so much worse to others. She had destroyed Afriel, most likely sold Michael and the Couriers to some horrible demon, and then killed who knew how many along the way.

Delilah snorted but otherwise held her composure. "If we need you, Ander, I promise I'll let you know. For now, I'll show you where you and Sytri can stay while you're with us." She guided Ander forward, and they passed by a home that smelled like freshly baked bread. "We made extra houses while we were building, so there are a few empty ones around. We have plans you know, to keep on adding and adding, to make a proper town."

Ander nodded and glanced over at Sytri, who was staring at him with bright, calm eyes, a delicate grin on his face. His composure was almost serene. But something else too. *Admiring*? Heat rushed over Ander's face. The gaze lasted only the briefest moment before they both turned away.

CHAPTER TWELVE

"This is like a legitimate house," Sytri muttered, dragging his fingers across an eggshell-colored wall. "Like a *new* house. There aren't even any bloodstains. That's crazy."

Delilah had departed minutes ago, seemingly unaware she had completely changed their world. She'd simply apologized for the home's small size before waving and trotting out the door, leaving them both in disbelief. Though the building had the same proportions as a shack, it was indeed, a *house*.

Ander walked around the tiny room, where a blue couch sat, along with a dark coffee table. They appeared like someone had just brought them home from the store, aside from the layer of dust that coated them. There was a working sink and a working bathroom hooked up to a sewage tank system; there was even a tiny metal wood stove. The whole thing felt rustic but still fresh. It was homey. The kind of place Ander hadn't been in a long time.

"This place is . . . nice," he said, pushing back a curtain and staring out the window into the rest of Millstone. The sun was beginning to set, but people were still meandering, talking to one another, clearly enjoying themselves. "I didn't know that life could be like this, after everything." How could he? The world had changed so drastically. "Why did I spend my life in Gardners?" he said out loud, but not necessarily to Sytri. "Why did the angels there keep us trapped, living like that?" All he had ever known there was survival, being constantly afraid, anxious, wondering if the next day would be his last, or if that even mattered. Ander's fingers tugged at the curtain a little harder, his mouth a tight line.

"Living like what?" Sytri asked. "I thought Gardners was a safe haven?" He flopped down on the couch, his tail falling the side.

"It was safe, but not a haven. Not by a longshot. There was a clear hierarchy. The stronger you were, the more useful you were, the more you'd be given priority." Ander thought back to his time there, waiting in lines for whatever food scraps remained at the end of the day. "My living quarters were cramped. I was basically living in a hostel with twenty other people. All of us were considered . . . I don't know. Expendable."

"You've never brought that up before," Sytri said. "Didn't you say you wanted to take Ronan back to that place?

"I did. Because it *is* safe. I thought that was the most we could get. But maybe it isn't. If Millstone is doing so well, maybe other places are too." Ander pictured him and Ronan, spending days together in a real house. Obviously, Sytri would be there as well. The image made his chest flutter.

"Even I didn't know this kind of town existed." Sytri sat up. "Or that it could. And I've been following Mayrez around for a while."

"What do you mean you were following her around?" Ander scrunched his nose up.

Sytri's ears went flat. "I mean, I wasn't in Afriel by accident, you know? You saw all the demons there."

"What, were you part of her group?"

"Not exactly? I wasn't one of her bootlickers, that's for sure. But I did want to . . . to get a blend." Sytri glanced to the side. "Not through one of her auctions; I didn't agree with her methods. But I . . . We all knew that Mayrez was good at catching blends, and we all wanted one."

There was a pit in Ander's stomach. Of course that was why Sytri had been there. He'd been waiting, like every other demon, to get a blend. And he'd succeeded.

"What was your plan, then?" Ander asked after a moment. "If you hadn't gotten me?"

"Eventually sneak some other blend out. Have them make a deal with me. I'm clearly a better choice than Mayrez, right?"

Sytri laughed, though the smile that held it wavered. "And I had to sneak one out. I didn't have anything to trade."

So he'd hung on the sidelines until he could snatch what he needed. The thought was sickening. Still, he had given Ander a choice.

Was it really a choice though? Ander faced the window, unsure how to look at Sytri. The demon had been the lesser of two evils, but that didn't mean he'd given Ander legitimate options. Sytri could have just let him free without forcing him to pick between making a deal or being thrown back into Mayrez's clutches. It was unsettling to think that Sytri would put anyone in that situation.

He wouldn't now though, surely?

But how could he have changed in the course of a few weeks?

"Dude."

Ander jumped—Sytri's hand was on his shoulder. When had he gotten so close?

"Yeah?" Ander asked, turning.

"You okay?" Sytri chewed on his bottom lip. "I . . . You don't think I'm . . . I'm— I am better than Mayrez, right?"

Ander stared into Sytri's bright green eyes. The ones that had both frightened and mesmerized him when they first met. They were uniquely Sytri.

"Yes," Ander said, voice tense. "Maybe now, as long as you try to be."

"What do you mean?"

"What I said. You put me in a messed-up position, Sytri." In a second he was back in the tunnel again. A strange demon with glowing eyes dragging him down the depths. "I was scared. And you knew that. I was a lost blend, and you took advantage of my desperation." It felt like there was a rock in his throat. "I want to believe you wouldn't do that now. That you're not still taking advantage of me somehow. You're not, right?"

Sytri's eyes were rimmed dark. "I . . . I don't think so."

They stared at each other, and Ander's heart ached. He wanted to trust him. He *needed* to. "What does that mean? You extorted me before and now you're saying you still might be, like, manipulating me?" Ander's words were strained. "That's almost as bad as you making me think I was going to die. And if I hadn't agreed to your deal, wouldn't you have let me?" He froze. "Would you have given me straight back to Mayrez?" Chains. Micah. Torture.

"I don't know! But I wouldn't now; I definitely would never give you back to her now. I swear." Sytri's eyes were wide. "Ander, I promise. Not just because of the deal, all right? But because I'm better and I like you—we're friends." His teeth dug harder into his bottom lip.

But the Sytri from back then *would* have tossed him right into Mayrez's arms. He didn't have to say it, the answer was simply there, a knot in the air between them.

Sytri is a demon. Ander swallowed. *He has been this whole time. Why do I keep trying to forget that?*

"I want to believe you. I really do."

"Then do, and I promise I won't let you down." Sytri's voice had steadied, and his eyes met Ander's.

Ander breathed in and out, heart racing.

Demon or not, surely Sytri deserved a chance to do better? Wasn't that what Ander craved himself? *I've done things that I would never do now.* Not nearly as shitty as what Sytri had done but maybe the human equivalent? *Should I be giving him more leeway because he's a demon? Or less?* Ander gritted his teeth. "It's fucked up," he said after a moment. "But I get . . . I get that you needed a blend to survive. And I needed you too, to make it this far. We were both desperate."

"'Desperate' is a nice word for what I was," Sytri muttered.

Ander laughed, the sound sour. "It *might* be too kind of one." There was brief silence, the air tight. "I don't think you're, like, *evil.* It's not as black-and-white as that. But even so, you abused my situation to get what you wanted, and that's—that's so fucked up." His tone went up a pitch as his heart raced again.

"I know! Do you think I don't?" Sytri threw his hands in the air. "But I was different. Barely better than that awful version of me that came crawling out of Hell."

"What was the straight-from-Hell version of you like?"

"More like Mayrez." Sytri paused. "I didn't . . . you know, want to talk about it. But it freaks me out every so often, when I remember."

"You've got to clarify more than that. *Why* does it scare you?"

"It's hard to describe." Sytri's voice cracked. "I don't have words for it. Like there are different angels, there are different demons. I told you that. The kind I am and where I was, made me *angry*. No, that word isn't strong enough. It was past that. This disgusting and violent desire to destroy and . . . and *ruin* everything I touched." He backed away from the window. "I wasn't sentient, more like an animal in a trap, furious without knowing why. I just wanted to *kill* things. And when the Gates broke, and I made my way to Earth, that was the first time I could properly *think*. Though it took me months to understand what rational thought even was." He gritted his teeth, his eyes dark.

Ander had never seen that expression on him before. "Sytri, why didn't you—"

"I didn't want to explain it to you; no demon does. How can you trust me if I say I was just a fucking monster? That I came from a literal hellhole full of fucked-up animals?"

"You're not some savage animal now. You're talking to me, for one."

"Maybe, but there were steps from that to this. Because you're right, Ander, I basically kidnapped you and it didn't matter to me at all. And now, just a few weeks later, it matters so fucking much. I can't imagine doing that kind of thing again. Everything in my head is changing so fast and I'm scared—" Sytri's words stumbled into each other. His eyes darted over to Ander. "I'm scared that it can all get undone just as quickly. What if the Gates get sealed and I get sent back and I can't . . . I don't get to feel like this anymore? What if I don't get to be a person anymore? I like it here, Ander. I like it here on Earth, I like it with you. I like who I'm becoming. What if that gets ripped away from me?" His voice cracked. He looked on the verge of tears.

Ander had never seen Sytri so *broken* before, and he never could have expected it. But he was still unsure of how much he actually trusted him in the first place. Unsure if he could ever truly get over what he'd done.

Yet this . . . this fear seemed genuine. Ander knew that same panic that dug nails into his throat, voice so raw from crying that the screams were almost silent. And he'd been left alone with his for a long time.

It would be cruel to let Sytri deal with his the same way.

"I won't let you get like that. And I wouldn't let anyone take you away."

"What?"

"I would fight every angel to make sure you got to stay with me. And I would never, never let you lose your mind." Ander walked toward him, then grabbed his hands as firmly as he could, pressing so deep that Sytri's skin turned white. "I'd make sure of it. If you're with me, I'll do everything I can to keep you, you. I want to watch you become the best version of yourself possible." He fought to look him in the eyes.

Sytri stared at him for the longest time. Ander's hands started sweating. Of course, his little vow didn't mean much; he was the weakest blend of them all, even if he was somehow a Half. But he stood by his words. They tightened in his chest, a heavy lock and key. A promise.

Sytri's face softened, the hard corners falling way. "Thanks."

Ander was on fire. "Don't patronize me. I mean it."

"I know you do, that's why I said thanks." Sytri glanced at their hands, and Ander quickly let go, shoving them into the pockets of his shorts. There was a faint chuckle. "I'm very lucky to have met a blend like you. Can't imagine it could have worked out better. Though, I do feel horrible about how we started, that I put you through that. I want—I want to work to make sure I'm someone you can trust. Distance myself from the demon I was, for you."

Ander's heart thudded in his chest so hard he almost clutched at it. Almost. Sytri's face was focused, his eyes bright.

"Not sure if I'm worth all that. You should do it for yourself," Ander mumbled. His confidence had wilted away to hard embarrassment. It settled in his legs and made them jelly.

"You're so much better than you think."

"Don't compliment me." Ander covered his ears, heat flaring across his face. "It's weird."

"Fine, fine." Sytri laughed. "I'll compliment you later." He sighed, his shoulders relaxing. "Sorry for that outburst. I feel kind of dumb now."

"Me too. Let's talk about something else, please." Ander's heart was still beating a thousand times a minute. Feelings were strange; acknowledging them was stranger. And being all sentimental made him feel as if he were floating.

"Like what?"

"Well . . . we h-have a house now, that's cool," Ander said, gesturing around them, still not looking at Sytri.

"That is cool. I always thought the house-life wasn't for me, but I dig this." Sytri cleared his throat. "I really like this town so far, for the whole three hours we've been here. The place smells like food and trees. And people are staying together; no one's eating each other." He paused. "It's weird how much I like it. I even want to stay, a little bit. Demons are normally like scavengers, always moving. Standing still is . . . strange for us. But the demons here choose to stay and live with everyone else." Ander felt Sytri's gaze on him as he continued. "Think we could live here?"

"I don't see why not," Ander said quickly. It was the perfect place. It was what he had dreamed about. "As long as you don't mind." He would have felt silly asking Sytri to settle down in some strange town they had just stumbled upon, but Sytri had asked first. The world was insane, chaotic, and they had found the closest thing to a home that they could. Why not stay? Be happy?

"What about Ronan?"

Ander had forgotten Ronan. He swallowed hard. "What about him? When we find him, he'll live here too."

"What if he doesn't like me?" Sytri asked, his voice low.

"Why wouldn't he?"

"We just talked about that; a good portion of people still don't trust demons. This is the first place we've found where they do. We're in a partnership and we're *still* working on the whole trust thing."

Ander stiffened. Fair points. He'd spent so much of his life in Gardners shivering at the mere thought of demons. But he wasn't like that anymore. Ander had said that he wouldn't leave Sytri, and he meant that. If Ronan was like most humans and blends walking around on Earth, then Ander would have to get him to change his view.

But what if that view is resolute? What would I do then?
What if Ronan isn't even alive?

Ander quickly pushed those thoughts aside. He couldn't focus on them yet, especially not the last one, not until they had at least made it back to his hometown. Until he had combed through the city and talked to every survivor.

"I'll make sure he likes you, Sytri," Ander said after a moment.

"You can't be sure of something like that."

"I have to be," Ander assured him. "Because I'm not leaving you. And I won't leave him." There was a strain in his shoulders, a tightness in his chest. He couldn't leave Sytri or Ronan behind. He would do whatever it took to have them both.

"You sound really determined," Sytri said with an awkward smile. "I like that. You're getting tougher every day, fuzzball. Maybe that's some of me finally rubbing off on you." With his shoulder, he nudged Ander, who almost fell down. Sytri caught him with his tail and grinned.

"Then is any of me rubbing off on you back?" Ander asked, smiling. "Any of the good parts, if I have them?"

"Every part is, fuzzball." Sytri's tail pushed against Ander, forcing him into a spin, as if they were dancing. Sytri intertwined their hands and tilted him downward, Ander's back almost parallel to the floor as claws gently curved into the dip of his waist. The lightest touch. Ander felt it to his center. "Every part of you is good."

Ander was drowning in something other than panic and fear. This strange new substance clung to his body, making it hot and flustered. Yet, he couldn't quit looking at Sytri and he didn't want Sytri to quit looking at him.

Sytri choked out a laugh before pulling Ander back up and letting him go. He spun away, scratching at an ear. Ander coughed and glanced at the window, trying to will the burning heat in his face down.

"It's getting late," Sytri said in one breath. "And this is the first place in like, what, since we met, where we might be able to both sleep without me having to keep watch and jump up at every sound? We should try to actually rest."

"Yeah, I want to get up early and talk to Delilah if I can find her," Ander mumbled. Wiped at his shorts, as if anything were there to wipe off in the first place. He just needed to do something with his hands. He glanced at Sytri before walking toward the small door across from them and opened it up to reveal the bedroom. It was quaint, cute: a dresser, a side table, red curtains, a little oil lamp.

One bed.

Ander stared at it for a long time. He and Sytri had often shared a bed; heck, even a cot. They'd simply left space between them, and Ander had gone to sleep without a care. But now he was overwhelmed with thoughts and all of them about Sytri. *Calloused hands, stupid grin, that cute way his ears fold back when he's upset— Stop that, stop thinking.*

Sytri hummed to himself, also eyeing the singular bed. Ander chewed on his lip. The mattress seemed cozy as hell, there were comforters folded neatly on the side, two thick pillows on top. And for some reason that made Ander think about Sytri's fingers at his waist. And how nice they'd feel again, under the blankets. He swallowed dryly. *Oh my god, quit thinking.*

"Looks nice," he said, somehow making the situation more uncomfortable. "I'll take the left?" he added, before going over to the bed, sitting on it, and kicking off his shoes. Fuck, it was plush. He lay down and— *Oh wow.* "Sytri, it's a *really* nice bed."

"Ahaha, yeah?" Sytri laughed, kind of. It was followed by a wheeze. It sounded like he needed a Heimlich maneuver. "Well, I'm not . . . that tired yet so I might stay awake. Also, we don't know if we can trust these guys yet. I should stay on guard for a little bit, right?" He crossed his arms.

"That makes sense," It did not make sense. Sytri had literally said the opposite not a minute prior. Ander went with it, however, because he wasn't sure he was ready to have Sytri under the blankets with him. Then he glanced over at Sytri. In the near darkness, his strange blue-green blush glowed, highlighting every feature on his face.

Ander was suddenly aware of how small he was in the bed, curled up in it, how Sytri was almost looming over him. How he never wore a *fucking* shirt. How immensely, painfully attractive the jerk was simply by standing there, with his perfect fucking physique, even with his dumb feather tail. There were other things he had never noticed much that were so eye-catching now; for one, the tight skin on Sytri's stomach, the visible curve of each muscle. Especially how nice said muscles looked now, in the dimly lit room.

He could pin Ander down, so easily.

Ander swallowed hard and rolled over, throwing the blanket over his head, then pressing his face deep into the pillow. *What the hell is going on?*

"Just don't stay up too late." Oh god his voice had cracked. "I'm sure we're . . . I'm sure we're fine here." He chewed on his fingernails. Where he didn't feel safe was in his own head. There were thoughts he couldn't stop, thoughts he hadn't known he could even have.

Fuck.

CHAPTER THIRTEEN

Ander woke up to soft light, a cozy bed, a plush pillow, and feathers in his face. He sneezed, and the plumage fluttered, twitching slightly. *Wait, where am I?* There was a jumble of confusion in his head before it hit him. *In a home. With Sytri.* His chest was light, almost weightless, even though Sytri's arm was lying over it.

Ander stopped breathing. Sytri was beside him, arms wrapped around Ander, one leg casually over Ander's thighs. His tail had curled up the other side of Ander's body, the feathers grazing his face. When had that happened? They were so close, which wasn't that unusual, but this was an embrace and maybe for that reason, Ander was hyperaware of every piece of Sytri touching him. Being the only one awake, he felt like he was taking advantage of the situation.

He coughed, and Sytri didn't move. What the hell was he going to do? He needed to make space between them. But Sytri was warm and his grip comforting, much more than it should be. Ander didn't want to break from it. Was that a strange thing for a friend to feel?

It has to be crossing a line.

"Sytri," Ander said, so quietly that it would be exaggerating to call it a whisper.

Sytri awoke immediately. "What? Is something wrong? Are you okay?" He rocketed up. Now he was right over Ander, hovering above him, their noses almost touching, his charcoal hair swishing down past his face to ghost Ander's own.

They stared at each other for a solid second before Sytri seemed to understand where he was. "Oh." He stumbled off Ander, almost throwing himself onto the floor. "Sorry, sorry about that, you—you said my name." Sytri laughed. "And I, uh, I'm used to thinking some demon is about to fuck us up." He looked around the room and shrugged. "But it seems . . . it seems we're safe here, so far."

"It's fine," Ander said, much too quickly.

The atmosphere was different now. Something had changed last night, yet nothing had at all. How was that possible? Ander pulled his knees up to his chest and squinted slightly at the sunlight, rubbing his eyes. He wanted to vanish from the thick air between them. Fold himself up until he disappeared. Had Sytri known how he was lying? That his whole body had been pushed against Ander's?

Ander flushed; he wanted . . . *more.* The feeling of Sytri against him had sparked a heat in his stomach, swirled it around. It was a sensation Ander had almost forgotten he could have.

"We should get up, right?" he asked, glancing over at Sytri. "And try to find Delilah. There's still a lot I need to know about . . . about all this."

"Yeah, this place isn't too big. I'm sure she'll be easy to find," Sytri said with a shrug. He tilted his head toward the door, his hair falling softly.

Ander focused on the strands. Delicate spiderwebs. He wanted to put his hands in them.

"—probably like a leader of this place anyway, right? People will know who she is."

"Yeah," Ander said, nodding. What the fuck was wrong with him?

"Come on, then." Sytri motioned for him to follow. Ander blinked before getting on his feet. He slipped on his incredibly worn-out shoes and stretched.

"You've got freckles on your stomach."

"Wh-what?" Ander blurted, swinging his arms down, and tugging at his shirt.

Sytri's right ear flicked upward, and he stared at Ander, expression unreadable. Ander held his breath.

"Let's go."

With that, Sytri turned and went out the door. Ander stood there, took a deep breath, and followed. Outside, the sun was shining as brightly as it could through the trees. Ander looked around, staying right beside Sytri as they headed further into town. No one gave them a second glance. Unbelievable. If new people had walked into Gardners, there would have been angry whispers, accusations. *More people taking up space.*

And if they were weak like Ander? Then they would have been deemed useless.

In the distance, there were the edges of cliffs and mountain ranges. And an endless, endless amount of trees and sky. The air was rich with oxygen and pine. Ander breathed it in and felt renewed. This was a good place for Millstone to hide, in the depths of a national park, in a forest full of hills, rivers, and canyons. The terrain made it hard for one to know their surroundings, and by extension, made it a place most would be unwilling to traverse.

"If we did stay here, we'd have to help in some way, wouldn't we?" Ander asked as they passed a demon who was casually using their tail to paint the side of a house. "They seem to be a community."

"What did you do in Gardners?"

"Nothing." Ander scowled. He'd spent three whole years staring into space, wondering about the ifs and whats. "I don't know what I'd be good at," he said after a moment. "Or what they need."

"I'm sure you could do something. I'm sure they need everything. People to cook, clean, farm, scavenge; you're not useless, Ander," Sytri said, patting Ander's back. "Quit thinking it."

Ander smiled to himself. His heart fluttered, sunlight grazed his face, and everything was warm.

"Hey," Sytri said, walking up to a trio of blends who were chatting around a well as one of them pulled water from it. "Where can we find Delilah?"

The three of them paused before the smallest one spoke up. Her eyes were a little cloudy and her stare not quite on either of them, though she had turned their way. "She's been talking with Vega and the rest of the council all morning in the town hall. Are you the one who brought the map? Is that why you're asking? They've been discussing it, getting some of the scouts ready."

"Ready for what?" Ander asked.

"I don't know, probably going to jump that jerk Mayrez." The blend's wings ruffled as she said Mayrez's name with clear disdain. "It'd be wonderful if they did. It'd be a miracle."

"Where is the town hall?" Ander said quickly.

"You keep taking this path and then turn right at the end. It's a large building," the girl said, before hesitating.

"It has no windows. Super noticeable," one of the other blends piped up. "I really wouldn't bother them if I were you, though. The council prefers to keep matters like that—"

"Thanks!" Ander shouted, already leaving. Sytri stayed by his side, tail swishing back and forth almost like a dog's, as they made their way past blends and demons. Ander's mind was turning. A group, taking on Mayrez? How would they stop her?

When he turned right, he could see what the blend had meant about the building. It definitely stood out. It was larger than the others they'd seen so far, and it resembled a large wooden block, not nearly as pleasant as the rest of the architecture that surrounded them. It looked like it had popped out of the ground, an imposing and rugged tree stump that refused to budge.

"So what's the deal?" Sytri asked as Ander walked over to the door. "Are you going to ask how to get to Atlasville from here?"

Ander's fingers twitched above the doorknob. Once again, he'd mentally pushed Ronan to the side. He had wanted . . . revenge? No, that wasn't important. It was something else.

"I want to make sure Mayrez is gone," Ander started. "But I don't know if . . .?"

Sytri's ears went flat.

The door swung open. Ander just managed to back away from it in time, stumbling toward the steps. Sytri grabbed him.

"I'll bring him here!" a voice shouted.

"Please don't!" someone yelled back. Delilah.

Standing in the doorframe was a tall demon. Well, he wasn't standing as much as crouching. His hair was a red mess, flaring in every direction like a wildfire. Sticking out of it were two large, thin onyx horns. *Black and red. Like a cardinal.*

He faced Ander and Sytri, who stared back. The new demon quirked his head to the side like a bird. A grin cracked across his cream-colored face, revealing rows of sharp, perfectly white teeth. They sent a chill straight down Ander's spine.

Sytri's grip on him tightened.

"Found him!" the demon yelled, and suddenly he snatched Ander by his wrist and turned, yanking him upward like a freshly caught fish. Ander's vision spun, and he caught a glimpse of a table, wings, and faces as he was swung forward.

Almost as quickly, Sytri tackled the demon. "Hey, what the hell. Give him back you twiggy fuck!" With that, the three of them fell into the room.

There was an assortment of sounds, all of them distressed. Elbows and fingers jutted into Ander's sides and stomach.

"Wow, he's fast," the red demon said, standing up and pulling Ander and Sytri with him. Sytri batted his claw at him with a snarl. Like an angry cat. "Spunky."

"Vega, what the hell?" Delilah groaned. "How did you find him that—"

"He was standing outside the door," the demon, presumably Vega, said.

"What?"

"Yeah, waiting there. Kind of weird. How did you know I needed you?" Vega asked, observing Ander with wide cobalt eyes. The blue rippled like an ocean of excitement.

"I, uh, what?" Ander stumbled, scanning the dimly lit room, trying to make out his surroundings.

Oil lamps hanging from hooks on the walls cast an orange light that feebly fought back the blackness. The amber glow made the place resemble a crypt.

At the table in front of him sat four people, two of whom he recognized: Delilah and Cerberus. Out of the strangers, one was a small child with a sheet of long white hair and painfully bright red eyes. Ander could only focus on them for so long, before quickly turning to the second mystery person.

An angel.

Ander's breath hitched. He hadn't seen one since they'd entered the town, and this one looked *just* like a blend. But he could hear the bells chiming around them.

"Hello," Ander said, waving. "I, uh, came here to talk to Delilah. About what's happening."

"Look! He knew," Vega said, putting his arm around Ander's shoulder. "How neat!"

Sytri immediately pried that arm off. "Quit touching him." He glowered and Vega tilted his head again, another jerky, lizard-like movement. Large eyes stared hard, pupils dilating.

"What did you want to talk about, Ander?" Delilah asked, leaning her head forward, pressing the tips of her fingers into her forehead.

Ander's face grew hot, and he found himself at a loss for words.

He honestly didn't know. He'd come here to see what they planned on doing about Mayrez. But how did he intend to assist? Could he . . . could he help fight her? His heart thudded, body going numb at the thought.

That would be stupid, ridiculous, suicidal. He gritted his teeth. *Ask something more useful.* How long could they stay? Where was Atlasville? How could he provide for this community, fit in? Anything other than asking if he could help fight Mayrez. Because he already knew the answer.

"We should bring him with us on the ambush, don't you think?"

Ander blinked. Vega had said that. The red puffball, who was grinning almost ear to ear. He winked at Ander, sticking out his tongue.

Ander's feathers perked up.

"Vega, I already told you. You see him, he—"

"He brought us the map. He deserves a say on if he gets to go with us or not." Vega pushed Ander and Sytri forward. "Sit down, sit down, this is a meeting after all." He clambered over the table with his long legs, almost like a spider, and sat across from them, right between the angel and the girl. "I'm very interested in your opinion on the matter little . . . Ander? Yes? I really liked your map. It's full of all these little paths that traders take and excitingly, their schedules. Quick thinking, I would say, for you to procure that. And if they don't know we have this information, it's a bonus."

His eyes were so wide they must have hurt.

"If it's even real," the child said quietly. "It could be a trap. Quit acting like we've already settled to head out there, Vega. This isn't your call alone. Anyway, we haven't decided if the new blend can be trusted." They turned to Ander with malice in their eyes. "Mayrez has already tried to catch some of us before. You could have been sent in here by her with this false map. A way to lure us out into one of her notorious little ambushes."

"What? No. I hate Mayrez, I would never—"

"You're obviously a weak blend. And Mayrez, well she's almost an Archdemon. Easily strong enough to break you into submission. And if she did send you here for some little scheme, you should know that Vega *is* an Archdemon." They glared for a moment. "And he can do more than break you."

Ander turned to the redhead—the Archdemon—who was smiling brightly, as if the child hadn't just made a threat on Ander's life. Did that mean he was on par with Tephera?

Beside Ander, Sytri huffed.

"It would be simple for her to make you follow her command." Blood-red eyes trailed over to Sytri. "And send one of her lackeys to keep an eye on you, under the guise of a deal. She knows we're eager to take fellow Partners in."

"I'm not one of Mayrez's lackeys," Sytri hissed.

"So you say. That's not really a lot to us, is it, stranger?"

"What can we do to prove otherwise?" Ander asked, looking around the room. They all stared back. Delilah raised an eyebrow.

"Good question," the child said, crossing their arms. "Provide a good answer."

Ander blanked. He'd never had to prove his innocence. Most people assumed he wasn't capable of harm.

"I . . ." Ander glanced over at Sytri, but he was still glaring at Vega. So, Ander faced the group alone, focusing on the oddly human-like angel. They looked almost like an ordinary human, with dark skin and gray eyes. It was only the tawny wings and chiming that separated them. *Angel.* Surely they would understand him better?

"I'm not sure what that would be. Isn't there someone who can like read my thoughts, tell how I feel?" he said after a moment.

"Would be a useful little power, wouldn't it? But unfortunately, no," Delilah said, followed by a *tsk*. "So convince us."

A hook latched on to Ander's heart, sharp and cold, and pulled it down to his stomach. He took a deep breath. "I only have what I believe, what I *know*. That she's a monster. She dragged me in front of demons to be sold, like an animal. And she's destroyed at least one of the last refuges around." He met Delilah's impassive stare. "I want to make sure she's stopped. And you all are the best shot at making that happen. So if the map I made could help you do that, I need you to believe me."

His words seemed to hang in the air. He took a gulp and glanced around the room. No one was talking.

Then Cerberus sneered. "What do you mean she held you up for auction? Your blood isn't worth the effort to her."

"What?"

"You're barely a blend. Mayrez would simply drain someone like you dry and go about her life. She wouldn't hold you up for auction. We know her process; she only does that for ones she thinks she can make a pretty penny from, someone who's at least one-fourth angel."

"I'm—" Ander's face flushed and he gritted his teeth, barely stopping himself from blurting out the truth. Saying he was a Half should have been no big deal, but his skin still crawled when he thought about the demons who had clambered for his blood, the desperation and hunger in their eyes. Once again, he glanced at Sytri for reassurance. This time he found Sytri staring at him, but his expression provided zero answers. His mouth was a tight line, his eyes cautious. He wasn't saying no though.

Ander turned back to the group and placed a hand on his chest. "I'm a Half."

Cerberus snorted. "No, you're fucking not."

"I am."

"Look at you. You don't even have a full set of wings, which is like the bare minimum for a Half to have. You almost had me believing you, with that weird rant of yours, about how sad you were. I *was* believing you. I don't even know why. But now? Claiming you're a Half. Fuck you." He glared at Sytri. "How much did Mayrez offer you to carry this piece of shit around with you?"

"Don't fucking talk about Ander like that," Sytri hissed, standing up, nails clawing into the table. Cerberus got up just as quickly, his chair clattering to the floor.

"Is that a fucking threat?"

"Boys, calm down, please." Delilah's wings swung out behind her, sending a ripple of air through the room. "Cerberus, you know better than this. Damn it." She studied Ander, eyes stern. "Being Half is a deep claim from a blend with barely any feathers. But it's easy enough to test. And if you are truly a Half, it would be a lot harder to believe that Mayrez would be able to control you like she could a weaker one. Isn't that right, Serene?"

The small child stared hard at Ander. "Mayrez isn't strong enough to control a Half. And she wouldn't send one off to us. That's too big of a prize to let go. Even to try to trick us."

"So if I prove I'm Half, you'll believe me, then?" Ander asked cautiously. "What do I need to do to prove that?"

"We need to have one of us drink your blood. Well, not me or West." Delilah gestured at the angel. "Obviously, we can't tell things like that from blood. We're not demons. We can sort of feel it usually, but I'll be honest, not feeling it with you."

Ander looked at the tiny kid with the white hair. "I'm Half and Half," they said softly.

"What?"

"Serene's part angel, part demon." Delilah glanced at Ander. "You haven't met one?"

"No." Ander raised an eyebrow. "Someone can be half demon?"

"Of course, just like someone can be half angel. What, did you not know— Never mind. Not important. We need someone to taste your blood."

Nausea hit him. "You can't do that, can you? Sytri and I made a deal. He said that meant we were bound, that other demons couldn't drink my blood anymore without it poisoning them or something."

"Yes, if the both of you don't give them *permission*. A deal just makes it where one would need yours and Sytri's consent. You know, instead of none."

"Oh." Ander glanced at the three demons. If demons could still drink from him, Sytri must have known. *Why had he never brought it up?*

"I refuse to do it," Serene said automatically. "I've never partaken in that activity, and I do not wish to start now. So our options are either Cerberus—"

"I'd claw out his fucking eyes before I let him—" Sytri started.

"Or Vega."

Ander paused before looking over at Vega, who was sitting with a wild grin, eyes full of sparks. He clasped his hands. "I'd be delighted."

"I don't like him," Sytri said instantly.

"It has to be someone in this room. It's him or Cerberus," Delilah said matter-of-factly. "They're the only ones I trust to tell me the truth. I'm not taking your word for it." She stabbed a finger in Sytri's direction.

"We could leave," Sytri muttered to Ander. "We're heading to find Ronan right? We don't have to stay here. We could find a different place, with less judgmental assholes."

"It's not just about Mayrez." Ander shifted in his seat. "She was giving those blends to Tephera." Cold crept up his body. "They could help put an end to that."

"I don't want that creepy dude drinking your blood."

"Me neither!"

"I'm right here, but that's fine, I guess," Vega said, laughing.

Ander cringed. "Sytri. I need you to tell him it's okay. Okay?" he pleaded. Why was Sytri so against this? Why had he kept this information away from Ander in the first place? It was *his* blood. A dark knot grew in Ander's chest.

"Fine. Fine, I fucking guess it's okay." Sytri threw his hands up in the air like a child throwing a fit. "But if you fuckers don't kill Mayrez after this, I'm kicking all of your asses."

This time West laughed. Ander wasn't sure he had witnessed a pure angel laughing before. The crystalline sound was distracting, if only for a second because, right after that, Vega had swung himself over the table, sitting on top of it, and pulled Ander so he was in between his thighs.

"For Christ's sake, Vega. Why are you like this?" Delilah groaned.

"That doesn't feel necessary," Sytri growled.

"Hello, tiny Ander," Vega said with a grin. Ander stiffened; they were too close, he and this strange demon who had one hand wrapped around his wrist, the other his back. He drew Ander's hand to his face and licked his lips. "It's been a while since I've had a nice snack. I really hope you're a Half; that would be *fantastic*. Such good blood, from such a cute blend."

Every part of Ander went hot as burning coals. He tried to stutter out a response but couldn't. What the hell was happening?

"Just drink his blood already," Sytri snapped, his voice cracking like stone; Ander's feathers stood on end—he hadn't ever heard Sytri sound like that. But his attention was quickly snatched away as Vega bit into the thin skin on his wrist.

Flesh split and Ander couldn't stop from curling over. The bite hadn't simply brought heat and pain like Sytri's had. An itch crawled through him. One he couldn't scratch.

He tried to breathe, but it only came out in desperate, heavy pants, and the noise horrified him. Why was the bite like this? Why was he so hot? His head so cluttered?

Ander barely realized that he was being dragged into Vega's lap. And the part of him that was aware didn't seem to mind at all. Vega suddenly seemed all right, *good* even. Ander bit his lip. If he could get closer to him, maybe Vega could take this craving away. Fuck, maybe they could do everything and *anything*. Yes, Vega could solve this, tease this heat out of him with practiced hands.

He glanced up at Vega through half-lidded eyes, and the demon smirked. Ander's blood was smeared on the side of Vega's mouth. It didn't bother him. Strange.

He was ripped away with such force it tore the air from his lungs.

"He's a fucking Incubus!" Sytri screeched.

"I didn't say I wasn't." Vega crossed his legs and licked his fingers. Ander's vision was a blur as he lay in Sytri's arms. *What the hell?*

"Don't you ever fucking touch him again or I swear to fucking god I'll—"

"You'll what?" Vega's voice had gone cold. "I'd like to see." He turned toward Delilah, who was rolling her eyes. "I'm not sure if he's a Half per se. But his blood is as strong as one's."

Ander leaned into Sytri's cooling touch and gulped as his senses slowly came back to him, his face on fire. What had he turned into in front of all these people?

"Are you serious?" Cerberus practically yelled. "What do you mean?"

"Completely serious," Vega assured. "Whatever kind of angel blood is in him, it's different. I haven't tasted anything like it before. Something new on the menu."

"He's not on your fucking menu," Sytri snapped.

"That's for him to say, don't you think?" Vega turned back to the rest of the group. "Anyway, kid's not lying. No way Mayrez could control someone with that blood. He'd only be here for her if he wanted to be." Vega raised an eyebrow. "And I think little Ander here meant it when he said he hated her. I think we've got a real map on our hands, guys. And we'd be idiots to not use the opportunity to take her down. We're the good guys, right?" Vega leaned on the table. "We should stop her. We might not be able to stop the Cast currently, given how big they are. But we can cut off their supply chain. No new blends means it'll be way harder for them to recoup their losses."

The other four stared at each other in silence. Ander could sit up a bit better but kept himself pressed against Sytri, as far away from Vega as he could. Yes, Vega was on his side it seemed, but whatever he'd just done had left unease in Ander's stomach.

"All right. We'll at least look into it," Delilah said after a moment. "From what you told us, Vega, she should be back through here in a week, correct? That gives us time to evaluate the situation and see if the reward outweighs the risk."

"You believe me?" Ander said. *Holy shit.* "You're going to try to stop her, then?"

"It's a possibility." Vega curved forward, his arm outstretched, his fingertips grazing Ander's chin. "Who knows, maybe with that blood you'll get a chance to fight with us later."

Sytri snapped his teeth at Vega like a shark while Ander tried to will down the blush on his face. His chest was cold though. This was a win, so why was he still worried?

CHAPTER FOURTEEN

"If they fight Mayrez, do you think they'll be okay?" Ander asked, sitting on the small patch of greenery they got to call their backyard.

"Sure."

"Sytri."

"What? I'm trying not to think about it, okay?" Sytri rolled over onto his stomach and stretched out his limbs like a cat. "Besides, even if their fight goes sour, we can just leave."

Ander scowled before lying down beside him, staring up into the cerulean sky.

It had been two days since he'd spoken to Delilah. Within that time, Ander had tried his best to integrate himself into the town. Running from place to place, seeing who needed help and how. Already he'd helped bake for the community and had taken a few guard shifts. But it was hard to focus. The world was bright and warm, air drenched in the smell of pine. Yet inside Ander's chest it was cold and tight, and his jaw was constantly clenched.

"We could leave now," Sytri continued. "You know, to find Ronan."

Ander chewed on his bottom lip. "I want to bring him here." He glanced over to their temporary home. "It's better than Gardners. Maybe less safe, but I think it's worth it. So I have to get them to like me." He had to find what would make him useful.

"I guess, but can't you do that afterward? We're not going to go fight. Though I wouldn't mind swinging a few at that bitch." Sytri yawned while closing his eyes. "Anyway, get Ronan first, then make them like you. It's five days until they *might* fight Mayrez;

that's a bit of time isn't it? Especially since you always seemed like you were in such a rush to find the guy."

Five days was a horribly long time to waste. Ander had spent years at Gardners on standby, and he was sick of it. Every part of him wanted to pack supplies and head out again.

Get to Ronan.

"I am in a rush. But I don't want to step on toes and screw myself over by bringing Ronan back uninvited. And it seems petty to ask them if I can right now. Just gallivant into a meeting to ask about my brother while they're figuring out the best way to keep everyone alive?" Ander groaned and threw his hands up into the air. "I don't know, Sytri; it's killing me. But I don't want to bother Delilah."

The air crackled like lightning. "You could bother me." Vega leaned over them, grin on his face.

"Shit, dude," Sytri yelled as he scrambled to his feet. "Get the hell out of here."

Ander jolted as he swung up to sit on his palms. Vega snickered and spun on his heels to stroll around them, giving off some heavy predator vibes. His tendency to pop up whenever he wanted had been another theme of the past few days. Though this was the first time he had done so at their house.

"You two have been so incredibly boring recently. I was expecting a lot of fun when you arrived, but all you've been doing"—Vega pointed at Ander—"is moping. And you"—he directed at Sytri—"have been napping in the sun like an animal."

Sytri bared his teeth. "It's *relaxing* but if you want me to be pissed, I can be."

"Your foreplay leaves a bit to be desired. Anyway, I didn't come here to fight. I'm a demon of love after all." Another crackle in the air, then Ander was jerked up by an arm and twisted around. There was barely time to process it before he was face-to-face with Vega. "You said you needed to pester Delilah. What about?"

"How long were you here? I, uh, whoa— You're really close," Ander stammered. Suddenly his head was spinning again.

"Fucking quit doing that, Vega!" Sytri grabbed Ander's other arm and yanked him, tearing him from Vega's hold. As soon as he had him, his claws gripped Ander's waist. "Can't you just fucking have a conversation like a normal dude? The fuck."

"Sytri, it's rude to interrupt." Vega's eyes narrowed briefly. "Anyway, I was just walking by and happened to overhear some things that caught my interest."

"You were spying."

"I inadvertently stood still for a bit and my camouflage kicked in. I wasn't trying to hide."

"Oh, like you suddenly forgot how your powers work, you piece of shit."

"Accidents happen. But this isn't what I want to talk about. Ander had a question for Delilah. What was it? Perhaps I can help."

Ander glanced at both demons. "Wait? For real?" He tilted his head. Vega was odd, but he was part of the council. Delilah trusted him. Anything was worth a shot. "I want to bring someone here, to live with us."

"Ah, so you'd be a trio. Threesome if you will."

"Not that!"

"No need to explain, I'm all about the more the merrier." Vega placed his palm under his chin, in a dramatic thinking pose. "Let me see . . . Usually that would be completely fine."

Ander's heart dropped. "Usually?" *Shit.*

"Yes, but with Mayrez and the Cast becoming a burdensome pain in our side, we've been struggling. The greater they grow, the less the blends here want to risk leaving for supplies. We run low on basic necessities constantly; filters for the water, medical supplies, building material, the list goes on. Delilah doesn't like to admit it, of course. She wants Millstone to be a magical little refuge." He spread his hands like a rainbow. "Admirable, but not feasible unless this fight with Mayrez goes well." His tone turned dark. "Very well."

"What do you mean?" Sytri asked. "Do you think it won't?"

"I think we'll lose lives." Vega paced on the grass. "I know we will, actually. And after that, we won't have the means to take on others, especially if they can't provide for us."

Ander paled. He would be a waste of food and space here, exactly like he had been at Gardners, and he'd be kicked out. The memories were all in his head at once. Cowering behind the wall as demons ravaged outside. Standing silently in line for rations as stronger blends brought in their finds for the day. Shivering panic-ridden in his wreck of house, agonizing over days long gone, while angels kept watch over the city. Always helpless. Always scared.

No, he wasn't going back to that, especially not with Ronan and Sytri.

"I wouldn't be able to bring my brother here?"

"Most likely not unless he was an extremely powerful blend. Or if you were. You know, in a way that we could benefit from."

"Ander doesn't have to exist for anyone's benefit, fuck-face," Sytri hissed. "It's not our fault if you guys can't take on Mayrez." He let go of Ander and shoved a claw into Vega's face. "If you don't want us, we'll fucking leave."

"I don't want to leave." Ander put a hand on his chest. "I said that already, Sytri. I like it here. You do too. And I . . . I don't want this place to end up like Gardners. And I don't want to go back there either. So, what can I do to help?"

"Ander, what?" Sytri said, ears dropping.

Ander ignored him, focused solely on Vega. "What can I do to help? To make it clear that I deserve to stay here and that Ronan can be with me. Even if he's not a strong blend, even if he's just a human." *If he's alive at all.* Ander swallowed that fear.

"That depends, little blend; what can you do?" Vega smirked.

"All I've ever been able to do is heal myself."

"Oh. Oh! That's interesting, and here you were saying you had nothing," he chirped. "And you've been hiding that from us?"

"Why's it matter? I can't heal anyone else."

"I'm sure you know the basics of what blend blood does for us." Vega smiled gracefully. "It's why you made a deal with Spots over there. We get stronger on it, if only temporarily. The problem is that blends can only give so much at a time. But a blend who can heal? What a fun game changer that is."

"What the fuck are you getting at?" Sytri sneered.

Vega disappeared in a crackle again and suddenly he was right in front of Ander, shoving him against a tree. The feathers on Ander's neck shot up as Vega smirked down at him. "You're like an endless battery. We can make you bleed and bleed and bleed, and you'll be ready to give more." He pushed back a strand of Ander's curly black hair.

Ander paled, mouth dry. His body did heal from wounds quickly; that meant he was making new blood, bone, flesh, every time it was ripped from him. "What are you telling me?" he asked cautiously.

"Quit touching him! You're not tossing him around like a blood packet!" Sytri shouted. The shadow arms swept from his shoulders, one bashing Vega's torso, one pressing on Ander, shoving them apart.

"He'd be so much more than that," Vega said, stepping back smoothly, seemingly unperturbed. His gaze returned to Ander. "Think about it. We could bring you on the field, out into fights and battles. You give your blood to poor demons like me who have no Partner, so we can fight better, be stronger. Do that and you'll be saving lives."

Ander clenched his fists. Twisting out of Sytri's grasp, he stared Vega down. "Is blend blood really so beneficial?"

"Yours is; you've got something real special under that skin. It's an honest waste to give it to one lone demon."

"He's my Partner," Sytri growled. "You're not having him. No one is; he's mine." His voice was a snarl now, dark and violent.

"Sytri, if I can help this way, then maybe we can stay. I can bring Ronan here!" Ander cried. "I want this to work. I can prove I'm not worthless."

"You're not worthless," Sytri argued. "And you don't have to give yourself to a bunch of random fucking demons to prove that." His tail thudded on the ground and sent dirt flying.

Vega threw his hands up in exasperation, shaking his head. "I'm sorry, Ander, if Sytri won't let you, we truly can't. As we said, now that you've made a deal with him, both of you need to compromise before someone can safely drink your blood. But the fact that you could give so much blood, continuously strengthen us during a fight, you could be of use to us."

"He doesn't need to be of use to anyone."

"Sytri! I said I want to help—this is a way I can help. Why are you against that?"

"I don't . . . I don't want them touching you," Sytri snapped. His face burned a sapphire blue. "I can't handle that." He glared at Vega. "Especially if it's someone who's just going to take advantage of the situation."

"Pretty rude for you to talk about yourself like that." Vega chuckled.

"Shut up!" Sytri tackled him.

Before Ander had time to be concerned for either of them, Vega had managed to kick Sytri off and stand up perfectly straight, a sharp grin cutting across his face.

Sytri snarled, fangs flashing.

"Sytri, calm down!" Ander yelled, grabbing him by the arm. "We came here to—" He gritted his teeth. They had come here for Ronan. "We've finally found a place where people don't attack us on sight and now you're the one attacking."

"Yes, Sytri, let the adults talk." Vega smirked.

"I'm going to kill him." Growling, Sytri swung out of Ander's grip. Vega rolled his eyes, dodging him in an almost ballerina-like way. Sytri chased him, swiping erratically, expression turning feral. "Stay still you fuck!"

"Are you being serious? You have to be faster than that. Even with all Ander's good blood, you haven't amounted to much. Really, you should just let me have him."

Sytri screeched into the air. He tried again, fruitlessly, to catch Vega. Missing horribly, his claws swiped into the tree, carving out half the trunk and sending it crashing. It thudded on the ground, thankfully missing the house. Sytri didn't stop to acknowledge what he'd done though, still dashing after Vega.

Ander gaped, face red. "What the hell are you doing? Sytri, stop! Calm down!" It hurt him to yell, his throat sore. The deal in his chest flickered.

Sytri halted, not looking at him but slowly, his arms receded. His breath was ragged, his stance that of a wolf, arched and watching.

Vega whistled, gesturing at the tree. "Quite a temper there. You think Delilah will want to keep you if you're destroying property?" Sytri's ears drooped. Vega walked past him, eyes on Ander. "Recapping what I said before he so rudely interrupted. We need your blood, Ander. You could help us stay alive. Prove your worth, and Delilah will let you live here and bring . . . Ronan? You said? The missing piece? Plus, you will assist in keeping Millstone the way it is. So think about it." He gave a halfhearted wave and crackled away.

Ander stood there, his body a tangled mess of emotions fighting their way to the top. Anger seemed the most prominent. "Sytri! Why did you do that? We want these people to like us and you start throwing shit around? You have to control yourself."

Sytri didn't face him.

"Are you listening to me? You can't be—be doing this; *we* can't be doing this. I want to live here. So we both have to do better. You need to . . . to not pick fights! I need to help them. If this town turns into something like Gardners, where they pick and choose who is worthy of care, if they reject Ronan because I stood by like a coward—" Ander's voice cracked. "I can't live with that."

Sytri swung around, his claws digging into Ander's shoulders. "So the solution is to become a tool for everyone? A fucking meal?"

"Isn't that what I was to you when we made the deal in the first fucking place?" Ander snapped. "It's only okay if I'm a meal when it's for you? You still just see me as food that you don't want to share? I thought we were closer than that!" A spike twisted in his gut. "Is that why you didn't tell me other demons could still drink my blood with permission?"

"No! That's not why I didn't tell you."

"Isn't it?" Ander retorted, face hot.

"I . . . No," Sytri growled. "I'm not— Fuck, Ander, you're not a meal to me, okay? And I would like to think I'm more than just a weapon to you."

"You are. So why didn't you tell me?" Ander chided.

"It didn't seem important in the beginning." Sytri faced away. "Like, I wasn't ever going to agree to do it, so I didn't need to fill you in on it. And then I forgot about it altogether. It didn't come up, and I didn't . . . I didn't think about how you might *want* to know. How you had the *right* to. I'm sorry. I fucked up. Okay?"

"Is there anything else I should know about the deal that just *hasn't come up*?" Ander put his hand on his chest, over the flickering heat of their pact.

"No. Not unless I don't know about it either," Sytri murmured.

Ander drew a sharp breath. "It's my blood, Sytri."

"I know."

"I have the right to it. I have the right to decide what to do with it."

"I know."

Ander studied him hard. "Sytri?"

"Yeah?"

"I have to."

Sytri's shoulders tensed. "I hate this."

"But why? Why is this such a big deal?"

"Because it puts you in danger!" Finally, Sytri looked at him, eyes wavering. "I've said this a thousand times. I don't want them . . . all those demons with their hands on you, treating you like a goddamn snack." His voice was tight and deep, and it struck a chord in Ander's heart.

Demons and their hands. *Mayrez.* Her claw slicing into his skin for a taste of blood. The crowd reaching for him with hunger in their eyes. The idea of demons wanting to drink from him would always be tied to her, to that horror as he stood on stage. It made his feathers stand on end; he couldn't deny that.

"I don't like it either," he said after a moment. "But I'm not going to stand by. If I can help other demons, help them fight Mayrez, then I should. Not only is it the right thing to do but it will prove to Delilah that I deserve to live here. Then we'll have a home. Everyone will live. We'll get a happy ending."

"Do demons get a happy ending?" Sytri muttered.

"You will," Ander said softly. His chest felt heavy and light at the same time. Resentment slowly mixed with something unidentifiable. Sytri's hands were so warm on him.

Ander ignored all of that. "You've got to help me do this, so we can get a happy ending together. That's what friends do."

Sytri's grip tightened. "I'm too selfish to be a friend, Ander."

"What are you talking about?"

"I can't do it." He bit his lip. "There's too much wrong in me."

Ander sighed. "Sytri, it's all right. You're okay. I don't know what you're saying, but you're not a bad guy, okay—"

"Even when I want to do bad things?"

Ander hesitated. "What bad things do you want to do?"

"Everything."

Ander stopped. His breathing. His thoughts. All of it came to a screeching halt.

Then Sytri kissed him with chapped lips and sharp teeth and it *burned*. Heat consumed Ander to the tips of his ears in an instant. *What?*

Not a second later, Sytri pulled away, face a wild blue, staring at Ander with a look that could only be described as . . . ravenous.

Then he covered his mouth with his hand and took a shaky step backward, his tail curled around his stomach. "I'm sorry, fuck, I'm so sorry. I have to go . . . I have to go . . . think." More words slipped through his lips but they were incomprehensible.

Ander was barely processing the moment. By the time he had lifted his hand to offer comfort, Sytri was gone. And Ander was left alone.

CHAPTER FIFTEEN

A nder lay on the couch for hours, staring at the ceiling. Moonlight slipped through the curtains, spilling into the small room, softly illuminating particles of dust hanging in the air. He formed shapes out of them like connect-the-dots. It was a familiar pastime from his days in foster care, when he'd gone to bed to hide from everyone. Because the only thing worse than being alone was being alone in a crowded room. In the packed houses at Gardners, it had been the same.

He'd forgotten that crushing loneliness since he and Sytri had met. Now it sunk back into him, into his bones, pushed him against the couch until he couldn't breathe. It compressed him until he was nothing. Sytri had bolted, and Ander wouldn't be able to find him if he didn't want to be found.

Ander touched his lips. *Why did he panic? He was gone so quick that I couldn't even say how I felt.*

One speck of dust connected to the next above him. Now the motes were friends, partners, *something*. Ander chewed his lip.

How do I feel about him?

It seemed impossible to find his own emotions. He'd spent years ignoring them, and love most of all. Such a fleeting affection that could never be reciprocated or worse, could be cleaved in two once his partner realized their mistake. Like every family who had taken him into their home and found out he wasn't worth the effort.

But Sytri is different.

Ander stifled a sob in his throat. He reached for his deal and found it fluttering in his chest. It had been a while since he had looked for it—its heat was so natural to him now that it could easily be forgotten. Now, he curled around the sensation, the odd softness of the warmth within him. It was like spiderwebs in the sun. The sparks off a fire. A firefly fluttering in a glass jar. Sytri. He shifted his thoughts elsewhere so the deal melted back into his body, from tips of fingers to tips of toes.

Ander couldn't identify all his feelings for Sytri. But if he pried long enough, he could make out some certainties. Like the fact he wanted Sytri back. He wanted to kiss him again.

That I like him. A lot.

There was a soft *thud* outside the house. Ander sat up, rubbing his eyes. In the darkness, he focused on the door, his heart pounding: a thump, followed by a thump, by a thump. It was overwhelmingly painful.

The door opened slowly, more moonlight falling in, coating the figure that stood there. Its dark gray hair was illuminated so brightly it was almost transparent at the tips, like watered-out ink in the air. Tan skin was edged with a glow, showing every cut of muscle with an almost white outline. Turquoise eyes were sharp and vibrant in the black.

"Sytri."

"I'm so sorry," Sytri said immediately, backing away from the door and into the living room wall.

Why, why was he distancing himself like that? Ander jumped from the couch, adrenaline in his heart urging him forward.

"I shouldn't have . . . I should have known better than to— Vega was right, I'm the worst—" Sytri stammered.

Ander kissed him so quickly it was barely a touch at all. "Shut up. Shut up and don't leave me again. Please," he begged, staring into Sytri's eyes. "You can't do that to me. I can't handle it." His heart was racing; he hadn't planned on kissing him. But it had felt so natural.

"What are you doing?"

"What do you mean, what am I doing? You were the one who ran away. What are *you* doing?" Ander grabbed Sytri's wrists. "You left me!"

"Because I shouldn't have— I shouldn't have kissed you! I thought you were mad at me. That you'd need time to decompress or something. Obviously you weren't as mad as I thought." Sytri brought his fingers to his lips.

Ander followed the movement before focusing back on Sytri's whole face. "I was pissed at you for throwing a fit and knocking down a tree. Why would the kiss be what makes me angry?" he huffed.

"It's what Vega said: I'm taking advantage of you. I've been doing it this whole time." Sytri craned his neck, his face glowing that strange blue-green. An unearthly blush. "It's wrong."

"Taking advantage of . . . What the hell," Ander snapped, placing a hand on his chest. "You didn't even talk to me about it or wait to see how I felt. You should be able to tell that I want you with me. I care about you." *Oh god, how do I say this?* "And I don't want you to leave. Don't you want to stay?"

"Of course," Sytri said instantly. "How could I not?"

A slight smile crossed Ander's face before he sighed. "I don't get you. I really don't. You kiss me and then you run off? Because you thought I'd hate you for it? Sytri, even if I hadn't . . . liked it, I would never *hate* you for it. You're such a drama queen." He snorted.

Sytri blushed harder. "I didn't want to see your disgust or resentment because I couldn't control myself. I was like a monster. I attacked Vega and then I practically attacked you."

Ander paused. "Sytri. Having strong feelings isn't the same as you being some uncontrollable monster." He placed a hand on Sytri's cheek. "When you're angry, it's not great. But that kiss wasn't out of anger. You wanting to be with me isn't the same as you wanting to tear a person apart."

"How can I be sure?" Sytri said darkly. A flicker in his eyes and suddenly the expression was so different. *Starved.* Ander couldn't turn away. "When I think I want to tear you apart too?"

"What?"

Sytri grabbed Ander's shoulders, forced him against the side of the couch. A heat surged through Ander that paralyzed him, tugged at him. Sytri leaned down, his breath on Ander's neck.

"Every time I'm with you, I want to rip at you. Leave marks all over." Sytri's claws dipped down to Ander's waist. "Even now I feel it, and it's disgusting, Ander. The things I want to do to someone as kind as you."

Ander gulped, arching as Sytri curved into him, their bodies barely touching. One of Sytri's hands slipped under Ander's shirt, and the skin-on-skin contact, as small and as insignificant as it should have been, made Ander shiver. This was further than he had ever gone with anyone, and the tension folded over itself a thousand times.

Sytri jerked away from him, a hiss between his sharp teeth. "You're scared of me."

"No." Ander clasped Sytri's wrist and they both froze. He chewed on his lip. "No. I'm not scared of *you*, Sytri. I could never be scared of you." He squirmed, unable to look at Sytri. He could feel his gaze. "This feels like a lot. It's just . . . I've never done *anything*." His face was burning. He was sweating. Why was the room so painfully stuffy?

"Oh god."

Ander glanced up.

Sytri had covered his mouth with his hand, eyebrows pressed together, eyes half-lidded. There was a clear brushstroke of blush across his face. "Then are you sure you want to do this?"

"Y-yes," Ander stammered. His ears were hot now.

"I don't want to do something you'll regret." Sytri wavered, and Ander tightened his grip on his wrist.

Ander's head was a mess of thick, warm fog. He had liked Sytri against him. He had liked the kiss. Now he wanted whatever this was to continue.

"I'm not going to regret this," he said breathily. "I liked it. I want you to touch me." His hands were at Sytri's hips now, feeling the tautness of that skin, the muscle, the movement. He had been waiting so long to do that.

"Ander, don't say shit like that to me." Sytri sounded *pained*.

It made every nerve in Ander quiver. "I already did." His voice was soft, pleading, *begging*. He stood up on his toes and kissed Sytri. "And I'll say it again and again until you listen to me."

"I won't want to stop."

"Then don't."

And he meant it. Love or whatever this emotion was, it didn't matter. It made him want to feel as much of Sytri as anyone ever could. He wanted Sytri to keep gazing at him as if he was the only person who mattered in the world.

"Do what you want," Ander whispered.

Suddenly Sytri shoved him onto the couch. "I want to keep you to myself." His hair fell down the side of his face like a streak of ash. "Tear into your skin and make you crave my touch and beg for me to start and stop everything." He leaned over, his teeth grazing Ander's neck, chills spreading from the spot like an infection. "It's why I don't want the other demons to have a taste of your blood. Because all of you should be mine."

"Helping them has nothing to do with us."

"Are you sure?" Sytri's hands tugged at Ander's shirt, slowly pulling the fabric upward, letting it fold around Ander's shoulders. He placed his palms on Ander's navel, his touch warm, delicate, barely there. Ander writhed. He was a wreck, coals burning on a fire, cracking apart in the flames.

"That's what makes me so terrible," Sytri whispered "I don't want you to be given to anyone else. Any part of you. Your glances, your smiles, your touch, your blood—I want it all. You make me incredibly selfish, greedy, and *desperate*. Isn't it disgusting?"

"I don't know, but I like it," was all Ander managed to say. He jerked his hips and Sytri's hands went downward, resting on the thin fabric of Ander's jeans. It was too much, that sliver of cloth, in the way. Sytri rolled his palms across it, and Ander couldn't stop himself from bucking his hips, trying to catch more of the pressure. "Please."

He didn't know he could sound so pathetic. Was that really his voice? He wrapped a hand around Sytri's shoulder, pulling himself closer.

Sytri licked his lips, a sharp gleam in his eyes. "If I start, there's no going back," he hissed.

"I wouldn't let you go back."

Sytri didn't waste a second. He tugged down Ander's jeans, his claws scoring the fabric. Ander yelped, a flush of embarrassment racing through his body. No one had ever seen him naked, at least not like this. He'd been in school showers where he'd been ridiculed for his stick-like frame or the way his curly hair was extra curly . . . everywhere. They weren't fond memories.

But Sytri stared at him with bright eyes, mesmerized, admiring, and Ander's shame slipped away, replaced with desire.

"You're so fucking beautiful." Sytri dipped down, kissing Ander's mouth, teeth nipping Ander's lips. His hands were busy shoving his own pants away and hiking Ander's leg upward.

Ander swallowed at the display: Sytri above him, his cock out, a trail of black hair going up his tight stomach.

"W-whoa." Sytri's dick was . . . different. Ander twisted his mouth, hesitant to reach out and touch it. Sytri was already half-hard, and it was clear that the strange blue blood he had was down here too. There were noticeable ridges on the underside of his dick, odd grooves. Ander laughed dryly. "Okay, so all of you has to be demon-ish, huh?"

Sytri tilted his head and followed Ander's line of sight. "Oh, I guess that is a bit different from yours, huh? Do you mind?" His gaze was still hazy, that blush still on his face.

Ander's chest was on fire.

"Not really." He looked into Sytri's eyes as he slid a hand over his dick, exploring the ridged texture, the hardness of it. Sytri let out a hiss and shivered, mouth open. Ander gulped.

Sytri nipped at Ander's mouth before moving down his neck again, tasting sensitive skin along the way, stopping above his collarbone, then biting into flesh, drawing blood. A surge of heat flooded Ander that instantly made him weak. He grinded against Sytri, grasped his back, his nails digging into Sytri's skin.

Their cocks rubbed together, both getting harder. Sytri's pulsed against his own, the grooves pressing into him deliciously, and he had to hold back his moans. *Holy shit.* Sytri ran his tongue over Ander's blood. One hand moved to Ander's chest, tracing his nipples with the tips of the claws. The other grabbed his waist, holding him in place as Ander panted, air spilling from his lungs.

"Fuck," Sytri whispered in Ander's ear. "Ander, you have to quit moving like that. I won't be able to control myself."

"You don't have to control yourself this time." Ander whimpered. "Sytri, I want . . ." He was too ashamed to finish that sentence. Everything? All of it; god, it was too much.

Sytri didn't need to be told anyway. One hand held up Ander's leg, the other stroked his cock, starting at the base, fingers leaving desire in their wake. Ander trembled, his head a haze of want and longing.

Sytri pushed against him, his dick rubbing against Ander's, thick and hard. Slick?

Ander glanced down and almost drooled. Sytri's dick had a good three inches on Ander's own, which was now fully-hard and dripping. Sytri's cock was stiff as a rock and the ribbed marks along it seemed larger, thicker. Along with that, however, was a viscous translucent fluid that appeared to seep from the ridges.

"What's that?" Ander asked timidly, running his hand across it. It was bizarre and silky. "Extra strange demon stuff?"

"You know." Sytri rasped. "Humans make stuff like that too, right?" Then, after Ander had raised an eyebrow. "Do you not?"

"Do we what?"

"It makes the process . . . *easier.*"

It took Ander a second.

"Are you telling me you, like, make lube?" he squeaked. "Your dick self-lubricates?"

"Yours doesn't?"

"No."

"Seems like a flaw."

Ander couldn't disagree.

Sytri snickered before continuing to stroke them. Ander was hyperaware of each touch, his body arching, his spine curving as he jutted his hips forward, starving for every graze. Every single grasp, bump, and nudge got him closer to coming; heat swelled in his stomach, dripping down to his cock, making him needy for more. Ander brought his hand up, cupping Sytri's face, brushing back his hair. He loved looking at him, was unable to stop. Sytri smirked before biting at Ander's fingers, taking one into his mouth, tongue swiping at it. Ander's body bloomed with heat.

"Can I?" Sytri asked and, before Ander could question what that meant, slid his fingers slid down Ander's spine and rested on his ass. Ander froze. *Oh god.*

"Yes." He answered before uncertainty could knot up his stomach. Sytri skimmed across his ass, sending goose bumps across Ander's back, before thrusting a finger inside. That slick lube covered it, but even with that it was still an *intrusion.* Ander yelped, moving his hands to Sytri's shoulders and dug his nails in. It was strange, painful, but not unwanted. Such a confusing pressure and it only increased as Sytri pushed in another, crisscrossing his fingers, nudging against Ander's insides.

"You okay?" Sytri checked. His back was tense, every muscle rigid against Ander's palms.

"It hurts," Ander muttered, his body craning, not sure whether to get closer or further away. He jerked, twitched, and chewed into his bottom lip as he whimpered. "But . . . I'm fine."

"Tell me if I need to give you a breather."

Ander nodded as Sytri leaned over and kissed his cheek. Ander barely felt it; he was focused solely on sensations downstairs. Sytri twisted his fingers again, and Ander kicked automatically, head spinning and face hot. His hands slid down Sytri's sides, nails leaving blue scores behind. He knew this was the process, but goddamn he was unprepared for all this . . . probing.

Suddenly, Sytri's fingers swept past a spot that made fire coil in Ander's stomach, forced his breath out of him in a heavy gasp. Sytri stopped for a second, then rubbed it again. The heat tightened in Ander's center, and he swallowed hard.

"Ah," Ander moaned. "There . . . there's nice. That's weird nice. Weird." He felt like an idiot saying it, but he wanted more of whatever the fuck that was. "There, Sytri."

"That's the spot, huh?" Sytri gave a thick groan. "You look real good like that, Ander; about to come from my fingers alone?" He laughed, but it was heavy, drenched in lust. Fuck, Ander could come from that sound, no fingers needed.

Sytri's free hand went to Ander's neck again, thumb pressing a bit too far into his throat. Tension and weight built around it, like Ander had swallowed lead. He choked, panic snapping through his body, but then Sytri's grip loosened and the world became weightless and his mind dim. Euphoric. His vision slowly blurred. *Oh fuck.*

Sytri thrust his fingers in and out, and Ander rocked his hips, biting deeply into his lip, eyes closed. He focused on the sensation, the pressure, the little shocks of lightning shooting across him each time. A bolt of pleasure with each graze, edging him on.

A harsher, more pleasing thrust made Ander yelp and bite down on his tongue. With blurry vision he caught Sytri staring at him. He was sweating, with creases under his eyes. His muscles flexed as he pressed his fingers into Ander, knuckle-deep. It ached but in way that seemed *right*.

Sytri's cock was thick and leaking, sliding past Ander's own as Sytri pushed another finger inside. Ander moaned, and Sytri licked his lips—sharp teeth glimmered.

Why the fuck was someone so beautiful doing this to him? Ander leaned up, his body trembling, tired, aching. He slung his arms over Sytri's neck and pulled him in for a kiss—heavy, breathy, messy, and perfect. Sytri's teeth stung when they nipped him, and made Ander shake, the small tuft of feathers around his neck standing up.

"Just do it, Sytri, please," Ander huffed, their noses touching.

"It's going to hurt." There was a drop of worry in Sytri's voice. "I want that."

Ander wanted to feel that pain; god, he would beg for it if that was what it took. He needed to have as much of Sytri inside of him as he could. Had these thoughts always been there, with Sytri only drawing them out of him? Fucking forced all this sinful desire to the top as he touched him, caressed him? Ander didn't know, and he didn't care.

Sytri removed his fingers with a slick *squelch*, taking away pleasure that Ander immediately craved again. He didn't wait too long. Sytri slid his tip against him, and Ander shuddered, the weight and throb of Sytri making him hot with anticipation. He bit his bottom lip, waiting. Then Sytri thrust inside.

Air was knocked out of Ander, his whole body stretched and stiffened at the hurt. *It's a lot bigger than fingers*, was his first thought. He was being pressed apart with heat and pain. Above him, Sytri shuddered, his breath coming out as a hiss. He tilted his head to the side, his neck slick with sweat, and took a deep breath.

"Fuck, Ander. Ah fuck, you feel *great.*"

Ander couldn't reply—hell, he couldn't breathe. The pain was too intense. All that came out was a sob as lights filled his vision. A strange mixture of pleasure and hurt overwhelmed him. He hated it, he *needed* it. Sytri remained still, but he had already filled Ander's insides till he ached. His knees jerked, tears welled in his eyes. Shit, he couldn't handle this.

"Can I . . . can I move?" Sytri asked, his voice steeped with want, husky and begging, so deep and thick. He sounded like he was falling apart, and his body was twitching. His claws pierced Ander, who flinched. Sytri let out a hiss. "God, fuck, sorry, I *have* to move, Ander. It's that or pull out."

"Y-you can move." Ander had no clue if he was ready. He couldn't even think. But how the fuck could he deny Sytri with a voice like that? "I'm ready."

Sytri seemed to take his answer at face value. Slowly, he pulled out, Ander huffing, panting, still with his arms slung around Sytri. Their faces were so close. Ander couldn't keep his mouth closed— it was too much effort. His dick was throbbing, harder than it had ever been. He was so fucking close, it was killing him; the sensation a burning, tight coil that wrapped around his center.

When Sytri thrust, Ander's whole world turned upside down. He cried out a mess of words and almost-words. The demon's lean stomach rubbed against his dick, creating perfect friction. The movement was synched with Sytri's dick forcing him apart. Each thrust was sharp, deep, hitting his stomach. Ander was practically blind from the pleasure of it.

Sytri growled something, his voice raspy, dry. He was pounding Ander, snarls breaking free, animalistic and dark. He hefted Ander's leg up higher, the stretch making Ander rigid. One of his arms fell, fingers clutching the edge of the couch, tearing into it. His chest heaved as he tried to breathe, his heart thundering in his chest.

Sytri thrust harder, faster, filling Ander up and then leaving him empty just as fast. Saliva slid down Ander's chin but he didn't care; he didn't care about anything. He only wanted Sytri to keep going. He wanted more nails, teeth, pain, *feeling*. He was being bruised, ravaged, and it was fucking fantastic. Every time Sytri thrust inside him, Ander saw white, his body hitched closer to that release he was dying for. Ander hadn't known he could be this hungry for a sensation, want it so bad he thought of nothing else, his whole being dripping with anticipation. All the heat in his stomach twisted, heavy and hot like liquid metal, pulling and hurting. His dick was on the edge, pulsing, right there, he needed it a little . . . harder.

"Sytri, faster," Ander slurred. "Please. Fucking please." He was addicted to the hurt, the teasing and heat and the fucking painful desire. And he was *begging* Sytri to give him relief.

"Ah, you're suddenly the greedy one," Sytri said, breathlessly. He chuckled to himself. "But I'm more than eager to obey."

Sytri's tail wrapped around Ander's dick, squeezed it tight. Ander choked out a moan that got stuck in his throat. His whole body was electric. *What the fuck, what the fuck.* Sytri's tail was perfectly curled around him, each thrust of his hips making Ander fuck it as Sytri fucked him. A sinful synchrony.

The pleasure made his tears fall. He craned his body, pushed against Sytri. There was a tension in Sytri, a straining that let Ander know he was close. Fuck, he wanted Sytri to come in him. The idea made him sweat, salivate. He wanted the sweet ache of that fullness.

Ander pulled Sytri in tight and bit his neck, urged his own hips forward, and pressed himself into Sytri as much as he could. *God, I want all of him. I want him forever.* The tail clenched and relaxed, clenched and relaxed before turning slightly, rubbing agianst Ander, getting under the tip of his throbbing cock.

"Fuck, fuck," Ander moaned, stars in his eyes. He nipped at Sytri's skin, down to his shoulder, where he bit into the inky skin.

Sytri came, his claws ripping down Ander's sides, splitting the skin easily, causing fresh blood to bead on the surface. A whine escaped Ander, his breath hitching right after. Come filled him up, hot, thick; it was disgusting. It was fucking fantastic. The ripple effect—Sytri clawing him, taking him, moaning his name—was the last bit Ander needed. Not a second later he came, orgasm torn out of him in a flash of heat, his body going rigid. His dick jerked, come hitting Sytri's stomach like a bullseye.

They were still for a moment, just breathing heavily, shivering from skin still prickling with electricity. Sytri's tail uncurled, leaving Ander shuddering. Cautiously, Sytri gripped Ander's thighs and began to pull himself out.

"Ah, slow," Ander murmured, clenching his jaw.

Sytri nodded but, regardless of his carefulness, Ander couldn't help but writhe, far too sensitive for anything at this point. Each individual ridge on Sytri's dick pushed past his skin. He whimpered, arching his neck when Sytri came out of him with a soft, wet *schlip*, come spilling onto the couch.

They both collapsed, out of breath.

Ander stretched his arms and stared at the ceiling. *Holy shit.*

After a minute, Sytri sat up with a groan that was, oddly, followed by a snicker. Quirking an eyebrow, Ander propped himself up to see Sytri seemingly admiring the come between them.

"What the hell?" Ander muttered. Sytri was too strange, too embarrassing. "Stop that."

"Sorry, it's just, it's a lot," Sytri said, turning his gaze to Ander. He cracked a smile. "Also, you're, like, stupid beautiful."

"Don't say that after whatever the hell that just was." Ander gestured at the couch, the soon-to-be-stain they'd left behind. They'd had sex. He flushed. *He'd* just had *sex*. Losing his virginity wasn't something he'd planned after the demon apocalypse.

"I wanna go again," Sytri said, voice *heavy* with need.

"What?" Ander yelped, scooting up onto his knees and then wincing. Moving hurt. "Sytri, I'm sore."

"That will heal soon enough, right?" Sytri asked, nuzzling Ander's face, rubbing his scruffy cheek against him like a cat. He slid his fingers down Ander's chest.

"Y-yeah." Fuck. *It's hard to say no.*

Sytri kissed him, much softer, more delicately this time. Ander couldn't resist it. He couldn't stop himself when it came to Sytri. He stared into those bright eyes, the gleam, the joy in them. Sytri was grinning, still blushing and covered in sweat. Ander wrapped a leg around Sytri's waist and pulled him close. It was so easy to want him, to want *everything* about him. "Yeah, I'll heal."

They'd worry about the rest of the world later. Ander had spent too long worrying not to enjoy tonight.

CHAPTER SIXTEEN

Ander lay in the crook of Sytri's arm, listening to his raspy breathing—a rough snore or two followed by a grumble. He chewed on his bottom lip, tearing into dry skin. Where did he stand right now? Not that he ever had much of a grasp on himself in the first place.

What the fuck had he just done? What the fuck had he just done *multiple* times?

He glanced at Sytri, whose mouth was partially open, revealing a sliver of sharp teeth. There was stubble on his chin, dark creases under his eyes, as if he was permanently tired. *He's so beautiful.* It made a warmth flutter inside Ander's paper-thin heart that risked burning him up.

They could stay like this, unbothered by the world. No one would blame them.

But Ander couldn't do that. He had to prove his worth by helping Millstone take down Mayrez. Yet, after last night's events, surely Sytri would be even less willing to share Ander with others.

Sytri was *territorial*. The aggression in bed was an evident sign of that. *I liked it, though.* Sytri's grip had been a sign of need, and Ander relished every claw mark it had left on him.

Ander swallowed. It was an understatement to say he had enjoyed their night.

But he hadn't come all this way for that.

He had come for Ronan.

Ronan wasn't here though, and Sytri could die trying to find him. That would be far too much to bear. So, was the answer to quit searching?

Ander sighed. He was supposed to be enjoying this moment, curled against Sytri. Not debating morality in his head, with a sick murky feeling clogging up his chest. Yet, there it was. What was he supposed to do?

"Hey," Sytri mumbled, adjusting his shoulders, eyes blinking open slowly. "What are you worrying about?"

"W-what?" *Oh god, am I that transparent?*

"I hear your heart," Sytri said nonchalantly. He probably didn't even realize how romantic that sounded. "It's beating way too fast. You nervous?"

"I'm—" Ander paused.

"Do you . . . do you regret what we did?"

"No," Ander said quickly. "No, no, I don't regret that at all. I just— I don't know." He leaned closer against Sytri. "It's only that it doesn't seem right. That I can be with you and be happy. I was supposed to do things. I was supposed to find Ronan."

"And?"

"And?"

"And what else? You said 'things.' Plural. That's one. And we can still do that."

"Hmm." Ander stared at the ceiling again. "Yeah." His plan had been to find Ronan and follow him, like before. He'd been the only person who'd paid attention to Ander.

Ander loved him for that. And his love had made him heed Ronan's every word.

Life wasn't like that anymore. He didn't have to wait for Ronan's command; he had chosen to go out into the world. He had chosen to travel across the state, investigate abandoned buildings, and join a weird Partner sanctuary in the middle of a national park.

All of them, his own decisions.

"We could try to find him," Ander said at last. "I definitely don't want to give up on him." Would it hurt to look at Atlasville when they were so close? Yet, if something happened to Sytri during the search . . . Ander sighed. His heart flitted about.

"What about my blood, though?" he said after a moment. "I know you don't like the idea of me sharing it with the other demons—"

"I absolutely hate it if that's what you're asking."

"But it wouldn't be the same thing that's between me and you. If I gave them my blood, it wouldn't break what we have, Sytri."

"Vega is an incubus. When he bites you, it's going to get you fucking hard, whether you want it or not." Sytri snorted.

Ander smacked his arm. "Hey! That's not my fault okay? I don't want that. I don't like that. It felt very . . . forceful. I wasn't fond of it." His throat seemed tight. "But it's all I can do to help them. And I want to help them. I need Millstone to be okay so if we do find Ronan, we can all live here, happily. If something happened—if they died when they went—I wouldn't get over it."

"It wouldn't be your fault if—"

"I *wouldn't* get over it."

Sytri went quiet, then rolled his eyes. "I suppose if we're in the middle of a fight, Vega can't really use it as an opportunity to feel you up."

"He wasn't feeling me up."

"Yes, he was! He's an incubus. That's what they do. Nasty sexual-harassment demons. Jerking it everywhere." Sytri did a hand motion to show exactly what he meant.

Ander laughed, covering his mouth. "I'm sure they don't do that."

"You'd like to think that."

"Is every demon a certain type of demon?" Ander asked. "If Vega's an incubus, does that mean you're a specific kind?"

"A demon's type is based on the sin they're derived from. Vega came from lust so he's an incubus." Sytri scowled, voice raspy.

"Oh." Ander blinked. "So, like the seven sins kind of deal? Why don't you guys talk about that more often?"

"It'd be weird to say it out loud for no reason," Sytri muttered. "It's not something you just bring up. I thought you already knew, honestly. I forgot you stayed in Gardners, where they taught you shit about nothing."

"So what sin are you from?"

"I already said it, really." Sytri's voice wasn't as lighthearted anymore.

What had Sytri said about himself? Not much really. That wasn't good; they'd had sex and he didn't even know Sytri's favorite kind of music. They'd have to fix that. But what had Sytri said about his demon type? Demons were based on the seven deadly sins so . . .

"Wrath?"

"Yeah." Sytri sounded less than pleased. "We're called Lucifers, after the Fallen Angel who controls our section of Hell."

"So that's why you used to be angry all the time?"

"It's why I'm scared all that rage will come back. Because it's what made me."

Ander couldn't even begin to fathom what it meant to be made of wrath. But he understood that the circumstances of Sytri's existence were fucking the guy up. "I don't think what had made you matters anymore." He gripped Sytri's hand. "That's gone by now. We're all remade every day, you know? New skin cells, new thoughts, new blood. You're all *this* Sytri now. Nothing else."

Sytri smirked. "You think?"

"Yes."

"You're not just being sweet on me so I'll let demons pass you around like a fucking juice bottle?"

"No!" Ander laughed. "That's gross."

"That's what they'd do!"

"It's not like that, you jerk, and you know it."

"Gah, I know, I know." There was a slight whine to Sytri's voice. "But I can't help but hate it. Like I said last night, I . . . I don't want to give you to anyone else. Does that make sense? Seeing the way Vega touched you fucking infuriated me. It wasn't fair. And I know, we demons have shit boundaries; like when we first met, I kissed you and I didn't think anything about it." He huffed. "But now kissing you, like, means something?" He covered half his face with his hand, the tips of his ears turning blue. "That's lame. God, every time I talk about feelings and shit I sound stupid."

"It's not stupid," Ander said quickly. "I like it." He kissed the nape of Sytri's neck. "And how I feel about you isn't how I feel about anyone else in the world. And I promise you, I'm not going to let demons make out with me."

"Even Vega? When he fucking gets his nasty incubus vibes all over you?"

"Promise." Ander chuckled.

"You seemed pretty into it the first time."

"I wasn't prepared. I had no idea the bite was going to make me feel like that."

"Feel like what?"

"Sytri."

"I know. It wasn't your fault." Sytri sighed. "Goddamn it. Fine. I'm aware this means a lot to you. And I kind of have a vendetta against Mayrez too. Yeah, her capturing you is how we met, but when you talked about how frightened you were when you were on that stage, I was pissed." Sytri narrowed his eyes. "See, there I go again, getting pissed. I'm constantly pissed at people. Are you sure that's normal?"

"Yes. You're pissed at them for good reasons." Ander tapped his toes against the bottom of the bed. "So . . . you'll let me, then? You'll be okay if I provide my blood?"

"I guess," Sytri muttered, gritting his teeth. "I just have to make sure all of them know that you're still mine, this is a temporary permission, and none of them better get creepy about it or I'll kill them."

"No one's going to get creepy about it. I don't know why you think that." Ander snorted, his face hot.

"You're too cute; it's dangerous." Sytri put an arm on the other side of Ander, kissed him under his jawline, trailing down his neck. "There's no way another demon around here isn't going to think it too." His fingers tapped against Ander's sides, slipping toward his waist.

"Stop! We just got up." Ander laughed, halfheartedly shoving at Sytri's shoulders.

Sytri simply snickered and kept going, nipping at Ander's skin. "I'm busy. Like I said, I have to make sure they know." He pulled at Ander's soft flesh, biting and tasting it. "Have to leave marks all over so everyone knows what's up."

"That's really dumb!"

"No, it's a genius plan. Absolutely no cons. I get to bite you and let everyone know that you're mine." Sytri raised his head and kissed Ander. "You are—you are mine, right?"

"Yeah," Ander said, almost faster than Sytri could ask. "Correction, we're each other's." He kissed Sytri back. "That's not going to change."

Sytri laughed, an airy, bright, and beautiful laugh. And it was ridiculous that after everything that had happened, such a small thing could make Ander happy. Genuinely, undeniably happy.

CHAPTER SEVENTEEN

"So, um what is it you've come to tell us . . . Ander?"

Ander couldn't meet Delilah's gaze. No matter which way he tilted his head or shifted his shoulders, the blue and red hickeys on his neck stood out like a collar. Sytri was smirking beside him, arms crossed.

It had taken hours to keep those marks there. Still, on the way here, Sytri had pushed Ander against a wall to make more. Not that Ander had minded in the moment, but now his hair was a mess, his neck was sore again, and he was horribly embarrassed. He was twenty-two, not some horny high schooler.

Though he hadn't really had a dating phase in high school, and Sytri never had any phase, so perhaps they were both just catching up. *At a mortifying time.*

"I was thinking about how I could be of use to you guys when you're ambushing Mayrez. I want to show that I can help, that I can be an asset to Millstone." Ander clenched his shirt in his fists, wringing off sweaty palms.

West coughed. "And what could you do, exactly?"

Great. Ander had made an angel feel awkward. That had to be a sin, right?

Eh, he'd fucked a demon last night; that was probably the thing he'd have to answer for if the time came.

"Oh, did you think about what I said?" Vega asked, sitting up in his chair.

Sytri snorted, rolling his eyes.

"What *did* you have to say to them, Vega?" Delilah asked, a great deal of concern in her eyes. She looked at Ander's neck and back at Vega.

"He has good blood, Delilah," Vega said, too cheerfully. "Someone down his family tree was an incredibly strong angel. The small taste of him I had a few days ago stayed with me for hours."

"And?"

"Use his blood on the field?" Serene asked.

"Exactly." Vega gave her finger guns.

"Would it really be that useful?" Delilah said.

"If he's a Half, then yes, no doubt." Cerberus stared at Ander curiously, tilting his head. "It'd be the strongest blood we have."

While being a Half was uncommon, Ander had assumed that a town of Partners would have at least one. But then Sytri had said that most of them had been torn apart on day one, before they had even known what they were. Demons had munched them like candy. Ander swallowed around the pit in his chest.

"Not positive he's Half, like I said." Vega tutted. "But it is by far the best blood."

Delilah crossed her arms, eyeing Ander. "You and Sytri would both have to consent to allowing an array of demons on our side to drink your blood. We don't have the means of safely storing it so we could just take it on the go. We also couldn't risk any of them getting poisoned because you hadn't given them permission."

"How many demons we talking about?" Sytri asked.

"We have six demons that come with us on stakeouts who haven't made deals with humans." She turned to Ander with her hands clasped. "They are the only ones, theoretically, that you'd have to give blood to. But there are fifteen demons total that would go; nine others who have made deals, but in the midst of a fight, you might be the one who happens to be close. You would have to be willing to give your blood to them too, just in case."

Ander grew a little nauseous. "That's a lot of demons, taking a lot of blood. I know I heal, but that still seems like too much."

"I'm not sure how much blood you think they'll need, but it won't really be a lot. And these demons are experienced in taking as little as required, as gently as possible."

Ander quirked an eyebrow. *Then why has Sytri been biting so hard? We need to have a talk.*

"Even if, for some horrible reason, all of them needed to bite you, they know the limit they're allowed. I'd imagine that altogether, it wouldn't be even close to a liter."

Ander had lost much more than that before. He gave a strained grin. "Okay, I'll trust you on that."

"Fifteen, though?" Sytri growled.

"It's fine. That's only hypothetical." Ander patted his arm.

"But I still have to like, say, out loud, that I'm fine with them biting you," Sytri huffed. "And I hate that."

"It's just for one day, I think. It's not like a permanent thing, is it? Can Vega still drink my blood?" He slid his thumb down his wrist.

Serene shook her head. "No, it wasn't a deal. You didn't make a pact or contract. You gave him permission for that moment, nothing more. The only way it can be permanent is through a deal."

"So like . . . how does that angel part of me know when to *stop* letting someone? It's all pretty vague. We give consent out loud, but how does my body know, my blood?" Ander pinched his wrist. "Not that I'm against this. I am completely for it. I came here because I want to help, but I don't like the idea of telling someone they can drink my blood and a couple of days later they can still do it because my blood didn't get the memo that I was done."

"You needn't overthink it. It's all based on emotion, words, and volition. The way of angels and demons is more psychosomatic than that of mankind. You and Sytri must agree on when someone else can have of you. If you both do, they can; if even one of you doesn't, they can't. Remember, the deal essentially gives you each part of the other's soul, and they must work in tandem, simple as that."

"We're sharing pieces of our souls?" A knot curled in Ander's throat.

"Yes. You accompany one another's will," Serene said. "Were you unaware of that before you agreed to the deal?"

"I was unaware of a lot of things back then," Ander muttered. "And that sounds . . . intense. Sytri didn't say the deal was soul-related."

"To be fair, I wasn't entirely sure how it worked." Sytri's voice was flat.

"A lot of demons aren't. The whole thing is a little mysterious," Vega piped up. "We're not even positive about how it all started, especially since deals can only be made by demons and we—"

"Regardless, the situation is still as I said." Serene coughed.

Ander wasn't positive he completely understood but, bringing his fingers to his chest, he managed, "All right, then."

"So does that mean you're willing to let the demons in our crew take your blood on the field if they need it? And Sytri is fine with it too?" Delilah asked, raising an eyebrow.

Sytri sighed loudly, slumping his shoulders. "Yes, I am, but only for the day we take down Mayrez. Also I have to see these guys, because there better not be another incubus among them." He glared at Vega, who snickered.

"I don't know why you hate my kind so much. We're the most loving of all demons, don't you think? Especially compared to brutes like you. Little vengeful things." Vega placed his chin in the palm of his hand. "All bark and all bite." He snapped his teeth.

"Better than a fucking pervert."

"Can you really say that to me when you've left such a beautiful ring around your blend's neck?" Vega smirked. "Which only makes me want to leave my own, honestly."

Sytri swung an arm in front of Ander and growled. "I'll make you bleed."

"Loving this dirty talk."

Delilah smacked her palm against the table. "Goddamn it, Vega, you're on the council, can you please not make every meeting go like this? Please? Can we have one conversation where you don't make it weird? I want us to be professional."

"It's hard for a demon of lust to do anything else," Cerberus said curtly. "I told you that when we let him join. I said, 'Don't let this creep in our group, please.'"

"You're all idiots, you know that? Whatever, fine. Apparently, Ander, your blood is important according to the demons in the room. So, if you're willing, and Sytri is willing, I have no problem with you joining us. Sytri has to help fight too though, and you both have to listen to me and Vega; we're the ones planning out the attack. Can you do that?"

"I'll listen to you, not Vega." Sytri scowled.

"Please," Ander said, nudging him.

Sytri rolled his eyes. "Fine! I'll listen. But *only* because this is what Ander wants to do. And I want to see Mayrez go down. She was always kind of a prick to me. Thought she was tough shit."

"She is tough shit. That's why we're taking this so seriously. Why *I* am, at least," Delilah said, with a stern glance at Vega. "We've lost blends to her before, and there's a reason she's been able to keep snatching them up. Even the Cast would rather have her working with them than against them, especially since she could be an Archdemon at this point. We know that last time she attacked Millstone that she only needed so much more blood."

Vega shifted in his seat with the slightest dip in his mouth. A frown? Ander bit his lip.

"You understand me, right?" Delilah reiterated, glaring at Ander. He had glanced away for a second and it seemed to have irked her. "She takes on full-blooded angels by herself. You have no idea how lucky you are to have managed to escape her grasp. It was pure luck."

"It was Sytri," Ander corrected.

"Then you owe him big time."

"I know." Ander grabbed Sytri's hand and the demon smirked.

Delilah sighed, rubbing her temples. "All right, two days from now, I need you back here, outside the building. You'll meet the other demons, and both of you will need to confirm, out loud to all of them, that they can drink Ander's blood if need be during the fight. No backing out from this point. I'd rather not be disappointed. Come on, Cerberus, let's go get a drink." She stood up, gesturing at the demon.

"God, yes," Cerberus said, swinging out of his chair.

West began to slowly disappear from his seat, and Serene was . . . already gone. Ander blinked. *What the hell.*

Vega waved a cheerful hand, and Sytri dragged Ander out of the building immediately.

"Well, that went okay, don't you think?" Ander asked, wincing as the sun hit his face. In the dark room he had almost forgotten that it was daytime. "Didn't get to talk to them about Ronan, but I didn't want to overwhelm them with demands. Have to do things in order. Prove my worth. Keep Millstone safe. Then we live here, happily ever after."

Sytri snorted. "Happily ever after if we get rid of Vega. I still don't trust him."

"Hey, come on now, he's . . . weird. But I think he means well. You said yourself you didn't like to be judged because you were a wrath demon, right? It seems hypocritical of you to judge him."

"Don't use logic on me."

"It is your greatest weakness."

"You bully." Sytri huffed and threw his arms up in the air. "It's just— He gets so touchy with you, and I remember how lust demons acted in Hell, all right? Fucking Incubi and Succubi crawling around. It wasn't pleasant." He shivered. "And you said it yourself, the guy is weird."

"Super weird."

"That's kind of rude of you to say, Ander. I thought we were friends."

"Holy shit!" Ander practically jumped into Sytri's arms as Vega's long, thin fingers pressed against his back. Sytri grabbed Ander, hissing at Vega like a snake, his tail going straight up into the air. But Vega only laughed loudly, a grin splitting his face. He shut up just as quick though, wide eyes snapping open. *The guy's a lizard.*

"Very cute," Vega said, stepping around them, eyes locked on Ander. "Very, very cute. I can't believe you've made a deal with this demon, of all demons." He looked at Sytri for a moment, twisting his mouth. "Your blood is a little too good for him, Ander, my dear."

"I don't know what you're getting at dude, but you better shut the fuck up." Sytri's tone had darkened quickly.

"I'm merely saying, it seems like a waste to keep that blood to yourself at all times. It's rude, selfish even. It could help. As we've discussed, Ander heals rather quickly. The potential he has to give is endless." He reached out to Ander, who jerked back. "Especially if we put some salt in you."

Ander's chest turned to ice. "What?"

"Salt would increase the strength of your angel blood. Get you high on that, let demons feast from you." Vega licked his lips. "What a delectable time we would have. Your blood is so unique, Ander, so fantastic. I've been thinking about it."

"Well, quit thinking about it," Sytri snapped. "It's not for you." He stabbed a finger against Vega's chest. "And it's only for the other demons in emergencies. Ander isn't going to have a weird blood orgy with you fuckers."

"I didn't say 'blood orgy.'" Vega laughed. "Though I'm not against the idea." His eyes hazed over. "That would be a great party."

"Like Sytri said." Ander stood as firmly as he could, ignoring the heat that had flashed in his face at *blood orgy*. "I want to help when it's important. Which means when we're out there fighting, not all the time on the whim of other demons. Come on, Sytri." He started walking, but Vega seemed unperturbed, trailing after them.

"Yes, and giving your blood to demons at a constant pace will continuously strengthen them. You'd be helping us grow an army that could fight back. No offense to the other demons here, but they're not that tough, honestly." Vega sighed dramatically. "And it's been a pain for me, to be here with these weaker demons. I have to worry about them constantly, especially with the Cast creeping closer and closer. But with your blood, who knows what they could be; who knows what *I* could be."

"If you keep talking, you could be dead, so keep that in mind," Sytri growled.

"We've been over this, little wrath. You wouldn't have a chance against me." Vega paused. "And you know that."

Sytri froze for a second. Like a quick gasp, and then it was gone. He went back to walking, at a faster pace this time. Vega grinned, eyes narrowing.

"Was that a threat?" Ander asked curtly. *Or do you just like to shove a bit?*

"I would never threaten friends."

"Are we friends?"

It took Vega a good second to reply. "Of course. It's why I'm so concerned. I mean, Sytri, don't you think you're being inconsiderate? Claiming to love this blend so but then keeping him restrained to *you*? Someone who's not nearly as capable of keeping him safe as I would be." Vega placed a hand on his own chest humbly. "And I would utilize him properly."

"He's not—"

"I'm not something to be *utilized*. I'm helping because I want to help. I'm not a tool or a weapon," Ander snapped. "Don't talk down to Sytri and don't talk down to me!" The feathers around his neck puffed up, and the deal in his chest flared oddly. He pressed his fingers over the heat, glaring at Vega.

Vega's eyes darted across Ander's face, then, hesitantly he said, "I'm only offering to provide support."

Ander raised an eyebrow; he hadn't actually expected Vega to sound remorseful. But he was still pissed.

"It's more than that," he huffed. "You said to prove my worth so I could bring Ronan here, so I could live here. And I listened then. But don't think I'm going to listen to every single thing you say because of that. Especially when you're clearly trying to take advantage of me. Come on, Sytri." He grabbed Sytri's hand and tugged him forward, leaving Vega standing there, stiffly, in the middle of the cobblestone path.

Ander's face was burning. He didn't know what had come over him, but there were hot coals in his throat and his heart was pounding painfully. He wanted everything to go smoothly, but Sytri and Vega would wreck that if Vega kept on doing . . . whatever it was he was doing. Guilt-tripping?

"You okay?" Sytri asked cautiously as they pushed their way through a crowd of people.

"Yeah. I'm fine, I'm fine." Ander sighed. "Why can't everyone be helpful without some underlying selfish reason?"

"I don't think the world works like that."

"Can't it? There's no reason for us to try and trick each other; we could all be on the same side." His face was even hotter. He often heard the way he wanted the world to be was impossible, but he didn't like hearing it from Sytri. "I know that it's absurd to think everyone can be nice. But this town is supposed to be different. It's full of like-minded people, blends, demons, and even angels, getting along and working together. I don't like that Vega was, like, picking at us, picking at you." He crossed his arms. "It was like he was trying to pry something from us."

"I told you, lust demons are sleazy."

"No, you can't say he's bad because he's an Incubus."

"What? Seconds ago you were yelling at him *because* he was being sleazy."

"I know! Yes, but not because of what kind of demon he is. I told you already, don't be hypocritical." Ander groaned. "Say he's weird because he's Vega, okay? And Vega's weird. Like you're headstrong because you're Sytri. Remember?"

"Yeah. Yeah, I got it. Vega's a fucking creep all on his own."

"Yes." Ander laughed.

"And you're fucking adorable all on your own."

He blushed but forced a scowl. "You're being lame again."

"I know, all on my own." Sytri snickered, his smirk a little crooked, his chipped tooth visible. Ander briefly wanted to press a finger against the nicked fang, and turned red at the thought. *Weirdo.*

Sytri was beautiful, that was why all these strange ideas entered his head. Ander had to stare at the ground; it was dangerous to look at Sytri too long.

Vega could be the stronger demon. He could be the strongest demon alive and it would mean nothing to Ander. He had chosen Sytri and Sytri had chosen him. Out of necessity or luck: it didn't matter. It had been a perfect match.

His hand tightened in Sytri's. He wouldn't give up him for anything in the world. And he would trust him, more than anything in the world, when they went to stop Mayrez.

CHAPTER EIGHTEEN

I *'m not going to war, but this has to feel similar.*
Sitting against the tree in the small courtyard of Millstone, as starlight glittered in the skies, all he could think about was how anxiety was making his fingers numb, how his heart weighed like a stone in his chest.

"Why'd we get here so early?" Sytri asked, arms crossed as he leaned on the same tree, one leg propped up. He looked fierce standing there, eyes sharp and watching.

"I just wanted a moment to myself." He could have taken it at home, but a part of him worried that Delilah would secretly change her mind about letting him go along, so he wanted to be at the rendezvous point as soon as possible.

Though, he trusted that Vega wouldn't let such information slip past them. As strange as he was, he had been making sure Ander stayed in the loop. Even after the incident a few days ago, he'd kept popping by their house every so often with news—and to bicker with Sytri of course. He was seemingly more harmless than before, but equally annoying.

"Are you scared?" Sytri asked. But Ander couldn't answer before Sytri spoke up again. "Don't be. I won't let anything hurt you. Least of all Mayrez. I plan on ripping out her throat. Though maybe also throwing in a thank-you for allowing us to meet." He nudged Ander with his foot and winked when he looked up. "After I rip out her throat."

"Thank you, Sytri."

"You're welcome."

"For everything. You didn't have to agree to fight Mayrez with me. You could have just told me to take Ronan back to Gardners. But I don't want that; I want Millstone and its people."

"Eh, you always made Gardners sound like a shithole anyway. Definitely didn't make me want to live there."

"No. They wouldn't take you anyway: big no-demon zone." Ander laughed dryly. "So really, our only options are this, or heading out to find somewhere entirely new. And this seemed like the right answer, you know? Especially because I can help for once, so I should."

"I'm sure you could have helped before. You just convinced yourself you couldn't. Trust me, I know these things—I'm a demon. Believing you can't has always been mankind's biggest downfall. And believing you should when you shouldn't has been your biggest sin."

"That's disturbingly insightful coming from you."

"What's that supposed to mean? I know things about stuff!" Even in the dark there was a clear flush across his face.

"Okay, that's a little bit more on brand." Ander sighed, running his hand through his hair. "But what you said . . . You think this is a *shouldn't* time?"

"Don't know that until it's too late," Sytri murmured and then tilted his head at him. "But I'll be here for you if it is."

"Here early I see." Sytri and Ander both jumped at Vega's voice. He always managed to catch them by surprise. He clasped his hands and peered at the two of them. "Sort of expected that. You seem like you were a studious kid back in the day."

"I dropped out of college," Ander said.

"Oh, how unfortunate. What for? The cost? Too hard? Were you *lonely*?" Vega slipped around Ander's right side, placing himself between him and Sytri, then he swung out his arms and pulled them both into a tight embrace. Sytri instantly pried Vega's arms off them with a grunt and went as if to shove the demon, but Ander caught his eye and glared, hard. Sytri huffed and crossed his arms.

Ander nudged Vega. "Does it matter? It's been over four years now."

"If it doesn't matter, then it shouldn't matter to talk about it. But I can see perhaps that it's still a sore subject." Vega put a hand on his heart and the other halfway in the air, like a boy-scout promise. "Apologies for bringing it up. Anyway, I'm glad to see you made it. Delilah thought you would chicken out."

"I thought she would change her mind about inviting me."

"No, no, Delilah doesn't do take-backs. Unfortunately." Vega clicked his tongue. "Unfortunately. Oh well. Everyone else should be here shortly. We need you and Sytri to confirm it's fine for them to drink from your blood." He winked. "Me included."

"It's fine, Vega. I give you permission to drink from me if it means keeping you up in the fight, keeping you alive."

"I agree but I hate it. And as soon as we're in the clear and away from the fight, you can choke for all I care," Sytri muttered.

"Only if you do the choking." Vega gave him finger guns, the signature Vega move.

Sytri growled. *Signature Sytri.*

"Oh! Is this the Halfie?" a voice called out. The trio turned to see another three heading their way. Presumably, the demons they were here to meet.

There were two females, one male. The one girl appeared to be walking on . . . deer legs? Ander squinted. Probably. Definitely legs from an animal with hooves. As they came closer, the one with deer legs put her hands on her hips and cocked her head.

"Nice to meet you. I've never had Halfie blood. I've heard it's a delicacy." She looked at Sytri. "You must be the lucky son of a bitch who got him. There's not a lot of these anymore. I mean, the Cast has a handful, which isn't good for us." She narrowed her eyes. The pupils were rectangular like a goat's. "The more angel blood you have, the more you think like an angel, and most angels seem to agree with the Cast."

"I a hundred percent do not agree with slavery and the trading of blend lives," Ander said, glaring. He wanted to add that he wasn't a verified "Halfie" but he still didn't know what his weird blood meant, so it was better to not cause confusion.

The girl laughed, her chortle filling up the silence of the night air. "Good. Good. I would hope. Besides, Delilah wouldn't let you with us if she thought otherwise. I'm Sunspot." She held out a hand. "And I would like to partake of your blood on this fine night, Halfie."

"Permission granted. Just don't kill me."

"You can drink but don't be creepy about it," Sytri added.

"Pft, I'm not creepy." She stuck out her black forked tongue.

Ander went through and greeted the other demons, who had varying opinions. Most were excited for the chance to drink blend blood, a few were wary of Ander as a newcomer.

Soon more demons arrived, some with their blends and some alone. The fellow Partners and their demons seemed to be a lot less enthusiastic about the transaction. In fact, they seemed as uncomfortable about it as he was. Most made a point to state they would only drink Ander's blood if it was a life-or-death situation. He appreciated that.

It was strange to see the crowd grow around him, curious faces and voices asking about him and Sytri. Where had they been before? What brought them out this far? How long had they been Partners? Their time together had been very short, compared to others, some of whom had been together since the first demons had slipped through the gates of Hell.

"So if you weren't in a sanctuary when it all started, how did you manage to live without a deal?" one of them asked. His eyes were a pure red, intense. "No offense, but you don't seem like the strongest blend, blood aside."

"Orion!" his Partner said, nudging him in the stomach.

"What? It's true, right? It's why we're taking his blood instead of expecting him to throw punches with the rest of us.

"I can vouch for it," Vega said, giving an okay sign. "It's top-notch stuff."

There was collective murmuring. They inspected Ander. Their words crept into his ears—they wanted to know more, wanted a taste. He was trapped in the crowd, now surrounded by hungry eyes. His thoughts tumbled. *Let's start the bidding. Who's got the salt.* His hands were tied.

Then Sytri wrapped an arm around him, tugged him to his chest, putting space between them and the rest. Ander let out a breath and blinked until the memories scattered.

"Everyone!" Delilah's voice called out. They all turned their heads in unison. She stood there, arms crossed, muscles obvious—Ander was a little envious. Cerberus was a thin and gangly stick beside her. "We're all here and accounted for?"

"Wonder what was with the delay?" Sunspot whispered to Ander, who scrunched his eyebrows. She continued, "Where's Serene and West?"

"Do they usually come on things like this?"

"Of course. They're like the strongest. It'd be weird for them not to help. West is an *angel*."

"Quit talking, please," Delilah said, her voice just loud enough to rise above the rest. "This is serious shit. You all know that. That's why I picked you. You're the ones I trust the most." She scowled. "And we're hoping to take out Mayrez. Because not only is she a fucking bitch—" Someone in the crowd cheered. "—but she's been a source of slaves for the Cast, who are the number one thumbtack in our shoe. They are actively against the world we hope to see built from these ashes, and they're after us." She stopped, surveying the crowd. She paused on Ander, and a chill went straight up his spine.

There was so much hate in her words.

Were her eyes always that dangerous?

"They've stolen our own. They've killed our own. We can't get back what they robbed us of or get rid of that hurt. But we sure as fuck can hurt them back!" She said each word of the last sentence loudly, individually, each one as important and furious as the last.

The crowd cheered. Ander could only stand and watch, his eyes bright.

"We're splitting into two groups, half of you with me and half with Vega. We'll cross into Mayrez's path in about an hour. She probably has strong demons with her." Delilah straightened up. "Let's move out. I'll relay instructions as we're walking and talking, but it's pretty basic 'cause I'm a basic bitch. Guerrilla tactics, a lot of surprising, and a lot of killing on sight."

She pointed at a few people, whistling for them to join her. A couple brushed past Ander as they walked by. He was not picked.

Vega strolled over to him and Sytri, and patted Ander on his shoulder. "You're with me, Ander."

"Of course we are," Sytri muttered. He gripped Ander's hand. "Don't worry, it's going to be fine."

"Yeah, of course." *"Kill on sight," though—won't our enemies do the same?*

Ander looked up at Vega, the strongest of them all, to see the same casual, smiling face. But the grin wasn't as bright as it should have been, held back by apparent apprehension. Their plan was dangerous. Death was a hard probability if not a certainty. Fear struck him so hard that his hands pricked with static and the world went foggy and distant. He had to dig his nails into his palms and heels into the dirt to ground himself.

What Delilah had said stuck with him, though, all of it. She wanted a better world, one where demons didn't crawl along the edges of trails to devour the unsuspecting. One where angels didn't try to drug blends into submission. An outlandish goal perhaps, but one worth fighting for. And it sounded like Delilah had been fighting for it her whole life.

"What did Delilah do? Before all of this happened?" Ander asked Vega, who was leading him, Sytri, and seven other people out into the forest.

"She was a kindergarten teacher."

CHAPTER NINETEEN

Forests at night were dark. Incredibly, densely dark.

The trees had done their absolute best to blot out the stars and moon. Their branches were spread out, intermingling like a crowd of snakes. Ander had to keep gripping Sytri's hand for fear that if he let go, he would wander off a ridge. There were a lot of them.

They trekked on upward, Ander getting repeatedly out of breath. Even after all the days and nights he'd spent walking, going uphill took the wind out of him. That wasn't even taking in the other annoyances. He ran his hand over his neck, wiping sweat off for the hundredth time. Vega appeared completely unaffected by the trek, as did most of the demons who were traveling in their smaller group.

Six unpaired demons, two pairs of Partners. It wasn't hard to guess why their crew was more uneven than the other group, which was composed almost entirely of Partners.

"So, I know the map was, well, a map, but how did you figure out what time she'd be coming by here?" Ander asked, glancing over at Vega.

Vega fanned out a hand. "There were dates written in the margins that were fairly regular. It wasn't hard to figure out there was a pattern to her trips. So, we sent scouts to track her and once they got back to us, we were able to confirm her current schedule based on her recent location. She might have stopped at a few places along the way, but now she's heading toward the Cast. At this point there's no one else between her and them besides us."

He grinned. "Based on the scouts' last sighting, she should reach the trail right under the cliff in the next hour or so."

"Which is where we get the jump on her," Sytri said, snapping his teeth.

"Exactly. But our main purpose is to disorient and distract so Delilah and her group can move around the other side without being noticed. Then we'll have Mayrez literally circled. And to ensure that she doesn't bolt before then, we have you." He shot finger guns at Ander.

"The bait." Ander grimaced.

"The bait."

"Which I fucking hate, by the way, thanks for asking," Sytri barked. "Thanks for clearing that aspect with us before we signed up for this."

"She's going to notice him anyway, might as well use it to our advantage." Vega hummed.

Ander glared. *Feels like that bit of the plan was kept from us until the last moment on purpose, though.*

Vega clapped. "Anyway, she'll be distracted by you, and while she's all frenzied up, Delilah and her gang swoop in and end her."

"You make it sound so easy," Sytri said, rolling his eyes.

"Yes, well, we know it won't be. But it sounds nicer if I leave out all the parts where we will probably be maimed or gravely injured."

"Thanks for the pep talk." Sunspot laughed dryly.

Vega gave a half-hearted bow. "You are welcome. I've been working on it. But it will be fine. Serene is traveling with Delilah, and she can heal our wounded."

"That's her power? I've never asked," Ander said. "It's still so jarring to me that she's half-angel half-demon."

"It happens more than you think. And it's good to be half-angel and half-demon when you could just be half-demon."

"There are half-demon humans?"

"What? Of course." Vega laughed. "You think demons didn't dip their toes in the water when they could? But when the angels first arrived, they killed the demon blends just as swiftly as they killed any full-blooded ones, even though those blends had thought themselves just regular humans their whole life. Her angel blood probably saved her from that fate. Did you never see angels take down someone who looked human?"

Ander shook his head slowly. But then again, the beginning had been so chaotic. All he could remember was blood and slaughter, that it had been angels who protected him in Gardners. But there had been poor souls killed by what they thought would rescue them? It made his stomach turn. *Angels and demons have never been black-and-white.*

"Ah, well, fewer demons made it to Earth than angels back in the day, so demon blends were a rarer occurrence. Still, they happened, those little hell spawn." Vega laughed bitterly. "And the angels killed them. Oh, look I've rambled and now here we are." He waved his hand in front of them, and they slowed to a stop. They were grouped together at the edge of a cliff. Thirty, forty feet high, perhaps? From this spot they saw all that the moonlight could show: Mountains, hills, crevices, the tops of trees. Underneath them was a scraggly trail jutting from dense forest, an expanse of dark green glowing in soft white light.

Ander shivered as a breeze brushed by. He was so small. A drop in this sea of wilderness. "So now we just wait?"

"We wait, and then we jump." Vega steadied himself on the edge.

"So straightforward," Ander muttered.

"How do you think an ambush works?" Vega gazed around, eyes wide, huge; an owl hunting for prey in the darkness. "Well, she definitely hasn't been through here yet. Remember, don't give any blood until we're seen. Smell of your blood could alert them."

"I know, I know," Ander said. "Where is Delilah and her group?"

"Farther down." Vega's tone was solemn. It made Ander's stomach turn. "They're coming in via a longer route so they don't accidentally cross paths with Mayrez before we're ready. Perhaps I moved our group a little fast. I don't think Delilah is where she's supposed to be, yet."

"How do you know?"

"I can touch minds, Ander."

Ander cringed. *The hell?* "Have you, uh . . . touched my mind before?"

"That'd be invasive without your permission."

Ander scowled; that wasn't a proper answer. "All you are is invasive. That power is why you're the one leading this. You can hide yourself and people or whatever." He scrunched his mouth. "It's how you managed to keep sneaking up on me and Sytri this whole time."

"I wouldn't say 'sneaking.'"

"I would," Sytri interjected. "Or creeping, lurking, slinking. Any of those."

"We are all free to pick different words for my skill. But I'd prefer to call it 'observing politely.'" Vega looked back into the forest. "Now, I don't mean to be rude, but we must remain quiet for the rest of this. We don't want to be heard."

Ander glared, tucking the new information about Vega away. If he lived through this, he was going to have to pry more out of the demon.

The group stood there in the cold for a few minutes, staring down into the forest. Ander kept glancing at the trail, his eyes and ears ready for anything at all. He followed it upward, almost past his field of vision. That was the path Mayrez was following; somewhere along its spine was the home of the Cast. The people who controlled Tephera. Ander grimaced.

"What's that?" Sytri whispered.

Ander matched his line of sight. His vision wasn't like a demon's. Still, he could see what Sytri was talking about: The smallest white speck. A broken pixel on a computer screen. Perhaps a mere trick of the eye. Ander stared at it harder just in case, but the dot remained. Then it moved.

"Vega," Sunspot said, voice tight.

"I see it," Vega said. "Don't move. Though I don't think this has anything to do with Mayrez. Wrong direction."

Great. That's what they needed: something else to worry about.

"Everyone, crouch down."

Immediately, they all kneeled, Ander carefully placing himself on the rocky and crumbling ground. Every pebble his body scratched against, the softest scrape, made him wince. His own breathing felt too loud. What was the speck, to worry Vega so? Was he simply being cautious?

From the edge of the cliff Ander saw the light getting closer and closer, forming a blurry figure. Four legs, slender neck: A deer. A solid white deer.

His nose crinkled. The doe had brought a strange scent with it, metallic and dry. And it had to be bursting from it for even him to smell it.

The creature tiptoed softly, almost hovering, from place to place. As it neared the cliff, its odd body became more distinct, practically glowing in the dark. Its legs from the knees down ended in exposed skeleton. Was it an angel, a demon?

It got closer, until it was almost right below them. Then it froze. A perfect statue in the middle of the forest.

Vega's leg shifted, just barely. Sytri's hand curled around Ander's arm in a tight grip.

Almost curiously so, the deer raised its head, inch by inch, centimeter by centimeter, until it should have broken all the bones in its neck, staring straight at them with closed eyes. Ander could feel its curiosity, its *hunger*.

It wasn't good.

The creature opened its mouth, and out spilled the laughter of hundreds of children.

Ander's body was ice. *What the absolute hell is that?*

Vega jumped down, faster than Ander could follow, and a second later white blood splashed across the ground, glowing like the moon.

Like Tephera's. Ander clenched his jaw.

The deer was twitching, skewed on one of Vega's long, thin horns. With a toss of his head, Vega flung the creature off, its body swinging to the hard ground with a *thud*, convulsing before it no longer moved at all. Then, casually, as if he hadn't just murdered something, Vega began to climb back up the cliff.

Halfway to the top, however, a voice called out below, "What's that?"

Vega stilled, his claws deep in the rocky crumble of the cliff. He scowled at Ander and the group.

"Looks like a dead angel."

Ander's heart stopped. He knew that voice, even after all this time. The sound of it was like a clawed hand around his throat. *Mayrez.*

Sytri's grasp on his arm became ironclad.

"Didn't know angels walked out this far. Thought that's why we took this way in the first place," replied someone coldly.

"It's not a normal angel. It's one of them weird ones. The basic ones. They just kind of wander around." Mayrez again. Ander gulped as she and a trail of disheveled companions appeared from under the ledge.

"But we haven't seen a dead angel on this trail before. Do you think we should be concerned?" Micah. Ander should have recognized him given that icy tone. He was almost as white as the deer, blending with the animal's corpse as he stood above it.

She walked over to the deer and bent down, her horns sharp in the moonlight, her tail swishing like a snake behind her. Like a demented child, she prodded at it with a claw and cackled. The sound brought acid to Ander's throat. It was the same laughter from when she had made him into meat, a plaything, on sale to the highest bidder.

"Don't think so. We have an agreement with the Cast. Their angels don't hurt us. Any angel that tries means they don't work for them and is a free target." She placed a hand on Micah's shoulder and snickered.

Micah brushed it off sternly. "Don't touch me."

"Prude." Mayrez sniffed.

"That wasn't what I was saying anyway. What I meant was, what or who killed it if not us?" Micah seemed to study the surroundings, but he didn't look up.

Vega's face was unreadable for the most part. However, his situation was clearly not ideal. If he moved, he risked rubble falling and his ability to conceal would falter. How susceptible the prey was to his motives in the first place probably played a part as well. Demons on edge—they wouldn't be blind.

Vega mouthed something to Ander's group. Ander had no idea what. But Sytri nodded and turned back to the others, who all nodded too. Ander swallowed down his nerves. There had only been one plan: ambush.

Sytri tossed Ander on his back and in the blink of an eye, everyone leaped. Sytri snapped his teeth into Ander's arm like an alligator. Blood poured out, and Sytri's long shadow arms wrapped tightly around Ander as they fell to the ground thirty feet below.

It was apparently a simple drop for the demons, but the impact rocked Ander's head, his vision completely spinning like he'd been thrown in a washer. He winced, hands tightening on Sytri's shoulders. It took a solid few seconds before he could take in his surroundings.

Vega had managed to pounce on Micah, but not Mayrez. Perhaps she had been too quick or the other demon simply closer. Either way, Micah had been caught and in an instant Vega had jabbed his hand through the demon's throat, almost decapitating him. Micah clutched at what remained of his neck, burbling, backing away. *How is he still standing?*

The scene was a flurry of demons attacking demons, Vega now trying to cut down Mayrez. Ander could barely focus; he was still on Sytri's back, being swung around with inhuman speed as his Partner joined the brawl. He saw the world through ripples.

"Taking a nab!" Sunspot yelled and before Ander could prepare himself, she yanked his arm and bit down. Pain shot up his arm like lightning, leaving a burning trail that spread across his skin. His fist curled against Sytri's back as she pulled away. *Fuck*, he hadn't expected it to hurt like that. But that was why he'd come here: to be a battery.

He gritted his teeth and tried to focus on not dying.

After a few breaths he lifted his head. Immediately his chest went hollow. Farther down the trail were an array of thirty or so demons Mayrez must have brought with her. Ander's group needed Delilah and her half here now.

Another demon ran up next to him, biting his wrist, and Ander threw his other hand over his mouth to stifle his shouts. Panic flooded him, his body shaking, mind darting from one fear to the next. This demon must come from a different sin. His own blood felt like poison in his body and it *hurt*—goddamn it hurt.

Another bite, another demon drinking from his veins. He choked on air. What the fuck—why did every bite have to be different? How could one body feel so many different things at once? It was *agonizing*.

He whimpered, trying to relax his breathing. This had to be worth it. They would be stronger with his blood, tougher. The demons he had helped, they had a fury in their eyes, power in their blows. All around him were flashes of sharp claws leaving blood in their wake.

Then something else caught Ander's eye.

"Michael?" Ander coughed, adrenaline lifting him up. Michael and a few other Couriers, all chained at the neck, were being led away from the fight by a demon five times the size of anyone else on the field. The Couriers' eyes were vacant, their movements sluggish.

A lump formed in Ander's throat. Michael was *alive*.

"Get the blends out of here," Mayrez barked. "I'm not losing them."

"I wouldn't worry about them," Vega yelled, slashing at her. They each seemed to be holding their own. Sytri was fending off demon after demon.

Yet Ander couldn't stop himself leaning back toward the Couriers, arm outstretched. "Sytri. Sytri, we have to go after them. We have to save them."

"What?" Sytri knocked a demon sideways, a spray of blood following his fist.

"Is that the halfie?" someone shouted.

Ander stilled. Fuck, now was not the time for them to take the bait. The Couriers were right there, if he could just—

"Holy shit! He came back to me." Mayrez laughed. "Guys! Come deal with the ginger." She clawed Vega's side, static flashing into the air as she carved him like a pumpkin. She followed that with one solid kick that sent him stumbling backward, and a swarm of demons crowded him.

Shit.

"Everyone else stay out of this." Mayrez pointed a claw between her and them. "The Halfie and the thief are *mine*." She stepped closer to them, flexing her claws.

"Where the fuck is Delilah?" Sytri hissed.

"Little Halfie, you got far, huh?" Mayrez snickered. "Not by yourself it seems. Sytri, you didn't pay me for that. You can't just go around stealing other people's property. I thought you knew better."

"Don't touch him, you bitch," Sytri snapped.

"Oh. Wow. Got attached, huh." A starved grin spread across her face as she neared, moonlight glowing in her animal eyes. "Well, that doesn't matter. You brought him closer to some better clients. I hadn't wanted to risk the journey with him myself, but the Cast will pay big for a Halfie." Her eyes were disturbingly wide, and the smile split her face almost ear to ear.

"Shut the hell up. How about you and your fucking minions get lost?" Sytri snarled.

"Not gonna happen. Though I won't need all these lowlifes soon enough. Once I trade that boy, I'm sure to get plenty of souls from the Cast." She licked her lips. "I'll finally be an Archdemon. I'll be able to handle everything myself—no more need to share *profits.*"

Ander had gone cold. Sytri had said that only higher creatures could take out a soul. Higher than Vega, than Tephera. What was beyond them? What did the Cast have?

Ander bit into his lip as Mayrez stalked closer. Sytri tensed, readying his ink-arms. Over Mayrez's shoulder, Vega was struggling to stand. Everyone was shouting; Sunspot was snarling, someone screamed in pain. Friend or foe?

A familiar presence pressed into Ander. Mayrez. *You're mine, Halfie.*

Her prying pushed his thoughts onto a microscope slide. Ander panicked, trying to stay blank, keep her out, to ignore her words, but they started multiplying, screaming, cackling.

Came back to me. Came to bleed. You fucking idiot. You stupid fucking human.

Over and over again. Ander's nails pinched into Sytri's skin. He was hyperventilating—he had to calm down. She wouldn't get him.

I will.

Sytri would protect him.

He won't.

This wasn't the end.

It is.

Sytri's voice broke the struggle. "You're insane if you think you're going to take him from me, Mayrez."

"You're insane if you think you can stop me. You've always been weaker than me. Isn't that why you tagged along?" She stretched her claws.

Catting seemed to take her out of Ander's mind for the moment, and he took a deep breath. He wasn't letting her back in.

Then Sytri bit into Ander's arm, and he had to hold back a yelp.

Sweat beaded across his brow as Sytri let go seconds later. *Damn it, I already feel like shit.*

Mayrez snarled, eyes dark. "That's *my* blood, Sytri. I caught him!"

"Fuck off, you bitch." Sytri hunched closer to the ground, like a runner. From his left, another shadow arm ripped from the one already there. The new one dripped liquid onto the ground that was so solidly black, it looked like nothing at all.

The fire of Sytri's bite reignited, making Ander trembling. God, he prayed his blood had done something. They had to win this. *Save everyone including—*

The Couriers. Ander spun. They were being dragged away. No, they couldn't get out of sight. He had to do something. But what?

"Sytri, I have to go after them," he said.

"What the fuck are you talking about?" Sytri snarled.

"The Couriers are here. The ones I left behind!"

Sytri didn't so much as glance at them. "What? No, you're not leaving." His grip tightened. Ander could barely breathe. "You have to stay here where you're safe."

"You think he's safe with you?" Mayrez laughed and launched herself, swiping at him.

The two demons darted back and forth, Sytri swinging his cold black arms, which Mayrez dodged with ease.

"Sytri, you're all off. Not used to the blood yet? You've either been drinking too much—or not enough." She snickered. "It's Halfie blood; it's not like anything you're used to." She rushed forward, striking at Sytri's face. His blood sprayed into the air as he growled and jumped backward. "If you can't use it properly, it'll only bring you down. How about you just hand him over and we'll call it even? I won't kill you too painfully."

"Shut up." Sytri jumped into the air, a third black arm flailing out from the stains on his shoulders wildly before it straightened up and slashed Mayrez across the cheek. Blood went flying, and she recoiled with a sharp hiss.

Ander's vision fluttered. He felt so weak. "Sytri," he muttered and scanned the area: smack dab in a ring of dead bodies lay Vega, motionless. Dark blood pooled around him. Shit, Ander had to help. He wasn't doing his job strapped to Sytri's back like a damn child. "Sytri, I need you to let me go."

"*No.*"

But Vega was hurt and the Couriers were getting snatched away, and they had been right in front of Ander's eyes. He struggled, but Sytri's grip was steadfast. Goddamn it. Mayrez wasn't letting up, her blows coming quicker and faster. She was gaining an edge. It probably wasn't helping that Sytri was carrying him. Everything could be fixed if he *just let go.*

"You have to. They all need help and I'm weighing you down."

"Fuck, I'm sort of—"

"Sytri, put me down!" Ander yelled and the force of it burned in his chest like a collapsing star.

And Sytri dropped him. "Wh-what?"

There wasn't time to question why. As soon as Ander's knees hit dirt, he bolted. He swerved around Mayrez, who reached for him, but Sytri tackled her and pinned her to the ground.

"Vega." Ander crashed beside him, barely missing a corpse. The demon had definitely fought with his all, but now he was crumpled over with a wound on his left side so large and deep that muscle was visible. Ander swung his head away, bile rising in his throat. *What am I supposed to do? I only have one thing.*

"Drink, okay, drink?" He shoved his arm in front of Vega's face, where the bite from Sytri was already closing.

Vega didn't even speak; he latched on to it with fervor, greedily pulling the blood into his throat. Heat and need flooded Ander, pooling in his stomach. *Fucking ridiculous, we're in the middle of dying.* He pushed them down, cringing, eyes watering.

Vega's hands curled around his arm, his waist, forced him close. He kept on until Ander's head was dizzy and every part of him ached to be touched.

"Delicious, Ander," Vega said, when he finally stopped, wiping his mouth. He stood up. His side was already healing, skin growing across it like moss on a tree. *So fast. My blood can do that?* Vega ran a hand down his new flesh and smirked. "Impressive. And a bit frightening. All right, let me go save your boy now."

"Yeah, go do that." Ander slumped on the ground as Vega dashed off.

Crap, the Couriers though. Got to get to them. But his whole body was twitching, dying. And Sytri— *Shit.*

Mayrez was still tangled in Sytri's claws but she was sending wave after wave of electricity down his arms and he was *howling.* Ander tried to stand and faltered immediately.

But then Vega was on Mayrez. He tore into her, skewered her through with his horns and left her swinging on them in the moonlight. With a visceral shriek, she kicked herself off, ripping her own body to shreds.

She was a mess of blood and tattered flesh, but still she stood. Delilah hadn't been lying when she said Mayrez was strong; she was beyond that. Even wounded she was like a god, danger and wrath wrapped around a vortex.

"You think you've won?" she snapped. "You think you can stop me? I ruled in Hell and I rule here."

"You weren't in charge there either, Mayrez. I remember you," Vega said, sneering. "You were below me there and you're below me here. And if I remember, the one time you did try to challenge your leader, you failed and went cowering in fear with your tail between your legs." He spat at the ground. "Like a fucking mutt."

"Shut up!" Mayrez screamed, blood spewing from her mouth. "You don't know shit. I would've taken that bastard down if he wasn't a fucking cheat." She bared her teeth. "This is Earth now anyway, you fucker, and it's my playing field. And no one can stop me here, not a fucking soul."

"I beg to differ."

Delilah.

In a burst of lightning and smoke, she was there, her fist colliding with Mayrez's face. It would have sent the demon flying if Cerberus hadn't been on her other side. He whipped each tail forward with precision, impaling Mayrez's head, her chest, and her stomach. Blood spurted out like a fountain as Mayrez choked out an inhuman groan. She swiped a few times in jerky movements before she slumped to the earth.

Even Ander, who hated her with his entire being, who'd wanted her gone more than anything, shuddered. Nausea hit him like a brick and he turned away, holding back bile. Cerberus shook her off his tails like mud.

All was silent for a few seconds, and then Mayrez's demons *scattered.* They rushed to the trees, but Serene and West were there. Serene made a wall of flame that circled the runaways, trapping them in a blaze that swallowed them whole. One managed to dodge it, but West grabbed it by the throat and crushed it.

Ander grimaced. West's face remained impassive.

"I didn't think you were going to show," Vega said with an evident sigh of relief, walking over to Delilah. "And holy shit when you did—you like to make an entrance."

"Sometimes I get to be dramatic too. It's not just you." She flicked Vega's shoulder. "We ran into a bunch of strange angels. All of them shaped like white animals and sounding like people."

She shivered. "We killed them but more kept popping up. Caused a bit of a hiccup."

Vega narrowed his eyes. "Odd."

Mayrez gurgled again.

Ander jumped as if hit by lightning and whipped his head around to where she lay. Even with half her face beyond recognition and more of her blood on the outside than in, she struggled to stand. Her eyes were bloodshot, her face a string of gore. Pieces slid to the ground with wet slaps, and Ander took an instinctive step back while bile inched up his throat. She was . . . strips of meat. Why and *how* the fuck didn't she stay down?

"You bastards. You fucking pricks—" She coughed. "Stopping me won't stop them." She lurched forward with a wet laugh, and Ander had to hold back vomit. *Fucking hell.* "At least I found a way to live with them."

"Did you, though?" Vega said.

Then he slashed her neck clean in half, sending her head tumbling to the ground. Finally her body went slack, and the world seemed to fall silent as everyone stared.

This fight had been won, but Ander's nerves kept singing.

Like there were still wolves around the bend.

CHAPTER TWENTY

The demon hadn't gotten too far with the Couriers, and West and Serene ended it quickly. Ander had been overwhelmed with joy, almost sobbing in relief as everyone gathered up the Couriers and guided them to Millstone in the morning sunrise.

His happiness, unfortunately, was short-lived. Something was wrong with the Couriers. When they all arrived at the courtyard, the blends hovered around, mouths slightly open, eyes unfocused.

"Why are they like this?" Ander asked as he stared at Michael, who was now a teetering zombie. His skin had taken on a sickish gray hue, his cheeks sunken. Dry blood coated the side of his head. It hurt to look at. Ander couldn't even face Michael eye to eye.

Delilah's mouth was a straight, stern line. "Salt. Too much of it. It gets us high, gets us strong, but an overdose causes, well . . . this. They'll recover, but it'll depend on how much they had and how strong they are. Also, they're probably dehydrated and starving. Mayrez didn't exactly take care of her victims." She snapped her fingers in front of Michael and he flinched, mumbling. With a grimace, she continued, "They should be out of the salt phase in a few hours. We'll time it. That will probably give us an estimate of how far away the Cast is. Mayrez wouldn't have used more salt than they needed. She was never one to go around wasting her supplies."

"What would've happened if we hadn't saved them?" Ander asked.

"Cast would have had them. Some people do join them willingly. The hierarchy of angels works the same way as the demons'. The higher the angel, the more likely another blend or angel is to listen to them, especially if they're blitzed on salt. The rest who put up a fight? Torture, more salt, starvation, closed spaces, darkness. Whatever it takes to get them to break." Delilah sighed, her voice heavy. She clearly knew what she was talking about, maybe a little too much.

Ander didn't want to pry, so he turned to Michael, as he asked her. "Can I stay with him?"

"Why?" Sytri asked, leaning over.

"He was the one who agreed to let me go with them." Ander paused. "I want to make sure he's okay. Like he did for me."

"Mayrez kidnapped you, so I don't think he helped you too much," Sytri muttered. Ander glared and Sytri froze. "I'm sorry. I just— Never mind."

"Yeah. You can stay with him if you want," Delilah said, holding out her hand. "I trust you, Ander. You saved Vega. Nobody against us would let that asshole live."

Ander grasped her calloused hand, and she gripped his tightly; if Ander didn't heal fast, her strength would've left a bruise.

"Vega's not all bad, I don't think." He glanced at said demon, who was currently checking on the others. Not a casualty on their side. Lots of injuries, but no deaths. Relief welled inside of him, and he let it out in a deep sigh. Everything was okay for a night.

"I guess not," Sytri muttered. "But I can still choose to not care for his personality."

Delilah smirked, rolling her eyes. "Don't blame you for that after he tore down a damn tree at your house."

Ander raised an eyebrow. Had Vega taken the blame for that? No wonder Delilah hadn't marched there that day and kicked them out. Ander's heart softened just a bit for the idiot.

Delilah motioned to Ander and Sytri. "Anyway, we're guiding the Couriers into the school, if you want to help. We have a medical ward, but it isn't big enough for a group this size. Building one that is should be our next step, I guess."

"Well, hopefully we don't have this many injured again." Ander took Michael delicately by the wrist. A simple tug forward and the Courier followed. His head swayed side to side with each step and he murmured something again. Inaudible, indecipherable.

They were brought into a building that was to eventually be a school for larger classes. The residents of Millstone hoped to make it a thriving place, and they planned ahead. For now, all the furniture and equipment had been pushed to the side to bring in mattresses, water, and food.

Ander helped Michael sit down, then brought a water bottle to his mouth, tilting his head back. Most of it made it down his throat, Michael instinctively swallowing even in his haze. A small sliver streamed down the side of his face. Ander wiped it with his sleeve, and his eyes narrowed. This wasn't right.

"Were you two close or . . . what?" Sytri asked from behind Ander. There was a scuffing noise, as if he was kicking the ground.

"I don't really know him at all," Ander whispered. He repeated the process until the bottle was halfway empty—he had to be careful not to give him too much. After dabbing at the dried blood with a cloth beside the mattress, he slowly eased Michael down. As soon as Michael's head hit the pillow, his eyes closed. Ander stared at him for a second. "He doesn't really know me either, though."

"You're acting like you're close."

"We weren't. We aren't." Ander looked behind him, into Sytri's eyes. "Are you jealous?"

"No! What? No. I mean, now I'm not. Now that I know you guys weren't like *real* close or something. Whatever." Sytri squatted next to him. "Change of subject. It's weird, right, how salt can do this to you if you're part angel. Blend blood can mess us up too. But instead of making us into lumbering zombies, we become more like the raging, biting kind." He snapped his teeth. "It's why I'm nervous every time I drink from you. I don't want to end up like that. I might . . . I might hurt you."

"You would never hurt me, Sytri," Ander said softly. He leaned back on the palms of his hands. Around him, six other blends were being set on their mattresses by other members of Millstone.

Four of the survivors were familiar—they were Couriers; the rest he couldn't place. Probably snatched at another time. The thought left a sour taste in his mouth. His nose crinkled.

Mayrez was gone now, though. Finding Ronan was the sole objective again. That had once been the only goal, the finish line, but so many things filled Ander's mind now. Other people he worried about—he had never had other people.

He smiled to himself; Ronan would be blown away by all the relationships he'd formed. Proud of him too, for fighting and saving fellow blends. And now that Ander had proven his worth in Millstone, hopefully they could stay here, together.

"Thank you, by the way, for letting me go during the fight," Ander said after a moment. "I didn't expect you to." Sytri was silent. Ander scratched at his feathers nervously. "I was scared you wouldn't."

More silence.

"Yeah. About that," Sytri said slowly. "I didn't . . . I didn't *do* that."

"What do you mean?"

"I didn't do that, Ander. When we were out there, I knew with absolute certainty I wasn't going to let you go. I was so afraid that if I did, Mayrez would take you."

"But you *did* let go of me."

"I don't think I did."

"What are you saying?"

Sytri peered around them, at the other blends and demons, currently preoccupied with helping the rescued. He turned back to Ander, his mouth a tight line. "I think you *made* me."

Ander's heart stilled. "I don't understand."

"When you yelled at me to let you go, something happened. I wasn't in control of myself." Sytri looked away. "It wasn't me."

Ander just sat there, then brought his hand to his mouth, tentatively touching his lips. "That can't be . . . true," he whispered, with a glance at Michael, who was thankfully still sleeping. "That's not an ability, is it? I haven't heard of an angel who could do that."

"Maybe it's not the sort of power an angel would tell anyone about. Why would they?"

He grimaced. "If it's real, what am I supposed to do with it?"

"What do you mean?"

"It's a horrible thing, Sytri. If you're right." He could feel his tongue in his mouth, heavy, foreign. "Commanding others and taking away their autonomy? That's not something I want to do. It'd be like— It'd be like when Mayrez was in my head. But fucking worse." He gazed around the room. No one was paying them any attention, but suddenly Ander felt watched, as if everyone already knew. "That's not the power of someone who is . . . who is *good*."

"Your powers have nothing to do with who you are as a person."

Ander remained silent. When was the last time he'd told someone to do something? He was never one to say much, much less demand anything from anyone. He dug his nails into the flesh of his knees.

"I told Tephera to leave you alone . . . I've yelled at Vega to leave us alone. And they did. Both those times were after Tephera had put that salt in me." Ander's pulse quickened. "Did that do something?"

"I don't know. Maybe. Salt does bring out the angel. If your power had always been there, even a little bit, the salt definitely would have made it a lot stronger. But maybe it wasn't that, or wasn't *only* that. It's . . . I'm thinking, what if you *have* done this before Tephera gave you the salt? Would they even have noticed?" Sytri paused. "Because my head tried to, like, tell me it was normal. If I'd had any doubt in myself, I'd almost believe that you just convinced me. That it wasn't strange."

Ander paled. That was worse; manipulation done insidiously. He gritted his teeth. He had to test his voice, see if what Sytri said was true. But how?

He didn't want to talk to anyone now. If he accidentally made a request, it would be a misuse of power. If Sytri was right about this, if Ander had an ability . . . an ability like that, he couldn't bring himself to test it on someone unaware.

Ander glanced over at Sytri, who was scowling at the ground, tail flicking behind him. Sytri hated the idea of losing control of himself more than anything; how could Ander ask him to be a test subject for this? *And if I can't ask him, the person who trusts me the most, who can I?*

"I just won't use it," Ander said out loud.

"What do you mean you won't use it?" Sytri blurted.

"What I said. I can't do that to people."

"You did it to me."

"Possibly. We don't know yet," Ander said. "And if I did, it was by accident."

"Yeah. So you should figure it out. Because if you *can*, if it's *real* it could be dangerous to not practice using it. Or you're going to accidentally use it all the time." Sytri's eyes darted around the room. "And then someone else will catch on. Or worse, you'll end up doing something far more damaging than making me drop you in the middle of a fight."

Why does he have to make sense? Ander sighed, closing his eyes. "This sucks."

"It's not that bad. I mean, if you can figure it out, you could do a lot of good." Sytri kissed him on the forehead. "And do less manipulating. Though I suppose it's a good thing you made me let you go. The fight could have turned out a lot different if you hadn't helped Vega. I'll admit it."

Ander couldn't argue with that, and he was glad Sytri felt that some good had come out of it. Perhaps it *wasn't* all that bad. Dread still twisted his stomach, though; how could it not? If what Sytri suggested was the truth, Ander's voice had more power than he'd ever wanted it to.

Cold sweat formed on his brow. How much strength did his words have?

He wasn't sure he wanted to find out.

CHAPTER TWENTY-ONE

E ven though Ander had planned on watching Michael until he woke from his drugged slumber, it proved impossible. The night had been exhausting, and after just thirty minutes, it hit him hard. Eventually he'd given in to the heaviness under his eyelids, and he curled up against Sytri, finding peace. Sleep.

He wasn't sure how much of it he got before it was interrupted.

"Ander?"

Not ready to be awake.

"Ander?"

Maybe whoever that was would give up.

"Ander, is it really you?"

Weird thing to be asked.

"I'm tired," Ander muttered, rolling over to the side, only to start falling. He lurched upward, stopping himself, eyes wide as he swung his head around. Wait, where was he? Big building, bunch of mattresses. Michael staring at him.

"Michael!" Ander yelped a little too loudly.

The Courier looked so much better now. Light had come to his eyes. His face was still thinner than it should be, but the pale raggedness had dissipated and a lovely red had filled in his cheeks. Behind him, solid white wings fluttered softly, as if trying to wave off dust.

"Ander, it is you." Michael's eyes scanned him. Heat rose in Ander's face. Why was it so pleasing that the Courier had remembered him? "What . . . Where are we?" Michael tried sitting up properly in his bed, but the strain made his arms shake.

"You're in Millstone," Ander said, grabbing Michael's elbow, helping steady him. "The people here rescued you from Mayrez and then brought you here."

Michael stared at him blankly for a moment and then looked to Ander's side. At Sytri, who was already awake, already glaring.

"Millstone. That explains the demon."

"Actually, he's unrelated. That's Sytri," Ander said, followed by a scratchy laugh. "I made a deal with him."

"Oh no."

"Fuck you too, buddy," Sytri sneered. His first words to Michael, great.

"I didn't mean it like that; it's just— Never mind. I apologize." Michael surveyed the room, then turned to Ander. "You did what you needed to, I assume. And saved my brethren?"

Ander nodded. "We saved everyone we could find, and there were a lot. Mayrez had more people than we thought she would."

"She was going to take us . . . to the Cast." Michael's voice was solemn. "I don't know much about them, but we've heard rumors during our travels. I wasn't fond of the idea. She picked up others along the way, trading weaker Couriers and capturing stronger blends." He stared at Ander. "We're so far from home."

"Yeah, turned out me and Mayrez had a similar path."

Michael glanced at his comrades, who were still sleeping. "We must return. We've been gone for what? Weeks? Months? Gardners must be in a state of panic." He tried to stand up, and Ander eased him back down.

"Michael, relax. It's okay. You need to rest. You're still suffering from the salt."

"The salt," Michael repeated, his eyes wide. "That disgusting . . . disgusting dark angel." He shivered, then keeled over, vomiting a familiar black ooze, before eventually bringing his hand to his mouth. "I'm sorry, I'm sorry." His feathers fluttered erratically, and he took a shaky breath. There were lines creased under his eyes.

"Tephera," Ander whispered, staring at the dark, strange liquid. He gingerly placed a hand on Michael's back, rubbed in slow circles.

Michael stared up at him with wide eyes. "You met them?"

"Yeah." Ander had to hold back his own repulsion. "Sytri, go get something so I can clean this up."

"Why do I have to—"

"Sytri, please," Ander snapped, and instantly regretted it. He had to watch himself. He couldn't talk like that. *Because what if it's real?* Sytri bristled for a second before walking off. *It scares him that I could be controlling him. I've got to figure this out.*

"If you weren't in Mayrez's clutches, how did you come by them?" Michael asked, wiping at the corners of his mouth.

"Was lucky enough to stumble into their nest." Ander laughed dryly. "And stumble away."

"You ran into that beast? And escaped all on your own?"

"What? No. I had Sytri."

"Still, incredible, even with a demon. I didn't think anything could get away from that creature." Michael lay back against the pillow, closing his eyes. "Mayrez brought us through there and that angel poured salt into our bodies one by one and weighed us in its cold hands before wrapping sacks around our necks. It told her how much to give us each day, to keep us in that mindless, horrible state. They're a little pitstop on the way I suppose." His eyes shot open. "Was it you who gave them their scar?"

"What?"

"Tephera had a scar down their eye, made of light. Mayrez asked them about it, and they said that a little cretin blend had escaped and left them with it."

Even though speaking about Tephera at all, thinking about them for a moment, made Ander sick, he couldn't help but laugh at that. "Yeah, I guess I'm the cretin." At least he'd made an impact. But it also made him nervous; Tephera didn't seem like the sort one wanted as an enemy.

Michael hummed. "Incredible. Seems you are far stronger than we gave you credit for."

"Once again, I wouldn't be here if it wasn't for Sytri," Ander corrected. "Anyway, where did you go from there? What's her process for moving blends?"

"Mayrez kept us in that state to deliver us to the Cast. Which is . . . absurd. To think there are angels helping a demon do such horrid things. When I tried to reason with Tephera, they said that after enough salt, we'd be so angelic we'd *understand* what the Cast was doing. But that can't be true, right? The angels that protect Gardners would never work with Mayrez."

"I don't think they would either. But after meeting Tephera, I can't put all angels into one box anymore," Ander said grimly.

"I suppose not. But what does that mean? That we can't trust angels at all?"

"I don't know."

"Here." Sytri appeared again, handing a damp rag to Ander, who took it from him and wiped at the spill on the floor. The black ooze was strange and had spread like sticky ink. He had to hold back an urge to vomit.

"So, I owe it to the demon for keeping you alive, then?" Michael asked with a forced chuckle. "It was weighing on me so heavily, Ander, that I had promised you protection, only to deliver you to the worst possible death: Mayrez consuming you alive."

Ander's heart thudded. "What? No, Michael, when I joined you, I told you, my blood was on my hands only. You shouldn't have felt guilty. And as you can see, I'm fine." He gestured at himself, patted a palm on his chest.

"It is mostly because of me," Sytri said, putting his hand on Ander's shoulder. "But it's also a lot of Ander too. We're a good team." He smirked. His tail swished behind him, kicking up dust.

Ander smiled at him.

Michael watched them with scrutinizing eyes. He stared at Sytri's hand for a solid second before turning to Ander, biting his lip. He had seemed like the most open-minded of the Couriers, but he probably had limits too. Ander couldn't dwell on that thought.

"If you're up, the others should be soon as well," Ander said, glancing back at them.

"I hope not. Louis will not be happy when they realize we're in Millstone."

"Won't they be excited that they're not Mayrez's prisoner at least?"

"Eh. Their feelings might be about the same either way," Michael said with a scowl. "They were the one who thought this was a gross town full of blends and demons engaging in intercourse. They're not . . . they're not fond of demons at all. The idea of a blend or angel willingly Partnering with one disgusts them." He quickly waved his hands. "Not me though, you know this." Michael's face turned a bright red and he avoided looking directly at Ander or Sytri.

Oh. Ander's ears went hot and next to him Sytri snickered.

"I can never thank you enough for somehow finding us, through everything we've been through, and saving us from Mayrez's hold. It was atrocious being her slave." Michael grimaced, his eyes dark. "When you have that much salt, you can't do anything but listen. You can see your body acting on its own, but you're . . . watching your actions through a foggy mirror. Mayrez used that to her advantage."

Ander couldn't imagine. It had been wretched enough to be on stage while she tried to auction him away to a crowd of hungry mouths. But to be blitzed out on salt as well? Aware of demons ordering him around but unable to stop himself from obeying? Sickening.

He bit down on his lip again. If Sytri was right, that's what his own power would do. He couldn't bring that pain to others. He couldn't be the one to deliver such a thing.

"Ander? Are you all right?" Michael asked.

"What? Yes. I . . . I'm glad we found you, Michael," Ander said, bringing himself back to the conversation. "You said you felt guilty, but I felt guilty for abandoning you at Afriel. I just ran. That's been weighing on me."

"It seems we both carried remorse, didn't we? I don't know if that's the angel part of us or the human part," Michael said with a laugh.

"Sounds human to me," Sytri inserted. He sat and leaned against Ander, staring at Michael with calculating eyes. "So, what will you do now? Now that you're free? Are you going to stay here in Millstone, or—"

"No, no, as I said, Gardners needs us. We can't leave our city behind."

"It's not right to keep hiding things from the people there," Ander said sharply. "You shouldn't do that. The world out here is so much more complicated than I could have imagined. I was . . . unprepared." Michael lowered his head, but Ander felt no remorse for his tone. "What was the point of hiding everything? What is there to gain? You said that telling them would frighten them, but that's the point, isn't it?"

"Tell them what?" Michael said with a dry laugh. "That demons look like us? That they'll drug you, traffic you? Sip your blood like cheap wine?" He groaned. "What use would that be?"

"So when they leave, like I did, they won't be caught off guard!" Ander brought his hand to his chest. "The world has so much going on, and I had no clue."

"And how would the news have changed the outcome?" Michael asked. "What would you have done differently?" He narrowed his eyes. "I guess I know one thing; you would've been petrified. You would have waited longer before traveling. Maybe you would have never ventured out here at all."

"Maybe I wouldn't have. Who knows. But going out here, knowing nothing? It made me a lot more vulnerable than I would've been if I had a sliver of a clue on what was going on. What would happen to a whole group of oblivious people? What would happen if a demon snuck into Gardners?"

"Our angels would never let that—"

"It happened to Afriel, and they're right next door. They got slaughtered!"

"They instigated it! They always fought every demon they saw—they made themselves a target."

"What, now you're saying they deserved it?"

"That's not what I'm . . . Ander, look, I get it. I see your side, but I'm firm on mine. If we tell them, they'll go mad. Every neighbor would be a demon in their eyes. It'd be like the Salem witch trials all over again."

"The angels would know who was a real demon and who wasn't."

"Do you really think logic is going to stop the paranoid?"

Ander fumed. He didn't understand. He did, but he didn't. Still, after a moment, he took a deep breath, laid his hand on top of Sytri's.

"You met Tephera," he said softly. "You know now that it's not just demons out here who want to hurt us. Angels, demons, fellow blends: it doesn't matter what we are anymore. We all have different ideologies, and if the wrong person crosses the wrong person, it ends in blood. Yes, when I left, I almost died. I've almost died every day." His shoulders stiffened, and his throat felt tight.

"But I wouldn't go back and change any choice I've made up until now, even if I knew the outcome. Because my choices led me to Sytri. They led to me learning about myself. Led me to a town where demons and blends have found harmony, built something I didn't know could be made anymore. They led me to rescuing you, Michael." Ander narrowed his eyes. "People can be scared and still make good choices. We've been doing that since the beginning of time. Why would we stop now?"

Michael was quiet.

Sytri wrapped his tail around Ander's leg. "Tell them if *you* want, Ander. We can head to Gardners."

"I can't yet. I still have to go to Atlasville."

"Atlasville?" Ander looked up to see Delilah hovering near them. She took a sip from a water bottle. "What were you heading there for? The Cast burnt that place down like a month ago."

CHAPTER TWENTY-TWO

A nder wasn't sure how many days he'd spent cooped up in his room. Sytri had brought him food at least five times; that had to have happened over a day, possibly over two. He also remembered a sunrise and sunset from the shadows and colors it had painted on the walls.

Even as time moved around him, he found himself frozen.

Ronan. The possibility of his death had always hung in the back of Ander's skull. He hadn't seen him in over three years—of course it had been a possibility. *Most* people were dead for fuck's sake. But somehow, in his head, Ronan had been beyond the statistics, incapable of dying.

But he was dead, everyone was. Ander was. Sytri was. Everyone.

"You need anything?" Sytri stood at the doorway, hand gripping the opposite arm like he was unsure of himself. He kept checking on Ander like that, timidly. Ander disliked it. But he disliked Sytri's distance even more. It created a hollowness in Ander's chest that burrowed deeper each day, threatening to pull the rest of him in with it.

He shivered and waved slowly in Sytri's direction. "Can you . . . can you come here?" he asked, steadying his voice as best he could.

Sytri nodded and walked over, then sat on the edge of the bed, mattress sinking with his weight. They sat there, side by side, and Ander leaned against him.

Sytri's form was a comfort and yet it was breaking him. It was too easy to fall apart when there was someone there to hold the pieces. He did his best to ignore the deep ache that permeated him, the agony in his bones. It was different to any other pain he'd felt. Like being squeezed to death by barbed wire. When would it stop?

Perhaps never.

Sytri wrapped an arm around him, tail curled up, encircling his leg, the end resting on the curve of his back. Ander tried to focus on that and anything else except the one thing barraging his mind.

Ronan had died a mere month ago.

Ander had wasted time. If he hadn't been such a goddamn coward, he might have reached Ronan before then. They could have returned to Gardners, safe and sound.

They could have been together right now.

Sytri was staring at him with glowing green eyes. Ander grabbed his hand, squeezed it tight. *Things could have been different.* He stifled the sob in his throat, pushing away those thoughts. Of course he loved Sytri and was thankful to be with him, thankful to have him.

But that didn't stop the hurt.

"Ander," Sytri said softly. He pushed back Ander's curled bangs, brushed a finger under his eye, wiping away a stream of tears. "Ander, it's okay. All right? You did everything you could do. You've done so much."

The words made Ander's thoughts coil and knot together. "I should have left sooner," he muttered.

"You don't know if that would have made a difference. Maybe Ronan was already gone in the beginning. There's so many ifs in the world, Ander; you can't make yourself the deciding factor on everything." Sytri pulled him close, kissed his forehead. "I know you want to believe you can change it all. But you can't."

"I could, though," Ander said, eyes wide. "Ronan might have been alive, and I could've changed everything. If I have an actual gift." He twisted his tongue in his mouth. Bit down on it. "I could have made the angels let me go sooner, kept demons away from me. I could have commanded my way through this whole Earth . . . I could have made it to him."

"Ander. You said yourself that you don't want to command anything."

Ander gritted his teeth. "I know. You're right. You're right. It's just . . . I could have." He was shaking again. His thoughts were sinking to dangerous depths. That happened when he lay in bed for days, thinking about all the possibilities, all the ifs, as Sytri had said.

If Ander's voice had power though, he could make his own ifs *real*.

Ander unraveled himself from Sytri, splayed out on the bed, and stared at the ceiling. He had saved Sytri, himself, and now Michael and the other blends. He had befriended Delilah and Vega, found a place in this perfect town. With power he could help defend it, he could keep the Cast at bay. He could prove himself.

But no matter what he did now, he had already lost Ronan. And saving him had been the point of all this.

"You told Michael you wouldn't change anything," Sytri said, holding Ander's hand. "Do you still mean that?"

If he could go back and pick saving Ronan over meeting Sytri, would he? It was fine to wonder, selfish to ask it out loud. But Ander didn't have the energy to be angry at Sytri. In fact, he wanted to answer but found himself at a loss for words.

He wanted both realities. The one where he was with Sytri. The other, unreachable path where he had left sooner, found Ronan. Lived happily ever after. *Never met Sytri at all. But I want him too.*

Now he was the selfish one.

"I don't know," Ander said faintly. "I don't want to think about it."

"Okay."

They lay there in silence again. Every so often, Ander's breath would come out in a sigh as he willed down the urge to cry again.

"Sytri. What do I do now?" he asked. "What do you do now?"

"What do you mean?"

"Our whole deal was made because I wanted you to take me to Atlasville, to find Ronan. Now that it's gone, that he's gone . . . what happens to us?"

Silence.

Then, with a gravelly voice, Sytri spoke. "We're still the same for the moment. We'd know if the deal had broken immediately. It has a feeling, and it's not a good one. Though our deal could weaken in time, with this new information." He swallowed. "And eventually fade away."

Ander didn't like that. The deal, curled up next to his heart, was the only warm thing inside of him. Sytri couldn't leave him with that promise made.

People left him all the time. But Sytri couldn't.

"Do you want to be with me?" Ander asked.

"Of course."

Ander's pulse quickened. "Then we should make a new deal, a stronger one. One that can't come undone."

"A deal has nothing to do with if I want to leave you." Sytri's eyes narrowed.

"That sounds like someone who wants to leave me."

"Ander, I don't want to leave you!"

"How do I know?" Ander sat up, clutching his chest. "How do I know that? I'm so useless, I don't have anything to give you, Sytri; I'm not enough. Everyone's always leaving." Thoughts were piling, falling, scattering. He couldn't hold on to them. He brought his knees to his chest, tears falling, words spilling. "People leave. They can say they want you and bring you into their home and still decide you're not good enough. They do it all the time."

"What are you talking about?" Sytri put his hand on Ander's back and brought him closer. "I wouldn't abandon you, deal or no deal." He smiled gently. "You should know that by now."

"Everyone's always left. My foster parents didn't want me. My foster siblings didn't want me. Ronan was the only one who ever—ever did. And now he's left me too."

Sytri stared. "He didn't leave *you*, Ander. He just . . . *left*. There's a difference. Sometimes people have to leave."

"But where did he even go?" Ander asked, his heart pounding fiercely, like it was threatening to burst out of his body. "Since the Gates of Hell are broken, where do souls go? Where did Ronan go?"

"Well, if he was a terrible fucking guy, he'll have gone to Hell and will probably get out pretty soon as a demon. That's what happens to sinners. But turning demon gets rid of all the human bits. Most people don't remember their previous life. On the other hand, if he was a blend or decent human, he'll have gone to Heaven, I'd assume. Angels are more likely to remember what Earth was like, but I don't know if humans-turned-angel have been coming back to Earth."

"What do you mean?"

"All the angels I've run into have acted like they've been angels all their lives. I haven't heard a single one talk about their past life as a human, have you? Maybe whoever is in charge isn't letting the newly turned out of Heaven. But also it is, you know, Heaven. So maybe they don't want to leave in the first place. As opposed to us demons who can't *wait* to get out of Hell."

"So either he's a demon who will want to leave Hell ASAP, or he's an angel who may or may not be able to—or want to—leave Heaven." Ander groaned. "Of course he'll be an angel! Ronan's like the perfect person. But maybe he could still get to Earth somehow and—"

"Ander, that's most likely not going to happen."

"Shut up. I know that, okay. But it could. I could still find him unless . . . What would happen if he died again?" Ander froze. "What would happen if you died?"

Sytri shifted uncomfortably, eyes downcast. "I die."

"And?"

"That's it. Humans get this weird corporeal, earthly body first that protects the soul. When they die, that soul is released and takes on the form of an angel or demon. And when you're killed at that point, that's it. Whether you had the first human life or not."

"You've got nothing left?" Ander's stomach churned.

"It's an absolute end." Sytri shrugged, face tense. "Never had that extra body. You're lucky."

Ander's mouth twisted and tears swelled up in his eyes again. *What the fuck. What the fucking fuck.* "That's not fair."

"What?"

"This is all you have." Ander held back a sob. *Oh god.* "That's not right."

"It's just how things are." Sytri's voice was hollow.

"But I've been making us do so much shit that could've gotten you killed."

"You didn't *make* me do anything. I forced you into a deal with me, Ander." Sytri glanced away, biting his lip. "Don't forget that."

"But you could've told me what it would've meant if you—if you got *hurt*." Ander hiccupped, wiped at his eyes. He couldn't say *killed* again, now knowing the horrible severity of it.

"What difference would it have made? I've known my whole life, and I haven't cared. And aren't you similar? Weren't you always living your life like you only had one? You said you weren't religious."

This was all too much to deal with at once. Ander dug his nails into his knees while taking deep breaths. Maybe Ronan could come back, but once Sytri left, he'd be gone.

"I *did* live my life thinking it was the only one I had." Ander's voice hitched. "And I was cautious with it. When I learned there really was an afterlife I was— I *am* scared of it because it's still so incomprehensible to me. But you don't even have that unknown."

"Maybe it's better that way. Because I do know about Hell, and I'd hate to end up back there." Sytri's eyes hazed over. "And I'm not getting into Heaven. So maybe nothing is better than something, sometimes." He laughed dryly. "Hell, maybe nothing is better than Heaven when you're a demon."

"It can't be, right?" *Tephera came from Heaven, though.* Tephera the angel with eyes white as the moon. Ander shivered, a cold finger walking up the knobs of his spine. "I don't know. Demons and angels can both be horrifying. Maybe Michael was right, maybe I would never have left Gardners if I knew all that I know now. Or maybe I would have left quicker."

"Why quicker?"

How could he answer that? Blood drained from his face at the thought of telling Sytri the truth. But Ander was broken enough to let the words out through his cracks.

Maybe they would heal him on the way.

"I was so sick of being alive in Gardners. Done with it. The only hope I had was that maybe Ronan was out here somewhere and maybe I could find him. And I figured that if I didn't, something eventually would end me and I wouldn't have to do it myself, you know? So if I'd known the world was such shit, that Ronan *wasn't* here, then maybe I would've left sooner to get it over with—" His own sobs choked him.

"Ander, wait." Sytri's voice wavered as if on thin ice. "Holy shit, what are you saying—"

"Because if I'd known Ronan was dead back then, I'd have wanted to be dead too. I still feel like that now but it's not as fierce as it would've been. Like, I don't want to leave you behind, like everyone left me. And maybe that's stupid and maybe I should just want to live because that's what I want to do, but I can't."

"It's not stupid," Sytri snapped as tears welled in the corners of his eyes. Ander couldn't recall seeing him cry before. "It's not stupid to want to live, regardless of the reason. For me or yourself—hell, fucking stay alive out of spite. I don't give a shit, just keep living." Sytri pulled him into an embrace, his chin resting in the crook of Ander's neck. His claws dug into Ander's back. "And if you need me, you got me. And I'm not leaving, Ander. Not anytime soon."

Ander nodded, slumping against him.

He didn't have anything besides Sytri's words. So they had to be enough.

He stared blankly across the room. Sitting on the bedside table was his camera, the lens shining even as dust settled on the edges. He had wanted to take pictures of him and Ronan again, like when everything had been normal.

God, he was going to throw up.

CHAPTER TWENTY-THREE

"**G**ot everything you need?"

"You make it sound like we're going on a trip." Ander chuckled softly. He grabbed his bag off the floor in front of the door and flung it over his shoulders. "It's just a walk."

"Don't say it like that. You're going to take photos and stuff right? That makes it a *romantic* walk. Like couples-on-the-beach shit."

"Except without the beach?"

"Except without the beach." Sytri nodded and Ander snickered again. Sytri immediately bristled. "What, I'm serious! This counts as, like, our first date. I got all dressed up."

"You're literally just wearing a new pair of pants." Ander scoffed. "You're still shirtless."

"They're *nice* pants." Sytri did a twist, and Ander was briefly distracted by his stomach muscles. "Vega even had someone sew a spot in for my tail so they weren't just jeans I had torn. So, you know, he's probably gonna say I owe him down the line or something. But anyway, I don't need a shirt. They're pointless. Can't use my extra arms in those things."

"I think you simply don't like wearing shirts."

"By the way you look at me, I don't think you mind." Sytri grinned.

Ander flushed and elbowed Sytri, but the slightest ripple of warmth beat through his heart. Sytri was good at making him feel normal again, at making things seem fine. *They are fine. I am fine.*

That was why Ander was doing this. He'd been cooped up in the house for so long, like a little hermit, and Sytri had been so patient. Enough time had been spent mourning, and Ander couldn't bear to have more slip through his hands. He took a deep breath and opened the door.

It was afternoon, the sun halfway between the middle of the sky and the horizon. A beautiful cast of orange and silky yellow light brought out the shadows and highlights of the earth. He was outnumbered by colors upon colors, overwhelmed by the smell of rich dirt and oxygen-soaked air. Ander tapped on the shutter button repeatedly. The softest bend of his index finger pressing into grooved, hard plastic. Not enough to take a picture, but enough so that the familiar motion sent a soothing wave over him.

Millstone was still beautiful. After everything that had happened, that had not changed. The world was still breathing and Ander was still in it.

He stopped in the center of the cobblestone street and took a picture of a home in mid-build. Its wooden skeleton stood strongly among all the other finished houses, ready to join them. After a moment, the image slipped out from camera, Ander extracting it with the tips of his fingers. "I've got the photo book in my bag; can you get it for me?"

Sytri opened the pouch, sliding out the red book. He'd brought it home one night during Ander's episode. It had been a gift, an offering for a better Ander, and was a bit beaten but still nice. He opened it now to be greeted by a picture of Sytri's face. His lovely face. Ander chuckled to himself and Sytri peered over him.

"It's that photo where I look really hot. What you laughing at it for?" Sytri grumbled.

"Nothing," Ander said quickly. "Nothing. I just—I just love that you were the first thing I took a photo of." He slid the picture of the house right next to it. Sytri scowled before tugging the camera off Ander in one fluid motion, almost knocking him off his feet.

"Whoa! Sytri!" he yelped, swaying on his heels.

There was a flash as he regained most of his balance. He squinted at Sytri, who was taking the photo out of the camera. Sytri then proceeded to yank the book from Ander's hand, remove the photo of the house, and slide the new one into its place.

"Better," Sytri said, grinning a little too smugly. Ander stared down at the book. He was a fucking mess in the picture, and it was kind of blurry. A lot blurry, actually.

"I look like a cryptid." Ander snorted. "Why'd you do that?" He appeared so flustered, one of his legs out of the frame, eyes wide. "It's so bad." He held back another snicker, covered his mouth with his hand.

"Hey! It's better now," Sytri said, pointing at the book. "Now we're beside each other."

Ander's laughter died off as he glanced back at the album. Sytri was grinning triumphantly in his photo, the sun making his hair fantastic even in that small room they'd been cramped in. He was so perfect, even caught off guard. *So beautiful.*

"Put it back in my bag," he said, handing it over to Sytri.

"I'll just hold it." Sytri tossed it in the air and caught it with his tail, which wrapped around it securely.

Ander smirked. "You're just showing off."

"Yeah. You think it's hot or what?"

"Shut up." He blushed, waving his hand, before heading over to the gates of Millstone, Sytri following suit.

"Hey, hey, where we going?" Sytri asked, staring at the gate. "I thought that maybe you'd want to meet up with Delilah or Vega. I don't know, go see someone . . ."

Ander shook his head. "No, not yet." His voice was soft. He did want to see someone, specifically Delilah. He wanted to interrogate her and confirm that there weren't even rumors of survivors from Atlasville. Sytri had already asked about the chances of someone being left in the aftermath. The answer had apparently been grim. But what if there was just a hint that *someone* had made it? Hell, what if Ronan had left before the fire?

Stop. Stop thinking like this. All Ander needed was that sliver of possibility to go clutching at some web-thin hope that Ronan had persisted through everything. It was dangerous and maddening.

Concern was evident in Sytri's eyes. Hell, how stressed was he to suggest talking to Vega? So, Ander had to . . . he had to move on. He couldn't and wouldn't pester Delilah with those questions. He wouldn't chase anymore ghosts.

He clenched his jaw and then sighed. "I'll talk to them later. I promise. Right now, I just want to go take pictures, okay?" *Talking has to wait until I'm not going to break.*

"Okay," Sytri said cautiously. He put his hand on Ander's shoulder. "I want to make sure you're fine, ya know? And Michael seems worried about you too. So I guess he's a decent guy. Too decent, for someone you said you barely knew, but whatever." He rolled his eyes.

"So he and the Couriers are still here, then?" Ander asked as they passed through the gates. A Demon gave them a once-over as they left but nothing more. Leaving Millstone was a lot less dramatic than leaving Gardners.

"Yeah. Though one of the Couriers is not fucking happy. Some dude named Louis has been throwing a fucking fit. Always yipping about how the demons make him uncomfortable and that he didn't want to be in orgy-town-Millstone."

Ander snorted. "Orgy-town?"

"Yeah. Which, as we know, is not true. But then Vega had to go and run his damn mouth and freak the dude out, so now he's extra determined to leave. But Michael and this girl Mercy still need time to heal. They were on a lot of salt; it hurts for them to move around, and every so often they'll have sudden . . . I don't know, delusions? They see shit that isn't there and freak the fuck out about it."

Ander shivered as ice crept down his spine. How much salt had Tephera given *him*? Was it close to the same amount as Michael and Mercy? He didn't think he had hallucinated, but maybe he *had* and hadn't realized.

How could anyone willingly go through that uncertainty, that loss of control?

"Do angels really just get high off the stuff? Even though it makes them act and feel like that?" Ander asked with a grimace.

"I mean, it's not like humans haven't always been getting high on things that make them feel like shit. I think angels take it first because they know it'll make them stronger, and then like any drug, it gets addicting."

"I don't feel stronger."

"I mean, you said you might have stopped Tephera."

"Might." *But that has to be impossible.* Even on salt, he shouldn't have been able to control an *angel*. An Archangel. A pure, unfiltered, straight-from-Heaven-itself Archangel.

But then again, what did he know? Ander touched his wrist. Maybe whatever angel was in him was *stronger.* Like Vega had said.

His skin pricked and his feathers bristled with static, as if a storm were on the horizon. He stopped walking and looked around them. He'd been wandering, not really paying attention to where they were going. The sounds of Millstone had long faded away, leaving a silence that sunk into his shoulders like heavy rain. *If I had strength in me this whole time, I could've used it.* A roll of thunder broke out overhead. *I could've saved him.*

"Hey, you okay?" There was an audible *pap* of grass as Sytri stepped closer. And the electricity in the air seemed to shirk back.

Ander gritted his teeth. "As okay as I can be."

Sytri went quiet. That was fine.

"It's just hard, you know? And I've even dealt with death before. I've been to my fair share of funerals, with open caskets, having to look at embalmed people I vaguely knew. And then when demons showed up, it was everywhere. All the bodies, all the empty eyes. They were unavoidable."

Ander pointed his camera upward. The glossy, soft orange of sunlight fell gracefully on the leaves, covering them like a splash of liquid gold. He snapped a photo of it, the sun shimmering between the dark and cold leaves of the forest.

He sighed. "And I told you. That I—I was in a bad place. Those three years *ate* at me. I was so sick of being alone. I ended in some weird limbo, too scared to be alive on my own and too scared to kill myself." His fingers gripped the plastic camera tightly. "But eventually I worked up the courage to leave. If I found Ronan,

I could be alive again. Really alive. If I couldn't, or if he was dead, then eventually something would get me and that would be it. Problem solved."

Sytri's breath hitched, clearly the beginning of a protest.

"I don't, by the way, want to die as much. I'd rather live," Ander reassured him, voice strained. "Even if this world sucks. A lot. And everything is horrifying, all the time. But that's okay. I think." He stared at his camera and then up at Sytri, who was closer than he'd been before, but still a good foot away. His expression was unreadable, though he didn't seem afraid. "Right now I want to live. For you, and to . . . I don't know, to figure things out."

"You know you can't find the answers for everything, right?"

Ander paused; he hadn't expected Sytri to speak yet for some reason.

"I know. I just want to find out what I can, like why the gates broke, why the angels won't tell us what this is all about," Ander said slowly. "I'd like to travel and see what this newer world has to offer. I want to try and make it better, like Delilah is doing in Millstone."

"How can you make it better?"

Since learning about Ronan, dealing with Tephera, and finding out who Mayrez had worked with . . .

Ander wanted to learn about the Cast.

They were the ones that had made his journey such an absolute hell. They were the ones who might have killed Ronan. But facing them right now would be dangerous and absurd. He barely knew his own strength. And more so since it would involve putting Sytri's life on the line for his selfish desires.

Ander clenched his fist. He wanted to *stop* them, but that was so far out of reach.

"If I have power in my voice, I need to work on controlling it," he said finally. "The best way to do that seems to be staying here in Millstone and learning what I can from Delilah, Vega, and all of them. Delilah has a grasp on how to be a good leader. I'd like to be like that too. Someone who seems to have situations under control, which means being strong and brave. If I know how to use my power correctly, I could be that." He licked his lips. "So I need to stay here, and I want you to be with me. But you're not obligated to stay, especially with our deal fading away. And there's no reason to make a new one, especially because of the backlash. So if you want to leave, I—"

Sytri was suddenly there, pulling him in tight, his arms wrapping around Ander and covering him in warmth. Ander's eyes teared up, and he didn't even know why.

"You're so stupid." Sytri laughed.

"What are you—"

"Of course I'm going to stay with you, Ander. We're not just Partners anymore. I thought that was obvious? We are . . . *partners*." Sytri cupped his cheek and Ander's face continued to burn. "You don't have to make a fucking soul pact for me to stay. I wouldn't give you up for another blend, for the world, for anything."

"Promise?"

"I promise. There's not a damn thing out there that could make me leave you." Sytri kissed him. The scruff on his face scratched Ander's smooth skin, and his chest fluttered with a lightness that almost made him feel guilty. Sytri shouldn't be able to make him this happy. Not after everything that had happened, not after Ronan.

"Though, to be honest, I've been wanting to make a deal again to make sure other demons couldn't have your blood." Sytri paused. "Does that make me a creep?"

"No, I didn't even think about that. I haven't had to worry about demons just coming up and taking it without my consent before. So why did you tell me we didn't need one when I asked the other day?" Ander raised an eyebrow.

"You seemed fragile," Sytri said, pushing back Ander's hair. "I didn't want to make a deal with you when you were in that state. That wouldn't be right. I want to make sure you're thinking properly when we do something so serious."

"I'm thinking properly now."

"I hope so." Sytri gazed at him, with such intense admiration it made Ander flush; a ripple of desire washed across him, hitting his edges and coming back.

"All right. So let's make a new deal, so no one else can have my blood. How about that?" Ander said, pressing against Sytri, feeling the heat of him. Comforting, perfect.

"I like that. But we have to think about what the deal will be for."

"Something new?"

"Something good." Sytri's hands sank lower on Ander's waist and Ander's body became electric, every touch static. Sytri tipped him backward and swayed with him sideways. He seemed to love to dance. "It has to be so brilliant that there's no way I wouldn't be able to keep on doing it. So there won't be any backlash and the deal will never break. Perhaps . . . I swear that I'll love Ander, my significant other, with all of my being and stay with him to the day I die, through sickness and through health."

"Those are like wedding vows," Ander said, covering his face. Damn it, he was getting teary-eyed again.

"Well, what's your vow?" Sytri said, quirking an eyebrow and grinning. He nuzzled Ander's neck and kissed him, leaving small fires behind.

"Ah, Sytri, stop! I—I don't know. What do you want me to give you in the deal?" His feather's fluffed up.

Sytri froze, the air stilled, the heat between them becoming thick and dangerous. Ander's heart might have stopped beating. "Everything."

Ander laughed, embracing Sytri. "Fine, for our deal, I, Ander Castillo, promise to give you *everything*."

Sytri cracked a grin and went back to kissing him, nipping at his ear, hands gripping his hip bones. Ander half-heartedly kept him at bay as he continued. "My love, my life, my stupid words and dumb opinions. The best and worst of me—isn't this all a little too broad and vague for a deal? Will it work like that?"

"Don't know, but I do like all that stuff you just said. Though I suppose we should narrow it down to make sure it works. So okay, my very simple and plausible deal." Sytri met Ander's eyes, his face firm. "I swear to protect you with all I have. No matter where you go, where you are, I'll follow." His voice was stern as he said those words and filled to the brim with sincerity.

Ander was far too flustered to even breathe. Their earnestness had wrapped around his core, his heart.

"I, uh . . ." What did he have to give now? It couldn't be just his blood anymore. "I promise . . . to protect you too, we'll be partners equally. You won't fight alone anymore. You'll have me." His vow cut into the air, determined and strong. Though it wasn't nearly as nicely-packed as Sytri's, it was real all the same.

"Ander," Sytri said softly, with a sideways toothy grin. The chip in his canine was extra noticeable, extra endearing. "You know I don't want you to—"

"I don't care. We're partners now. And I'm going to help you in any way that I can. So take the deal or leave it, Sytri."

"Of course I'll take it." Sytri leaned closer.

Ah yes, the kiss to seal it. Ander's face lit up. Would this one burn as much as it had the first time they made a deal?

"You guys always have to sneak away to make out?"

Ander yelped and clambered onto Sytri.

Vega laughed almost maniacally, swinging into view from behind a tree a few yards away, stretching his arms and popping his fingers. "You two are weird."

"What the *fuck*, Vega," Sytri snapped.

"I was bored and I saw you guys leaving town, so I followed. But then I stumbled into one of those strange pale angels walking around and had to dispose of it. Then I checked for others just in case. Never ran into one that close before. Sorry, tangential. Doesn't matter, I'm here now." He looked over Ander, his expression almost sincere, with wide docile eyes, furrowed eyebrows. "How are you doing? I know you were distraught after talking to Michael and Delilah."

Ander straightened his shoulders. "I'm better. Thanks for checking on me, Vega."

Vega smiled, a much bigger smile than Sytri seemed capable of. It was unnerving.

"I didn't mean to make people worry." Ander nodded at both demons. "I'm fine. I am. It was something I should have expected."

"You can expect death every day, at every second. It doesn't make it more comfortable. It would be unnatural for you to not be affected." Vega walked closer, then leaned down so he was eye to eye with Ander. "We can only regroup and kindle new, blossoming relationships. Move each other forward with compassion and empathy. Like how you chose to risk your life to save me. I am forever grateful that you acted so benevolently." He grinned. "As far as I am concerned, you and I are close."

"But not too close," Sytri interjected.

"As close as I say," Vega said, licking his lips.

"Vega, I swear—"

"Swear to include me in your new deal?" His eyes lit up, and Ander almost stepped backward in surprise.

"What?" Sytri yelled. "No! Why would you think that we would ever, *ever* make a deal involving you? Were you hiding in the woods just to try and pull this kind of shit, you scumbag?"

"Cruel words, Sytri. I'm not scum of any sort." Vega stuck out his tongue. "I'm merely restating what I've said before. If we were to make a deal, the three of us, you'd benefit greatly. I'm a very talented and wonderful demon, if I do say so myself. And I do say that. I just said it."

"You can say whatever you want. You said you followed us because you cared about Ander, but this is what you really wanted to say. You didn't even wait five fucking minutes!"

"How long I waited to say it does not matter. And I did come here because I wanted to check on Ander. He's been in an emotional state and what good am I as a demon of emotion if I don't make sure he is well?"

"A demon of emotion? Is that what we're calling it nowadays?" Sytri snorted.

"You can be as rude as you want, that doesn't change the fact that I'm being sincere. I just also happened to hear you talking and this idea floated by that perhaps I could also—"

Bells rang out.

Everyone stopped. Even Ander, and he usually didn't notice anything. But the noise was loud, as if thousands of chimes were set off.

"An angel?" Sytri hissed. He wrapped his tail around Ander's arm, curling and tightening it like a leash before pulling him close.

"Angels," Vega whispered, eyes wide. "The Cast." He swung his head back to where they had come from. "What the hell?"

"How can you tell?" Sytri said, a curl to his upper lip.

"Who else has that many angels nearby?" Vega met Ander's eyes. "I'm sorry, I must request some of your blood? This feels dire."

"Permission granted," Ander said instantly.

"Fuck, I guess," Sytri muttered.

Vega pushed the collar of Ander's shirt down and bit into his shoulder, drawing blood into his mouth. Ander could feel it leaving his body and being replaced with heat and desire. His vision blurred, and he clung to Vega for a moment before willing himself to move and lean on Sytri instead. Fuck, why did Vega's bites have to make him feel so weird?

"I suggest you do the same, Sytri," Vega said as he pulled away from Ander. "The Cast will not give you the time to take his blood while we fight." Then he kissed Ander's forehead. "Thank you, be brave."

"Dude, what the hell," Sytri snapped, but Vega had already run off, gone in the blink of an eye.

Ander's hands were going numb now, pricked by pins and needles. What was happening?

He stared at Sytri, then at where Vega had gone, at the darkening sky. He could still hear the church bells ringing, growing louder with each second. How many angels did it take to make such a deafening clamor?

"We have to help defend Millstone." He gripped Sytri's hand. "Take my blood and let's go."

"All right, all right, of course we do," Sytri said, his voice a little frantic. "And you're going to . . . you're going to see if your voice works?"

"Yeah." Ander nodded.

"Good. Okay." Sytri stiffened.

Ander raised an eyebrow, it wasn't like Sytri to look so unsure before a fight. But he didn't have time to question it.

Sytri tossed him on his back, and as Ander settled, he put his arm in front of Sytri's mouth. The usual pattern: the same snap of teeth into his skin, then the strange and violent heat that Sytri poured into his being. Anger, confusion, an ache indescribable. He whimpered, biting into his lip. He had to focus. If it was the Cast attacking Millstone . . . Ander saw Tephera in his head again and shuddered. They had to hurry.

CHAPTER TWENTY-FOUR

Even from a distance, the destruction befalling Millstone was devastatingly clear. Sections were on fire, the blaze rushing upward into the air, whipping in the wind. Above Millstone, angels whizzed around, their feathers glistening in the setting sun and burning city.

The clamor of church bells was so violent it made Ander nauseous. He pressed closer to Sytri's back as they ran through the gate.

"What the fuck is going on?" Sytri snapped. "I thought Delilah said the Cast didn't bother them. What the fuck is all of this?"

Ander couldn't respond; he was too busy staring at the chaos. All around him, people were shouting, screaming. An angel flung itself at a demon, tackling it to broken earth, provoking a painful screech from both of them.

"Stop him!" Ander yelled, urging Sytri forward as the angel sliced at the demon's rib cage with sharp claws.

Sytri swung a shadow arm, knocking the angel off. The demon cried out and clutched his ribs as blood seeped between his fingers. Ander jumped off Sytri's back as his partner began to tear into the angel. "Let the demon drink my blood, Sytri."

"Fine!" Sytri huffed, not even looking back as he ripped the wings off the angel.

"Come on," Ander said, holding out his shaky arm. "Drink my blood, hurry up."

The demon almost tore Ander's arm to shreds as he chewed into it. Ander hissed, digging his heels into the ground. He tried to focus on anything other than his pain, but that only opened his mind to the yelling and shrieking, the sound of buildings crumbling—and that was worse.

The demon's frantic breathing had eased, and he let go of Ander's arm, muttering thanks. Ander feebly helped him up and after a moment was able to settle him between two buildings that weren't yet on fire. He was clearly still hurt, but it looked like his wounds were already starting to repair.

Ander's own ripped-up arm, sore and matted with a mixture of dry and fresh blood, was doing its own mending. He grimaced and tried to ignore the ache, attempting to spot Sytri among the chaos.

Sytri had just lifted himself from the body of the angel, blood pouring down his arms, his eyes flickering between their normal brilliant green and something else, something darker. It made Ander halt for a second, only a second, before running toward him, skidding to a stop at his side. "Are you all right? Did he hurt you or—"

Sytri turned to him, teeth sharp, his pupils like a cat's. "I'm fine, but where did all of these fuckers come from?" He looked at the sky.

Ander followed his gaze. The darkness was growing by the second, but the whiteness of the angels and blends never diminished against it. Nor the silver of the gowns they wore, making them resemble a storm rolling in on the horizon. *There must be near a hundred.*

"The Cast has always had a big crew."

Ander perked up. *Delilah.* He and Sytri swung their heads around, then Ander flinched. Even with Cerberus's help, she was swaying on her feet a yard away, blood oozing from the stump of her elbow.

"Delilah!" Ander gasped. "Oh god. What the fuck happened?" *Shit, I can't even heal her.* Since looking at her arm made him want to vomit, he focused on her face. "We need to get you out of here."

"We need to find Serene." Delilah coughed. "They can fix me up." She scanned the crowd, eyes dim.

An angel came screeching from the sky but Cerberus flung his tails forward, impaling it in midair with a growl. It squirmed like a dying insect, and he pushed it into the ground, ending it.

"Find Serene!" Cerberus snapped. "I'll protect Delilah. I'm going to take her into the school."

"On it," Ander shouted, tugging Sytri with him. They jumped past other fallen comrades, dodging the grasps of angels and blends alike. All the while searching for one of the smaller and less noticeable members of Millstone. Ander tried his best to spot Serene, but he confused every flash of white wings for their hair. Fire was constantly billowing around them, making his head spin.

Then an angel rammed Sytri from the side, sending him crashing to the ground, where it clawed at him fervently.

Ander spun, snatched the robe, and yanked the creature as hard as he could. "Stop it!"

The angel stilled, eyes wide.

Cold vines wrapped around Ander's spine.

Fuck. Was Sytri right? *Do I have power?*

After all this time of praying for strength, why didn't that possibility seem like a good thing?

His clenched his jaw. There was no time to think. If he had this ability, he had to use it. "Don't move," he hissed, yanking the robe again.

The angel was frozen in place, eyes wide as it remained half-hunched over Sytri, who managed to scramble to his feet. As soon as Sytri was up proper, Ander let go of the robe and dashed to his side. As he did, the angel's arms started to twitch.

Ander stomped his foot. "I said don't fucking move!" The words sent fire down his lungs this time, making him choke. "Okay, Sytri, I don't know how long I can do this. It feels . . . *weird.*"

Sytri drove a claw straight into the angel's throat.

Ander let out a strained breath as it slumped to the dirt. He glanced at Sytri, who met him with stern eyes.

Was that right, what I did?

Ander opened his mouth, but Sytri already seemed to know the question. "We'll talk ethics afterward," he said, using his tail to push Ander back. "Right now we have to find Serene."

Ander grimaced.

They ran deeper into the town's center. They were darting past a line of demolished homes when a sudden streak of fire whipped past Ander, almost singing his ear. He swung his head around to see—*Serene.* They stood in a bonfire, apparently of their own making, as flames lashed out from their hands, lighting an angel ablaze. Their small frame seemed ethereal amongst the inferno, in its own holy light.

"Serene!" Ander yelled, as loudly as he could. "Serene, Delilah needs you!"

Serene froze, before whisking the flames away and dashing toward them, leaving the charred remains of their foe behind.

"Where is she?" They asked as they staggered to a stop, worry creasing under their eyes.

"She went to the school to hide out. She's not good," Ander said honestly.

Serene's mouth pursed, and then they started running again, Ander and Sytri keeping pace with them.

Ander winced as someone cried in the distance. "How did this happen, Serene? How did everything get so bad, so fast?"

"I don't know. We didn't hear them until they were here. None of our guards spotted them. It's like they all just appeared in the sky." Two struggling blends collided into the building in front of Serene, and they yelped as wood splintered off like shrapnel. They turned sharply in the other direction. Ander started to follow but not before glaring at the Cast blend for a second.

"Stop moving," he hissed and the Cast blend seemed to seize up, staggering for a moment before the Millstone one took the advantage.

I did it— Ander's stomach twisted, and he buckled over. *Shit.*

"You okay?" Sytri rasped, grabbing him.

"Y-yeah, just . . . actually, I don't know." He swallowed hard. The sickness eased a little, but he could still taste acid on his tongue. "I feel weird."

"Maybe stop using your power. It might be too much for you right now, and the last thing I need is you keeling over."

Ander nodded as Sytri helped pull him forward.

They stopped in front of the school building, which seemed thankfully, miraculously, unharmed. Serene swung the door open wildly, only for two demons at the entrance to jump up, snarling.

"It's me you idiots," Serene snapped. "Where is Delilah?" The demons recoiled and started rambling, panic in their voices.

"Over here!" Cerberus shouted. Serene dashed over to the corner with Ander and Sytri following. On a table against the wall lay Delilah, propped up on multiple pillows, her bloodied arm soaking the sheets. As Ander neared, he had to avert his gaze.

"Oh god, oh god," Serene said, hands shaking. "Delilah, who has done this to you?"

"Would you honestly be surprised if I said that fucker was still alive?" Delilah gave a bitter laugh before wincing and breaking into a cough. "Ah, *fuck*."

Ander went cold.

"Mayrez?" Sytri asked.

"No, that bastard Micah. I guess we should've found all their bodies and burned them. I didn't even think about it." Delilah grimaced. "I didn't think . . . I didn't think he'd have a *reason* to come here. Mayrez is gone, Micah didn't seem like he was in charge. Much less working with the Cast." She groaned, her body curling like a piece of paper crinkling to flames. "I can understand them being pissed; we took away a source of blends. But why is Micah with them?"

"Don't worry about that now," Serene said, placing their hands on Delilah. They hummed to themselves, before their claws pierced Delilah's skin.

Cerberus fidgeted, his face a concerned scowl. "You'll be fine, Delilah." It wasn't clear if he was saying that for her or himself. "I'll kill him this time. For sure. He's not getting away."

"So that's why they're here?" Ander asked. "For revenge?"

"I assume so," Delilah muttered, her eyes fluttering open and closed. "They're pricks like that . . ." Her voice ended lower than a whisper.

"D-Delilah, stay with me," Cerberus stammered.

"She's fine." Serene pressed their claws in further as sweat dripped down the sides of their slim face. "Healing tires the body. But I have her stabilized. Just don't let anyone else get to her." They glanced at the door. "Someone has to stop the chaos outside. Where is Vega?"

"He ran ahead of us," Ander said. "He should have been here by now."

"We need him," Serene said, thumb on Delilah's wrist. "He's one of the best fighters besides Delilah, and she has to rest."

"What about West?" Ander asked.

"They're better as a shield than a spear," Serene said. "Even if they're a pure angel."

"Well then, what *can* they do?"

"They're mostly in charge of concealing Millstone's presence."

"Then where are they now? How did the Cast still spot us if they shield us?"

"I don't know," Serene snapped. It was a strand away from a cry. "I don't know. If . . . if they found us so easily, caught us off guard so quickly, they might be—" They were whimpering now. "They might be dead." It came out in a sob. *Oh fuck.* It had been a long time since he'd heard that dreadful sound: a child crying.

He had to do something.

The door exploded into pieces.

Cerberus flung his body over Delilah, shielding her as daggers of wood impaled him. Ander held up his arms in a feeble attempt to protect his head. The skin there was shredded, flesh ripped apart like fabric.

"Ah, this is where the party is."

Micah walked into the room. Sleek, solid white, cold.

Cerberus snarled at him, fangs sharp. Sytri hissed, and the other demons in the room all braced themselves, surrounding Delilah.

"Delilah, you ran away from our fight. I was having a good time making sure— Oh. There you are." He wasn't looking at Delilah now. He was staring at Ander, with pure blue eyes that drowned him like the sea.

Before Ander could speak, there was a flash and Micah was in front of him, ivory wings unfurling from his back in a rush of feathers, brilliant and blinding. He grinned as Ander barely jolted backward in time to avoid colliding with him.

"Stop!" Ander yelled, full of unbridled panic. For a second his stomach rolled. But still, Micah faltered, and Sytri used the moment to slash at his face. Dark blood sprayed across the room, and Micah tumbled to the ground, gasping.

Ander glanced at the demons beside him. "Get Delilah out of here."

"Already on it," Cerberus said, lifting her up. She groaned, snapping awake for a second, confusion in her dim eyes. "We're leaving. Serene, come with." It wasn't a question, and Serene followed him, the two other demons right behind.

It was just him and Sytri left to deal with Micah. He wasn't as afraid as he should be. He had his power and he had a partner now. That was more than he'd had the first time he'd met Micah. *How many times can I try to control him, though?* The nausea hadn't dissipated, and now his head was getting woozy.

"I was right." Micah laughed. "Oh the rest of the Cast will be so pleased."

"You sure have the creepy villain act down," Sytri snarled.

Micah immediately quit laughing. "I'm not a villain. You're the demon."

So he's not? Micah's white wings fit the bill of most angels. But he had wanted Ander's blood; he had tasted his blood.

"You're half-and-half. Like Serene," Ander whispered.

"I'm not half-and-half!" Micah snapped. "I'm more angel than filth. And with your blood, I'm going to achieve the perfect purity of the divine."

"I have no idea what you're talking about," Ander said. "Get out of here. You and the Cast have to leave *now.*" His head spun and he bit down on his tongue, ignoring the bitter taste. Using his voice was stranger now; it was beginning to *burn*. Like it was fire he was threatening to vomit.

Micah twitched, scowling.

"Fucking leave!" His stomach rolled with heat, and he wrapped an arm around it, gritting his teeth.

Sytri ran at Micah, swiping with his claws, but Micah dodged with a wince.

Ander grimaced; clearly he wasn't strong enough to stop Micah completely.

Am I still just weak?

"Stop it!" Ander yelled louder. He was teetering now. The nausea was hitting him full front and center, and it was bringing fire with it— His lungs seemed to be smoldering. *Damn.* "You're not as strong as you think. You asshole." His throat burned again but much less this time.

Sytri pounced on Micah, who jerked away far too late. Ander blinked. *Wait, did that work? Holy shit.* Maybe he and Sytri could hold an edge. "You feel . . . slow and weak. Scared." He swallowed again. Speaking didn't hurt as much that time.

Sytri grabbed Micah by the shoulders, flipped him over, and tossed him across the room, sending mattress springs and chairs flying. He landed with a powerful crash, breaking through half the wall, part of his body dropping outside.

Elation bubbled up in Ander even as he stumbled backward, slipping on his heels. "You're not getting Delilah! You won't ever hurt her again. You're going to regret that you did, Micah. You're going to regret everything you've done." The world was smudging together like smears of charcoal—God he was going to faint.

Micah chuckled, and Ander glared through his smoky vision.

"We didn't come here for Delilah. What do you think this was?" Micah pulled himself out from the building, as bricks fell to the ground in heavy thuds, dust curling in the air. "A petty revenge tactic? As if the Cast gave a shit about Mayrez." Like lightning, he dashed forward and slammed Sytri to the ground, pinning him by his throat. "Or her lackeys?"

"Sytri!" Ander cried. He tried to run toward them, but he fell to his knees, bile rolling in his stomach. *Fuck.*

Sytri hacked, trying desperately to swipe at Micah's face but missing. His black arms writhed weakly like fading smoke,

"Sure, they gave us good blends, made it easier than crawling around ourselves to filter out the worthy ones. But we didn't risk fighting Millstone for her benefit before. Why would we now?" Micah glanced over at him, and Ander could *feel* his smug grin.

Ander paled, as the world spun around him. "Then what the hell do—"

Bells clanged and a voice echoed in his head. *Hello, tiny blend.*

Familiar cold, dark fingers pried into Ander's mouth. He tried to jolt away, but he tripped again, hitting the floor. Everything was swirling like it was being twisted by a tornado. *Shit, shit, I fucked up.*

Not a second later, monstrous hands clasped all around him. Fear he'd thought would never come again shot throughout his body, making every hair, every feather stand on end. He tried to yell but the words were muffled.

It was almost motion-for-motion, an exact reenactment of before as he was lifted into the air by the angel. Then he was turned around and found himself face to face with Tephera. There was a lone white line slicing down one of their eyes. Its light was mesmerizing.

The gift you gave me. A reminder.

Ander bit down as hard as he could. He tasted salty blood, hot and thick. Tephera didn't budge though, didn't even wince.

No speaking, tiny blend. I have learned that now.

"Ander!" Sytri yelled. "What the fuck? Let go of him, you asshole!"

Sytri was out of sight, though. And Ander was rigid in Tephera's hands, trapped. Tangled in a frigid tree and its vines.

"Not now, demon." Micah laughed.

There was a crash, and Sytri shouted obscenities. Tephera turned, and their large body slunk away like a snake's, bones snapping as they did. They weaved their way out of the building and into the night, Ander desperately twisting in their hand.

"Bring him back!" Sytri's voice was splintered into pieces. Pain struck Ander's heart so hard it broke. "Let him go!"

"Stop fighting," Micah shouted.

Ander gave a muffled yell, his blood and drool dripping from Tephera's hands. Suddenly Tephera squeezed him, and something *bad* cracked inside Ander. He crumbled as pain seeped into every inch of his body. Panic flooded his chest. *Am I going to die?*

It is okay, tiny blend. We will make you pure. You will be a beauty in the Cast. Magnificent. You are a long-awaited gift. We have been needing you.

Tephera took long steps forward. Around them and Ander a fire raged, flames spreading from house to house. The sky was painfully dark, the red and bloody edge of the sun the only light. It looked like Hell.

Let us go to the Cast. To your rightful home, tiny blend.

Tephera took another step, and their body shifted. The world split in front of Ander's very eyes, fragments and shards rearranging themselves. New lights, new earth, new everything, until in a loud bang, they were gone.

CHAPTER TWENTY-FIVE

Ander's body reassembled itself, and with the final click, a spark went through him. It was strange and discomforting. He wanted to vomit but held it back. *Don't know why.* Throwing up on Tephera's hands would have made him feel a little better. But not really.

Where was he?

Where was Sytri?

Ander searched inside of himself. Tucked next to his heart, the little fire of the deal burned, delicate yet strong. He held on to that sensation. With it, he knew Sytri still breathed.

His vision was spinning, but he didn't need it to tell Tephera was moving. The sky was still dark, so they hadn't gone through time, like it had seemed. But they had traveled a distance. The oxygen here was noticeably thinner and colder than that of Millstone; there were fewer trees too.

The Cast will be so pleased to have you, tiny blend. We have been waiting a long time for a blend like you.

Ander didn't understand. What made him so much of a rarity that a group that kidnapped blends wouldn't have found one by now? He tried to focus on his voice again but, combined with Tephera's dizzying stride and having exhausted himself against Micah, it was impossible. Didn't really matter anyway, with Tephera's fingers still jammed in his mouth.

Make you pure, make you pure.

Tephera seemed to be talking to themself. *All right.* Ander took a deep breath, ignored the spit and blood on his chin, and tried to think.

He was fucked. Super fucked. If he could use his power again then he might be able to get a handle on the situation, but Tephera knew that, which meant the Cast probably knew as well and wouldn't give him the opportunity to talk either.

And even if he could speak at the moment, he didn't know how much he could say before he passed out. He needed time to build back whatever power fueled his voice. That was unfortunate. But it wouldn't stop him.

He would get back to Sytri.

Ander stared up at Tephera, at the void of their body blending into the dark sky. The only way to differentiate them from the endless space behind was that the endless space had stars, bright and burning stars. Tephera was nothing, absolutely nothing, besides their two white eyes, one with a thin scar.

Pride and fear flared inside Ander; that wound was his doing.

How strange to be proud, while captive.

"Tephera," an unfamiliar voice called out. "Did you bring the Seraph?"

Tiny blend is in my hands.

Seraph. The word was familiar—from where?

Ander squirmed again. Nothing. He couldn't escape while he was in Tephera's grasp. He would have to wait until an opportunity showed itself.

"Excellent! Oh, this is great. Where are the others, though?"

Behind. I did not waste energy in shifting them with me again. Tiny blend has been acquired, and that is all that is important. Micah said to wait for his return, so now I will wait.

"We can't really afford to wait, Tephera."

It is what Micah requested.

Silence. Presumably Tephera was the type of angel one didn't want to argue with.

Micah said the Seraph is for him and him alone.

Oh. He didn't like that at all.

The loud groan of a door opening startled Ander, bright light making him wince. The world above him and Tephera changed. This was a huge, *huge* building. White wooden pillars arched to a ceiling so high up that Tephera was able to stand straight and still have a giant empty space over them. All around them footsteps and conversation echoed. It was a bombardment of noise. Insects busy at work.

Underneath it all, bells rang out.

Angels. Everywhere.

"Set them down over here, Tephera," the voice commanded, disgruntlement evident. "We will . . . wait for Micah's arrival before we proceed further."

Ander was lowered until his feet touched the ground, turned so he wasn't just facing Tephera's chest. Unfortunately, he was still unable to move. Tephera's thick snake-like fingers remained curved over him, and the tip of one of them remained in his mouth, making it impossible to talk. And really hurting his jaw.

At least he could look around. He was in a church. A gigantic one, brilliant and overwhelming—a megachurch, perhaps. There were towering marble angel statues in front of him. They were at least twenty feet tall and lined the walls that led up to spiraling staircases on each side. It was all huge beyond belief. *I'm a speck in this.*

Everywhere, angels and blends were pacing the floor. They had stacks of books in their hands and crosses swinging around their necks. Every single one seemed to glance at Ander, if only for a fraction of a second, before whispering to a companion nearby.

They *had* been waiting for him.

"Hello, Seraph!"

Ander blinked. Looking straight at him, with four wide eyes, was an angel. He appeared *so close* to human but his aura—dense and hot—*hurt*. Like the air encircling him was thick with fire. No blend felt so powerful. *He has to be an angel.*

"I'm extremely pleased to be the one who welcomes you to our home."

The angel was clean-cut, hair perfectly brushed to the left, teeth in unnervingly straight rows. Two brown wings were folded neatly behind him, and his four brown eyes consisted of two on each side, one almost directly on top of the other. He resembled a very proper spider. As Ander stared, he tilted his head, a smile on his face.

"We've been waiting a long time, Seraph. You would not believe our excitement when Micah informed us of what he found. A real, living Seraph, walking around on Earth, after all of this chaos." The angel laughed a little too loudly. "A miracle, absolute miracle. Oh. I haven't introduced myself. I'm Tabbris." He held out his hand.

Ander still couldn't fucking move.

"Ah-aha! Oh. My apologies. We have you confined at the moment. How rude of me." He stuck his hand on one of Ander's fingers that stuck out at an angle in his captured position and shook it as much as he could. Ander cringed inside. *What the hell is up with this guy?*

"Anyway, I am Tabbris, you are the Seraph. Tephera, does the Seraph have a name?" Tabbris looked up at Tephera, who had been silent through this whole ordeal. Were they capable of secondhand embarrassment?

I am sure they do. But I do not know such a thing.

Ander scowled as much as he could. Surely Tephera knew his name? Were they being a dick?

"Well then, we will go with Seraph for now, I suppose. Which is fine. Ha!" Tabbris pressed his shoulders close together when he laughed. It appeared uncomfortable.

A few angels and blends walked by, their eyes staring into him, and he wanted to ask if there was anyone else he could talk to for the moment, someone who was more in charge than . . . Tabbris.

"It will take Micah a while to return." Tabbris tapped his foot on the floor, the *click* and *clack* getting faster and faster. "Tephera. What exactly are we waiting on him for?"

He ordered that we wait.

Angry silence. Tabbris kept huffing to himself like a peeved child. Ander wasn't sure if Micah could make this situation any more uneasy. Though he could definitely make it more horrifying.

Ander took a deep breath through his nose and attempted to focus again. The room was huge, yet that somehow made Ander feel more confined. He was suffocating in the space of it all. It pressed in on him. That and Tephera's fingers.

Around him were only enemies or potential enemies. They wanted something from him, but what? He was a Seraph—what did that entail? What did they have to gain from him? Whatever it was, he wouldn't give it away willingly.

"Tephera. I know that Micah said wait for him, but don't you think that Ezra would want to be informed as soon as possible about the Seraph being here?"

She is aware.

"Ah." Tabbris grumbled. "Then wouldn't she want to meet him right away? Surely she doesn't like to be kept waiting."

Tephera tensed, their fingers pressing harder into Ander's skin, into his mouth. He choked. *Gross.* As he gagged, Tabbris's eyes flickered to him for a moment, mouth forming a straight line.

"The Seraph is in distress; we shouldn't keep him like this. So what if Micah said wait; he isn't the one in charge. Ezra is." Tabbris seemed to sneer at the thought. "You yourself, Tephera, are a pure Archangel and Micah is just *half* of one." His jaw clenched at the word. "Why are we listening to him?"

You speak of treason, Tabbris. Ezra will not be pleased. You question her.

"I do not question Ezra, I would never question Ezra!" Tabbris's wings fluttered. "It's only that we are a place for the holy, and Micah's blood is not purer than yours or mine. I do not understand why Ezra would allow him to—"

"Allow me to what, Tabbris?"

The voice boomed throughout the whole church: loud, powerful, stern.

There, in front of the door, stood Micah. A splash of blue blood coated his pristine silver robe, sweeping across the front, over half of his bottom jaw, and a bit onto his ear. A perfect stroke of paint.

Ander's hair stood on end; there was fire in his bones, and he could do nothing with it. Where was Sytri? That was *his* blood. He had to be alive though, had to. The deal still burned in Ander's chest. But it was so faint. Because Sytri was dying or because

Ronan was already dead? The uncertainty made the world flicker like a dying light bulb.

The other beings inside the church had frozen at Micah's entrance before scurrying faster. They steered clear of him and his path across the room to Ander, Tephera, and Tabbris.

"Micah. You made it back faster than I thought you would," Tabbris said, clasping his hands. He smiled politely, but it was strained, like his face would snap any second.

Whatever tension these two had going on, Ander did not want to be in the middle of it.

"Once I knew that Tephera had the Seraph secure and back at the Cast, I had no reason to stay. And while I can't shift like Tephera does, I have my own means of getting where I need to be." Micah smiled. His teeth were sharp.

Ander obviously didn't care if someone was a demon. But there was a sickening part of Micah that stood out like tar on snow. He had the same vile and dangerous energy as Mayrez. Sytri, Vega: their demonic traits were tamer. They were feral sometimes, yes, but more curious than bloodthirsty.

Micah was bloodthirsty, figuratively and literally.

"Why are you so close to my Seraph?" Micah asked with another, sharper, smile.

"I . . . It's not your Seraph. They belong to Ezra. They belong to the Cast. We all need the Seraph to make Ezra's pure future a reality." Tabbris's voice held strong as he stared Micah down. *Impressive.* If only the two of them would bicker themselves into a distraction, he could escape. Maybe. Tephera's grip wasn't exactly getting looser.

"Ezra." Micah's eyes went wide. "Come on, Tephera, we must bring the Seraph to her. She will be overjoyed to see him."

As you wish, Micah.

Tabbris's upper lip curled. "So, you get to deliver the Seraph all by yourself and get all the credit then, I suppose? Even though I helped coordinate the attack against Millstone? Even though countless others went with you to help retrieve the Seraph?"

"This isn't about something as childish as *credit*, Tabbris. Ezra and I must discuss future plans. We have been working on this for a long time." Micah ignored Tabbris's stares completely as he bent down and pushed back the curls from Ander's face. His touch was cold. "We have been waiting dearly for someone like him."

Micah had never been this close before, and Ander had never wanted him to be. This close, he could see the specks of white in Micah's eyes, the unnatural smoothness of his unbearably pale skin. It was all unnerving. He seemed to be cut from porcelain and ice. Ander wanted to spit in his stupid frigid face.

And he wanted to speak, to show that he wasn't afraid. But what could he do all tangled up in Tephera's long fingers like a butterfly in a spider's web?

"You are a beautiful creature, Seraph," Micah murmured. His breath was like frost. "And I have been *longing* for a blessing such as yourself to become mine."

"He's not yours!" Tabbris shouted, his voice snapping through the church like a gunshot.

A tense line crossed Micah's forehead, and there was the smallest twitch of his upper lip. He pulled himself away from Ander and faced Tabbris, who had launched into a rant.

"The Cast works together. We are a family, we all work for the betterment of this world, for Ezra, for the angels. How can you ever expect to be as pure as Ezra requires if you only think about yourself? That is not the Cast way. I will never understand why she allowed you to be in charge. You blend in too well with the demons." Tabbris spat on the ground.

Ander didn't have to see Micah's face to know that Tabbris's words had gotten to him. Because Tabbris's own face changed to one of pure regret.

How *didn't* they know that Micah *was* part demon? Though Ander himself had thought the man seemed angelic in appearance amongst Mayrez's posse. But Micah *felt* like both.

Maybe that makes it easier to lie to both sides.

"Micah, I—"

"No, shh, I get it, Tabbris. I blended in seamlessly with Mayrez's pack of mongrels for Ezra's sake. I hid my wings, I kept the glow of my spirit down to a flicker. But let us be clear: I was playing a part." Micah wasn't yelling, but his voice was all Ander could hear. "I am of angel blood, like the rest of you. Or do you doubt Ezra's words?"

"No, I would never doubt her of course—"

"Then how about you shut your filthy mouth instead of coming at me with such blasphemy? I am the voice of Ezra until the cardinals return. The Cast knows the truth. That demons are horrible, despicable monsters made of sin, death, and urges they can't control." Micah took a step closer to Tabbris. "It frightens you all to think that I could be one."

"Micah, I didn't say you were a demon, I only—"

"Ah, but you do think it, right? And it disgusts you." Micah turned on his heels and stared straight down. "Yet as I said, Ezra sees only angel in me. Because that's all I am. And if you want to question her yourself, you may."

"What are you saying?"

"I'm bringing the Seraph to Ezra. You may join."

Hushed whispers all around. A knot grew in Ander's stomach. Who was this fucking Ezra they kept talking about? An angel, and the creator of the Cast as well? What kind of angel did it take to make a cult?

Ander really didn't want to meet such a being.

Tabbris seemed enraptured by the thought, however. There was obvious light in his eyes. "You mean it?"

"Of course." Micah wasn't looking at Tabbris, though. His eyes were focused solely on Ander now. There was an emptiness to them, something lost. He reached into his pockets and pulled out a few strips of leather with metal latches on them. "Tephera, would you mind?"

Ah. Yes.

Like vines unwinding, Tephera's fingers pulled away from Ander's mouth and throat, slowly. But as they were removed, Micah snapped the leather strip onto Ander's mouth, another strap onto his wrists, and one around his neck, painfully tight. They all snapped together, and even knowing he couldn't break free, Ander attempted to anyway, only proving himself correct.

Micah smirked down at him. "Cute that you even tried, Seraph." He patted his head, and Ander fumed, taking a step backward only to be yanked forward. His stomach dropped. The collar around his throat had a leash on it that was wrapped around Micah's thin hand. "Can't have you running away and ruining my plans, can I? Or any of that commanding nonsense. At least, not until you're commanding for *me*." He winked.

Ander wanted to be brave. He really did. But everything about Micah made his body cold, his heartbeat echo in his head in a painful panic: *run*. The terrible side effects from using his voice were dissipating, but now fear was messing with him.

"Come along now, Tabbris, as we deliver the Seraph to Ezra for approval." Micah walked ahead, and when Ander refused to budge, he yanked so hard on the leash that Ander went flying, stumbling onto the ground, head slamming into the marbled floor. Something in his neck snapped and jolted through the back of his skull. White lights streaked like lightning through his vision.

"I know about that little healing power of yours. I have no reason to be gentle. Don't make me be rough."

Ander kneeled there, twitching. It was like electricity was fizzing around his skull. Then, there was a *click* near the base of his skull, followed by another and another until the ache began to subside. He coughed, eyes watering.

Micah stood there smiling down at him.

"Come on, we've got to go now." He said it so *sweetly*. Like a teacher comforting a child.

Ander's shoulders shook as he managed to stand back on his feet. *I've got to get out of here.*

Micah led them through a hallway, Tabbris walking beside him, fidgety but obviously excited. Ander didn't focus on the two of them, though; he searched for an exit. There had to be one—fuck, there had to be multiple; this building was like five mansions pressed together.

But all Ander could see were long hallways with huge stained-glass windows above his reach. Thick pillars of dark wood kept the building up, their tops curving along the rooftop, and smooth boards below their feet made every step echo. Starlight flickered through the windows, and Ander was illuminated by passages from the Bible, along with paintings of horrors and wonders. There was no exit.

Where the fuck was God now anyway? While Ander was being carted off to a lunatic angel, bound in leather like some sort of BDSM snack?

Where was Sytri?

Alive. The presence of their deal confirmed that at least. And Ander had to get to him, had to escape from this damn megachurch on top of a fucking mountain, in the middle of a forest.

Micah came to a set of doors and pressed a key into the lock. There was a loud *clink* and, as he pushed them open, a cold breeze swept past. It smelled strangely sweet. The scent brought up memories that Ander couldn't place, foggy and off. Nightmares and daydreams. Where had he been before, with this fragrance? Had he even been alive? Had he even possessed a form?

Micah turned to Tabbris. "Do not speak to Ezra, please, she will not appreciate it. She might be upset that I brought you in the first place. Do you understand? You are an unexpected guest in her residence."

"I understand," Tabbris said softly. His voice sounded like it was breaking.

Ander didn't want to go past those doors, further into the black where that cold and the strange smell came from. But he had no choice. Micah tugged him along, and into the darkness they went.

Immediately the path went downward on broad wooden steps that didn't stop for ages. When they did, it was at another door that Micah unlocked with an additional key to reveal another set of blasted stairs. Ander tried to count them as they went. It seemed like forever between each momentary rest as Micah unlocked the next door.

One door. Two. Three. Four. The smell was so strong; it felt like a heavy syrup in the air. It clung to Ander's clothing, his skin, making his eyes and mind drowsy. The smell was familiar but from so long ago. And when he thought he'd identified it, it twisted and changed into something new: Apples, baked pies, pastries, soft rain, cold, ice, sugar, molasses, maple. It never stayed still.

Five. Six. Seven. Ander was going to pass out. How long had they been walking? Half an hour? More? The fragrance was making him dizzy now, and not only that but his thoughts and memories blurred together. As if he had done this before, but he *hadn't.*

He wanted to ask Micah what the hell this smell was, what kind of angel Ezra was. He also wanted to tell him to fuck off. He searched for that part of himself again, the fragments of his power, and found them burning. They seemed to come back quickly. Was that related to his healing abilities? He only had a little bit of strength, but he recovered it fast?

He held on to the fragments. Had to be ready to press magic into his words as soon as he could. And make sure they were the *right* words. A few commands, then he'd most likely be too tired to give any more.

"We are here," Micah said as he unlocked the last door.

On the other side of the door was the largest empty room Ander had ever seen. It must have been as long as the whole building; the end of it was past his vision. But from what he could see it was completely bare. Only a string of faint lights hung along the top of the high ceiling.

And then a white rabbit was sitting on the ground a few feet ahead.

Ander blinked. It hadn't been there a second ago. He stared as it sniffed around, glowing faintly in the dim light. It looked at them, at Micah, then twitched an ear and scurried over to a wall. It went up it like a spider, and out a pipe near the lights. Oh—there were pipes. They were various sizes and lengths, but all up near the ceiling.

Where a white fox was.

What the hell?

Micah. You have brought it. A voice practically cooed. The sound was so like Tephera's—everywhere all at once—but it was so much slicker, sneakier. Like water slipping between concrete, slowly breaking it apart, making way for the weeds and undergrowth.

Ander's chest sank. On the ground, merged into the blackness, was an even blacker blackness. Like Tephera, but it had no shape or form. It was a huge stain on the ground, spread out almost the whole stretch of the floor.

Micah led them toward it. And the voice spoke again.

Give me a moment, my love. Let me see.

It was a hole. *No.* As they reached its edge, its depth became obvious, and Ander froze down to the bone.

It was an unimaginable pit of horror.

Hundreds of feet below, countless skeleton-white animals all squirmed. They pulsed against each other like maggots festering in a sticky wound. Every so often one would latch onto the wall of the hole and walk up it, defying the laws of gravity and nature. A deer had just crested the top and was staring at them. It opened its mouth the smallest bit, and the laughter of children wheezed out. Then it headed straight for a pipe.

Ander was shaking. He didn't want to be here. With these monsters, with Micah, in this building.

An aura thrummed all around him, the air shaking with a power that made him choke, his skin grow hot, and the animals in the pit began to writhe as something moved under them.

Run, run now. But he couldn't, not tethered to Micah.

"I'm so glad I was able to find a Seraph for you, Ezra." Micah sounded like a love-struck husband coming home. "I couldn't believe my eyes when I found him. Well, my tongue really—that taste. But I wasn't sure, until I heard him speak. He used the voice you told me about. The one we need."

I have not heard the voice of a Seraph in a millennium. Oh, the voice of life, to hear its sweet sound. My heart is aflutter.

"Taste? What do you mean taste, Micah?" Tabbris snapped.

Ander couldn't look away from the mass of white animals. There had to be hundreds or thousands of them in the depths of the chasm, thrashing about. Now they pushed together on the sides of the wall, a mass growing and growing, with a boil forming on top.

A hand the size of truck shot through the creatures at the bottom, fingers outstretched.

Ander jolted backward, eyes wide. He could hear the hand clawing against the wall of the pit.

Then all the animals started screaming.

Shush, my darlings. Shush. I am simply going to have a look.

Ander couldn't bring himself back to the edge of the pit. Frantically he yanked against the leash still in Micah's grip. Micah huffed and pulled Ander back, sending him tumbling once more, his knees hitting stone.

Bolting clearly wasn't a viable escape plan, but he *had to escape.* The thud and scrape of Ezra in the pit was growing louder. He had seconds till she made it out. *What can I do? Can't talk right now. All I can fucking do is heal.*

Heal from almost anything.

Ander smashed his face on the jagged stone.

"What the—" Micah started.

The leather ripped and so did a large portion of Ander's face, as blood and skin grated off him. He scraped his face again, tearing at the leather until it finally fell from his mouth.

There was a flash of movement as Micah reached toward him.

"Don't touch me!" Ander screamed, his voice slicing into the air as blood oozed down his face. He met Micah's wide eyes. "Drop the leash!" Hot shards pricked his throat.

With a twitch, Micah's hand uncurled from the tie that kept him and Ander connected. Ander swung his attention to Tabbris, who was still standing by the ledge. "Set me free! Now!"

Tabbris swung around like a zombie, eyebrows pinched together.

"Fucking hurry up!" Ander yelled, panic swelling in his chest, which was ready to burst. Acid hit the back of his throat, but he swallowed it down. Ezra's deafening grating was getting louder, almost violently so.

"Seraph, you don't know what you're doing, please, calm down—" Micah began.

"Shut up!" Ander shouted again. "Shut the fuck up and stay still!"

Suddenly his gut rolled and he dry-heaved, shaking. Shit, he had done too much too soon.

Tabbris struggled with the binds on Ander's wrists, clearly fighting against the orders.

Seraph. Are you not pleased to see me? The voice was closer now.

At the edges of the pit, large pale fingers appeared, gripping into the edge, breaking the stone. They were so pale they were translucent at the tips, blue veins visible underneath, as thick as ropes.

Each finger was practically ten feet long, and small animals came scurrying off them: insects, mice, snakes, birds. All of them blinding white. Slowly, a head lifted above the rim of the pit, its feathery hair falling down, and its two onyx eyes staring. Ander's heart stopped.

Shit.

"Ezra!" Tabbris shouted. "Oh, you are so beautiful." His hands twitched, and the last strap on Ander's wrist came undone, though Ander barely noticed.

Ezra rose higher, and her mouth was split into a large grin, full of millions of tiny sharp teeth. She tilted her head so far down that it looked like it'd snap right off, as she gazed at Tabbris. Without her mouth moving, she spoke again. *Who is this in my home?*

"What the fuck are you?" Ander whispered. Her eyes were like wide pools of black ice, turning him into a bag of cement.

Oh, Seraph. Do not speak so crudely. You are of pure blood. And I have been waiting. We all have been waiting.

"I'm not staying here. Tell them to let me out." Ander breathed. One last attempt. Words as strong as he could make them. But bile and fire coiled in his stomach, and he crumpled over hacking again. *Fuck.*

Your bloodline is tainted by the human stock that made you. I am solid angel. I am Throne. A perfection most desired. Your words may try, but they cannot bend me. However, I will bend you.

Her long arm snaked its way over to them. Ander scurried back on his hands and feet, getting as far from her fingertips as he could. It was like a tree was coming at him.

She snatched up Tabbris.

"Ezra? My queen?"

She popped him into her mouth like a mint. The crunch of his bones and squelch of blood being squeezed from his body resonated in Ander's head. Bile rose in his throat.

What the fuck.

What the fuck.

What the fuck.

I am sorry to hear that one had been giving you trouble, Micah. Unfortunate. But I do love a small snack every so often.

"It is not your fault, Ezra. The others fear the vile blood in me, even if they cannot confirm it is there. No one can see the bigger picture like you. The purity in me like you." Micah brushed dirt off his torso and glared at Ander. "The Seraph doesn't wish to follow me, I'm afraid. He made a deal with a demon, but I ended it."

Ander flinched.

No, I still sense the deal, throbbing under the Seraph's skin. You did not end the demon.

"What? No. I thought I had. I'm so sorry, Ezra. I will go find the demon right now and make sure of it this time. I'll—"

It is fine, Micah. It is dying, this deal. I can pull it out of the Seraph. I might take some soul along the way, but I can do it. Then he can make a proper deal with you. What do you say, Seraph? I take out the old deal so you can make a new one with my dear Micah. Or will you perish here and now? She smiled a bit wider, crinkles forming in the corners of her cheeks.

Ander couldn't think. She could take the deal out of him. She could take out his soul. His breathing became ragged. Make a deal with a demon he loathed or get eaten by a fucking monster of an angel—these were his choices? He bit his lip. His body was trembling, each breath hitching in his throat. Why wasn't he stronger? If he had just known about his powers sooner, had tried harder, then maybe he would be strong enough to stop her.

What did Ezra want with him? Would it be better to die? He didn't know the harm she could cause with him, with his voice.

Ander clenched his jaw. God, he wanted Sytri back so badly it *hurt*.

A hand touched his shoulder. He looked up to see Micah gazing down at him.

"Let Ezra take the deal out, Seraph. If you don't resist, it won't hurt. Then you can form one with me. Make this easy."

Ander opened his mouth; words wouldn't come out. He turned to Ezra, with her wide eyes staring endlessly. Blood still stained her teeth. A piece of Tabbris's shredded clothing was stuck between two of the sharp blades.

All Ander could hear was the pulsing in his ears. All he could feel was the soft fire in his chest. The small fire beside his heart where the deal struggled to stay alive.

That space wasn't for Micah.

"No."

"What?"

"No." Ander stared at Micah, who was a statue of white in the black. "I won't let you take out the deal so you might as well kill me. You can't have my blood."

"I don't think you understand the position you're in," Micah hissed.

"I do. And I don't care." Ander stood up. "I'm not helping you maniacs do whatever the hell it is you're trying to do. It's fucked up. I won't be a part of it. I'd rather die right here and now than know that anything you take from me could help fuel that monster's ideas." Ander glared at Ezra. She kept smiling back, but it felt different. There was a heaviness about that grin.

Seraph. You are making a grave mistake.

"So? That's all I've been doing up until this point." Ander took a few steps backward and turned to Micah. "Get me out of here." The blend flinched. "Micah. Get me out of here." Stronger. He had to be stronger. He gritted his teeth, as the nausea hit him hard again, and he stumbled backward in a fit of dry-heaving.

Micah walked toward him.

You do not command what is mine, Seraph!

There was a rush of air as Ezra swung her hand toward him. Ander couldn't dodge it, and she snatched him, squeezing the air right out of his lungs.

Ezra brought him right to her face; he could see his reflection in her black eyes. Up close, she smelled like icy steel. Fear bubbled in his chest, but he shoved it down. Fear wasn't useful.

Besides, Sytri wouldn't have shown any.

Ezra's breath was like frost. *You will show respect to your betters.*

"I thought I was the better angel?"

I could swallow you whole.

"Then do it."

The sound that came out of her was like a car crash: metal against metal, rubber tires screeching on concrete. She *crushed* him and bones cracked, fire lighting up his insides and sending him reeling as his rib cage shattered. *Oh fuck.* Everything was white-hot pain.

She pressed her thumb against his chest. Inside of him the deal flared, fireworks sparking across his chest. She was trying to pry it out of him.

No. "Don't you fucking touch it!"

She hissed back at him, mouth still unmoving. Then she screeched. She dug her nail in harder, and Ander cried out as blood poured.

"It's not yours! You can't have it! And even if you take it from me, I won't make another fucking deal. I'm not for Micah." He groaned, breath shaky as blood continued to stream down him. But the fire by his heart burned, catching his bones alight. It was fighting her. *He* was fighting her. That burn was the embers of an angel inside of him. He stifled another hack, another heave.

Ezra crushed him again, like a soda can. Pure agony shot through him like electricity and blood filled his mouth.

The world went black.

If he hadn't been able to heal, he would've been dead right then.

After a few blind blinks, the world flickered back into view and there was a horrible twisting ache as his body desperately tried to repair itself. He could *feel* bones rearranging under his skin, the scraping and pressure. But his deal remained intact.

Micah. I need you to do what it takes to get the Seraph to make the deal.

Ezra reached below into the pool of overflowing animals and stripped a layer of skin off a deer with one, effortless pull. It laughed horrifyingly into the darkness, kicking its legs. Ezra yanked on Ander's chin with her thumb, opening his mouth like a nutcracker and then stuffed the furry white skin into his mouth. It was coated in thick blood that slipped down his throat. He tried to hack it out, but the skin was wedged in, choking him. As he lurched downward to dry-heave, he paled at the sight before him. There was the rest of Ezra's monstrous body.

It was mangled beyond belief. The left side of her torso was completely open, and animals rested inside, nipping at her raw meat. Her rib cage jutted out, covered in eyes spiraling around in their sockets.

God, I'm going to vomit again. Was this the damage Sytri had spoken of, when something too powerful tried to cross the Gates?

Take him, cleanse him. Ezra's voice was ice cold as she dropped Ander to the ground, and he thudded on the floor, racked with pain. Before he could get his bearings, Micah had grabbed the deer skin and wrapped it properly around Ander's mouth, then snatched his wrists, re-tying his loosened restraints.

"You've fucked up now, Seraph."

Ander could have guessed that. But he had managed to avoid making a deal with Micah, and he hadn't gotten eaten by a huge cannibalistic angel. So honestly, he was two-for-two so far. Sytri would be proud.

If he ever saw Sytri again.

CHAPTER TWENTY-SIX

M icah locked Ander in a four-foot-by-four-foot closet. Thick ties bound his hands, and a gag had been strapped around his neck and ears. All he could do was sit cross-legged, stare at the door, and think. Why had Ezra failed to get his deal out?

Hell, first off, how had she been able to attempt it? Sytri had said there was no way for a creature that powerful to make it to Earth, yet, here one was.

Obviously, she was the angel who'd been supplying Mayrez with souls. Ander's stomach rolled. *Fuck.*

He had to get out of here, but had no clue how. In all his life, he had never felt so powerless—which was saying a lot after all the shit he'd been through.

Hours passed and the door in front of him didn't so much as creak. Fear and desperation kept him awake for as long as they could before the urge to sleep won over, his thoughts rambling until the end.

He wasn't sure how long he'd been asleep, when the door cracked open, jolting him awake, a line of drool slipping from the sides of the gag. It was hard to swallow his spit with the damn thing. Really didn't help him feel sane in the situation.

"Seraph. Have you calmed down?"

Micah, the bastard. Ander didn't know if Micah honestly expected him to respond. It was obvious he couldn't, but he glared at the man, hoping that conveyed his feelings to the maximum.

"We have to go through training today, Seraph," Micah said, leaning forward with a metal clip in his hand. "Stand up, please."

His voice was stern and flat as a frozen river. Ander sneered before obeying. Micah pushed Ander's curly hair back, snapping the metal hook around the latch on his neck. Then he tugged it. "Now, come on."

Ander was not enjoying his new dog status.

His bones ached as he stepped into the light, wincing at the flickering flames throughout the hallway. It had been completely dark inside the closet. Outside the window the sky seemed gray, rain clouds blotting the sun and sky. Maybe he'd been in that closet for days. What did he know?

"If you would just agree to my terms, everything would be going a lot more smoothly. I wouldn't have to treat you so disgracefully. You are a Seraph, after all; it seems cruel to lock you away like a bad pet." So the resemblance hadn't been lost on Micah either. The man ran his hands through Ander's hair. "We could get along real well."

Ander jerked away, slamming a heel on Micah's toes.

"Ah, son of a—" Micah hissed. He yanked Ander's collar, choking him. "Don't be so childish! You are of divine blood. Act like it."

Ander continued to glare at him.

He'd never been talkative. But now that he'd been robbed of the option to speak, all he wanted to do was yell. He was past caring about using his voice as a weapon; he just wanted to tell Micah how much he fucking hated him.

"We have a lot to do to make you pliable, Seraph." Micah led him through a large white room filled with spacious tables covered with food. It was like a log-cabin eating area, or a cozy mom-and-pop southern restaurant. Unfortunately, that coziness was dampened by the fact the room was full of cult members wearing matching gray-gold robes. Almost a hundred? Most of them seemed to look Ander and Micah's way as they passed, but they kept their voices to a whisper, perhaps not daring to speak any louder.

Presumably they knew about him, about his Seraph blood, but what beyond that? What did they know about him that he didn't?

Ander laughed to himself. Everything probably. He had discovered his ability a few days ago and hadn't even known what it meant. Micah seemed to have been aware that Ander was a Seraph since they first met.

"As we've said, the Seraph blood in you is so minuscule that it's barely there. Not surprising really, it's been . . . over a millennia since one has been on Earth. But that fragment is still so powerful. And it will take effort to tune it correctly. But once we do, you'll be singing praises in the holy gestalt."

Whatever that was, Ander didn't like it. *Gestalt?* Some gross combination of angels?

They passed by one more table of food on their way out, and Ander's mouth watered. He was starving. How could he voice that? *Micah has to know I'm . . .*

Ander's shoulders slumped. Of course Micah knew. It was another form of torture, like the dark room and the claustrophobia. Starvation and dehydration were just checkmarks on the list. What was next?

"Now, let's get that beautiful blood in you going."

They entered another room. Ander paused, unsettled by the sudden darkness and the soft, aching moans. The smallest windows were at the top of the walls, letting only fragments of light in. The space seemed foggy, like he was peering through a haze.

Little divisions were made in the room by wispy white curtains. Behind one there was the silhouette of someone on a bed, their knees jerking, hands going to their heaving chest.

"Come on now, don't be shy," Micah said smoothly.

Ander's feet stayed planted. His nose was burning from whatever was in the air. Tears welled in the corners of his eyes. This was wrong.

"Seraph. As I said, you don't have a choice." Micah pulled, the easiest flick of his wrist, but it sent Ander toppling toward him. He managed to regain his balance, only to almost lose it again when Micah grabbed him by the arm and tugged him to one of the curtains.

As Micah drew it back, Ander was greeted with a wooden table with straps on the sides and dark black stains covering the entire thing. The sight of it made him want to gag. An IV bag swayed like heavy, swollen fruit on a creaking pole beside it, the liquid inside almost milky in color. Shivers went down his spine.

"Now, you've been through this process before," Micah said, rubbing Ander's shoulder, like pressing ice against him. "This time will be a little different, though. For one, it'll be much more . . . humane, I think. No force-feeding like a sickly pet; instead, we'll get you hooked up and give it time."

Ander stiffened. *Wait.*

But before he could even attempt to run, someone behind him grabbed him under his arms, lifting him with ease. Ander kicked, but Micah snatched his legs and together his captors slammed him onto the table. It took them seconds to bind him completely, pulling straps so tight he could feel the bruises already forming. He gasped and struggled against the restraints as the table *clack*ed and groaned beneath him.

"Can you take Hans out of here?" Micah said, gesturing at whoever had helped immobilize Ander. A brown-feathered angel passed through Ander's vision, and he heard the person who'd been on the table next to him being taken away.

Micah smiled. "I'm going to have Carter here take off your binds in a moment, okay, Seraph? So you don't choke. They're deaf, so hopefully your pleas won't reach them. But just in case, we're getting you settled first so they can leave the room as quickly as possible."

He cranked something on the table, raising Ander's head. Across the room was the source of the fear that had been building in Ander's heart. There, half-hidden behind more curtains, were bags and boxes of salt. He swallowed hard.

A prick in his arm made him flinch. He turned his head as much as he could and saw a needle being pushed deep into his flesh. The attached plastic cord twisted around to the full bag that was obviously more salt than water. A piece of duct tape went over the tube, locking it on his arm.

"It's amazing, you know, that we can take this salt," Micah cooed. "The human part can't handle this much at all. The salt kills it. That's why it hurts so good every time you take it. The human part is dying, and the angel part is thriving. You thirst and hurt, and desire and want and beg, all at once." He sighed. "It is the purest ecstasy. Your own body craving a power that's destroying it." He leaned closer, near Ander's neck. "I relate, in more ways than one. I've tasted your blood before, and I would like to again. But alas, you've made it dangerous for me, though it would be hard to have a drink with the rest of the Cast around anyway." He grinned. "But be assured, Seraph, I will eventually devour what is mine. And once I do, you will make me the first blend turned pure angel. Get rid of all this filth inside of me." His voice was so low at the last part, almost sorrowful.

What the hell is this freak going on about? Ander wanted to kick him in the stomach and run. But once again, all he could do was glare, praying that the anger sparking in his chest was visible in his eyes.

Micah tilted his head as he pulled away, but whatever he saw, he didn't comment.

Fuck you.

"He's strapped up, Carter," Micah said, while moving his hands again—sign language, of course. "Start the IV, give him about ten minutes, and then remove the gag and leave quickly. His voice could still be potent even if you can't hear it. We don't know yet. He is a Seraph, after all." He patted Ander's arm. "I'll be back to check on you in . . . a few hours? Perhaps a few days. We shall see. Who knows? However long it takes for you to become docile." Micah chuckled. "Be good for me, Seraph." Then footsteps trailed away and a door closed.

Ander knew the moment the salt hit his blood. There was a hot pressure as it forced its way where it shouldn't, spreading like a wildfire and turning his whole body into burning webs.

Ander hacked violently. Every breath was raspy, painful. White bursts dotted his vision while he struggled to swallow the sludge that bubbled in his throat. It wouldn't leave the gag, and he desperately didn't want to spew it out his nose.

As he panicked at the thought, calloused hands pulled at the muzzle. His mouth opened, tasting the salt-drenched air, and the sudden freedom gave him a spark of energy.

"Let me go!" Ander shouted, voice strained and pained. Instantly he vomited heavy globs that tasted of iron. Sweat rolled on his face and he heaved again, body lurching at the effort, pulling against his binds.

A door shut with a *click* and Ander screamed. It tore his vocal cords, brought a tremble to his body. "Get me out of here! Get this shit off me!"

Over and over again he cried out.

But apparently no one remained to hear.

Hours passed. Ander lay there, writhing and hacking up tar. It sank into his clothes, turned so cold it made his bones shake. His body burned with a tiredness he'd never felt before. His wrists were scraped raw from the straps.

Where was it all coming from? Was it really his sin like Micah had said?

Hours more. He fell into a slumber and awoke only to throw up. He forgot his name. Then he grabbed hold of it. He forgot where he was and, when he remembered, he wished it had stayed forgotten.

For an hour or so he felt clear and strange. Angelic? Perhaps. He thought of Michael and the other Couriers. They had been dazed by salt. Was he?

He began muttering to himself between bouts of vomiting. Things he could remember: names. Sytri, Ronan, Vega. Over and over, the repetition helping him to stay calm. Not long after he started, however, his throat became dry. On a better note, his vomiting finally ceased.

Ander stared at the bag, once bulging with water, now slack and drooping. Had all of that really traveled inside of him? He wanted to prod his body with his fingers, find the pools where it had settled.

How long had it been?

There was no light outside. But there was one in the room. A candle, a bit to Ander's left, was flickering. Just like the deal in his chest, which seemed so weak and far away at the moment. Was that part of the plan too? Make him weak, make his deal weak?

He stared at the flame, at the shadows that raged against the wall from its desperate waving. It was fighting to stay alive. *Ezra said I had the voice of life. What counts as life?*

"Hey," Ander said to the flame. It did not respond. "Hello." It continued to waver and wisp about. "You're alive." He licked his lips. He was thirsty. Probably from the salt. "Can you grow for me?" For a moment, the fire stilled. Ander's eyes widened. "Can you grow? Eat up the wick, the oxygen in the air, whatever it is you need? Grow. Burn." He focused on the sliver of angel in him, tugged it out. Its light curled upward until it reached his tongue. "Burn."

The flame kicked up with a loud *clap*, touching the ceiling, leaving a scorch mark in its wake. It was the brightest flame Ander had ever seen, and for a moment that same sort of heat swirled in his heart. He could almost grin. *Fire fucking counts.*

But as quickly as the blaze had come, it left, and it took everything with it. The wax had melted into a slick puddle dripping onto the floor. Its metal holder had been burnt black.

Ander stared, his chest tight. He had hoped that the flame would catch the whole room on fire, and then when the Cast burst in, he could somehow escape. But perhaps that wouldn't have worked anyway. What if no one had noticed in time and he'd just burned to a crisp?

Could he have told the fire to stray from him? Controlled it so it only burned across the leather wraps on his wrists? What could he do if he focused?

The question drifted in and out of Ander's head. Learning the full potential of his power could be his way out. Maybe the Cast would get careless and leave him alone and ungagged in the right room. He clutched onto that thought, that bit of hope as the world faded out and he fell back to sleep.

He awoke with a start, opened his mouth to speak, and couldn't. The muzzle had been brought back. *Fuck.* He'd passed out hard enough for them to gag him again. He stared up at the ceiling. This was a different room. It was more comfortable too.

He was on a bed. He twisted to rise and grimaced: his hands were tied together. With some effort, he managed to sit up and place his feet on the ground.

"Hello, Seraph."

Ander jumped—Micah was sitting across the room.

A lamp flickered above him as he leafed through a dense book, barren of a title. "I hope the salt treatments weren't too unbearable. You puked a lot more than most. I think it's because of the Seraph blood, but I'm not sure. Anyway, how do you feel? Better after the shower?"

Shower? Ander glanced down at himself and turned red. He was in *Cast* clothing—a stupid fucking robe. He glared at Micah, face aflame. Had that creep put his hands on him while he was unconscious?

"Your feathers grew, Seraph. It's a beautiful thing to see the salt finally going into effect. It took a lot to provoke a physical response. Your powers though, are still up for debate. We won't know the extent of them until later, unfortunately. When you're willing to make a deal with me."

Ander twisted his head, trying to look at his shoulders. The robes didn't really let him see, but now that Micah had mentioned it, he could feel feathers bending under the weight of the fabric, grazing his skin. Not wings, just feathers, but more than before. They had spread down his shoulder blades.

He tensed; the salt *was* changing him.

"So, are you willing to listen to me now?"

Ander didn't move.

"I suppose that's a no, then. How dreadful. It's clearly going to take a lot more salt to make you pliant." Micah stood and stretched his arms. "Well, I hoped you enjoyed sleeping on an actual bed. Because until I can trust you, it's back in the closet." He walked over to Ander and snatched up the leash around his neck and pulled.

Ander dug his heels into the ground, tears filling his eyes. The thought of returning to the confined space of the closet made his shoulders stiffen, and a thick curl of tension wrapped around his throat.

"All this fuss, when you could let Ezra pry your deal out and make a new one with me. Would be a lot less of hassle. Wouldn't you prefer that?"

Ander could say yes and not mean it, but Micah wouldn't just take off the muzzle here, risking Ander's definite betrayal. He would drag him to Ezra to get the deal out first. And it seemed unlikely that one salt dosage was enough to make him stronger than her. Probably not.

He glared.

Micah seemed to understand that. "Then, Seraph, it looks like we have a long journey ahead of us. And it's going to get harder, you know. Carter said they almost listened to you when you spoke, which means we can't ungag you anymore for the treatments." He sneered. "For your sake, I hope you're done with that vomiting nonsense. Or the next couple of saltings will be most miserable for you."

He yanked the leash hard, pulling Ander and all his fear with him.

CHAPTER
TWENTY-SEVEN

The deal was vanishing.

Ander leaned against the wall of his prison, his breathing slow and shallow. He'd spent days trying to coax life back into the deal, but it was a faint flicker in his chest now that flared meekly if he focused. Like a dying animal gasping when prodded. Ander didn't like that, but death was all he could associate the feeling with. The thought made the walls close in around him.

Don't do this. Don't give up now.

As if summoned by Ander's despair, the door to his cell opened.

And there stood Micah.

His eyes were wild with excitement, like he was watching the world catch fire from his own match. Ander grimaced.

"What a wonderful day it is." Micah hummed, snapping the leash on Ander. "Things are finally moving forward."

Ander raised an eyebrow, but Micah did not elaborate. Could he or Ezra feel the dying deal? In this state, was it weak enough for Ezra to pull it out?

Ander's feathers stood on end as Micah dragged him into the hallway.

He stumbled down the corridors like a man on death row. His attempts to concentrate crumbled with every step. The recent saltings had been harsher and longer. The time to recuperate between each one had been minimal. When he had been able to think, he'd focused on the need to find Sytri, to escape Micah, to stop the Cast entirely. But in between those moments he'd lost awareness.

What had he been doing?

If it wasn't for his deal with Sytri, Micah would have no doubt taken advantage of one of Ander's blackouts to form his own pact. How long did he have until Micah managed to wedge his cold self in Ander's chest? Strike a deal that he wouldn't even remember? He dreaded the thought of reaching for the spot next to his heart and only finding a shard of ice.

I won't let that happen.

"I've got a gift for you, Seraph," Micah cooed as they walked. Ander rolled his eyes and bit deeper into the leather strap in his mouth. He had broken through one before, so they kept having to get more. The current one was finally beginning to tear.

Maybe he could— *Oh fire.*

A candle was flickering perilously close to a curtain.

This time, this last time, it had to work.

Burn. Burn. Burn. Burn.

The flame fluttered unperturbed.

Damn it. Ander clenched his jaw. He had hoped thoughts alone would have worked now that the salt had simmered and thickened that angel part of him. He could feel the divine sparks when he had tried to command the fire, the way they floated up his throat. The angelic light wanted out.

If only it had worked. Unlike his mouth, his thoughts were unfettered. Unfortunately, they were also turning strange. So often he found himself wanting to . . . to *cleanse. Get rid of all the sin inside me.*

Ander shook his head and breathed through his nose. No. He couldn't think like that—like some sort of scrutinizing angel with a purity complex. *À la Micah.* No matter how much salt they gave him, he would stay in control of himself. No weird ideas.

Especially when he was in such clear danger. He was *definitely* being brought to Ezra. She was going to use her horrible hands to try to rip the last bit of fire from him. Did he have to vocally agree to a deal? Would he have the opportunity to try his voice on her again?

Will I be strong enough?

There had to be a way out of this fucking mess. He couldn't risk taking more salt. He could feel the human part of him slipping under the angel part. Being brushed aside neatly and folded into a corner.

Ander needed his human part to get out of this bullshit.

"I was beginning to get a bit worried that we'd never get to make our deal, Ander. You've been putting up so much resistance."

How far could he get if he jumped out the windows? They seemed to be a little closer to the ground this time around. Perhaps he wouldn't splatter completely like an egg on pavement.

"But thankfully everything will be sorted out nicely today."

Ander glared at Micah. *Fucking choke and die.*

"I know you think poorly of me, but you'll see how much I just want to treasure you. The way only an angel can treasure another angel. With a deal, we'll both get what we need," Micah said, almost softly. Ander shuddered.

Obviously in Micah's mind he was already a pure angel or some bullshit. Even though he wanted to make a deal, which only someone with demon blood could do. The man was delusional, fucking delusional, and Ander didn't like anything he was saying. He couldn't fathom being bound to this man.

Can you kill the person you make a deal with? Ander's pulse spiked.

They were in an unfamiliar hallway now. Was this the way to Ezra? It seemed so long ago, so washed out in his mind from the torture, the salt, that Ander couldn't remember.

Micah opened a heavy door, and on the other side was a dark stadium. The whole dim room curved downward into a bowl, an arena. A thousand people could have fit in there. However, only a mere dozen were present, possibly the higher-ups. They wore robes with intricate gold embroidery, like Micah did . . . and Tabbris had.

The Cast elites all seemed closer to the spotlighted center stage, but some were in the balconies overhead, staring down.

High overhead there was a large, stained-glass dome ceiling. It should have been letting in the morning sun, alleviating the uncomfortable atmosphere of the room. However, whatever the glass had originally portrayed had been covered up, and instead a massive, thick white painting of Ezra had been put in its place.

Her feathery hair had been lifted to form actual wings that spread over the communion. The bones of her rib cage were scattered with black eyes and from them spilled white animals. The feathers and creatures bowed with the dome, seeming to embrace everything below in a suffocating hold. Ander could almost feel Ezra herself locking onto his frame. Her wicked mouth hungry for a bite of flesh.

"Beautiful, isn't she? We had our best artists work on it," Micah praised, as if he were talking about a community project and not a weird art tribute to a murderous angel. Ander tugged on the leash to disagree but just kept on pulling. "This is a holy place. We come here to pray to her—to her and the other Thrones. And soon you will join us in our worship at my side. We will wait together."

What the fuck did that mean?

"In the meantime we will make the necessary sacrifices."

The angels and blends down at the stage were all chattering, their voices getting louder and louder with each step Ander and Micah took. All of the angels wore dark cloaks; they were a mass of shuffling storm clouds.

"We will cleanse the Earth."

A slumped-over figure was on the platform, with two angels on either side of it. Ander squinted.

His heart stopped mid-beat.

"We will obtain purity."

The world closed in around Ander until there was only him and the light on stage. His feet skidded on the slick oak as he tried to run toward the stage, before Micah jerked the leash, yanking him to the floor. His head collided on the hard ground with a thud, rippling his vision and thoughts.

"We all have to lose something for this world to get better, Ander. And if we are to achieve perfection, we must rid ourselves of the stains that hold us back." Micah sneered at the stage. From the ground, Ander gazed up to the light, his heart racing, adrenaline coursing through him.

Sytri.

Sytri was at the pulpit, covered in that blindingly blue blood.

Ander struggled, trying to get up with his tied hands. Micah lifted him by his shirt and cupped his face, those thin cold hands on his hot flesh.

"No more waiting. We're here to remove the stain," Micah whispered. "And then make you mine."

Ander yanked himself free.

He tried to run once more, only for Micah to jerk the leash again. This time, however, Ander kept his balance and pulled harder, screaming as loud as he could behind the gag, the muscles in his throat straining, his whole body rigid and desperate. He yelled every word imaginable, every command, every demand, every plea. All of them too smothered to hold power.

Sytri.

There was so much blood coating him that it was hard to make out his details, but it was definitely Sytri; those horns, that face, those piercing eyes. Well, now they were hazy as he stared at the floor below, where a pool of blue was forming at the base of the chair he was tied to. They had beaten and bruised him, left him like roadkill. Ander could *feel* Sytri's agony.

Ander would kill them. He would kill all of them.

"Once we free ourselves of our burdens, our sins, our past regrets, we can move toward purity," Micah said softly. "And once pure, you will be able to accept us."

Accept *him*. That was what he meant. The fucking monster.

Ander pulled harder. Sytri didn't seem to have noticed him, he was so hurt.

Get to him.

Once again Ander tried to yell but no words could form. They had silenced him, stolen Sytri, all these things they had *no right* to do.

Immoral acts, deserving of punishment.

Were these his thoughts or the angel part's?

Sytri.

His voice was barely his to control.

Sytri!

Sytri stirred. Time seemed to halt. He blinked, lifted his head, slowly.

Have to save him.

That empty spot in Ander's chest pulsed, tugged at the tense rope between him and Sytri. He had to close this gap. The distance was too much to bear.

Light flickered in Sytri's eyes. He mouthed a word, lips barely moving. *Ander?*

Tears welled on Ander's cheeks. *Fuck.*

Sytri yanked against his restraints, only to hiss and bare his teeth. The crowd heckled him.

"Ander!" Sytri coughed, voice raspy and dry. Ander's heart lurched. He wanted to call back, but all that came out was a smothered cry.

"Hello, everyone," Micah called, waving his arms out to the side, yanking Ander with the motion. The Cast turned to him immediately in unison. "Ladies, gentlemen, beautiful beings, we are here this early morning for another sacrifice to our beloved Thrones. This time, however, the sacrifice is a little different. Not only is its blood a gift to our Masters, but it's the removal of sin from our Seraph. They made a deal with this demon in front of you."

"A demon made a deal with a Seraph?"

"Disgusting!"

"Sacrilege!"

The insults sprang from everywhere, venom in their voices. Ander stared into the crowd. Mouths curled into sneers, eyes like ice, feathers puffed up in disgust. They were vultures, scoffing at their meal. They would still eat, however.

"Now, some of you made deals before we saved you." Micah put his hand on his heart. "And once we removed your stains, you were worthy of the Cast. We cleanse the demon, we cleanse his stain." Micah pulled Ander's hair, yanking him, straining his neck. "We make the Seraph purer for the Cast."

"For the Cast!" they all shouted, hands raised.

"Who else will you make a deal with, Seraph," Micah whispered into his ear, "to keep you safe, when you don't have your demon anymore?"

Ander couldn't move. He was pulling with all his might against Micah's grip, but it accomplished nothing. Less than thirty feet in front of him, Sytri sat in a chair on the raised platform. On each side of him, the angels held sharp sickles in their hands. The blades curved around Sytri's battered form, like teeth closing in.

"He wasn't even that hard to find. He has been desperately looking for you. But his little rescue attempt was all in vain. No demon is as strong as the Cast, as strong as the will of Ezra."

Micah's face was too close to Ander's. One of his hands was a little too low on Ander's waist, chilling him to the bone. All he could see was Micah pushing the salt into his veins, feel his gross and disgusting teeth piercing his flesh. How could the rest of the Cast be so blind? How could they not tell that something was off with this man?

Why would they, when something's off with all of them?

Micah let Ander go and started talking to everyone again. "Now, as we continue with our sacrifice, let us start our prayer." The angels at the pulpit were shifting their shoulders, readying their blades near Sytri's neck.

Ander's heartbeat began to echo in his head, louder and louder.

"Angel Ezra, my guardian dear—"

The angels were jeering the prayer. Sytri was still pulling at the binds in vain. But even if he gathered enough strength, there was no way he could take on this whole room by himself.

Ander was shaking now, and he couldn't feel his legs. It was like the world was breaking apart— *Damn it!* He needed his hands free, the gag gone, but he wasn't strong enough to tear them off.

"To whom Her love commits me here—"

Ander stilled. *He* wasn't strong enough.

"Ever this day be at my side—"

He twisted toward Micah. His legs were weak and his chest hurt, but he jumped and slammed his head straight into his face. He felt the crunch of bone as Micah's nose burst like a can of soda. The bastard cried out, his scream turning to a gurgle as rose-red blood poured down his face.

Ander bolted past confused angels and toward the stage. Adrenaline powered each step. He leaped onto the podium as realization seemed to hit the Cast. They grabbed him and tried to snatch him away from Sytri, whose wide panicked eyes met his. Ander pulled himself closer, glancing desperately down at the gag and then back at Sytri. *Please.*

Sytri blinked. Then he leaned back and then jerked forward, this time the chair teetering on its legs. His teeth latched on to the thick leather strap that pressed into Ander's mouth, and he snapped it free.

Ander yelled, "*Stop!*"

Everyone halted.

Ander panted, face red, heart in his throat. Fire flitted about his lungs like a sparkler had been lit. The angelic blood in him had tasted freedom, after so long.

But more importantly, Sytri was right there.

He stared at him in disbelief. Everything was quiet. There was only the light shining down on the two of them, and a swarm of the Cast frozen in their clawing.

"Sytri," Ander breathed. "You look terrible." He sniffed.

"You too."

An angel to Sytri's right flinched.

"Don't fucking move," Ander snapped and the angel froze.

There hadn't been any nausea or heat when the power left Ander's throat. The salt *had* made him stronger. Good.

He held his bound hands up to Sytri, who bit down, ripping the leather in half easily. Around them the crowd of angels stood immobile with dark and twisted faces. But Ander ignored them and embraced Sytri. "I've missed you."

"I missed you too, but we've got to go," Sytri rasped.

Ander grimaced, before yanking down his robe to show a strip of his shoulder. "You're hurt, drink first."

There was the briefest hesitation before Sytri nipped at Ander's skin, and Ander shivered at the familiar and welcome pain. This was how it was supposed to be.

Sytri detached himself, and in seconds he had ripped himself free from his ties. He was rubbing at his bruised wrists, when he turned to Ander, his eyes bright.

God, I love him.

Suddenly Sytri cupped his face and kissed him. It was brief and urgent but *needed*.

"Okay, now we leave," Ander muttered as they pulled apart. His face had gone hot.

"We can't let the Seraph leave—they're ours!" someone cried, their voice strained as if they were being choked. Sytri growled, flashing his claws.

"Stay still! Don't move!" Ander yelled again. "Sytri, we *have* to go."

"I want to kill all of them," Sytri hissed. "They took you from me, Ander. Tephera just ripped you from me. And now they think they fucking own you?" His jaw clenched.

"We don't have time to keep on talking. I don't know how long I can keep them like this." Ander grimaced.

"Fine, fine," Sytri said through gritted teeth.

He hefted Ander up, slinging him over his back, and Ander wrapped his arms around Sytri's shoulders tightly. The handful of days apart had felt like a lifetime, but here Sytri was, pressing against Ander. Would have been perfect if they weren't in a cult of sadistic angels.

Like a dream and a nightmare all at once.

Sytri spun and punched one of the angels with the sickles in the face, sending him straight into the wall behind him.

"Sytri!" Ander cried, even as Micah's mouth began to twitch.

"Just one guy," Sytri gasped as he ran. "Had to vent some anger real quick."

"Don't let them go!" Micah yelled, blood still spewing down his face. The effort left him coughing, but he staggered forward ever so slightly. "Ezra needs him!"

"No one move," Ander shouted as Sytri leaped over the crowd. Nausea swirled in his stomach, and he grimaced. But it wasn't overwhelming this time—he could focus.

Sytri sprinted toward the door and kicked it open, revealing a handful of angels on the other side. "Shit, shit," he muttered, sliding across the floor and then turning down the hallway.

"Don't follow us!" Ander shouted back at them. His stomach rolled with sickness. "Crap, not yet." How many Cast members had he already commanded? How many more could he?

The sickness and heat were only the beginning of the effects though. He probably had time.

Just then an angel came crashing through the walls in front of them. Sytri yelped and jumped, clinging onto the wooden frames overhead and avoiding chunks of wall, before swinging over the large winged creature and darting down another hallway. Yelling and screaming followed them.

"It's like when we first met." Sytri laughed. "A crowd of people chasing after you. Is this how we'll spend all our date nights from now on?"

"I mean, if you like it so much!" Ander cried as a door flung open. "We can plan the same for next week, I suppose."

An angel sprang down from the rafters, hands outstretched to grab and swipe. But Sytri jumped back, two shadow arms ripping from his shoulders and slicing into them. They were torn to shreds almost instantly.

"They said you were a Seraph," Sytri yelled over the shouting of the Cast in the distance. "Is that fucking true?"

"I guess." The Cast certainly seemed damn sure of it. "What does that mean?"

"It means we're in a shit ton of trouble."

"Good. Wasn't sure I was in quite enough yet, so I'm glad to know I've found more." Ander grimaced. "Where is everyone else? Did you really head out here alone?"

"No. I was with Vega. He was the only one willing to come with me to scout the place out." Sytri panted. "He was actually supposed to sneak in here using his weird camouflage shit. Unfortunately, we got separated. That big fucking monster angel—"

"Tephera!"

Seraph, you cannot leave.

Tephera had materialized in front of them, shifting into view from a static void. They swiped with claws that Sytri barely dodged, rolling to the floor and covering Ander with his shadow hands.

"Don't touch us!" Ander snapped. He swallowed hard, tasting bile. *Shit.*

Tephera flinched.

"Don't get near me," Ander yelled as loud as he could even as fire leaped up his throat. But Tephera was an Archangel and they continued to move, albeit more slowly, their hands stretching like spiders toward Ander and Sytri.

"Get us out of here, Sytri," Ander shouted.

"What the fuck do you think I've been doing?" Sytri slid under Tephera's arms and slammed sideways into a wall behind them with a grunt. "But there's a bunch of lunatics chasing us, and it's making it rather difficult. Especially when one of them is Tephera." He turned and darted up a narrow staircase, leaving said angel clawing the doorframe below.

That's true. Shit. It was just them, two against at least a hundred? Ander hadn't exactly been doing a headcount in his days as a hostage. They needed a wild idea to escape.

"We need a distraction," Ander muttered, scanning around them for anything that could help. He stopped on the flickering flame of a lantern. *Yes.*

"Knock every candle you see to the floor," Ander said.

"Wait. We're burning it down?" Sytri's voice rose.

"Yeah. We're lighting it up."

"Ah man, I fucking love you."

As they ran, further and further up the stairs, Sytri used his shadow hands to send every candle holder, lamp, and flicking chandelier to the floor. Ander watched as the fire spilled out on the floorboards, clung to the wood, trying to drain the life out of it to fuel its flames.

"Burn," Ander whispered at the patches of light. "Please, burn stronger." It took less effort than commanding a person, didn't make his nausea worse. The fire didn't want to resist—it wanted to spread.

As if oxygen had been pumped in, the fire obeyed, sprouting and growing, grabbing the dusty curtains and old bookshelves. Like red flowers blooming. Soon a path of hell followed them as they ascended the church stairs, darting past floor after floor. Handfuls of flames turned into a roaring blaze in seconds, heat drying out the air, smoke reaching toward ceilings.

"Fire!" someone called out from below them. "The demon has set us on fire!"

Ander closed his eyes and envisioned the flames. "Don't give up," he said urgently. "Keep burning and find Micah."

A trio of blends spilled out of a doorway in front of them, and Sytri instantly grabbed one, practically ripping them in half. He tossed the body behind them—more food for the flames. He snatched another member, snapping their neck with a growl. Ander's breath hitched. Sytri's snarls were . . . feral.

"Hey, focus. We're getting out of here. You said it yourself: can't stop to kill everyone," Ander said, voice tense.

Sytri tackled the third blend who had been trying to leave, his claws splitting their sides open. Their screams were silenced when he chomped into their throat, spitting out the flesh with a growl.

What the fuck. Ander glanced behind them. The fire was catching up. "Stop it! We've got a fucking inferno to escape."

Sytri wavered. Then, he pushed himself off the ground, panting. "Sorry, I . . . I was just . . . They *stole* you."

"I know. You were angry. Now get us the hell out of here."

"R-right." Sytri ran a bloodied hand through his hair and then dashed up a spiraling staircase. His speed made Ander's head spin.

A lone angel blocked their path, but Sytri knocked him out a window.

At the top, Sytri stopped abruptly. Dead end. Nothing around them but glass windows. The sun outside was still half-hidden by the earth, the rest by trees. As they looked out the nearest window, there was only a drop of seemingly miles to the ground. *This church is stupid high.*

"Fuck. Wasn't paying attention, should've jumped out a window a while ago," Sytri muttered. He swiveled back toward the door they'd come from, but the orange hue of the fire could be seen dancing up the steps. *Oh, this sucks.* Sytri would die if they jumped from this height—fuck they both would. If they only had enough time to climb down or—

Glass shattered, shooting across the room.

"Give me back my Seraph."

Micah's voice was solid as ice.

He was on the other side of the now-broken window with rippling white wings beating from his shoulders. Pushing through the remaining shards cut through his shoulders and arms, nicked his feathers, but he didn't react as he stepped inside. His dark-rimmed eyes were focused solely on Ander, the hollowness pulling him in.

"Hell, you don't give up, do you?" Sytri hissed.

"I could say the same for you, rat. Now hand over the Seraph. I saw him before you did. I tasted his blood first. He is mine."

"You don't own Ander. He's not property, you fucker." Sytri snarled. "Does the rest of the Cast know they're being led around by a crazed half-demon? Seems like something a demon-killing cult wouldn't really be keen on."

"I am not half-demon. I am half-angel," Micah barked, slamming his hand on his chest. "And I deserve the Seraph. He will make me pure. It is *sacrilege* for him to give his blood to a monster." Ander gritted his teeth as Micah carried on. "You are nothing but a violent demon, one so useless and wild that even Mayrez didn't want to deal with you."

"Get out of here, Micah," Sytri said coldly.

"This is my territory. I'm not going anywhere. Not until you give me the Seraph. You've broken him, tricked him with your devilish words, and now I have to fix him."

"You're out of your fucking mind."

Micah flinched, then clenched his jaw. "I'm stronger than you. It's a simple fact. So why risk your life for blood you can't possibly understand? Blood you'll squander away. Grab another blend and hand over that one."

"Over my dead body"

"It doesn't have to come to that," Micah said, almost reassuringly. "His deal is fading. I don't have to kill you. I could just wait until I can use him *properly*." He licked his lips. "So be a good boy, give him up, and you'll get to live. Win-win."

"Shut the fuck up," Ander yelled. There was fire in his throat again, followed by the taste of acid and smoke. He swallowed it down with a flinch before speaking again, voice raw. "You're a monster, Micah. It doesn't matter if you drink my blood. You're not capable of being pure, or whatever it is you're trying to achieve. It's not the demon in you that makes you so vile. It's just you. You're disgusting. And no matter what you do, you will always be." Ander's stomach turned. "And I can't wait to see you die." He glared at Micah, heat rising in his lungs. "Now don't move."

The man froze, eyes going wide as his face paled. Satisfaction bloomed in Ander's chest. Despite the urge to vomit, it felt *good* to see that.

Then the floor began to crumble.

SERAPH.

"What the *fuck* was that?" Sytri yelped.

"Ezra," Ander and Micah answered in vastly different tones.

"Ez-what?"

A whole chunk of floor clattered beneath them. Sytri backed up against the wall, but that side began to cave in. It felt like the whole building was collapsing.

"She'll fix this," Micah murmured. A grin split across his face, the stretch of it too wide for comfort. Too many teeth, too much gum. He spread his wings, arms open. "Ezra, I have the Seraph with me! He is mine."

And with manic eyes, he charged them.

"Stop!" Ander screamed, and immediately broke into a violent cough. His lungs were on *fire*.

But Micah hesitated for a second. Long enough for Sytri to jump past him, his feet landing on wood just outside the window, which immediately gave way.

They jolted toward the ground. Ander was flung from Sytri's back like a kite whipped by a hurricane.

"Ander!" Eyes wide, Sytri reached for him. Then his back slammed into a chunk of wall, sending him into a spiral, and his eyelids fluttered.

Ander's chest dropped. *Shit. Shit.* "Sytri! Stay with me!" He grabbed for Sytri's hand and missed. Tried again and again. He gritted his teeth—air and debris and everything was hitting him full force. He stretched his arm out so hard it felt like it would snap off his body.

Then his hand latched on to Sytri's. He pulled him close and wrapped his body around him. If he could roll over, take the blunt of the blow— No, that wouldn't matter.

They were going to die.

Do something! Save him!

Be stronger.

The skin of his shoulders split like dry paper, and he cried out in agony before his body ripped upward so hard it snatched his breath.

The fuck.

He flapped his wings.

CHAPTER TWENTY-EIGHT

A nder blinked. There really were *wings* stretched out around him. *Multiple.* Four? They were huge and onyx black and hung heavy on his shoulders. He could feel them as he moved his arms. *Holy shit. Are these mine?* Ander fluttered them, the motion as simple as flexing a finger as he and Sytri drifted downward.

"Ander," Sytri whispered, "did you just upgrade from a fuzzball?"

"I don't know what I did." Ander peered below. "Ground! Ground!" He flapped furiously, catching a strong wind and pushing them farther away from the church. They tumbled onto the dirt, rolling on each other. Ander folded his wings, feathers ripping out of them as they skidded across rocks.

Breathing heavily, they untangled themselves. Ander groaned and pressed his palms into the rough dirt. Then he latched on to Sytri, embracing him so hard he thought they would both crack.

"Fuck, we're alive," Ander muttered. "Oh my god. Never doing that again."

"You were flying," Sytri said, eyes wide. "What the hell?" He ran a hand over one of the wings, which sent a shiver down Ander's spine. "Ander . . . you— They're beautiful."

Ander's feathers fuzzed up. And what was this odd and giddy sensation inside his chest? He flicked his wings, tears welling up in his eyes.

"Whoa, y-you okay?" Sytri stammered.

"Yes. Fine." Ander wiped at his eyes and gave a strained grin. "Just feel weird."

"Understandable." Sytri placed his palm on Ander's cheek. "But as soon as—"

A thunderous crash shook the ground, and they turned to where they had fallen from. The building was crumbling apart, fragments plummeting to the earth like meteors.

The church was huge. Grander than Ander had imagined from inside. He and Sytri had managed to light up a whole section on the left, but the majority of the massive building remained.

Its shadow clogged Ander's heart. Even with the fire clinging to it brightly, the dark wood seemed like a stain among the forest. And worse, Ezra was inside, festering away in the depths. Ander gritted his teeth. *The leader of the Cast and all the horrors it's brought.*

She needed to be stopped. The fire had to swallow her whole.

"Burn faster! Get to her!" Each word knocked him closer to throwing up or catching fire. Maybe both. But he had to do this. "I am a Seraph and you will obey me!" He gasped, swaying on his feet.

Lightning crackled through the air, sparking an explosion across the roof that made Ander and Sytri recoil. The fire at the edge of the steeple rocketed along the top of the building in a string of flames and force. Walls burst apart, sending boards and glass into the air like fireworks. The church groaned in pain, its old bones charring and collapsing.

"Holy shit, Ander," Sytri rasped.

Ander's chest heaved, his breathing loud and his lungs aching. It felt like fire-tipped needles were in his throat. But he'd done it. *That'll have to get to her now.* He leaned on Sytri, legs shaking.

Then angels and blends spilled out from the wreckage in a panicked frenzy, their screams filling the air. Ander's blood went cold.

"Wait," he whispered, voice raw. *This isn't what I meant.* "Wait, I just wanted Ezra. I didn't . . ." He clenched his jaw. What the fuck had he been thinking? He couldn't just burn hundreds of people to death even if they were from the Cast. This—this wasn't right. His heart raced, vision flitting from one person to the next. Scared. Hurt. Dying. *I didn't—*

Seraph!

Out from the burning church came a huge white hand, its skin bubbling and boiling. Ezra pulled herself out of the building, shrieking as animals fell off her, their pale bodies aflame. Ezra's head swiveled around, the permanent sharp smile still engraved on it even as she screeched. The church fell apart more, her huge limbs easily snapping the thick wooden planks like twigs.

"What the fuck is that?" Sytri yelled, getting in front of Ander.

"That's the Throne," Ander shouted back. "We should run." He took a step toward Sytri and floundered. His feet seemed to be slipping from underneath him. "Fuck."

"Ander." Sytri grabbed him, held him up. "Fuck, you feel like you're on fire."

The tips of Ander's wings dragged on the ground as he tried to get on Sytri's back.

"Come on, I have you." Sytri's voice was tense.

Leave, my children. Hurry. Ezra desperately swiped into the air.

And it ripped like fabric, from the top of the church to the ground. Suddenly, a hole in the middle of nothing. Ander's heart dropped; the other side seemed . . . brighter.

Surviving angels and blends scurried to it, stepping through and vanishing from sight. A portal—the monster had made some sort of portal. *She's too powerful, even injured like she is.* Worse, she was escaping. No. No. She wasn't *supposed* to be able to leave. He reached forward.

"Stop," he tried to command, but his voice cracked and he dry-heaved. *Son of a bitch.* Was it because he'd used so much? Or because he couldn't control someone like *her*?

"Ander, it's okay. We have to leave. Before—"

Tephera, my child. Bring me the Seraph.

Ander gripped Sytri as Tephera formed in front of them.

Yes, Ezra.

The angel raised their head into the air, and a terrible screech seemed to come from nowhere. Within a matter of seconds, dark clouds began to form above them, the wind whipping upward in every direction, thunder roaring.

Tephera had brought a storm.

Hand me the Seraph.

"Fuck outta here, dude," Sytri snarled.

"Stop, Tephera—" Ander tried to whisper, but the air burned up in his lungs, cut him off.

Tephera swung an arm, but Sytri dodged it, leaping into the air and slashing Tephera's flesh as they swiped again. White blood spilled from their wound and they screeched.

Hand me the Seraph.

"Ezra needs him!"

To the right, Micah: bloody, pissed, still very much alive. *Shit. No.* This wasn't supposed to be happening. Micah and Tephera were supposed to burn inside the church. What was the point of it if they got out?

"Stay back!" Ander attempted but the words splintered as he spoke, with no power behind them. Worse, his insides seemed to be melting. Fear welled up in his chest, and he slumped over.

Out. I'm out.

"Ander, quit trying to fight! I need you stay here with me," Sytri barked.

Suddenly they were both slammed backward into a tree. Sytri yelled as Tephera's grip around them tightened, smashing them together. Micah stood in front of them, leaning over Tephera's huge hand, and he grabbed Ander by his throat. Ander gasped as the breath was crushed out of him.

"You're not escaping me, Seraph," Micah hissed.

Sytri bit down on his wrist, and Micah shouted, pulling away too fast and leaving his arm in shreds. Sytri snapped his jaws, bits of skin and blood between his teeth. "Don't fucking touch him. Ever again." His shadow arms swung out, one swiping Micah aside, the other one clawing at Tephera's throat, forcing the Archangel to drop them. They hit the ground with a heavy *thud*, and Ander wheezed, trying to draw the air back into his lungs.

Tephera and Micah stood their ground. The rain started to come down harder, and Sytri stumbled in the slick mud forming underfoot as he tried to stand. This was bad.

"For somebody that was just a leech clinging to Mayrez, I didn't expect you to turn into such a fucking problem," Micah spat as Sytri slashed at him. "You're getting stronger on the Seraph's blood. And it should be me." He gritted his teeth. "So learn your place!"

Then someone crashed into Micah, sending him flying straight into the woods.

"That guy gives the most boring of speeches. But, hey, now the gang's all here. How pleasant."

"Vega!" Ander and Sytri shouted. Ander's heart reignited. Vega stood there, red hair as slick as it could be in the rain, his shirt clinging to him. He turned to them with a good, if eerie, grin.

Quit talking. Tephera swung an arm down in the midst of the conversation, their voice echoing all around. Vega knocked it sideways with brute force that made Tephera topple to the ground with a *boom*. Ander couldn't help but stare.

Vega turned to them and clicked his tongue. "Inappropriately late, I apologize. I was inside the building that one of you set on fire without warning me."

Ander laughed nervously. "My bad."

"Delilah and the rest of Millstone should be here soon. I informed her of the Cast's location as soon as I was separated from Sytri." Vega cocked his head as Tephera began to push their large form off the ground. Before Tephera could even get straight, Vega grabbed them by the leg and swung them across them across the ground, sending them skidding into the rubble of the church. He was the size of Tephera's hand, yet he did it effortlessly.

"Holy shit." Ander whipped his head around to look for Micah. There was no movement in the trees. *Is he down for the count?*

Vega picked up a slab of concrete and flicked it through the air with a laugh like it was nothing but a baseball. It smashed into the head of Tephera, who groaned in agony.

Ander winced. "Wait, but how'd you tell Delilah where we are? More mind stuff?"

"Flare gun." Vega cackled. "The idea *was* to discreetly evaluate the estate, then form an actual plan. But it was sort of an emergency. Also, there appears to be no estate now. Good job, Ander. I'm always a fan of fire."

The rift is closing, Tephera. I cannot hold it longer!

We must hurry, Seraph.

Tephera raised their head from the debris, and a ball of light formed between their horns. It was the brightest thing Ander had ever seen, like a small white sun. Tephera plucked it out with two fingers and curled it in their hand before rolling it onto the ground softly.

It was hypnotizing. Ander wanted to touch it. Simple as that. His body moved on its own, and he stretched forward, hands greedy to grasp the sphere.

"Ander, don't!" Sytri snapped.

The light exploded before Ander could even get close.

Then everything was white. There was an airy, bubbled brightness inside of him—it was all there was.

He stumbled onto an ivory plain. Where had everyone gone? Where was he?

"Sytri? Vega?" Ander yelled. His own voice hurt. It was too loud. He whimpered and tried to curl away from agony. Panic flooded him. His breathing became frantic. What was this place? Had he died?

Calm now, Seraph.

Tephera had him. Ander couldn't see them, but he could *feel* them. Tephera was gripping him like a doll and lifting him. He squirmed in their invisible hands as sensations came back in pieces. The chill of cold rain drew goose bumps on his bare skin. But he still couldn't see anything besides white.

"Tephera, don't—" Ander started, but acid hit the back of his mouth. Fuck. He couldn't even *begin* to use his power anymore. Panic shot up his spine. He'd always been so weak, so useless. Just like this.

"Sytri!" Ander yelled groggily. "Vega!" The rain grew louder; other sounds slowly came back. He could hear his friends, in the distance, groaning and gasping. Ander tried to pry himself free. Were they blinded, just as he was?

Not good.

"Hey, Tephera!" Ander coughed. "I'm a higher angel than Ezra, right? Then shouldn't you listen to me anyway and not her? I am your Seraph."

She is my Maker.

Ander stiffened. What else could Ezra do then, if she was healed once again? He couldn't let that happen.

The air became static, and even unable to see, Ander recognized the sensation. Tephera had shifted again, breaking him apart in seconds to place him somewhere else. Then just as quickly, Tephera's fingers uncurled. Ander flung his wings out, but they were smashed against him as he was grabbed again by *much* larger hands. His chest went cold—he was only too aware who was holding him this time.

My Seraph.

Ander violently twisted in Ezra's white hands. The world was back in view, and he did not like it. She brought him close to her face, rain pouring down on them both, her feathered hair flat and stringy against her skull. Her black eyes shimmered with the remains of the fire behind them.

Ander stared; he hadn't been this close to her before, even when she had tried to pry his deal out. Her existence felt wrong, the space she occupied tainted.

The light behind her burned him, and he winced at it before seeing something strange, just for an instant, on that other side—a flash of familiar blond hair.

"*Ronan?*"

The world closed in around him, and the person just past Ezra was all he could see.

Ezra clicked her teeth. *You thought you could leave me, Seraph?* She hissed frozen air onto him.

Ander struggled, trying look beyond her. "Ronan?" he yelled this time, pressing his palms into Ezra's hand, attempting to push himself out.

Do not ignore me!

Ezra squeezed him and Ander cried. Fuck, his organs felt like they were being *crushed*. He tasted iron on his tongue. Could he heal from this?

You have destroyed my home, Seraph. If you were any other creature, you would die the most painful death. Instead, I am going to ensure you live the most painful life.

She staggered toward the rip, curving her mangled body to enter it. Shit.

"Fuck," Ander groaned. He could barely speak, much less attempt to command. His insides were *bleeding* and he didn't . . . he couldn't feel them fixing themselves this time.

Am I dying?

Was Ezra just going to take him over there to die? *For real? After all this shit?*

In the corner of Ander's vision, the blurry smudge of the blonde figure moved. *Ronan.* He tilted his head though it felt like snapping his neck in half. That hair with that sharp nose, cut jaw—it all matched.

His heart lurched. *It's him—oh my god.* He broke out into a sob from pain or joy or whatever the fuck. *I'm so close to him. And I'm going die.*

Maybe he could just go with this. If he was going to die, wasn't it his dream to do it at Ronan's side? Hadn't the point of all this to be with him? Hell, maybe if Ander lived the two of them could escape. Ander bit his lip, choking back another cry. He stared at Ronan, and it was as if his breath had been stolen.

Or that's my lungs being crushed. I really am dying.

But that's Ronan and I can fucking get to him.

Suddenly his chest blazed, fire running through his veins and then snapping back to his center in an explosion. He jerked backward. *The deal.*

It burned in his core like a star. *Sytri.*

How the fuck could he think about dying, when he had promised Sytri he wouldn't?

When I said I wouldn't leave him alone.

The rift began to close, Ezra ambling toward it with Ander. The dark rain continued to cascade down, and his hands slipped on her slick fingers. He was hyperventilating now, and his blood was pumping frantically in his body like it wanted to leave him. No, he wasn't giving up, and like hell he was leaving Sytri behind. *We made wedding vows, goddamn it.* And he intended to keep them.

Even if that meant turning away from Ronan.

The bright light on the other side was burning Ander's face. Every desperate attempt to hurl himself free made Ezra tighten her grip, caused his world to go white. *Fuck.*

"Let him go!"

Sytri. He jumped, and his claws and teeth tore into Ezra's wrist like a savage animal's. She yelled and tried to shake him off, but as soon as she moved, Vega was on her other side carrying a huge-ass piece of concrete like it was made of air. He slammed it down into her wrist. The cement punctured right through, and the bone gave a *crack* as gold blood squelched out in ribbons. Ezra threw her head back with an agonized screech.

She dropped Ander, whose body pulsed with adrenaline. He flung his wings open again, barely managing to stay aloft. Mostly he was thrashing about. *Shit, I'm no good at this.* Below, Sytri grabbed the slab and twisted it, popping half her wrist out, making her hand hang like a piece of loose meat. She withdrew her mangled flesh with a violent sob, backing into the rift as it began closing.

As Sytri started to fall, Ander caught him, locking his arms under Sytri's and lifting him up into the air with strained effort.

"I got you," Ander said with half a grin, before gazing back at the closing space. He stared, not at Ezra, but at Ronan, whose face had gone ashen upon nearing the Throne. He came up to her huge form, soft brown wings ruffling behind him. For a moment he searched through the rift, as if to see the villains who had done the damage.

He saw Ander.

"Ronan," Ander said one last time.

But neither moved toward the other.

He was *right there.*

Down below, closer to the ground, Tephera slipped into the closing light, a gasping Micah on their back. The white-haired bastard glanced up, glaring straight at Ander. There was a hunger—a desperation in his eyes that made Ander shiver.

Then with a shuddering rumble, the whole earth shaking, the rift closed like a sticky wound until it vanished.

The rain ceased.

And there was silence.

Nothing moved. Behind them, another chunk of the church fell in on itself with a loud crash. Ander wearily glanced at Vega to check on him.

Vega just kept staring at where the hole in the sky had been. "So a Throne, huh?" he called out after a moment. "That's not good."

Ander nodded with his final drop of energy.

Then he plummeted. Sytri fell with him, rolling underneath to take most of the impact. They hit the dirt with a thud, gasping.

It took Ander a minute before he could push himself over onto his back. He wheezed and stared blankly at the sky. The gray clouds were fading away, the sun trying to edge its way through.

Sytri spoke up. "I can't believe we lived through that and our deal bounced back? That's fucking crazy—why'd it do that?"

Ander turned. Sytri was staring at him, eyes so bright.

"I think it's because . . ." Ander paused. Everything was so calm. Sytri's body was warm and comfortable next to him, smelling of cinnamon and rain. If Ander said what he knew, the moment would be ruined. But that wasn't a good enough reason to lie or wait.

He grimaced as he spoke. "I think it's because I saw Ronan."

"What the hell do you mean you—"

But Ander was out.

CHAPTER TWENTY-NINE

I'm all different now.

Ander twisted on his heels, strained his legs, and bent weirdly to get a better view of his back in the mirror. Four wings, pitch-black, jutted out from his skin. Two were opposite each other on the tops of his shoulder blades. They were only about three feet long when unfurled.

The second pair were the more cumbersome at eight feet long. They lined up with the first duo and were settled at the indent of his waist.

A trail of down lined the path between all four wings. *Extra fluff.* He'd always envied wings like these on other blends. *Now I have my own.*

"You going to turn into one big bird on me?"

Ander yelped, sweeping his wings in quickly to cover his half-nude body. Sytri laughed from the doorway and then strolled into the room, eyes shining.

"Give a warning, Sytri. Swear to god, you're taking after Vega."

"Oh, wow, those are fighting words."

Ander reddened as Sytri eyed him and his bare chest.

"So many freckles. So many feathers." Sytri leaned close and pressed his fingers against Ander's collarbone. Delicately, he slid them up to the nape of his neck, claws grazing the odd crook where the wings connected to Ander's back, eliciting a shiver. "I've got all these new spots to explore."

"Don't be a creep," Ander said, unable to look Sytri in the eyes, his face burning. He grabbed his shirt off the bed and slung it on. The sleeves had been completely cut off and slits had been made down half the sides to accommodate him. It was a great gas station find, displaying three wolves howling at a moon. And it hung almost equal with his cargo shorts.

Stylish.

"Are you ready, then?" Ander asked.

Sytri's smile fell a notch. "I guess. But do we really have to?"

"Yeah, or else we wouldn't be." Ander laughed, a tad bitterly. He grabbed his new (to him) messenger bag and hefted it awkwardly over his shoulder. It was heavy with everything he'd scrounged in the past week: new clothes, food, water, plus his camera. He scanned the room, though he knew he hadn't forgotten anything.

A deep sigh came from his soul; he hadn't even been able to make the house a proper home.

Sytri sounded hesitant again: "Delilah said we could stay."

"Doesn't matter. I'm a risk to them." Ander's voice was a bit firmer, and he took a breath before continuing. "The Cast will come back if they know I'm here."

"Then we'll be ready."

"Millstone can't be ready for Ezra."

"What if the Cast comes here anyway?"

"They might." Ander hesitated. "But they don't have a church right next door anymore. So maybe without me here, they won't think it's worth the effort. We have to do whatever we can to keep Ezra away from here."

Sytri groaned but there was a dark crease under his eyes. He had seen her too, witnessed the force of the Throne who had somehow made it to Earth. She was a walking nuclear bomb.

She would wait and heal, however long that took, so that when she returned, she wouldn't be a damaged thing, burning in distress. She would be whole and not a soul in Millstone would be able to survive her.

He grew cold. "We've got to go, Sytri. For their sake."

Sytri's ears flicked back, and he bit his lip.

"You don't have to come with me. I wouldn't blame you if you—"

"Oh shut your goddamn mouth, you know I'm coming with." Sytri rolled his eyes. "We've already had this conversation, you idiot. Don't know why you'd think I'd leave you now, unless you're trying to throw me out at the last moment. And anyway, we're back at full force, so you can't get rid of me even if you wanted." He tapped his chest, right where the deal sat.

Ander felt his own. Seeing Ronan had proven that Sytri could still complete his part of the deal, and the flame had lit anew.

It was a wildfire, bright and unhindered, like Sytri himself.

However, that fire next to Ander's heart had only reignited because he'd realized Ronan was out there. Alive and within reach.

But then there was Sytri. He turned to his partner, who eyed him with concern.

He couldn't go to Ronan.

Not in the midst of whatever encampment the Cast had set up. It would be a death sentence, and Ander couldn't make Sytri face that. And Ronan was a part of the Cast. Maybe willingly. He hadn't seemed salted.

But what if he'd been drugged and brainwashed? What if Ander could talk him out of it with his voice? *Could I use it like that?* A shiver ran down his spine.

"Ander?"

"What."

"You're doing it again."

Ander froze. He turned slightly and checked himself in the mirror. His wings had unfurled and puffed up like the fur on an angry cat's back. His eyes had faded from their usual amber to something paler, foreign. He almost didn't look like himself. As if someone else popped into his body and manned the wheel.

But as soon as he saw the difference, it vanished, and he was back once more. Eyes normal, wings relaxed, just Ander. He sighed before glancing at Sytri, whose face was tense with worry. Would he always be like that now? Anxious and wondering as to what the Cast had done to Ander?

Ander wasn't even sure himself. The memories were hazy at best, drowned completely at most. All he did know was a lot of salt had been put in him and now sometimes his head wandered, more so than ever before. If Ander drifted, if he blinked . . .

He could see the Heavens.

"Sorry. I'm fine. I'm—I'm nervous. Thinking." He headed out the door with Sytri, then peered back one last time into the house. Small. Cute. Perfect. He could have lived there—he had wanted to live there. Now, as he left it, it seemed to reach back for him.

"I'm gonna miss having a proper house with you," Sytri said softly.

"Me too."

"Maybe we'll get another one someday?"

Sytri's optimism was needed, but Ander didn't know how well it was working. He couldn't imagine a world where Ezra hunted him and he still managed to settle down. He would always be a rabbit, running away from the fox. Her mouth open wide, ready for the next bite.

"Maybe."

They closed the door behind them.

The world was just beginning to breathe. Purple haze teased the arrival of the sun, and birds called out to each other meekly. Overhead, a handful of the brightest stars managed to be seen, still fighting for their spots. There was a calmness in the fresh air. Ander admired each house they passed, and the little lantern lights that illuminated some of the pathways. Millstone had repaired itself quite well after the attack. Though not all things could be fixed.

Ander's breath hitched in his throat, and he froze. A few feet from where he stood, a dozen wooden crosses were planted in the ground. Though he had passed them before, it hurt afresh every time. They were inscribed with the names of demons and blends he had spoken to during the fight against Mayrez. They had trusted him.

"You okay?" Sytri said, his hand grazing Ander's wrist.

"Yeah. I'm fine." Ander turned to the mulberry sky and sent a silent prayer to whatever listened nowadays. Then they continued their solemn walk.

At the gate stood Delilah, Cerberus, and Vega. Ander scowled. He hadn't wanted a little going-away shebang. It would've been easier to just wander away. He focused hard on the spot between Delilah's eyebrows, keeping his eyes away from the strange stump of her arm. Serene had healed her the best she could, but even with angels and demons, sometimes things were beyond repair.

"You two really are leaving, then?" Delilah asked.

"Yeah." Ander could still see her bleeding. Laid out on that table, as Serene's tiny shoulders shook. *My fault. They came for me.* "Yeah, it's for the best, I think."

Both parties were silent.

"You would've been a hell of guy to have," Delilah said after a moment. "I'm sorry you can't stay." Her mouth was tight when Ander finally looked her in the eyes, her thoughts clear as day on her face. *I need you to get out of here. Millstone isn't safe if they come back for you.*

He didn't blame her for them. "I'm sorry too."

"I hope you find what you're looking for." Cerberus's gaze turned to Sytri. "You as well." It was the nicest he'd ever been.

Sytri nodded.

Ander studied Vega, whose expression was pinched, as if words were bottled up inside of him.

Ander gave a soft grin. "I'll miss you." His chest tightened at the realization, which hit him just as the words came out. "I think we're friends. I hope you think so too, and that it stays that way, even if we never see each other again."

"We are very much friends," Vega said, the bottle apparently broken. He clasped Ander's hands in his own. Then he bent his body at an odd angle to meet him eye to eye. "And I wish to go with you and Sytri." He grinned, mouth full of razors. "Please?"

"What?" Ander sputtered. Odd laughter bubbled out of him, and he turned to Delilah, who shrugged.

"We've already talked about it with him," she answered, a twitch in her lip. "I guess he's had his fill of Millstone. He's a grown demon, so I can't stop him. But it's your choice whether you let him ride along." She wouldn't face him properly. Ander straightened his shoulders.

What did he want?

"Are you kidding me?" Sytri whined. "Oh my god, Vega."

"What can I say?" Vega said. "Delilah's right. I've been in Millstone for most of my time on Earth. Settled down too quickly, I suppose." He straightened up, eyes shining. "And I have a feeling you have a goal in mind, Ander. I want to be there for it." His smirk was dark for a moment.

Sytri sighed. "What are you saying?"

"I'm saying, Ander is a Seraph," Vega said excitedly. "Never met one before. That's a high-up-there tier. And it's made him a target. He'll need someone like me to help. But also, to be honest, Millstone will be stagnant now. No Cast about to fight if Ander leaves and has them follow his breadcrumbs. You do have a plan for that I imagine?"

"A little," Ander admitted. "It's not the greatest, but it's what I have and they'll definitely know I'm not at Millstone." He glanced at Delilah. "That's a promise."

"It's dangerous," Sytri said. "They're basically going to know where we are all the time."

"We just have to stay on the move; it'll be fine." Ander gave a strained smile.

"Sounds like a bad plan. But fun!" Vega said.

"My misfortune should not be a source of entertainment for you," Ander said lowly.

"It shouldn't," Vega agreed. "But it does sound like you'll need help out there. And I'd like to partake in that helping. As you said, Ander, we are friends."

Vega had to know what he was asking. He had seen Ezra with his own eyes. Yet, that didn't seem to spark fear in him—the opposite in fact.

Ander chewed his lip. Taking Vega with him seemed counter-productive to his goal of protecting people. But Vega was obviously willing. And he was right: Ander was going to need help.

"You know you can't make a deal with me? My deal with Sytri is fully intact." Ander tapped his chest, where sparks kicked to life.

Vega's grin didn't falter. "I'm aware. But it's not about that."

"Sytri?"

"I guess," Sytri huffed, throwing his arms in the air.

Ander hadn't expected a yes so quickly, even if it sounded reluctant. Maybe Sytri also was scared that it'd just be the two of them out there against the whole Cast. Ander fiddled with the thought of more help. *Me, Sytri, and Vega.*

"All right." He nodded. "But be on your best behavior."

Vega flung himself onto him, yanking him into a tight embrace. Then, using his spindly long limbs, he latched an arm around Sytri and roped him into the hug.

"Yes!" he shouted with a cackle. "All right then, gang, let's get the show on the road." He spun on his heels, grabbed Delilah's hand, bent down, and kissed it. "Thank you for your time, Delilah. I've appreciated every moment of it. Be sure to miss me, because I'll miss you." As he stood back up, he gazed down at her. "I think you knew I'd leave eventually. But I'm glad you let me stay until then." His voice was solemn. Almost quiet, which Vega never was. Ander felt like he had witnessed something he shouldn't have.

The scene ended as quickly as it had begun. Vega withdrew his hand from Delilah's and turned toward the gate, waving for Ander and Sytri to follow.

"Seriously, let's go now! We haven't time if we want to cover as much ground as possible during daylight." He trotted away a bit before twisting his head to peer at them. "Come on!"

"He's too excited," Sytri said, grabbing Ander's hand.

"He's been cooped up. You said it yourself that demons don't like that." Ander looked over at Delilah, who was staring at Vega's back. Her eyes were vacant, hand digging into her shoulder. "Delilah?"

She jumped slightly. "He was right, I knew he wouldn't hang around long, but I'll still miss him. Even though he was a complete ass." She swung her hand down hard on Ander's shoulder. "Don't let him die or I won't forgive you."

Then she walked away with Cerberus, back into the heart of Millstone. Vega kept skipping out into the wildness of the woods. Ander stood there gazing between the two of them, his throat tight, air gone.

Sytri squeezed his hand. "Whatever happens from this point, I'm with you."

Softness eased back into Ander's being. He could breathe again. "Thank you."

"Your idea really does sound dangerous," Vega called out from up ahead. "I'm not quite sure what it is, but anything that lets the enemy know where you are? Not good. Perhaps you should think of a different plan."

"That's what I said! Damn, can't believe we're agreeing on something."

"If you can think of a better one—" Ander started.

"I'm sure I can," Vega interjected. "See, we haven't even started the journey and you require my help." He sighed dramatically, placed a hand on his chest. "You're so lucky I wanted to come with."

"Never mind. Ander, send him back."

"Send me back yourself."

"Don't think I won't."

"It's more like you *can't.*"

The bickering got louder and Ander glanced at the two of them, at the half smiles on their faces. Same bickering, but vastly different tones than when they first met. He chuckled to himself, though his chest was suddenly tight. Once again, he was venturing out into the world with only half a clue to what he was doing.

Ander brushed his knuckles against Sytri's, making him pause. He glanced down at their hands, a blue blush crossing his face before he intertwined their fingers. Ander smiled.

The world was still monstrous. But now he and Sytri would face it, together.

RIPTIDE
PUBLISHING

ACKNOWLEDGMENTS

Thanks to every LGBT+ weirdo out there that just wanted a book about some anxious gays with cool powers—this book was mostly for y'all. It might be a little deeper than that, it might not. Who knows?

Also shout-out to Carole for not coming to my house and killing me over all the edits.

ABOUT THE AUTHOR

Chely Penn is a Hispanic creator who gets wrapped up in too many interests. Between writing, drawing, and illustrating, she still manages to pester her girlfriend, dogs, cats, and singular tortoise. You can catch her on tiktok.com/@chelypenn or instagram.com/chelypenn. She goes to comic and anime conventions often and would love for fans to stop by her booth!

Enjoy more stories like
Deal in Divinity
at RiptidePublishing.com!

www.ingramcontent.com/pod-product-compliance
Lightning Source LLC
Chambersburg PA
CBHW030641020726
47493CB00006B/1819